PRAISE FOR DONNA GRANT'S BEST-SELLING ROMANCE NOVELS

"Grant's ability to quickly convey complicated backstory makes this jam-packed love story accessible even to new or periodic readers." *–Publishers' Weekly*

"Donna Grant has given the paranormal genre a burst of fresh air…" *–San Francisco Book Review*

"The premise is dramatic and heartbreaking; the characters are colorful and engaging; the romance is spirited and seductive." *–The Reading Cafe*

"The central romance, fueled by a hostage drama, plays out in glorious detail against a backdrop of multiple ongoing issues in the "Dark Kings" books. This seemingly penultimate installment creates a nice segue to a climactic end." *–Library Journal*

"…intense romance amid the growing war between the Dragons and the Dark Fae is scorching hot." *–Booklist*

Dragon Night ~ Dragonfire ~ Dragon Claimed
Ignite ~ Fever ~ Dragon Lost ~ Flame ~ Inferno
A Dragon's Tale (Whisky and Wishes: *A Holiday Novella*,
Heart of Gold: *A Valentine's Novella*, & Of Fire and Flame)
My Fiery Valentine ~ The Dragon King Coloring Book
Dragon King Special Edition Character Coloring Book: Rhi

DARK WARRIORS SERIES

Midnight's Master ~ Midnight's Lover ~ Midnight's Seduction
Midnight's Warrior ~ Midnight's Kiss ~ Midnight's Captive
Midnight's Temptation ~ Midnight's Promise
Midnight's Surrender ~ A Warrior for Christmas

CHIASSON SERIES

Wild Fever ~ Wild Dream ~ Wild Need
Wild Flame ~ Wild Rapture

LARUE SERIES

Moon Kissed ~ Moon Thrall ~ Moon Struck ~ Moon Bound

WICKED TREASURES

Seized by Passion ~ Enticed by Ecstasy ~ Captured by Desire
Books 1-3: Wicked Treasures Box Set

<u>**HISTORICAL PARANORMAL**</u>

THE KINDRED SERIES
Everkin ~ Eversong ~ Everwylde ~ Everbound
Evernight ~ Everspell

KINDRED: THE FATED SERIES
Rage ~ Ruin ~ Reign

DARK SWORD SERIES
Dangerous Highlander ~ Forbidden Highlander
Wicked Highlander ~ Untamed Highlander
Shadow Highlander ~ Darkest Highlander

ROGUES OF SCOTLAND SERIES
The Craving ~ The Hunger ~ The Tempted ~ The Seduced
Books 1-4: Rogues of Scotland Box Set

THE SHIELDS SERIES
A Dark Guardian ~ A Kind of Magic ~ A Dark Seduction
A Forbidden Temptation ~ A Warrior's Heart
Mystic Trinity (a series connecting novel)

DRUIDS GLEN SERIES
Highland Mist ~ Highland Nights ~ Highland Dawn
Highland Fires ~ Highland Magic
Mystic Trinity (a series connecting novel)

SISTERS OF MAGIC TRILOGY

Shadow Magic ~ Echoes of Magic ~ Dangerous Magic

Books 1-3: Sisters of Magic Box Set

THE ROYAL CHRONICLES NOVELLA SERIES

Prince of Desire ~ Prince of Seduction

Prince of Love ~ Prince of Passion

Books 1-4: The Royal Chronicles Box Set

Mystic Trinity (a series connecting novel)

DARK BEGINNINGS: A FIRST IN SERIES BOXSET

Chiasson Series, Book 1: Wild Fever

LaRue Series, Book 1: Moon Kissed

The Royal Chronicles Series, Book 1: Prince of Desire

MILITARY ROMANCE / ROMANTIC SUSPENSE

SONS OF TEXAS SERIES

The Hero ~ The Protector ~ The Legend

The Defender ~ The Guardian

<u>**COWBOY / CONTEMPORARY**</u>

HEART OF TEXAS SERIES
The Christmas Cowboy Hero ~ Cowboy, Cross My Heart
My Favorite Cowboy ~ A Cowboy Like You
Looking for a Cowboy ~ A Cowboy Kind of Love

<u>**STAND ALONE BOOKS**</u>
That Cowboy of Mine
Home for a Cowboy Christmas
Mutual Desire
Forever Mine
Savage Moon

**Check out Donna Grant's Online Store at
www.DonnaGrant.com/shop
for autographed books, character
themed goodies, and more!**

HEART OF GLASS

SKYE DRUIDS

THREE

DONNA GRANT

CHAPTER ONE

After her parents and the London Druids told Ferne relentlessly never to set foot on the Isle of Skye, and that the Druids who called the isle home were not to be trusted, she ignored them all to follow an instinct she continued to question.

The closer she got to Skye, the more her stomach churned. She could turn back. She had yet to reach the isle. Sure, her brother knew where she was going, but Mason would accept if she returned before going farther. Yet she didn't turn her car around. She kept driving.

The bridge that connected mainland Scotland to the Isle of Skye came into view. There was still time. All she had to do was pull over and turn around to head back to England and Mason. Generations of Druids knew never to come to Skye. It meant immediate banishment by family, though Mason would never do that to her. He supported her. Always. Still, she felt a gnawing uncertainty that made her want to retch.

"Last chance," she whispered as she came upon the bridge.

Her foot lifted from the accelerator, but she kept driving. Her heart slammed erratically against her ribs when she reached the top of the structure, and then she was on the descent. Before she knew it, her tires rolled onto the Isle of Skye.

She shook so badly she thought she would have to pull off the road, but as quickly as the shaking had begun, it slowed and then stopped altogether when she was on Skye. Ferne's gaze swept around her, taking in the shops, houses, cars, and people, not to mention the unimaginable beauty everywhere. The navigation system directed her toward the cottage she had rented, but she ignored it and just drove. She wasn't supposed to be here. Not only because it had been ingrained in her from her earliest memories but because there was a really good chance the Skye Druids would force her out as soon as they learned who she was. Ferne would take whatever time she had to see Skye while she could.

The sun remained hidden behind soft gray clouds that intermittently sputtered drizzle. The sea whitecapped in some coves, while others had smoother water. The mountains rose like stony giants watching over the isle. There were lochs, waterfalls, and a landscape of such rugged splendor that she began to understand why so many tourists frequented the isle. But there was something else, as well. Magic.

Ferne had once heard a London Druid whisper about how a friend of theirs had said they could sense the magic on Skye. She had dismissed the claim as an exaggeration. Now, she knew they hadn't lied. While she wouldn't say she actually felt the magic, there *was* something different in the air. And she wanted to feel more of it.

The only thing missing was her brother. Mason loved their Druid side more than she did. She had shied away from her magic for several years. Not Mason. He went all-in on everything. There were no half-measures for him. He would love it on Skye.

Her intention to drive and take in the beauty of the isle was soon cast aside by her need to get out and experience the majesty for herself. The instant she saw the signage for the Fairy Pools, Ferne turned off the road and headed toward them. It was a main tourist attraction, but she didn't care.

Her mobile rang as she maneuvered down the lane to the nearly empty car park. She glanced around, searching for the pools. All she saw was a path. The insistent ringing brought her thoughts to a halt. She didn't need to look to know who called. Only one person ever rang her.

She answered through her car. "Hey, Mason."

"Is everything all right?" His deep voice held concern. "It took you longer to answer than normal. By my calculations, you should've reached Skye. Have they given you problems?"

Ferne maneuvered her Mini into a parking slot. She squashed the irritation that rose at her brother's overprotectiveness. She was the same with him. They had been that way since they'd lost their parents in a plane crash. "I'm here. The drive was uneventful."

"Have you gone to the house yet?"

She grinned, shaking her head as she put the car in park. "I haven't."

He released a long sigh, and she could well imagine him running his hand down his face as he did when he was restless and agitated. Or worried. "There's still time for you to come home. No one has to know you're there."

"I'm not afraid of them."

"Ferne," he said, reminding her of their father when he chided her. Very British, with his voice dripping disappointment.

She closed her eyes to the gorgeous backdrop of the Black Cuillin mountains. "I had the same argument with myself the entire ten-hour drive here. I *have* to do this."

"You're all I have left."

"And you're all I have, but that doesn't mean we should shut ourselves away from the world. Or stop doing what's right. The Druids on Skye are in danger. If they're toppled, the rest of the Druids around the world will fall."

Another sigh. "This is a dangerous thing you're doing."

Ferne opened her eyes. "So is what you're doing."

"Excuse me?" he said after a slight pause.

"I admit, it took me longer to sort through things because I was preoccupied. If it weren't so important for me to be here, I would've turned around and come home." She took a deep breath and released it. "Tell me I'm wrong. Tell me you're not looking into whether Mum and Dad's accident was more than that."

There was silence on the other end of the line. Then a soft, "Bloody hell."

"What you're doing is much more dangerous, Mas. You should've told me."

"The elders—"

"Can bloody well sod off," she snapped. Then she pressed her lips together. "They want to control everything and everyone. Neither of us has ever been satisfied with the reports from the plane crash. If the London Druids had anything to do with the accident, then they'll be watching you."

"Us."

She winced at the truth of his words. "They don't care about me. It's you they've always had their eyes on."

Mason chuckled, surprising her. "You sound just like Mum." The smile left his voice. "Just as you have to do what you're doing, I need to do this. I know what I'm doing. Trust me, Ferne."

"I do."

"I'm going to get us answers, and while I hate that you're on Skye without me to watch your back, it's better that you're not here. Not after they kicked you out of London."

She rolled her eyes. "If they do anything to you, I will burn them to the ground."

"That's how I feel about the Skye Druids."

She grinned. "I almost feel sorry for anyone who comes against us."

"I don't," he replied, no humor in his voice. "It's what happens when tragedy strikes a family, and all they have is each other."

Ferne wanted so much to reach out and hug him. "I'll ring once I'm at the house."

"Stay in touch as you promised."

"I'll be just as worried about you."

He paused. "Find out all you can about the Druids there. Just…"

"I know," she replied. "Be careful. The same goes for you."

She disconnected and turned her attention to the landscape. Her worry for Mason wouldn't lessen until she returned to the family estate in Derbyshire, but she couldn't do that until she finished on Skye. But now that she was here, she knew it would be harder to leave than she'd ever anticipated.

Ferne unbuckled her seat belt and stepped out of the car. The air was damp and chilly, made more so by the soft wind. She grabbed her purse and walked around to open the car's boot. After she'd tucked her keys and mobile into her pockets, she hid her purse and dug out her hiking boots from her suitcase. Once she'd changed shoes, she put on her coat and secured the car. Then, she walked around the vehicle.

"So. This is Skye," she murmured.

She started across the road to the trail that wound through the land. A path that millions of feet had walked. Like all of Skye, the pools had originally been for the Druids. But there was no stopping change. Now, the Fairy Pools were a popular tourist stop for anyone who visited the isle. Not that Ferne could blame them.

After tripping a couple of times, she had to force herself to look away from the mountains and watch where she stepped. She crossed a small trickle of water that grew wider and deeper the closer she got to the pools. In her excitement, she hadn't taken the time to look around to see who was about.

As much as she dismissed Mason's worry, he had a point. Many wouldn't want her on Skye. Ferne paused next to a boulder that towered over her and took out her mobile. She recorded a video, turning in a slow circle to get everyone in. From what she could tell, only a couple with two young kids was at her back toward the car park. As for the other car besides hers, she guessed it was the lone figure in the distance. She couldn't make out if it was a male or a female, but she was on guard regardless.

Ferne continued walking. She contemplated getting pictures for Mason, but she couldn't tear her eyes from the land. With every step, she thought about the generations of Druids who had walked the path, seeking the pools. This was the land of her ancestors, a territory that had beckoned to Druids long, long ago. And she finally understood why.

She also understood why the London Druids were so adamant about no one visiting. The land was stunning, yes, but it was also magical. It felt like home. The magic within her recognized Skye and found contentment here, which meant she was relaxed and comfortable. After years of being twisted with grief, it was like coming out of hibernation. The air was fresher, the wind like a caress upon her skin. Her steps were lighter, her mood brighter.

A few minutes later, she passed the young family. The kids, twin girls, held hands as they walked, singing in what she thought was Swedish. The mother and father gazed adoringly at their children and flashed her a quick smile. Ferne knew how well some could deceive, so she once more pretended to take pictures and watched the family out of the corner of her eye until they were gone.

She reached one of the first waterfalls. She stood for long minutes, simply watching the rush of water as it poured into a waiting, crystal-clear pool. As she climbed higher, the waterfalls became grander, the pools bigger and deeper, and the rocks below larger.

She spotted one that jutted out in the distance and headed there so she could stand over the waterfall and look down the gorge where the water had cut into the rock and land, carving out the pools. A glance around showed she was alone. She looked behind her at the car park and saw only her Mini. She had the pools to herself. She almost broke out in a dance. If Mason were here, he would've egged her on. Her father would have, too. Only her mother, laughing all the while, would've hurried them along.

Knowing she was alone, Ferne lowered her guard and took her

time climbing the path. A smattering of rain came quickly and ended just as rapidly, but even that couldn't get her to return to her car. When she reached the rock she had seen, she lowered herself onto it, letting her legs dangle over the side. It was quite a considerable distance down.

Ferne leaned back on her hands and considered Rhona, the leader of the Skye Druids. She probably should've been Ferne's first stop, but she would go see Rhona first thing in the morning. It was already late afternoon, and Ferne still needed to get to the house she had rented.

She lifted her face to the sky and closed her eyes. The magic of the isle pulsed here. It was what had initially drawn the Fae when there had been an alliance between the Skye Druids and them. The rumors swirling around the London Druids was that an alliance might be intact once more. However, whether she could believe anything her old group said was something else altogether.

The London Druids had their fingers in a lot of pies. They believed they were more powerful than the Skye Druids, who probably didn't even know they existed. Every group of Druids around the world compared themselves to Skye. It was hard not to when it was the land on which the Druids had settled in the beginning.

Until her ancestors and countless others had been banished from Skye forever.

Yet here she was, wading into dangerous territory to save the very people who had turned their backs on her relatives. Ferne had tried to reach Kirsi, one of the Druids on Skye, and while she had connected with her through magic, she wasn't sure if she would go to Rhona as Ferne had urged. There was also a darkness swirling around Skye that prompted Ferne to come herself.

She wasn't here just to save the Druids on Skye, but *all* Druids. She would need to convince Rhona of that—however long it took. She wasn't leaving until she knew the Skye Druids had their enemy in hand. Ferne hadn't told her brother that she was prepared to fight alongside the Skye Druids to achieve that, but he already knew. Because he would do the same.

SKYE DRUIDS

Theo Frasier slammed the door of his vehicle too hard as he got inside. He blew out a frustrated breath and rested his hands on the steering wheel. It had been a particularly wearisome day with still no leads on who was controlling the Druid-murdering mist.

He yanked his tie loose and tossed it into the seat beside him before starting the car. His stomach was sour from too much coffee. Still, a part of him wanted to stride back into the station and pick up where he had left off. The other part knew he needed to find a decent meal—something besides what was in a vending machine or he could pick up as takeaway. He also needed a long shower and a decent night's sleep. He hadn't had much of any of that since the murders had begun.

Theo drove out of the police station's car park, but he didn't turn toward home. He needed somewhere quiet where he could think. And he knew just the spot. His father had taken him to the Fairy Pools on numerous occasions. Sometimes, it was just to enjoy the day. Other times, it was to have serious conversations. There were also the times when his father needed to think through things. It wasn't long before Theo took up the habit himself.

Joel Frasier always said the magic of the isle allowed him to put aside the noise of the world, as well as his thoughts, and get to the heart of a matter. It had led Theo's father to become one of the best detectives in Skye's history. Those were large shoes to fill at times—well, all the time, really.

The drive to the pools was quick. With dusk falling soon, and the intermittent weather, Theo knew there wouldn't be many tourists—just the way he liked it. He noted the black Mini Cooper convertible with its red racing stripes as he parked. Theo looked toward the pools but didn't immediately make out where the individual might be.

He climbed out of his vehicle and locked the doors behind him as he set off at a quick pace. Almost as soon as he crossed the road and his foot hit the soil, he felt the tension ease from his shoulders. He didn't slow as he made his way to his favorite spot.

There was nothing quite like the Fairy Pools when no one else was about. Each time he came, he experienced something different. Today, he felt small and insignificant against the backdrop of the Cuillins and the clouds growing darker by the moment. He had often wondered who'd first found the pools. He imagined the Druid had borne the same awe and appreciation as he did every time he saw them. Any season, in any type of weather.

Theo was bound to Skye and the pools, just as every ancestor through his bloodline had been.

He released a long breath, feeling the muscles in his shoulders ease a little. He was nearly to his spot when his gaze lit upon a figure. She stood on a rock out in the middle of a waterfall.

Many people made their way to it. He had done it himself multiple times—but when the rocks were dry, not damp from recent rains.

She looked at the mountains, her hands in the pockets of her olive-green coat. Her long, curly, black hair was gathered at the base of her neck and fell down her back. His steps slowed. He didn't want to surprise her, lest she slip and fall. The water below was deep enough that she could jump, but there were also many rocks and boulders she could hit unless she was experienced.

The roar of the water drowned out the sound of his approach. Her attention was on the subtle shades of the sunset penetrating the thick cloud cover. He moved ahead of her, keeping his gaze locked on her face, waiting until she noticed him. Her head swung to the left, their gazes connecting. Even from a distance, he could make out the green color of her eyes. He saw her stiffen slightly. She was a woman alone, and he instantly took steps to ease her concern.

Theo lifted his hands before him. "Hi. I just wanted to be sure you could get back to safety. The rocks are slippery."

"I did notice that once I got out here," she said with a twist of her lips.

He noted her British accent. Theo glanced around to see if any others were about, but he didn't see anyone. He slid his gaze back to her. "I'm happy to leave, but I'd be remiss if I didna ask if you wanted help."

"Actually," she said, glancing at the sky, "I think I might take you up on the offer. The water is a tad chilly for me."

Theo walked to the rocky edge. He bent, using his hand to steady himself as he dropped to the boulder below. He carefully crept closer and extended his arm to her over the rushing waterfall.

"Inch closer. Be mindful of the edge of the rock, it dips slightly. I slipped on that once."

"Once?" she asked as she did as he instructed, her eyes locked on the rock in question.

"It only takes once."

"What happened?"

He watched her, letting her take her time. "I fell on a rock you can't see because of the waterfall. Broke my arm in two places."

She stopped and peered into the water before looking up at him. Now that she was closer, he saw that her eyes weren't just any green. A band of dark olive ringed an iris two shades lighter.

"Getting out here is a lot easier than getting back."

He inclined his head. "Aye. The pools can be deceptive."

"Are you sure you can get me out without both of us falling in?"

Theo flashed a grin. "I've swum in the pools my entire life. I know exactly what to do. You're almost to me. Just a little more. Once I have your hand, I'll pull you over."

"Sounds easy enough."

It was, but Theo couldn't stop thinking about his fall and how easily he could've died that day had he tumbled a half inch more to the side. He steadied his feet and stretched his arm out a little more. His other hand gripped the wall of rock. Her arm lifted, and their fingers brushed.

"Almost there," he urged.

She looked at him the moment he wrapped his fingers around her hand. "I'm ready."

A shiver ran down his spine at the words. He ignored it and tugged her over the rushing water. He yanked harder than necessary, and she crashed into his chest. Instinctively, his arms went around her, steadying them both. He felt her heart pounding. Or maybe it was his. He wasn't certain. Her hands gripped him tightly, and she looked up at him. They stood as close as lovers. Strands of dark hair had moved to curl around her cheeks. His gaze swept over her oval face, taking in her brown skin, gently arched brows, and thick lashes. His attention dropped to her full, slightly parted lips.

A swell of desire hit him so hard it seized his breath. He told himself to loosen his arms and put some space between his body and hers, but he couldn't. His arms were locked in place. His gaze moved slowly up her face. The roar that was ever-present in his mind as he tried to sort through the puzzle of whatever case he was working on silenced for the first time. Ever. The drumbeat of his heart grew louder. Or was it hers?

He fell into the color of her eyes. It was a dark, warm, yellowish green. Inviting. Curious. Earnest. Years as a cop had taught him to read people, and he liked what he saw in her. He liked it a lot. That alone should've jerked him out of the stupor he'd fallen into. Yet she felt good against him. She held his gaze, seemingly as dazed as he.

To his surprise, her chin lifted. Without even realizing it, he lowered his head to her. He didn't go around kissing strangers, no matter how beautiful they were. But Theo couldn't stop himself if he tried. And he didn't want this to end.

Their mouths met in a gentle brush. She sighed softly. He went back for another taste, letting his lips linger. A deep, wild yearning filled him in response. The answer was the woman in his arms. She was the responding song to an invitation he didn't remember crafting. The calm to his storm.

The spark to his desire.

And just like kindling, he went up in flames. They wrapped around him, consuming him as he deepened the kiss. She melted against him and kissed him back with just as much fervor and need as what surged through him.

He wanted her. *Needed* her. To have their bodies joined, their souls mated. He'd never felt such deep-rooted lust before. It shook him to his core to have such a visceral reaction to anyone, but especially a stranger.

Theo slowed their kiss and eventually lifted his head to look at her. He bit back a groan at her kiss-swollen lips. She was breathing as hard as he was, her hands clutching his arms. Her tongue peeked out as she licked her lower lip. He fought against the urge to take her mouth again.

He swallowed and looked away, trying to get control of his body. Theo realized it had grown dark. He shook himself for leaving them both out in the open in such a perilous spot. "I should get you back onto land."

"Land?" Her brow furrowed as she blinked. Then she nodded. "Yes. Of course."

Theo loosened his arms, his hand sliding down to grab hers. He tried to feel nothing with her fingers tangled with his, but he felt everything, and it was all magnified by a hundred. Her soft skin and long digits, the easy way she took his hand...

"Place your feet where I do," he instructed.

She nodded once more.

Theo forced his gaze from her and began the climb. He took the easiest path, helping her up even when she didn't need it. She followed his instructions without question. Once they were back on land, there was no reason to keep hold of her any longer. He reluctantly released her but missed her instantly.

"Thank you," she said with a smile. "I feel quite foolish for thinking I could get back and forth on my own."

"You probably could've made it."

She swallowed and glanced at the ground. "Do you often come to others' rescue?"

"A few times," he replied, feeling his lips ease into a grin.

"I owe you. If not for you, I might have had to spend the night out there."

"Anyone would've helped."

One slim eyebrow rose. "I'm not so sure."

The conversation lagged, and he wasn't ready for her to leave. He said the first thing that came to mind. "Is this your first time on Skye?"

"Is it that obvious?" she asked with a laugh.

"No' at all. Just be mindful that our weather here is a wee bit wild. We can get all four seasons in a day."

"Really?"

"I dress to expect the worst. I can always take clothes off."

Her eyes twinkled as she raked him with her gaze. "Just how many do you take off during the day?"

Theo opened his mouth to reply and found his mind had gone blank. He had been out of the dating scene for so long that he wasn't sure how to do it anymore.

"I think I've embarrassed you."

"No' at all."

Her brow lifted again as she stared at him, a half smile on her lips.

"Rain is coming," he said after hearing a faint rumble in the distance. He thought of their kiss and how neither of them had said anything about it.

"So it would seem."

The last of the meager light was fading, bringing on full night. And with it the mist. Suddenly, he forgot about the kiss. He needed to get her back to her car quickly and safely. It didn't matter if she was a Druid or not. The mist was killing, and it was his duty to protect.

"I'm headed back if you'd like to walk with me," he offered.

"It has gotten dark quickly. I think I will."

"We need to hurry if you doona want to get wet."

"It's just water."

"Aye, but it's a wee bit nippy out. You'll get cold quick."

She flashed him a smile as they began their walk. "I've never been one to race out of the rain."

A memory from long ago flashed in Theo's mind: his mother dancing in the rain. It had been ages since he'd thought of her—or remembered that. The recollection shook him. He tried to push it away as they started walking.

"This place is special. You can feel its m—mystery."

She had almost said *magic*. He was sure of it. Many visitors said that about the pools, whether they were Druids or not. It even stated as much in the brochures. But the fact that she had made sure *not* to say the word made him consider why. "Aye. It is a verra special place."

"I'm sorry if I interrupted your evening," she said.

He pulled out his mobile to turn on the light to use as a torch. She followed suit. Theo glanced at her. "I'm no'. I can come here anytime."

"Do you often have the Fairy Pools to yourself?"

"No' often, nay. They're extremely popular. You should see them in late summer when the heather blooms."

"I imagine it's spectacular."

"It really is. Most of our attractions call to tourists for various reasons, but there are a few places no' listed in brochures that I could tell you about. Unless you've already made your plans."

She paused for a moment. "I've not made any plans, actually. I'm not sure how long I'll be here."

Something in her words struck him as odd. Or maybe it was just the cop in him searching for things that seemed off. It was another reason he didn't date. He could never turn his police brain off.

But he had with her.

CHAPTER THREE

What were the odds that a handsome stranger would come upon her when Ferne hadn't realized she needed help? Slim, indeed. Ferne didn't entirely let her guard down, though. She couldn't. She *wouldn't.* Yet this man only seemed to have her well-being in mind. Mason would have no doubt come up with a dozen or more reasons why she shouldn't have trusted him.

And even more why she shouldn't have kissed him.

Ah, but that kiss. She could still taste him. Could still feel his warmth and the strength of his body against hers. She hadn't wanted the kiss to end. In fact, she had been so enamored she had forgotten where she was.

At least she'd gotten more time with him on their trek back to their vehicles. Ferne found herself wanting to reach for his hand. Something about him was comforting, genuine. It wasn't a particular thing, but him in general. She didn't even know his name. And she wanted to. She hesitated to introduce herself.

Maybe it was better if he didn't know her name. Then again, they had shared a rather fiery kiss hinting at mutual passion.

Ferne took the opportunity in the soft lull of their conversation to look behind her. The mountains loomed like dark giants now. She could still hear the waterfalls, but could no longer see them. Still, there was no denying that something special and *magical* had happened at the Fairy Pools.

Before her rescue…

And definitely after.

It had felt as if the magic had been all around her, holding her…welcoming her. Had it brought the man?

"Whoa. Careful."

A large hand, gentle but firm, took hold of her arm and stopped her. Ferne swung her gaze back around to see the stranger's shadowed face creased in concern. She followed his gaze in the mobiles' light to see a drop down. Her next step would have sent her tumbling forward into an awkward and possibly injuring fall.

"Well," she said, mortified. "That was foolish. You've saved me again."

He waited until she'd regained her footing before releasing her. For just a moment, she thought he might slide his palm against hers once more, but he eventually—reluctantly, maybe?—dropped his hand.

"It's a simple path in the day, but once it's dark…"

"Yeah." It was why she had taken the opportunity to walk back with him.

"Did you leave something back there? We can turn around to get it," he offered.

She shook her head. "No, it's just…I wasn't expecting this place to touch me as it has."

"It does have a way of doing that."

The look in his deep brown eyes wasn't easy to make out in the darkness, but Ferne wondered if his words held a double meaning. Was he a Druid? Those without magic outnumbered the Druids on Skye now and had for some time. She had been careful earlier when describing the area as magical, and she felt as if he were being just as careful with his words now.

Ferne wished there was more light. She had gotten a good look at him when he walked up, and a closer one when she was in his arms, but she wanted more. He had deep brown eyes with a warmth that surprised her. Thick hair so dark it appeared black was cropped close on the sides and the lower back of his head, while the top was longer, holding just a hint of wave. Thick brows sat atop astute eyes. He had sharp cheekbones that accentuated his even sharper jawline and chin. And lips that were neither full nor thin but somewhere perfectly in between.

And a deliciously hard body.

"Shall we continue?" he asked.

Ferne inwardly shook herself. "Yes, of course."

Once more, they pointed the light from their phones to the ground before them. He had situated himself on her left, maybe so she didn't fall into the water. Not that she could blame him with the way she had been acting. It was difficult to explain that she felt as if she had come home yet discombobulated at the same time.

And then flushed with desire that seemed both new and recognizable.

She glanced at his clothes. A charcoal gray trench coat with a black suit beneath. It was a classic pairing, but she noted the exceptional fit of the coat and pants. Either he had the kind of body that fit perfectly into something off the rack, or he'd had them tailored. Then there were his dress shoes. They weren't bargain loafers but more on the upper end. And well cared for.

They were making good time back to the car park. The wind had cooled, and the air was heavy with rain. Their gazes met briefly before he helped her cross the stream.

"It seems disingenuous to have someone come to my aid twice, as well as share a kiss with them, and not give my name. I'm Ferne."

He paused, their hands linked. "Ferne," he said as if testing the noun. "I'm Theo."

She smiled. "A strong name. It suits you."

The first fat drops of rain landed on their hands. It seemed to pull Theo from his thoughts. He released her and continued walking. She fell into step beside him, noting how he shortened his strides for her. She added *considerate* to his list of attributes. Who was Theo? She suddenly wanted to know every detail.

After kissing him for a solid week.

A wall of rain suddenly struck, soaking them. Ferne threw back her head and laughed, letting the water splash onto her face. She had been locked in sorrow for too many years, living through books. With its magic and handsome rescuers who knew how to kiss, Skye reminded her there was so much life yet to live. She didn't care that the icy water fell between the collar of her coat, drenched her sweater, and then rolled down her back. She was *alive*.

And the London Druids had no sway here.

Her thoughts turned to Mason and it sobered her. She lifted her head and caught Theo watching her. Water dripped off his thick lashes. His waterproof trench kept most of him dry, but he didn't seem to notice the rain. He blinked, droplets falling to his cheeks and rolling to his jaw before dropping once more.

As quickly as the wall of rain came, it moved past them. She heard it hitting the cars before fading. The intensity of Theo's gaze sent a shiver through her. She thought about the fire that had blazed within her at their kiss and found she wanted it again.

"You're drenched now."

His voice was soft, barely discernable. Almost as if the words were difficult to say. She nodded. "So are you."

"I've only ever known one other person who loved getting caught in the rain."

"If rain waters the world, why can't it water us, as well? I feel it's a gift."

He blinked and lowered his gaze to the ground for a heartbeat, then two. "Aye."

Ferne watched him, wondering what was going through his mind. Then he seemed to come back to himself and drew in a breath as he looked at her. He quirked a brow, silently asking if she was ready to continue. They fell into step once more.

"I'll be happy to pay for any dry cleaning," she offered.

"There's no need."

"Are you sure? I disturbed your night and got you caught in the rain."

He looked at her, a crooked smile on his lips. "We got watered. There's a difference."

She couldn't help but laugh. "I wasn't sure what to expect coming to Skye, but it's been more than I could've hoped for already. And it's just my first day."

"The isle rarely disappoints. People come from all over the world, and Skye seems to know what everyone needs."

It appeared the island did indeed know that. She had needed help without knowing it, and Theo had suddenly appeared. "You don't mind all the tourists?"

"It keeps our economy going."

"That didn't exactly answer my question."

Another flash of a grin. "It gets tedious at times, but we've learned to live with it."

"Especially tourists who do stupid things without thinking, unknowingly putting themselves in dire situations when they're alone?"

He laughed softly. "I can honestly say that this evening was just what I needed."

"I'm happy to be of service. If you need such an event again, just let me know. I'll get back on that rock to await you."

He smiled as she intended, but the heat to his look made her squeeze her legs together. Oh, yes. She would definitely, *eagerly* take another of his kisses. None of this was her normal—or at least hadn't been for some time. She had shut herself away from others and stopped living for any but Mason. Being on Skye had reminded her how she used to embrace all possibilities. She never used to let embarrassment or humiliation hold her back.

"I might take you up on that offer," he replied.

She was sad to see they had reached the car park. Ferne wanted to stop and continue their conversation, but Theo was right. She was cold now. It was all she could do to hold back her shivering. It was time to remember to live again, throw caution to the wind, and take chances once more.

"I still need to find my rental, but I'm famished. Can I take you out to dinner as a way of thanks?"

He turned his head to her. "I'd like that."

"Perhaps we could talk about the kiss," she offered as she paused beside her Mini.

"What would you like to discuss?"

She shrugged. "More of them."

His eyes darkened. In an instant, they were again in each other's arms, their mouths meeting. His tongue swept inside, tangling with hers. His hard body pressed her against the car, allowing her to feel his arousal. The wetness of her sweater squished against her back, making her shiver.

Theo ended the kiss and moved away from her. "You should get out of those clothes."

"Probably." She cleared her throat and tried not to shiver again. "I don't really know a good place to eat. Any suggestions?"

"The Claymore is one of my favorites."

"The Claymore, it is. Would an hour be adequate?"

"Aye," he said with a nod.

"I'll see you there."

"I look forward to it."

They stared at each other for another moment before he inclined his head and walked around the Mini to get to his vehicle. She waved before opening her car door. Ferne took the time to shrug out of her coat and toss it into the back. She was still entering the address into the navigation for the rental when Theo drove away. Ferne wasn't long behind him. She would come back to the Fairy Pools. How could she not after such an encounter?

The magic hadn't shunned her, and she hoped Rhona and the Druids wouldn't either. A nice dinner with Theo—possibly more kisses—and conversation was just what she needed to fortify her for the following day. It might be wise to call Rhona instead of just showing up. Then again, if she alerted the Druid leader of her intentions, Rhona could refuse to see her.

Ferne found the cottage easily enough. The rain had begun again, but she didn't mind. The car lights lit upon the whitewashed building. Thankfully, there was a covered area off to the side for her to pull into. She put her coat back on and hauled her luggage from the boot. After a quick look at her emails to ensure she remembered the lockbox code for the keys, she walked in the rain to the door. She was inside in no time.

CHAPTER FOUR

SKYE DRUIDS

"Am I really going on a date?" Theo asked his reflection.

Was it a date? She had asked him to dinner. And they had shared a couple of kisses that made his blood burn even now.

"Bloody hell," he said as he ran a hand through his damp hair.

It was just dinner. He didn't need to make a big deal out of it. He ran his hand over his now-smooth jaw. Since his hair tended to curl when he didn't want it to, he put in some product to keep it in check and then dried it. He returned to his room and opened his closet door to grab a pair of dark jeans and a cream, cable-knit sweater. He tugged on his favorite brown leather boots before taking a deep breath and looking in the mirror again.

"Why did I say the Claymore? Everyone will be there."

Theo walked from his room and grabbed another coat. An indignant meow reminded him that he hadn't fed Basher. He'd found the injured and sick white cat a few years ago. Theo had intended to foster him and find Basher a home once he was on the mend, but he bonded with the feline and couldn't let him go.

"I'm coming. Hold your horses," Theo chided teasingly.

Basher bumped his head against Theo's leg, weaving between his feet and purring loudly as Theo readied the cat's food. He set the bowl on the floor and gave Basher a good rubdown. It was only after the cat turned to his food that Theo swiped his keys and started for the door.

"I'll be back, Basher. Watch the house," he said before walking out, turning the lock, and setting the wards.

Theo never left without saying goodbye. He knew the cat couldn't understand him, and the words were more for him than Basher, but Theo felt better voicing them. He strode to his car and slid behind the wheel.

His hand shook slightly as he started the engine. It was only dinner with a new friend—a sexy new friend he couldn't seem to stop kissing. He hoped the night turned into more, but he wouldn't push. First, dinner. He could share a meal. He ate with others. Sometimes. Well, rarely. Usually, he grabbed a bite at his desk during lunch. Breakfast, when he remembered to eat, was with Basher. Dinner was usually with the cat, as well. But Theo used to go out. He used to have a life outside of work. Maybe it was time he remembered what that was like.

"Here goes nothing," he said as he pulled out of his drive and headed to the restaurant.

Even after driving around for ten minutes, he was early. But he couldn't stand not being inside. So, he parked and made his way into the building. To his surprise, he spotted Ferne already seated at a table. She smiled and waved to him.

Her dark hair was down and parted to one side, the long curls framing her face. Once more, he was struck by her eyes. He wondered if her parents had named her after the plant because of the color of her eyes. They were a perfect match.

He heard someone say his name. He glanced to the side and spotted Scott and Elodie. He gave them a nod in greeting and continued toward Ferne.

"Hi," she said when he approached.

"Hi."

Fuck. She was gorgeous. She wore a wide-necked, rose-gold-colored sweater and black jeans. Two gold necklaces encircled her neck. Each wrist held an array of different gold bracelets. Surprisingly, she only had two rings. Both simple, thin, and gold—one on her left thumb and another on her right middle finger. Medium-sized gold hoops adorned her ears.

He removed his coat and hung it over the back of the chair before lowering himself onto the seat. Theo placed his forearms on the table. "You found the place all right?"

"I did, yes." She glanced down at the menu before her. "I…um…I should've asked earlier if you were seeing anyone."

"Nay, lass. You doona need to worry about that." He paused then, realizing he should ask her that, too. "Are you?"

Her laugh was part snort. "No."

"A definite nay, then."

Her lips widened into a smile. "You could say that."

Silence stretched, and she fiddled with the menu. This was why he didn't date. It was just so awkward. He was trying too hard. And why? For a holiday romance? Ferne didn't live on Skye. He might see her for a week, maybe two, and then never again. So why not relax and enjoy things?

"If the pools were your first-day stop, what do you have planned for tomorrow?" he asked.

She bit her bottom lip for a moment. "I'm going to play it by ear. It's been some time since I've been on holiday."

"Did you come alone?"

One slim brow quirked. "That's one of those questions I won't answer. What if you're a serial killer?"

Theo had been taking a drink of water when she answered. He choked on it, causing guests near them to look his way. He turned his head away and coughed before meeting her gaze. "That I'm no', lass."

"But I only have your word," she said innocently.

"Who's to say *you're* no' the serial killer?"

She jerked her head back, insulted. "Me?"

"Aye. It's rare, but it happens. About five to seven percent of all serial killers are female."

Her eyes narrowed on him. "And how do you know that?"

The arrival of the waiter saved him from answering. Ferne ordered a gin and tonic, and he asked for Dreagan whiskey. If he were going to do this dating thing, then he would do it fully. There wasn't a whiskey in production that could touch what the Dragon Kings produced.

"Well?" Ferne pressed when they were alone again. "Are you a writer? There are a few genres where I could see a person using that information in a book."

"I take that to mean you're a reader."

Her mouth softened in a smile. "Absolutely. My father used to travel a lot, and he'd scoop up as many books as he could everywhere he went. We have chests and chests of them. My brother said we need to get rid of them, but I refused. Since there was no more room in the library, I had to think of something."

A library, huh? The clothes, her accent. He was leaning towards Ferne coming from money. "What did you decide?"

"I was going to open my own bookshop. There are certainly enough books in all genres to do it."

"Did you?"

She looked down at the table and shook her head. "I intended to open it in London, but things didn't work out there."

"Then open it somewhere else."

Ferne laughed softly and met his gaze. "You make it sound so simple."

"It is. You have the books, and you have the ambition. Just find a location."

She tapped a finger on the table. "Hmm. I hadn't thought of that." She blinked and focused on him. "You still didn't answer my question."

He should've known she wouldn't let it go. Not that he could blame her. People could never be too careful nowadays. Some truly horrific individuals were out there doing appalling things to others. "I'm a police officer."

"Ah. That makes sense."

"Does it?"

She nodded her thanks to the waiter as he brought their drinks. Her long, slim fingers wound around the glass to lift it to her mouth. "It does."

"How?" he asked as she sipped. He had his own hand wrapped around his lowball where the amber liquid sat.

"The way you were careful to ensure I felt safe. And how you see everything in one look."

He lifted his glass and inhaled the scent of the whiskey before letting it sit on his tongue and then slide down his throat, warming his stomach. "You seem to notice quite a bit, too."

"I'm a woman in the modern age with an overprotective brother who won't rest unless he knows I'm safe."

"He doesna sound like the type who would've been happy about you being out on a boulder like you were earlier."

Ferne shook her head as she laughed. "Not at all. I'll tell him eventually."

"You doona keep secrets?"

Something shuttered in her eyes, and her smile lost some of its luster. "No."

A succinct reply that held a wealth of meaning. Theo longed to question her about it, but he recognized she'd end the exchange quickly. In his years as a cop, he had learned to read people. Specifically, when to push and when to relent. Now was a retreat. That discussion was one for a committed relationship, not a holiday fling. He needed to let it go.

Even if he knew there was a story there waiting to unfold.

"Do you keep secrets?" she asked.

Theo thought about his fellow cops and how they had no idea he was a Druid. He thought about the cases he worked with the Druid community, all with details like *magic* being kept out of reports. He thought about his last relationship and his omission of how bad his job could get and the strain it caused on others.

He fought not to toss back the rest of his drink. "Sometimes, the only choice is a lie to protect others."

"That's walking a fine line."

"Aye."

She studied him for a long moment. "You're talking about more than lying to a suspect to get a confession, aren't you?"

"I know people who see the world in black and white, but it isna ever that simple."

"Sometimes, I wish things could be set in such easy categories."

He pushed aside his drink. "Ferne," he began. The vibration of his phone interrupted him. He inwardly cursed as he held up a finger to her and checked his cell. As soon as he saw that it was the station, he sighed. "Excuse me. I have to take this."

She nodded as he rose and went outside. The call was quick, a desk sergeant informing him that he had to come in to the station immediately. Theo pocketed the phone and reentered the restaurant. He glanced toward Scott and Elodie's table, but the couple was already gone. Then his gaze met Ferne's.

"You have to go," she said as if reading his mind.

He really didn't want to. "Aye. I'm sorry. I'd much rather stay."

"You have an important job. It's fine."

"At least let me buy the drinks."

She waved him away. "Nonsense. I've got this."

"How about a rain check?"

When she didn't immediately reply, his heart sank. But then her gaze softened. "I'd like that."

He licked his lips, unable to look away from her gaze. "I'll be in touch."

It wasn't until he walked into the station that he realized he didn't have her number or even her surname to look up her mobile. He was a detective. He'd find it somehow. Theo strode toward his office, only to have his name called. He paused and turned to see Alisha Cunningham, the chief superintendent, standing in her doorway, waiting for him.

Theo pivoted and started toward her, steeling himself as he did.

It was never a good sign when the chief was in the office late at night.

He paused at the threshold. "Ma'am?"

"Come in and shut the door," she said as she walked to the window and stared out at the night.

Theo did as he was told and waited. He got on well with the chief, though not everyone did. She was hard and exacting, but the station needed that. As long as her cops did their jobs correctly, the chief superintendent didn't have a problem. If you didn't…well, a few had lost their positions for thinking the rules didn't apply to them.

"I may not have grown up on Skye, but I'm not oblivious to its roots," she said.

Theo frowned at her back. "Ma'am?"

"You're very good at your job, Frasier. But I expected no less from Joel Frasier's son. Your father was one of the best cops I've ever known."

Theo shifted from foot to foot. He didn't like where this was going. "Ma'am, I—"

"Do you think I don't know, Theo?"

He stilled, unease chilling his blood. "Know what?"

She slowly turned to face him. "That you're a Druid."

CHAPTER FIVE

SKYE DRUIDS

It suddenly felt as if every eye in the restaurant was on Ferne. She made herself casually recline in the chair as if it were no big deal to eat alone. In fact, it wasn't. Though, admittedly, she didn't do it often. But this wasn't London. Or even the local village in Derbyshire. This was Skye.

Where everyone was a potential enemy.

Including Theo.

She reached for the gin and tonic and took a drink. She really didn't want Theo to be an adversary, especially when they had something so magnetic between them. But even she had to acknowledge how utterly insane it was to flirt with someone at a time when she should be preparing for the worst. Maybe it was for the best that Theo had gotten called away. He'd asked to have dinner later but failed to even get her full name, much less her mobile number. She had started to offer it when he walked away.

"Would you like to wait for your friend to return before ordering?"

Ferne looked up at the waiter and shook her head. "He was called away. It'll just be me tonight."

"In that case, would you like to put in your order?"

It was on the tip of her tongue to decline, but the bit of her old self that had shown up at the Fairy Pools nudged her, reminding her that life was too short to shrink away from things. Ferne gave the waiter her order and returned to her drink as she moved her gaze around the restaurant.

No one looked her way—at least none that she could tell. She might think everyone was a local, but they were most likely tourists. Which meant they wouldn't care about her. She chuckled, shaking her head at her wild thoughts.

She heard the soft chime from her purse, the sound she had chosen for Mason's texts. Ferne dug out her mobile and opened the message.

I FOUND SIX MORE CRATES OF BOOKS. THAT'S TWENTY SO FAR. I'M DROWNING, FERNE. DROWNING.

Ferne bit back a laugh as her thoughts drifted to her conversation with Theo about the bookshop. It wasn't as if she'd wanted to live in London. It was just a practical place for a bookstore. Then the London Druids had to go and interfere with her life. Though she was beginning to think it might have been for the best. She quickly sent off a reply.

DON'T YOU DARE GET RID OF ANY. I STILL HAVE PLANS FOR THEM.

WOULDN'T DREAM OF IT. THERE ARE MORE ROOMS THAT HAVEN'T BEEN OPENED IN SOME TIME. I'VE A FEELING BILLINGS AND THE REST OF THE STAFF WILL LOCATE MORE CRATES.

She almost wished she was there to find them herself. IF THIS IS YOUR WAY OF GETTING ME HOME SOONER, IT'S WORKING.

I KNOW.

She rolled her eyes and tucked her phone away. When she looked up again, she found an older woman staring at her. She, too, ate alone. Her graying brown hair was cut short around her full face. She nodded, her sly smile unsettling Ferne. Ferne returned the smile and looked away, but she could still feel the woman's attention on her.

Ferne didn't let herself linger on that. Tomorrow was a big day. She wondered if she should find Kirsi. The Druid had powers she hadn't tapped into yet—not fully, at least. It wasn't Ferne's place to teach her, but it would be helpful if the Druid mastered it sooner rather than later.

So many things could go wrong. The London Druids' animosity and complete loathing of the Skye Druids was drummed into everyone in the community. They believed that the fall of the Skye Druids was inevitable. Wanted, even. Because then the London Druids would be the ones to claim the spot at the top as the most powerful. At least that was their belief. Ferne didn't believe that. Neither had her parents.

Ferne didn't only need to convince Rhona of the dangers surrounding Skye, but she also needed to impart how lethal the London Druids were. All while hoping the leader, or any other Druid on Skye, didn't attack her or force her off the isle for some long-ago debacle involving their ancestors.

The arrival of her food broke into her thoughts. She glanced across the table to the chair Theo had used, then to his glass of whiskey. Dreagan had been a favorite of her parents, as well as Mason. It didn't surprise her that Theo also liked the brand.

She took his glass and let some of the liquor settle on her tongue before swallowing. Maybe it was because it had been a few years since she'd drunk any, or perhaps because she was in Scotland, but it tasted better than she remembered.

Ferne chose to drink the rest as she ate. The food was delicious, and she imagined the conversation with Theo would've been just as good, if not better, had he remained. She wondered what had called him away.

She paid the check and stood to pull on her coat. As she did, her gaze darted to the table where the older woman had sat. Others occupied the spot now. Ferne didn't know what about her had been so disturbing. It would be too easy to dismiss her reaction as nothing more than her being overly cautious, but Ferne knew better. Not now.

And especially not on Skye.

Ferne grabbed her purse and left the restaurant. She immediately looked up as she stepped outside. The clouds were dispersing some, giving her a glimpse here and there of the stars staring down at her. A lively hum came from the restaurant, yet the stillness around her was unsettling. It hadn't been there before. Not when she'd first arrived on Skye, not at the pools, not at the cottage, and not when she reached the restaurant. But it was there now. Like a wet blanket draped over the isle.

She hoped she hadn't gotten to Skye too late. She should've come as soon as she realized the danger instead of trying to reach Kirsi, which had taken far longer than expected. Ferne wondered if she should visit Rhona now. It was late, but too much time had already passed.

The decision made, she unlocked her car and opened the door. As she was getting inside, she glanced up and saw the older woman from the restaurant watching her from inside a vehicle. It made Ferne's heart skip a beat in panic. She hurriedly shut the door and started the engine. As she put the Mini in reverse, she dialed Mason.

He answered on the first ring. "I swear I'm not harming the books," he said, a smile in his voice.

"I'm going to Rhona's tonight."

Half a beat of silence passed. His voice lowered and turned serious. "What happened?"

"A woman at the place I was eating stared at me. She nodded as if she knew me," Ferne explained as she turned left. She had memorized the directions to Rhona's house. "And her smile. It was chilling, Mason. I dismissed her, but then I saw her again when I left the restaurant. She was in her car watching me."

"Forget all of it. Come home now. Don't go back to the cottage. You can replace anything you've left."

"I'm not leaving without talking to Rhona."

"Ferne," he said tightly, his words controlled and even. "Kirsi may have already spoken to her. You're risking your life for people you don't know."

She glanced in the rearview mirror but saw no lights following her. "I'm doing what's right. I have to do this."

"You could just call her. You could've done that from here. I should never have let you go."

Ferne tightened her hands on the steering wheel. Mason was overreacting, but they had both done that since their parents' deaths. "This has to be done in person. Besides, I won't give them a reason to attack me. I just want to talk. And they're going to want to listen to what I have to say."

"Bloody hell, Ferne."

She imagined him fisting his hands at his sides in an effort to control the helplessness he likely felt. It was a habit he'd had since boyhood. "Neither of us is happy with what the other is doing at the moment. I promised to keep in touch. I've told you what's happening and what I think."

"And I'm supposed to just sit here with that?" he snapped.

It was always better when he let his anger out. It was when he kept his voice measured and his words restrained that everyone needed to worry. "You could always come here."

"I'm tempted to do just that."

She would prefer that, rather than have him investigating the London Druid elders. Those bastards were ruthlessly calculating and brutally callous to any and all who stood in their way. They also had zero tolerance for anyone who broke their rules. Hence why she had been kicked out of London. "I could use your help."

But she knew he wouldn't come. It would mean him being removed from the London Druids, and he needed to stay within the group to search for the truth.

"Are you really going to see Rhona now?" he asked.

"I am. And no one is following me. I've been checking."

He released a long, drawn-out sigh. "You don't need me there. You just want me to stop digging into things until you're here."

"So perceptive."

"You could be done tonight. All you have to do is tell Rhona—"

"*Convince* her," Ferne interjected.

"Convince Rhona. And then your job is done. You could be back on the road tomorrow morning."

She could be, yes.

"Right?" Mason pressed.

She scowled. "In theory."

"I know that tone. You may want to stay, but when Rhona finds out who you are, you may not have a choice but to leave."

"True. Hopefully, Rhona won't be that kind of leader."

He snorted. "They're all those kinds of leaders."

"That's all we've known, yes, but—"

A wall of mist dove at her from above. Ferne screamed and slammed on the brakes, the tires squealing as the vehicle slid to a stop.

"Ferne? Ferne! Goddammit, answer me!" Mason bellowed through the speakers of her car.

She couldn't find her voice as she stared at the thick mist that just stopped short of crashing into her windscreen. It unfurled what looked like an arm, and then a hand that lay flat against the glass before the mist surrounded the Mini.

"Ferne!!"

Her heart thumped wildly. She could sense something in the mist. It moved almost sensually around the vehicle before returning to the front of the car. Then it was gone, shooting straight up into the sky.

"Billings!" Mason yelled. "I need the helicopter immediately!"

Ferne drew in a trembling breath and uncurled fingers that gripped the wheel tightly. Her hands shook dreadfully. Adrenaline surged through her, turning her blood to ice.

"Ferne, if you can hear me, I'm coming," Mason said.

She swallowed. "I…I'm here."

"Ferne? Fuck. Are you hurt? What happened?" he demanded.

"I think I was confronted."

"By who?"

His measured voice was back. She saw lights coming up behind her. Ferne's leg trembled as she moved her foot from the brake to the accelerator. "Not who. What. Mist. A wall of mist."

CHAPTER SIX

Theo blinked at the chief, unsure if he had heard her correctly.

"Don't look so shocked," she said and motioned to the chair. "Sit."

He lowered himself while trying to think of some reply.

The chief leaned back in her chair and crossed one leg over the other as she regarded him. "It appears you need context. I came to Skye from Inverness right after I made detective sergeant. They paired me with your father for a short while, and I saw him use magic during one of our cases. At first, I didn't want to believe what I'd seen, but there was no dismissing it. He didn't try to make excuses or act like it didn't happen. I didn't know what to do, so I didn't ask questions. When our shift ended, he suggested we go have a drink. That's when he told me about the history of Skye and the Druids here."

Theo wondered why his father had never shared that bit of information. He ran his hand over his mouth, trying to take it all in.

"I told you all of that so you know you can trust me. I never outed him," the chief said. "I'm certainly not going to say anything about you. The fact is, there's a murderer on Skye. Is it the Druids who have been targeted?"

Theo nodded. "Aye, ma'am."

"Do you have any suspects in mind?"

"I wish I did. Right now, nearly everyone is a person of interest. I can no' even say it's one of our Druids."

She pulled a face. "Right. Because it could be a tourist. However, it's someone with magic."

"There's no denying that bit."

"Do you have any ideas for how to catch them?"

Theo shifted in his seat. "I've got nothing." He hesitated. "How much did Dad tell you about us?"

"Just facts. I know that Corann led the Skye Druids until his death. I'm unsure who took that position after." She raised a brow, waiting for an answer. "This is the part where you tell me who it is, Frasier."

He blew out a breath. "With all due respect, ma'am, I'm coming to terms with the fact that my boss knows the secret I've had to keep my entire career. And that my father was the one to share the information after drumming into me that no one could ever know."

"You're intelligent. You'll get used to it," she stated.

Theo held her gaze. "My community is being targeted, and I doona know why. Our new leader was nearly killed recently, and we've yet to discover who all was a part of that. There's a lunatic out there using magic to control mist that gets into a person's home and horrifically ends their lives. For all I know, you could somehow be a part of things."

"And you can't check my story because of your father's dementia."

"Precisely."

Alisha Cunningham sat forward, resting her arms on her neat desk. "The only way I can prove to you that I'm on your side, Frasier, is to help you. I've spent the better part of the day on the phone with my boss, who is far from pleased with current events. I never told you what I knew because there wasn't a need. There is now. You've been working this case with your hands tied so no one will know your connections. I'm prepared to change that. If other Druids are on the force, they're yours to use. Create your own team. I'll give you anything you need. But we have to stop this serial killer before others lose their lives."

Theo briefly closed his eyes. It would benefit him to have a team around him. Maybe then he could actually get some rest and think clearly instead of doing everything alone. There were two problems with that, though. He would have to trust the chief with another's secret, and there was only one other Druid in the department.

If he did nothing, others would be killed. But what if the chief couldn't be trusted? What if she disclosed everything? Theo would lose his job. He loved being a cop, but at the end of the day, this was about more than his career. This was about lives.

"There's only one other on the force, ma'am," he answered.

A deep frown furrowed her brow as she slowly leaned back. "I was afraid of that. Is there anyone else you can trust?"

"No' in the department."

"But outside of it?" she asked hopefully.

He nodded once. "Aye."

"Then do whatever you need, wherever you need to do it. If you need something specific, come through me. I'll approve it."

Theo started to rise, then stopped. "You're no' demanding names from me?"

"I told you, I want to help. I also want you to know you can trust me. I'll earn that. Your people once ruled the isle. I don't understand why things have to be secret now. Who cares if people know you have magic? Maybe some of the crimes would stop around here if they did."

"Or there would be more Druid crimes."

The chief smoothed a hand over her auburn hair without a strand out of place in her tight bun. "Druids and regular people knew of each other and coexisted for decades. When did the secrets begin?"

"When new people moved here. It isna exactly easy to welcome someone and deliver our history while informing them there's no reason to be afraid that many on the isle have magic."

Her lips widened into a grin as she chuckled. "Fair point."

Theo glanced at the floor. "I'll find who's controlling the mist and killing, Chief."

"I know. Now, go set up your team."

He stood, looking at his boss differently. The restrictions from before had been lifted. Nothing held him back now. He gave her a nod and strode from the room. Theo didn't bother going to his desk. He didn't need anything from there. He pulled out his mobile as he made his way down the hall and headed out of the station. His call was answered on the first ring.

"Tell me you have something," Rhona said.

"I will soon. We need to meet."

"Tell me where."

Theo paused next to his car. "It needs to be secure and private. Somewhere no one will think to look. Somewhere people willna see."

"Carwood Manor."

Theo grinned as he climbed into his car. Bronwyn Stewart's ancestral home was not only private but also protected in ways few places on Skye were. "Should I call Bronwyn?"

"Balladyn and I will talk to her."

"I'll meet you there."

Theo ended the call and drove out of the car park. His thoughts turned to Ferne when some restaurant lights caught his attention. He'd find her. Somehow. The isle wasn't that big. For the first time in weeks, he felt as if he had a direction. He didn't, of course, but now he would at least have a team. *His* team. Together, they could get to the bottom of the mist and find its master. One way or another, it would be stopped.

He still wasn't sure how he felt about the chief knowing his secret. It could be advantageous, but he wasn't naïve enough not to realize there would also be drawbacks. Right now, though, she was on his side. He wouldn't let this opportunity slip past him. He could deal with whatever happened afterward. There was no use worrying about something that hadn't happened.

As he drove down the dark road, his headlights shining before him, he wished everyone knew his secret. He longed for the days when every resident knew of Skye's history and the Druids who had lived and died to find a place for themselves in a world that didn't know what to do with them.

That world still didn't know what to do with them.

Mostly because it didn't know about them. Or the Fae. Or the Dragon Kings. There were too many secrets that would eventually come out. And whenever that happened, there would be chaos. Those without magic would feel threatened and do what humans always did—search out those different and kill them. It had been done countless times throughout the millennia. Humans had even attempted it with the dragons. Which hadn't turned out well.

Hence why the secrets remained.

Theo turned onto the long, winding drive to Carwood Manor. Several vehicles were parked out front. He recognized Bronwyn's older SUV, and beside it were three others that he had come to recognize well, each belonging to one of the Knights. They were a group of Druids who brought justice to other Druids killed by their kind. The Knights had found their way to Skye to help one of their own—Elias MacLean, who happened to be in a relationship with Bronwyn.

Elias and his family were from Skye, though he'd left long ago after a horrific tragedy. His younger sister, Edie, and her family had remained on the isle, but the youngest MacLean sibling, Elodie, had also left. Only to return recently. She'd faced the past to discover the truth and found love with Scott Ryan in the midst of it all. Theo should call the couple and ask them to join him.

But first, he wanted to fill Rhona and Balladyn in. If Bronwyn and the Knights were willing to assist, he'd gladly welcome it.

He parked, and one of the double doors of the manor opened before he had even exited his vehicle. Bronwyn smiled in greeting, her brunette hair falling straight to her shoulders.

"I hope you doona mind the use of your home," he said as he walked up.

She shook her head and stepped aside. "Of course, not. After our run-in with the mist, we're willing to do anything to get rid of it."

Theo glanced skyward, looking for the mist, before stepping inside the entryway to find Rhona and her mate, Balladyn—a Fae who was also a Reaper—speaking with Elias. Elias's team wasn't too far away—Sabryn Beaumont, the American who led the Knights; Carlyle Oliver, a British aristocrat; and Finn O'Connor, an Irishman. The missing member who preferred to remain private was their hacker, Sabertooth.

"We'll leave you to speak in private," Bronwyn said.

Theo held up a hand to stop her. "Actually, I'd like to speak to all of you. Chief Superintendent Cunningham just informed me that she knows I'm a Druid. Apparently, she worked with my father some years back and saw him do magic. He told her who he was. *What* he was." He paused and blew out a breath. "She has given me permission to set up my own team to end the killings. Anyone I want. I'm looking at the best group I know on Skye to help me."

"You don't need to ask me twice," Rhona said with a smile.

Elias nodded. "Nor me. Elodie and Scott would also be willing. And Filip."

"Get everyone here," Theo urged. He turned to Bronwyn. "Can we use the manor as our base?"

"The house is more than willing to be of use," she replied.

There had been whispers that Bronwyn and the manor communicated. It wasn't out of the realm of possibility. This was Skye, after all. The manor had been built with magic, on land infused with it.

"Thank you."

Balladyn's red-and-silver gaze caught his. It was still strange to see a Fae on Skye after they had been exiled for so long. Then again, Balladyn wasn't just any Fae. He was a Reaper—a group of

Light and Dark chosen by Death to keep the Fae in line. Balladyn was also Skye's Warden, which made him significant.

"You should know the mist was seen tonight," Balladyn stated in his deep Irish accent.

An image of Ferne at the restaurant flashed in Theo's mind. "Was anyone killed? Injured?"

"Not that we've heard. Yet," Rhona answered.

Carlyle slapped his hands together. "Let's get started, shall we? I'm eager to catch this bastard."

CHAPTER SEVEN

SKYE DRUIDS

Mason closed his eyes and braced his hands on the desk, struggling to keep his emotions in check when all he wanted to do was race to help Ferne. His phone lay before him on speaker, and it was all he could do not to pick up one of the heavy crystal figurines his mother had collected and smash it against a wall.

"Tell me everything," he demanded of Ferne.

Three years separated them. As children, they had fought constantly. She'd always wanted to be with him, and he had hated it. Then, he went away to school and rarely saw her. Ferne had written him often—letters, emails, texts. She had kept him in the loop of what was happening at home, even when he hadn't cared.

Despite him not replying to anything she sent.

But that was his little sister. It hadn't taken him long to realize that most of his friends came to the estate for Ferne. Not all of them, though. One friend had also thought of Ferne as a sister. Mason had developed an intense protectiveness for Ferne during that time. That's when they started growing close. He became her defender, keeping his licentious, lustful friends away from her.

He really began to worry when she left home and started university. The first year had been the worst of his life. Their father repeatedly told Mason to trust Ferne. Said she could handle herself. In an effort to keep in contact, Mason began corresponding, while her messages trailed off as she embraced her freedom.

That went on for almost three years before their parents died—and everything changed.

"The mist didn't hurt me," Ferne answered. "It just moved around my car."

Mason felt the band constrict around his chest when he heard the tremor in her voice. Ferne was attempting to put him at ease, but he knew her too well. "Mist isn't supposed to move like that."

"True."

"What aren't you telling me, Ferne?"

She sighed loudly. "The mist…it almost seemed alive. It formed an arm and a hand."

"A what?" he exploded. This wasn't normal. He had to get to her immediately.

"I know it sounds bad."

"Do you?" he snapped. He wasn't sure she truly grasped the situation.

"It felt as if it were investigating me."

That made him pause. "Because you're a Druid?"

"I think so."

"Is this the evil you sensed in your vision?"

"Not exactly. I don't know what malice is here, but there's a lot of it."

All the more reason for him to get to Skye immediately.

"I think…well, I think it could do harm if it wanted," she added.

And he had let her go alone. What the fuck had he been thinking? But he knew. It was safer with her away while he investigated the London Druids. She was out of their reach because they would never go to Skye. Though he regretted his choice now.

He was taking a huge chance, but he had looked at it in every way. Ferne couldn't be around as he investigated things. When she said she was going to Skye, it was a godsend. Or so he'd thought. She could have stepped into an even more dangerous situation.

"I know what you're going to say," Ferne continued, her voice growing stronger. "I can do this, Mas. I *have* to do this. No one else can."

He straightened and opened his eyes to look at the ceiling. He caught movement out of the corner of his eye and turned to the door to find their butler, Billings, waiting silently. "Just because you can do it doesn't mean you should." Even as Mason said it, he cringed.

How many times had his father said those exact words to him? Words that used to rile him beyond comprehension. And he had just said them to Ferne.

She snorted. "Nice try. I'm fine. Just startled. Not hurt at all."

"This time." There would be another. Mason was sure of it. "I can be there in a few hours."

"Are you coming to help? Or attempt to make me leave?"

Billings made a face at her last statement. Ferne did what Ferne wanted to do. The only way Mason would get her off Skye was by throwing her over his shoulder and carrying her away, and he wasn't that kind of brute.

But he didn't want to lose her either.

He wanted to uncover the truth about the plane crash, but it would have to wait. It wasn't worth Ferne's life. Mason would tell her everything and hope to hell he could convince her that he didn't need help with the investigation. It was a long shot. Ferne would probably insert herself completely. Just as he would in her place.

"Mason?"

"I'm coming to help," he replied.

The sound of her blinker came through the phone before she said, "Wait until morning. I'll feel better about you flying in then. It'll also give me time to talk to Rhona and better understand things here."

He wouldn't get any sleep that night worrying about her. Mason walked around his desk and pulled out the chair before opening his laptop. He did a quick search and saw the headlines of the recent murders on the isle. "Ferne, did you know about the deaths on Skye?"

"Yes," she said after a short pause.

"Why didn't you tell me about them?"

"The same reason you didn't tell me about your investigation."

Billings lifted a brow at her response. Mason deserved the retort. "I was trying to protect you."

"I love you dearly for that, but I can't live in a bubble any longer. I could fall down the stairs at home and break my neck. There are dangers everywhere."

Not to mention people who didn't think twice about taking lives if it suited them. Was this how their parents felt when he and

Ferne left home? Bloody hell. He was never having children. The worry would kill him. "You're right."

"I'm pulling up to Rhona's house now."

Mason released a slow breath. All Ferne wanted to do was warn Rhona. Once he did that, then his sister could come home. He'd fly up to Skye tomorrow, get her, and pay someone to drive her car back.

"Well?" he asked when she remained silent.

The Mini's headlights illuminated the house. It was only a little larger than her rental but had the same quaint, charming look. There didn't appear to be any lights on inside, but Ferne didn't let that stop her.

"I've not gotten out of the car yet," she told Mason.

"Let me hear."

She rolled her eyes at his protectiveness, but she wouldn't have it any other way. Ferne switched the call from her car back to her phone and shut off the engine. "Just stay quiet while I talk."

"Fine," he bit out. "Look for the mist."

Ferne exited the vehicle and glanced at the sky as she did. A shiver ran down her spine when she thought of the mist. It had come out of nowhere and vanished just as quickly. It could do it again. She wondered what it wanted. Or was it just part of Skye? Maybe she was overreacting. She'd have to ask Rhona. Ferne lengthened her strides to reach the door, then knocked and waited. After a few moments, Ferne rapped again. Still, no one answered.

"I don't think she's home," Ferne said as she lifted the phone to her ear. "I'll have to come back."

"We can do it together tomorrow."

Ferne made her way back to the Mini and started the engine. "I'm fine with that."

"And I'm going to stay on the phone until you reach the cottage."

"Should I leave the call connected overnight so you can hear me sleep?" she asked sarcastically.

Mason's voice dipped in agitation as he said, "Ferne."

"I'm teasing." She sobered. "I know the dangers here, Mas. But if the Skye Druids don't stop their enemies, we're next."

They kept up small talk as she drove to the rental, but she didn't bring up Theo, the kiss, or the Fairy Pools. Not because she didn't want Mason to know but because she was still sorting through it all herself.

She took the time after parking to make sure things were as she had left them outside. Once inside, she did the same. Nothing appeared to have been moved or messed with.

"Ward the cottage," Mason told her.

"Planned on it as soon as we get off the phone. And before you ask, I checked every room."

He blew out a breath. "All right. Have a good night. I'll finish making the plans for the chopper tomorrow."

"The meeting, sir," she heard Billings say in the background.

Mason grunted. "Bloody hell."

"Take the meeting," Ferne urged. Then she realized her mistake. "Wait. What is it for? If it's about the accident, then cancel it. I want to be there."

Her brother hesitated.

"Mason? Who is the meeting with?"

"It's estate business," he finally answered.

She couldn't tell if he was lying. There were many reasons he would, and that concerned her. "Is it really?"

"The meeting should be over before noon. I'll text you my arrival time."

That gave her all morning to explore more of Skye. And maybe run into Theo again. Or go to the station to look for him. "Sounds good. Now, go get some sleep. And, Billings?" she called to their loyal butler. "Make sure he doesn't work any longer tonight."

"I'll do my best, Miss Ferne," came the cool reply.

There was a smile in Mason's voice when he said, "Good night, sis. See you soon."

"Night," she said and disconnected.

Ferne then let out a sigh and looked around the cottage. The evening hadn't gone at all like she had hoped. She was more rattled by the encounter with the mist than she let Mason know. She wasn't sure if wards would keep it out of the rental, but she would try. Ferne spent the next twenty minutes warding every window and door that led outside.

She then made her way into the bedroom and looked at the open suitcase on the bed. Her intention had been to unpack this evening, but now she wasn't sure what to do. She'd come to warn Rhona. That was all. Even if the Druid leader believed everything Ferne had to say, there was no reason for her to ask for her help.

After her encounter with the mist, Mason would stay until she left Skye. She'd do the same to him. Yet, she wanted to remain on the isle. No, *wanted* was too light of a word. Staying almost felt like a necessity. As if she didn't have the option to do anything else.

She had been so enthralled with the Fairy Pools and then Theo that she hadn't taken the time to *feel* Skye. It was time she did. Being a seer hadn't always been easy. The images shown to her never revealed the entire picture. There were only fragments and bits of information she had to decipher. She had gotten it wrong so many times when she was young. For a while, she even ignored her gift, which had been the worst thing to do. If she hadn't turned her back on her magic, she might have known about her parents' deaths and been able to stop them.

Ferne embraced her magic completely after the accident, which was why she was so adamant about helping the Druids on Skye. At least Mason wouldn't banish her. So much of their thinking had changed after their parents' deaths. Would she be here if her mum and dad were still alive? Ferne couldn't answer that. But she did know they would've disowned her if she had come to Skye when they were alive. They might not have agreed with everything the London Druids did, but they wholeheartedly believed everyone should stay far away from Skye.

Ferne pulled a black pouch from her suitcase. She withdrew each crystal and set them in a circle on the floor around her. Then she changed to get comfortable and lowered herself into a cross-legged position on the floor. She would rather be outside, sitting on the ground for direct access to the earth, but this would have to do for now.

She closed her eyes and rested her hands on her knees. A smile pulled at her lips as her magic unfurled like a flower when she reached for it. It spread through her, welcoming and abundant. Then she urged it into the ground. Almost immediately, she felt the magic of Skye.

It was heady and strong for a heartbeat. Intoxicating. It reached for her, and as she extended her magic more, it paused for a long minute before connecting with her. Ferne gasped at the surge that ran through her. She recognized it from the pools earlier, though it had only been a brief touch then. Suddenly, flashes of faces and locations on Skye zipped through her mind, and through it all, she felt distressed. Overpowering, nauseating terror.

She saw the mist as if from Skye's own eyes, moving from house to house, leaving carnage in its wake. She saw the mist attack a manor house, only for the home to strike back. The magic tried to show her more, but it was murky, the face indiscernible. And then the magic of Skye retreated, leaving her bereft.

Ferne sucked in a mouthful of air and bent forward. The isle knew the cause of the mist. It had tried to show her, but Ferne hadn't been able to make out the face. She couldn't even tell if it was a man or a woman.

Her visions had never been anything like that before, and she knew that was all because of the magic of the land. Ferne didn't know if it had shown others, but she had more than just convincing Rhona to do now. She intended to find the one controlling the mist.

CHAPTER EIGHT

Theo squeezed the bridge of his nose with his thumb and forefinger as he closed his eyes. He released a breath and longed to crawl into bed and sleep for a week. Maybe two. The past three and a half hours had been spent comparing what he had compiled about the mist and who might be controlling it against everyone else's thoughts and notes.

And he still hadn't narrowed the suspect list down to anything meaningful.

"Tea?"

He jerked his head up and pushed away from the wall in the hallway as he looked at Rhona. "I couldna stomach more caffeine right now."

"That's good since this is herbal. It's also one of Ariah's blends."

Every Druid had some kind of gift, and Ariah's was creating amazing teas. He accepted the cup. "I never refuse one of Ariah's."

"Smart man," Rhona said with a grin.

He took a drink and noted sage, cinnamon, lemon balm, and a

hint of mint. Theo bought this energizing tea himself. It was one of his favorites. He returned to leaning a shoulder against the wall. Rhona's green eyes locked on him. Hers were a brighter green than Ferne's, yet he thought Ferne's more arresting.

She had wormed her way into his thoughts many times over the last few hours. And each time, his body heated as it recalled their breath-stealing kiss and how they had clung to each other.

Theo halted those thoughts as he took another drink and studied Rhona. "We've known each other long enough that I know that look. You're trying to figure out how to say something. The best way is to just spit it out."

Rhona laughed softly and glanced at the floor. "You look ready to collapse. I put too much on you, and that wasn't fair."

"It's my job."

"That doesn't mean you should kill yourself to do it."

Theo shrugged and stifled a yawn. "I'm no' the only one who has overexerted themself. I see the dark circles under your eyes."

Her lips flattened as she looked down the hall to the room where some of the others still talked among themselves. "I never wanted this position. It nearly cost me my life. If Balladyn hadn't found me..."

Theo knew the entire story, but few others did. They had come very close to losing Rhona right on the heels of Corann's death. Who would've led them then? Thankfully, she had been saved.

There was a movement within them who called themselves the Druid Others. They mixed *mie* and *drough* magic to create a kind of hierarchy within the ranks so they could become more powerful. The Fae had tried something similar and were taken out by the Reapers. The original Others had set their sights on destroying the Dragon Kings to take Earth. That hadn't gone to plan either. But the Druid Others had attempted to kill Rhona and brought things clearly into focus for all Druids on Skye.

If only they were fighting against the unknown faces of the Druid Others. If that were the only worry, Theo might be able to get some decent sleep. Especially since Balladyn and Rhona were mated, and the Reaper watched over her. But then the mist came, and with it, an entirely new set of rules that they were still attempting to figure out.

Rhona visibly shook herself and swallowed as she met Theo's gaze once more. "Corann chose me, and while I'm here, I'm going to do the best job I can protecting Skye and everyone on it."

"You've got me and a lot of others standing with you."

"I appreciate that. You're important, Theo. Not to just the Druids but to everyone on Skye. You need to take care of yourself. You have your team together now. Let us shoulder some of the work. I can never think clearly when I'm too exhausted."

He finished the last of the tea. "Aye. It's a wee bit difficult to rest when I dread hearing about more deaths."

"The mist didn't attack tonight," Balladyn stated as he strode up. "That's a win in my book."

Rhona reached for him, their fingers tangling as their gazes met. Balladyn's mouth curved into an easy smile, one he reserved for only Rhona. Theo's thoughts went to Ferne once again: how easily she had laughed and teased him, how good it had felt when she was against him, their bodies pressed together. And the kiss... He wondered if she had remained to eat alone or if she had found someone else to spend the evening with. If only he had thought to get her number.

Theo blinked and shook his head. When he looked up, Scott had joined Rhona and Balladyn, and all three were staring at him expectantly. "It's been a long week," he said in answer to their silent question.

"Get some rest," Rhona reminded him before she and Balladyn walked away.

"So," Scott said with a sly smile, "who was the woman at The Claymore?"

The query was inevitable. "Someone I met today."

"How was the dinner?"

"Cut short when the chief called me into her office."

Scott's brow furrowed. "That's too bad. Surely, you'll get to take her to dinner to make up for it."

"She said as much." But should he? He was juggling enough right now. He didn't need to add romance to things.

"Doona sacrifice your personal life," Scott warned, his deep blue eyes troubled.

Theo snorted. "Personal life? What's that? I've no' had one in years. I wouldna even know where to begin."

"All the more reason to make sure you get one. And quickly. Call the woman."

If only he could. "She's only visiting. I need to focus on the mist right now so no more people die."

"I didna plan to stay either. Look how that turned out."

"You're right." He would keep on until Theo relented. "Aye. I'll ring her."

Scott's narrowed eyes said he didn't believe Theo. Thankfully, the Druid changed the subject.

"There are twelve of us looking at this now. You doona have to tiptoe around the department to get what you need. We'll find whoever the wanker is and put an end to them and the mist before you know it."

"I hope you're right. I doona want to carry the weight of any more deaths."

"Those are no' just yours to bear. All of us feel responsible. Though I think you and Rhona shoulder the heaviest burden."

Theo straightened from the wall. "Something else will be worse than the weight of the dead."

"What's that?"

"If the culprit is a Druid from Skye. That would mean one of ours turned against us."

Scott's brow furrowed. "You make it sound as if it hasna happened before."

"It has. *Mies* who willingly gave their souls to the Devil to become *droughs*. All for power." Theo shook his head. "Until Bronwyn, we didna know there were other ways a Druid could become *drough*."

"Speaking of Bronwyn teaching us about the different ways to become *drough* and using blood magic, I've no' been able to stop thinking about the book where she learned that. Or whose hands it might fall into."

Theo didn't have time to think about that book or where it might be. They had enough foes around Skye. They didn't need to add another to the roster. "I admit it would be a nice to have it in addition to Bronwyn's instruction."

"But your focus is elsewhere." Scott grinned. "I understand."

"We'll look into it once we've caught who is controlling the mist," Theo promised.

Theo followed Scott back into the room to make sure no one had any questions before he left for the night. He stood to the side and listened to their conversations. There were a plethora of ideas being floated around. More than most were viable. But this case was different than others. He couldn't go to a suspect and ask them questions because he wouldn't have any way of knowing if they lied. The only way to find who controlled the mist was to catch them in the act.

Bronwyn had seen someone at the manor when she, Elias, and the Knights were attacked before. Theo needed that kind of scenario again. But that meant putting someone in danger. No doubt any of them would volunteer, but it would have to be a perfect setup. And he was all too aware that there was never such a scenario.

"What are you thinking?" Elias asked.

Theo moved deeper into the room so everyone could see him. "At first, I thought the murders were random, but the more I think about it, the more I believe those killed were targeted." He nodded at Bronwyn and Elias. "Just as the two of you were. Bronwyn believes someone was here during the attack."

"We need that again, then," Finn pointed out.

Theo flattened his lips. "Agreed. But again, the mist is going after certain people. If we can figure out why, that would help us gather a list of those who could be in danger."

"I'm fairly certain you can put my name on that list," Rhona replied.

Theo twisted his lips. "My gut tells me the mist willna come for you yet. No' as long as Balladyn is around."

"Then I'll let them think I've gone," Balladyn stated. "As a Reaper, I can veil myself for as long as I want."

Carlyle grunted. "Isn't that advantageous?"

"It is," Balladyn said coolly, shooting him a side-eye.

Sabryn sat forward on her chair. "I've been thinking about

getting Saber to do a deep dive on our murder victims to see if we can find anything. A financial link, perhaps."

"There could be other online links, too," Elodie said.

Theo fought against another yawn. "That's a good place to start. Tomorrow."

"What time do you want to begin?" Rhona asked.

He shrugged, his gaze moving to Bronwyn. "It's your home."

"Which has been opened to the Knights. All of you are welcome to stay," she announced.

"In other words," Elias said, "we're on your schedule. Tell us when you need us."

If only he'd been able to do this weeks ago. The case might be solved by now. But he wouldn't think like that. "I'll be here first thing in the morning. Whoever can come, be here. If no', come when you can."

"We'll be here," Filip told him.

Everyone nodded. It was just one more reason Theo loved Skye. The connection of their magic bound them, but it was more than that. They were a community, one that was shrinking by the year, but it was a place where a person could find a home and even a family.

Theo said his farewells and headed downstairs to leave. He heard his name being called and turned to find Bronwyn trailing after him. He paused and waited for her to catch up in the entry hall.

"The manor will welcome you if one of us isn't here," she informed him.

He knew she didn't give such consideration lightly. The manor had been her sanctuary, keeping everyone she didn't want out with magic. By allowing him entry, she was trusting that he wouldn't bring anyone unworthy into the house. "Thank you."

"I meant it. About you staying. The mist can't get into the manor. It might be the only truly safe place on the isle."

Theo thought about his father and the countless others who had no idea they were in danger. "I appreciate the offer, but I doubt it'll come to that. The mist doesna want me."

"We don't know what it wants. You should take care."

But it wasn't him he was thinking about. It was Ferne. "I will."

Bronwyn closed the door behind him, the lock clicking into place softly. Theo looked around at the dark sky on his way to the car without seeing anything. He spent the drive back to his cottage studying the sky as he drove. The longer he went without seeing the mist should have been a good sign, but he knew it was only biding its time.

Basher stood inside the door when Theo entered. The cat yawned and stretched before walking toward him with his tail up.

"I missed you, too, buddy. There's going to be some long nights ahead for both of us until we catch this killer."

The feline wound around Theo's legs and meowed softly before running to the jar of treats.

Theo laughed as he followed. "I'm hungry myself."

CHAPTER NINE

Edie looked on helplessly as her husband, Trevor, finished adjusting his tie. "You can't deny that something has changed between us."

"I agree. It's you," he stated, not bothering to keep the anger from his voice. He looked at her through the mirror. "You see things that are no' there. You have no' laughed in days. All you do is yell at the kids. And me. For the smallest things."

That wasn't true, was it?

"Even the kids are talking about how your no' the same," Trevor continued while slipping on his suit jacket and staring at himself in the mirror. "Everything we say is wrong. Nothing we do is right. You snapped my head off last night because you didna think I kissed you goodnight when I had done it twice already."

She swallowed and parted her lips to speak.

But Trevor talked over her. "It's been like this ever since Elodie returned." He moved to the dresser and put on his watch. "You'd think after complaining about your siblings being gone all these years, you'd be elated they're back on Skye."

Edie should be, but she wasn't. Her siblings had lied to her, and she could never forgive them for that. They thought they were so clever, but she knew who was responsible for their father's murder—and it wasn't their mum, who was in prison for it.

"That," Trevor stated as he turned and pointed at her. "That face right there. You want to know what's wrong with you and me? With you and the kids? Take a look in the mirror."

"Everyone has always said we have the best marriage. We can get back to that," Edie said.

He drew in a deep breath and put his hands in his pants pockets. "Something has to change. The kids are upset. They cringe when you walk into the room. I might take a lot of shite, but I willna continue putting them through whatever this is."

She frowned and took a step toward him. "What are you saying?"

"I'm saying that I'm doing what any parent would do—what *you* would normally do—and putting the children first."

"Trevor," she began.

He held up a hand. "I doona want any more excuses. If you want us to remain married, then please, for everyone's sake, sort yourself out. And quickly. I want my wife back."

Edie watched him stride from their bedroom. She followed him, shoving aside her emotions so their two kids didn't see. She grabbed her keys to take the children to school when Trevor called for them. They came immediately, something they never did for her, ready with their lunches to follow him out. No one told her goodbye.

She rushed to the door and opened it. "Have a good day, kids. I'll see you at pickup. I love you, Trevor."

The kids raised their hands in a wave without looking back. Trevor paused before getting in the SUV. His gaze met hers, and he gave her a little smile, but it wasn't the type he normally gave. He said she had changed, but so had he. He claimed it was because of her. Before this morning, she would've argued that her recent reactions were due to him forgetting their lunch dates, which he had never done before. Not to mention his workload increasing, which kept him traveling more for the firm.

She wrapped her arms around her middle as the SUV drove away. She had asked Trevor to take the kids to school many times, but he always had some excuse or another. Now, he wanted to do it. And the kids were dressed, ready, and waiting. For him. Never for her. It was an act of God to get them out of bed every morning, not to mention getting them to eat their breakfast or get dressed.

Edie needed to talk to someone about all of this and get another perspective. She had to know if she was seeing things that weren't there or if she was validated. She closed the door and went to find her mobile. She decided not to call every name in her contacts for one reason or another, most because they were horrible gossips and would spread anything she told them.

Then it dawned on her that she didn't have any close friends. The kind of girlfriends who would drop everything when you needed them. She *should* have that with her sister. She had always wanted that. Elodie had all but ignored her for fifteen years when she was away. Now, while her sister might be back on the isle, that didn't mean she had time for Edie. Sure, Elodie would always be up for dinner when Edie offered, but it was awkward when they got together.

Maybe she should confront Elodie and Elias with what she knew. She hated feeling as if she were being left out, and that was exactly what they were doing to her. Edie had always been the one to stay in touch with them. She had been the only one to go and see their mother in prison. Yet their mum had asked Elias for help in finding her a house once she got out. After Edie had been talking to her for years about giving her one of their rental homes.

It stung.

Deeply.

Now, her other family was turning against her. It felt as if the entire world had shoved her out into the cold. Alone. She didn't have any friends she could trust, and she was sure Trevor wouldn't want to hear any of this. He'd think it was all just an excuse. And it wasn't as if she could confide in her kids. Or her siblings.

There was her mum. But Emily MacLean had also tossed her aside in favor of Elias. So, that wasn't an option either.

Edie walked around the sofa and sank onto the thick cushion. She had some rentals she needed to get ready for upcoming stays, but she couldn't get motivated to do anything. How could she think of anything when her life was crashing down around her?

Her gaze moved around the living room, noting the pictures that presented them in the best light, showing the world how happy they all were and how well they got along. Like most families, it was a sham. Their kids fought from the time they woke up until they went to sleep. She was sure they continued fighting in their dreams. The older they got only changed what they argued over. It was difficult to keep up with who had wronged who on any given day. Sometimes, it was easier just to ignore them.

Edie always had Trevor, though. He was the calming influence that could quiet the kids with a look or a single word. He could pull her out of a bad mood with one of his dirty jokes. And no matter how stressed or frazzled she was, he could make her feel beautiful and wanted in the way he wrapped an arm around her and looked into her eyes.

Where had all of that gone? If it was her fault, she wanted to fix it. She *had* to fix it. Without Trevor and the kids, she didn't have anything. Trevor was right. She needed to sort herself out. The sooner, the better.

Edie rose and walked to the coat hook by the door. She slipped on a jacket before putting her phone into the pocket. She grabbed her keys and locked the door behind her. Then she set out for a walk. She used to walk several times a day. At first, it was when she got pregnant, but she continued with the kids in the pram. Later, they joined her, though the walks were always shorter. Once the children started school, she extended her strolls. When had she stopped? *Why* had she stopped? Walking helped clear her head, and right now, that was exactly what she needed.

She started past her vehicle when she saw something sticking out of the driver's side door. Edie used her keys to unlock it and then opened it. A piece of paper fluttered to the ground and into a puddle. She quickly bent to retrieve it. Edie carefully unfolded the note to find a typed message.

I can help.

Meet me at Wild Point at 9 am.

Her stomach dropped to her feet. She looked around, wondering who had put the note in her vehicle. Her gaze returned to the stained paper, and she reread the message. She couldn't imagine who would leave such a thing. Obviously, they thought they knew something. She was desperate to return to the life she'd had.

Desperate enough to meet someone who left hidden notes.

Unless it was meant for Trevor. But it had been *her* vehicle. Which meant it was for her. She crumpled the paper. Either way, Edie would find out. She pulled out her phone and looked at the time. Then she turned on her heel and returned to the house to grab her purse. Within moments, she was backing out of the drive and heading to Wild Point.

The entire way there, Edie tried to think of who she might be meeting, but she quickly rejected everyone she thought of. All of them would've called or texted. This person obviously didn't want to leave a record of their correspondence, and that concerned her. And who wouldn't want others to know?

"Cheaters. That's who," she mumbled to herself.

She winced at her words. Once, when they were dating, she'd thought Trevor was cheating and called him on it. He had come unglued. They had a good marriage. Or they did. He wouldn't turn his back on her. He wanted to fix things. He was giving her time to do just that. Besides, she would know if he was cheating. He was aggravated with her, though. That much was clear by his lack of kiss goodbye that morning. Edie thought back to when he'd begun acting weirdly. Sadly, it was almost exactly the time Elodie returned to Skye.

"Shite," she said and slammed her hand against the steering wheel.

So, it was Elodie's and Elias's fault that her marriage was in shambles.

No, no, that wasn't right either. The fault lay with *her* for letting her anger fester instead of confronting her siblings. She would tell Trevor everything tonight—including about the fateful day her father was murdered. He'd be angry that she hadn't been truthful all these years, but she would do her best to explain why. She needed him—his strength and his calm outlook on everything.

Edie reached the narrow road that would take her to a pull-over for Wild Point. No other cars were around, but she was early to the meeting. She pulled the vehicle to the side and shut off the engine. There was still time for her to leave before anyone showed up, but she knew she wouldn't. She had always been the type of person who needed answers, especially if something was right in front her, and all she had to do was meet someone to discover what it was.

Either she would discover that Trevor was cheating, or she would find out who thought they could help her and why. And who knew? Maybe they could. She needed help. That much was evident. Skye's magic worked in strange ways, and she wouldn't turn away from such a gift.

Edie got out of the SUV and slipped her hands into her pockets. Her mobile was in one, and her keys in the other. She locked the vehicle and started walking. It was nice that she'd gotten here first. It allowed her time to walk while preparing for the meeting. If whoever it was came. All of this might be for naught.

There was a hint of blue in the sky as she made her way over the trail. Her mood lightened when she spotted the gulls ahead. She was so focused on them that she didn't immediately notice the person. Edie jerked to a halt as they turned, and Edie looked into a familiar face.

"I'm glad you came," Kerry said with a knowing smile.

CHAPTER TEN

Ferne stood with the mug of tea in hand as she looked out the cottage's window to the sea just steps away. The clouds were gone, and the morning sun was on full display, promising a beautiful day.

She longed to walk to the beach to sit and listen to the waves gently rolling onto shore, almost as much as she yearned to explore more of Skye. But she needed to do other things before Mason arrived. Ferne knew her brother would balk at what she planned, but there was no getting around what had to happen.

The tea was exceptionally good. She went back to the cupboard to see what brand it was so she could buy some. To her surprise, she found it was from a local store called Tea Talker. Ferne made a mental note to check it out once the rest was sorted. She sighed and leaned back against the counter.

Sorted.

It made it sound as if she were filing papers or doing laundry. If only things were that simple. So much was going through her mind right now, and she needed to simplify things. If she didn't, she would never be able to convince Mason of anything. But he needed to be here. It was the only way he would truly understand.

She rinsed her empty cup and set it aside before checking the time. She had a few hours before Mason contacted her. She had a lot to do in a short time. Ferne walked past the bedroom doorway. Her crystals remained on the floor from her earlier attempt to connect with the magic of Skye as she had the previous night. Unfortunately, she hadn't felt anything. Not a single stirring. Not even a little tingle. She couldn't help but feel it had used up everything the night before. Maybe she just needed to find a new spot.

The Fairy Pools called to her. There were answers there. She could *feel* it. However, if she went now, she would stay for hours, and she had things she needed to do first.

"Right," she said, shaking herself.

Ferne put on her coat and grabbed her purse and keys. She paused to reinforce the house's wards after locking the door. As she walked to her car, she cast one more longing glance at the cove. She couldn't help but imagine herself there during the summer, swimming and sunning beneath a bright blue sky. Or under a full moon with the stars on full display.

That thought vanished as she slid into the driver's seat. Her first destination was Rhona's. Hopefully, she would catch the leader of the Skye Druids this time. Ferne went over the key points of the conversation in her head. The Druid would be suspicious of her, which Ferne understood. It was why she had to get everything out clearly and succinctly, along with providing as much proof as she could gather.

Which, sadly, wasn't much.

The closer she got to Rhona's, the more nervous she became. Ferne had been disturbed by the mist the night before, but she'd had hours to think about this conversation and all the ways it could go wrong. Her mother used to tell her to think positively about a situation to manifest what she wanted. And that's exactly what Ferne had been doing since she woke.

She shifted anxiously in her seat as she slowed to turn onto the road that led to Rhona's house. Her heart beat faster, her stomach churning in a way that made her wish she had skipped breakfast—and that last cup of tea.

Ferne debated whether to drive away and come back later. She was too tense and apprehensive. She knew herself well enough to know that she would muddle things in this condition.

A car honked behind her, startling her. Ferne realized she had been sitting in the road. She quickly turned onto the lane and waved in apology to the car that zoomed away. Her foot hovered between the brake and the accelerator. She could stop and turn around. The Mini continued slowly moving down the narrow road.

"You can do this," Ferne told herself as she kept driving to Rhona's. "All you have to do is lay it all out for her. Just talk slowly. Don't ramble."

She really hoped she didn't ramble. It would make her look unsure of things, and she really needed Rhona to understand the depth of the danger everyone was in. Ferne slowed once more and turned onto the drive. She saw a car outside. That gave her hope that Rhona was there.

"Well," she said aloud after turning off the engine. "Nothing will happen sitting out here."

Ferne unfolded from the vehicle and softly shut the door. On her way to the house, she glanced at the numerous flower beds that would undoubtedly overflow with blooms in the spring and summer. Once at the door, Ferne took a deep breath and rapped quickly on the wood. Then she waited, her heart beating like a drum in her chest.

The London Druids taught that those on Skye couldn't be trusted. They said they wielded power like a blade. And that any of those sent from Skye so long ago who returned would be met with death. Ferne was taking a huge chance. Rhona wasn't the leader of those on Skye for nothing. She had to be exceptionally powerful to take over for Corann.

Ferne wasn't without skills, but she didn't want a fight. However, she was prepared if Rhona attacked. Ferne could only hope the Druid leader was smarter than that and would listen before she made any decisions.

Seconds ticked past. No one came to the door. Ferne tapped her toe nervously. She knocked again, but still no one appeared to greet her. She decided to go around to the side of the house in case Rhona was outside. There was no sign of anyone.

"Bloody hell," Ferne muttered.

What was she going to do now? She didn't know Skye or the residents. It wasn't as if she could go around asking where Rhona was. Well, she *could*, but the locals most likely wouldn't tell her.

Yet there *was* one person she could talk to. Someone she probably should've seen first. Kirsi.

Ferne strode back to the Mini. She might have found Kirsi with her magic, but that didn't mean Ferne knew where the Druid lived. She closed her eyes and searched for the remnants of what her visions had shown her. Ferne let them play out in her mind a few times before she recognized the inside of a co-op. It could be nothing, but it was all she had at the moment. And when one grasped at straws, they clung with everything they had.

She did a search on her mobile and found the co-op's address. Ferne followed the directions through the navigation. She had hoped to talk to Kirsi when she was here, but she hadn't been sure of the welcome she might receive. She had heaped quite a lot on the Druid, and Kirsi hadn't seemed at all sure of any of it. Perhaps Ferne had been too cavalier about what she had dropped into Kirsi's lap and asked her to handle. She hadn't been more detailed because Ferne hadn't had any specifics. She still didn't. Not really.

The drive was beautiful beyond compare. Everything about Skye was a contradiction. She had felt the magic at the Fairy Pools and even at the cottage the night before. Now, a sense of dread was rising. Or perhaps her emotions were distorting her thoughts.

She passed the police station, her foot lifting off the accelerator. She thought about pulling in and asking for Theo. Now wasn't the time. Later. After she spoke with Kirsi and Rhona, and before Mason arrived.

Ferne found a parking spot outside the co-op. She took a few moments to study the area from inside the Mini. It was a busy spot next to several other buildings and nearby homes. People milled about. She wished she knew which were Druids and which weren't. After ten minutes, Ferne got out.

She started for the store after she'd hooked the loop of her purse in the crook of her elbow. As she neared the door, it opened, and three children charged out followed by a man she guessed was their father. He held the door for her while shouting for the kids to wait for him. Ferne nodded her thanks, but he didn't look her way again.

She pushed her sunglasses up onto her head and stepped to the side, away from the door. An older gentleman with a graying beard was behind the counter, chatting with someone as he rang them up. Ferne's gaze roamed the store, noting the shelves and the array of goods offered. There seemed to be a bit of everything, but it wasn't London, or even Derbyshire for that matter.

"Can I help you?"

Ferne turned at the voice and found an older woman with her graying auburn hair in a cute pixie cut, sitting in a wheelchair. She had a bright smile and soft green eyes. "I…um…I'm not sure."

"What we have on the shelves this week might not be here next," the woman said with a laugh. "Matt likes to change things up."

The man at the counter said, "I heard that, Nora. You never tell people it was originally your idea."

Ferne looked over to see Matt smiling. She slid her gaze to Nora to find the two looking at each other with such love that it was obvious they were a couple.

"Forgive us," Nora said with a laugh. "We're just two old people who forget others are around."

"I think it's lovely. My parents were similar."

Nora's smile slipped. "I'm sorry. Now. What can I help you with? Or were you just browsing?"

"Actually, I was hoping to find someone."

"There are plenty of men around here who could use someone like you," Matt said as he walked up. "Or women."

Ferne smiled, flattered. "You're very sweet. I'm not interested in a relationship, though." Yet as she said the words, Theo's face popped into her mind. Because she was definitely interested in something with him.

"We know a lot of people around here. We can probably help," Nora said.

Matt laughed, the corners of his brown eyes creasing as he crossed his arms over his extended stomach and stood beside his wife. "No doubt we can. We know just about everyone."

Ferne looked between the two of them. "I don't know her surname, but her first name is Kirsi."

The couple froze, their faces going slack.

Ferne drew in a breath as she realized there was only one reason for them to act that way. "She's your daughter."

"You're the one," Nora said. "You're the one who spoke to her."

Ferne glanced at the door as it opened, the bell ringing above to announce any new customers. "I don't mean any harm. I promise. I'm here to help. You have no reason to trust me, I know, b—"

"She's in the back sorting mail," Matt interrupted.

Nora touched her hand. "Follow me, dear. I'll take you to her."

CHAPTER ELEVEN

SKYE DRUIDS

Theo stared at the whiteboard. The *empty* whiteboard. He'd hoped to have at least somewhere to begin, maybe even some names to start investigating. Instead, he had every Druid on Skye.

And visitors he didn't know, who were also Druids.

In other words, he was trying to find a needle in a mound of needles. How was he to begin when all the threads he could pull were knotted together into one huge ball? He knew he was mixing metaphors, but he didn't care. He crossed his arms over his chest and tried not to let despair tangle his feet.

"I thought I'd find you here."

Theo looked toward the door at the sound of the American accent. Sabryn walked into the second-floor bedroom they'd commandeered as their headquarters. The furniture had been removed sometime during the night and replaced with tables and chairs, along with the whiteboard and several other standing boards. Sabryn had a piece of half-eaten buttered toast in one hand, and a mug of something hot in the other. She leaned a hip against a table, wearing her favorite color—black. Today, it was a sweater and dark jeans. Her straight, chin-length, black hair was parted down the middle and tucked behind one ear to show the many earrings that ran up the lobe and shell.

"Hungry? Carlyle is in his element with so many to cook for." She held up her toast. "Though he's not happy with my choice. Somehow, he thinks bread isn't a decent meal."

Theo grinned and dropped his arms. "He ushered me into the kitchen as soon as I arrived, wielding a knife in one hand and claiming it was to chop tomatoes for the omelet. I wasna taking any chances."

"Probably smart. Carlyle is adamant about breakfast being the most important meal of the day. We've all learned to just give in. It's a lot safer that way."

Theo chuckled, but as soon as his gaze returned to the empty board, he sighed.

"We'll get somewhere soon. You have all of us now. I've got Saber looking into all those murdered. If there's a connection to be found online, he'll dig it up."

"That'll help. We just need to start removing people from our suspect list."

Sabryn moved to stand beside him. "We threw around a lot of ideas yesterday."

"Aye," he said with a nod as he met her deep blue eyes. "Good ideas."

"The Knights don't know Skye. Elias might have been born here, but he's been gone a long time, so I include him in things. You, Rhona, and even Balladyn know the people here the best. Sometimes, you just have to start with your gut."

Theo grunted. "Knowing everyone is the problem. I'd like to

think no one on the isle could be a killer. The truth is everyone has it in them."

"That is a fact, unfortunately."

"And it means I have to look at everyone except those in this house. Each of you was marked off the suspect list because either you were no' on Skye when the killings began, or the mist attacked you."

Sabryn ate the last of her toast and wiped her hand on her jeans. "Rhona gave Bronwyn a list of all the Druids on Skye. She's printing it now. We go through them one by one, if we have to. You have eleven of us at your disposal. And don't forget, Saber could actually count as two. He's ready and waiting for instructions."

"I keep forgetting about him since he isna here."

"I never do," she said with a smile. "He's saved our asses more times than I care to admit. None of the Knights would be here without him."

Theo nodded. "Will he come if asked?"

"Nope. We've never seen his face."

"Never? Have you spoken to him?"

"It's usually by coded message, but there have been occasions. I know he alters his voice when we do."

"And that doesna bother you?"

She took a sip of her drink and raised her brows. "Tell me, Frasier, do you mind when someone saves your life?"

"Point taken. Still, he's part of your team and you doona know him."

"I recognize strength in others. I've noticed you do as well with how you direct us. Sabertooth's is computers. There is little he can't do. We accept that and the fact that he doesn't want to leave his bunker or wherever he resides. He's never let us down. He answers us at all hours of the day, and, as I've said, he's saved each of us multiple times."

Theo twisted his lips. "I can no' argue with that."

"Give him a direction. He'll do a deep dive on anyone you need."

Theo heard movement behind him and turned to see the others beginning to make their way into the room. He met Rhona's gaze. "We start with the obvious person. Kerry."

"I was going to suggest that," Rhona replied.

Bronwyn's brow furrowed as she sank onto one of the chairs. "But as you said, it's obvious. If it she were controlling the mist, she would know she'd be the first person we looked at."

"That doesn't mean it isn't her," Finn replied.

Balladyn looked from Theo to Rhona. "I could trail her."

"It may come to that, but I don't want to pool all our resources on her," Theo said. "Sabryn, please ask Saber to dig up anything and everything he can on Kerry. We've got thousands of names to get through."

Bronwyn handed him a sheaf of papers. "I printed out everyone and divided them by their deputies."

Theo glanced at the list, leafing through the printouts. There were so many names. Too many.

"Maybe we start with the deputies," Carlyle offered. "Each of them holds a position of power, right?"

Elias nodded once. "Rhona chooses them—or Corann before her. There are five of them, each living in one of the five sectors the isle has been divided into."

"They remain in their positions until death or they can no longer serve," Filip added.

Elodie twisted her lips. "Like Kerry."

"Aligning with the Druid Others and attempting to kill Rhona ended Kerry's service immediately," Balladyn said in a hard voice.

Theo grunted. "Which is why she's a suspect."

"Carlyle has a point," Finn said.

"I usually do," Carlyle added in a not-so-hushed tone.

Finn rolled his eyes before returning his attention to Theo. "The deputies hold power positions, but if they're chosen because of their magic, then beginning there seems promising."

"Rhona pointed out downstairs this morning that some Druids probably don't let others know of their abilities," Sabryn replied.

Bronwyn shrugged and nodded. "I didn't let anyone know I had turned *drough* or used blood magic."

"Or could open a portal between dimensions," Elias said with a wink.

"That either," she replied sheepishly.

Elodie lifted a hand. "I didn't announce I could do what I do either."

"To be fair, your mother's spell made you forget," Scott told her.

Elias caught his sister's eyes. Theo watched a silent exchange happen between the siblings. Both were still managing the trauma of their childhood, and probably would for years to come. They had a good support system in each other, as well as Scott and Bronwyn, which gave the two a fighting chance.

Theo suddenly had a thought as he looked between the siblings. "Neither of you mentioned bringing Edie into these meetings."

For a moment, neither Elias nor Elodie spoke. Finally, Elodie said, "Things have been…"

"Weird," Elias supplied.

"Tense," Elodie corrected, "with our sister. It's something within her family, I think. I'd rather not divide her attention."

Elias's brow knitted briefly. "She could be beneficial, but I agree with Elodie. Leave Edie unless we absolutely need her."

"I hate to be blunt," Carlyle began.

Finn snorted. "No, you don't."

Theo hid his smile at the constant ribbing between the two friends. It was good they were there to lighten things up, because they would need it.

"No, I don't." Carlyle shot a smug expression toward Finn. "But Edie hasn't been removed as a suspect."

If Theo thought Elodie or Elias would balk at that, he was mistaken. The siblings nodded in agreement.

"So, back to the deputies," Finn said. "Starting from the top and working down usually works."

Rhona scratched her neck before shoving her long, red hair over a shoulder. "That's what we did when looking for the one who tried to kill me."

"We found nothing at first," Balladyn added. "It took the help of those at Dreagan, as well as MacLeod Castle."

"As much as I'd love to meet the Dragon Kings and their mates, the thought of having a MacLeod Druid and one of their Warriors to help is exciting," Sabryn said.

Bronwyn, Carlyle, and Finn nodded in agreement. Theo slid his gaze to Rhona. If anyone could get the Warriors and Druids to Skye, it was her. As for the Dragon Kings, that would likely fall to Balladyn.

"As a last resort," Rhona said. "I'm not being territorial. This is about fixing our own mess. No matter how I've looked at this, I can't dismiss the fact that whatever is going on began here."

Elias made a sound in the back of his throat. "Other Druid murders happen around the world."

"Not like this," Rhona insisted.

"Something is killing Druids. We can all agree on that. Whether it's the mist or something else," Sabryn stated.

There was another round of nods.

Theo cleared his throat. "I agree. Let's start with the deputies."

Sabryn pointed at the paper. "Mark the names, and I'll give them to Saber, along with Kerry's."

"Meanwhile, let's split up and follow the deputies and Kerry for the day. We need to know everything. Their schedules, who their friends are, who their enemies are, and if they do anything suspicious."

Balladyn leaned a hand against a wall. "It's only because we're searching for a murderer that I'm offering, but I could get inside their homes and listen."

"Let's hope it willna come to that," Theo said.

Rhona nodded once. "Agreed. That's an invasion of privacy."

"I'm pretty sure most wouldn't care, as long as we caught the killer," Elodie pointed out.

Rhona's lips flattened for a heartbeat. "Last resort. I have the deputies looking into everyone in their sectors. They've been doing it for about a week now."

"Let them keep looking," Theo said. "They may find things we doona. They may also corroborate other things." He paused and looked at each of them. "For some of you, you doona know the people here. It willna matter who they are. For the rest of us, there's a good chance someone we know—a friend, maybe a neighbor—is controlling the mist. I doona need to tell any of you no' to let your emotions get in the way. They will, no matter how hard we try. We have thousands of names to eventually get through. The mist was seen last night. For whatever reason, it didna attack anyone. I doona know how many more nights we'll get without a murder. We need to work fast, aye, but also smartly."

Bronwyn got to her feet. "And if the one we're after isn't from Skye?"

"My guess is they don't plan to leave until they have what they want," Elodie said.

Rhona squared her shoulders. "First things first. We check our people. Once everyone is cleared, then we'll turn our attention to visitors."

CHAPTER TWELVE

Ferne was unsure what to think about Nora's and Matt's reactions. They seemed almost happy to learn who she was. It could be a trick, though. She prepared herself as she followed Nora, and Matt fell in a half-step behind the wheelchair.

The bell chimed, announcing another customer. Ferne glanced over to see a couple enter. Her gaze went to the man first. He was tall with auburn hair and a face that made everyone do a double take. Yet it was the woman who caught Ferne's attention. Eyes a unique nutmeg color met Ferne's. Something about the woman caused Ferne to trip. The moment broke when Matt excused himself to help them.

Ferne hurried to follow Nora. Right before they entered the back of the store, Ferne glanced over her shoulder to find the woman staring at her. Something about her was familiar. It felt as if Ferne should know her.

"Did you know the couple who just came in?" Ferne asked.

Nora shook her head. "Sorry, lass. I didn't get a look at them."

There was no time for more as they turned a corner near some crates of mail. A young woman with light brown hair with hints of red amongst the strands lifted her head. Pale green eyes met Ferne's. She knew that face.

"Kirsi," Ferne said.

The woman stood still as a statue for a moment. Then the mail slipped from her limp hands as she walked around to them. Kirsi's gaze ran over Ferne from head to foot and back again.

"Ferne wants to speak to you," Nora said in a soft voice.

Kirsi startled as if just realizing her mother was there. She looked at her mum before returning her attention to Ferne. "Have you come to help?"

"I have. Though I'm not sure how long I can stay."

"What? Why?" Nora and Kirsi asked at the same time.

Ferne fought not to grin. It was clear the two were very close. "There are things you don't know. Things from the past I'd rather not bring up."

"You're here. That's all that matters. Now you can tell me what to do," Kirsi said.

Nora motioned to a door that led outside. "You two go. I'll finish here."

"Mum, no," Kirsi said. "I can work and talk."

Ferne turned away as the two spoke in quiet tones. She felt a stabbing ache in her chest when she thought of her mother and their shared confidences. It was worse now with the thought that someone might have been instrumental in taking her parents' lives.

"You're as stubborn as your father," Nora said in a normal voice, the words dripping with love.

Kirsi shrugged. "I know."

Ferne turned back to find them both looking at her.

"I hope you'll stay for supper," Nora said. "Matt and I would love to speak with you ourselves."

Ferne bowed her head. "That is very kind of you."

Nora made a sound and waved away her words before turning herself around and wheeling the chair back out the door.

Ferne waited until they were alone before facing Kirsi. She set her purse on a table and removed her coat. "I expect you have questions."

"First, how the hell did you contact me like that?"

She smiled, liking Kirsi instantly. "With a lot of magic. It's something I only do in the direst of circumstances."

"I'd like to get into that more, but right now, I just want to know what you think I'm supposed to know how to do."

Ferne briefly dropped her gaze to the floor. She had spent so much time thinking about what she would say to Rhona, but she hadn't given Kirsi the same benefit. That was a mistake. Ferne decided to start with what she knew. "Something is wrong on Skye."

"There isna a Druid here who doesn't know that. Surely, you've read about the murders."

"I did see some headlines."

Kirsi grunted as she picked up a pile of mail and began sorting it. "Several Druids have been killed by mist."

"Mist?" Ferne had to grab hold of the table near her to remain standing.

Kirsi's head snapped to her. "You've seen it?"

She nodded, her mind racing as she thought of how the mist had acted around her. "Last night."

"What happened?"

Ferne wished she could forget, but she never would. "It came out of nowhere as I drove. Suddenly, it was in front of me. I slammed on the brakes because it looked as if I couldn't get through it. Then, an arm and a hand appeared. It touched my windscreen before it began moving all around my car."

"And then?" Kirsi asked, urgency in her voice.

"It left."

Kirsi stood there for a moment. "Shite. I'm not sure if that's a good thing or not."

"You're sure it's the mist that's been killing?"

"Without a doubt. It has attacked others. The mist *is* killing, but everyone is sure someone's controlling it. And by everyone, I mean Druids."

Ferne turned and perched on the edge of the table. "Fuck." As soon as Mason found out about this, he would physically drag her off the isle if he had to. She looked at Kirsi. "Some call me a seer. I suppose I am. Like any seer you speak to, it isn't always easy to determine what it is we've been shown or why. When I was younger, I took my magic for granted. It was there and fairly easy to wield."

"Lucky you," Kirsi mumbled.

Ferne didn't take offense. "There was a time about six years ago when I turned away from magic altogether. I can't remember the exact reasoning. It might have had to do with Mum pressuring me to learn more, do more. The fact is, I ignored my abilities. Anytime I could even sense that I might get a vision, I did everything in my power to make sure I didn't. Then an accident took my parents. Not a day goes by that I don't look back and wonder if I might have seen the accident and prevented it." Ferne straightened from the table. "After my parents…well, I immersed myself in my magic as never before. I didn't ask for help from other Druids. Maybe I should've sought their knowledge instead of going it alone, but by doing it on my own, I developed certain skills."

"Communicating through dreams."

"It's not really in dreams. I need someone relaxed. The place between dreaming and waking when you're fully aware of many things. As I said, I rarely use it because of the strain it puts on my magic and my body. By doing such magic, it leaves me utterly drained and vulnerable."

Kirsi finished with the stack of mail and grabbed another as she glanced Ferne's way. "If it does that to you, and you were coming to Skye, why do it?"

"I didn't plan on traveling here. And the fact is, I knew if I rang Rhona and told her what I knew, she'd likely dismiss me."

Kirsi's lips softened. "Maybe. Though Rhona is great. Have you spoken to her?"

"Not yet. I've tried, but I've not caught her at home."

Kirsi briefly looked up again. "You're here, which means you don't have to be so cryptic with your words."

"I wasn't cryptic on purpose. It's not always easy to get words across. The link is difficult to maintain. I never know how long it'll last."

"I didn't think of that. We don't need to worry about that now. So, what am I supposed to do? And what have I always known how to do? I'm also curious about all the lives before that I've supposedly led. How do you know about those?"

"I saw them."

The younger Druid stilled and slowly turned her head to Ferne.

"Not all the lives," Ferne explained. "Just flashes. I'm not like regular seers, Kirsi. What I saw with you was the past and the present all mixed together. I *knew* you had lived many lives without actually seeing each one. It took me over a week to sort through the images that came to me as I tried to put them into a coherent package."

"Did you?"

Ferne shook her head. "There were too many, and I couldn't remember them all."

"Then how do you know it was me?"

"I saw you standing over a waterfall. That could've been anywhere on Earth, but I had a hunch. A few searches of Skye later, I found that exact waterfall at the Fairy Pools."

Kirsi shrugged and set aside the mail.

It was with the history Ferne knew, but there was no need to disclose that to Kirsi. "Once I knew the location, I suspected you were a Skye Druid. That was when I first tried to reach out to you."

"You make it sound as if I'm special."

"Because you are."

Kirsi rolled her eyes. "Trust me, I'm not. I can barely do anything magical."

"There is evil surrounding Skye. It's been above the isle for some time and slowly enveloping it. You can find it. Destroy it."

A full minute went by without Kirsi making a sound. Then she looked away, shaking her head. "Did you not hear me? I don't have unique magic. I can do the basics, but that's it."

"I know what I saw," Ferne insisted. She didn't bother saying that it was Kirsi in another time period. That would only freak the girl out more. "I know this is a lot for you to take in."

"Take in?" Kirsi yelled.

Ferne saw the fear in her eyes. "If the Druids on Skye fall, the rest of us don't stand a chance."

"Then you've come to the wrong place. I'm just a girl trying to figure out her life. I know nothing of the world. I've not traveled, and I'm certainly not some kind of special Druid who will find this evil you speak of. If it's even real."

Ferne knew she had handled things badly, but there was no going back now. "If you need reminding that things aren't right, remember the mist."

Kirsi said nothing as she turned back to the mail, sorting it with angry, jerky movements. Ferne realized the conversation was done for now. She grabbed her jacket and purse and walked away. As she emerged from the back, she found Nora waiting for her.

Ferne saw a pen and paper near the register and jotted down her name and number. "I can be reached here. In case Kirsi wants to talk again."

"I take that to mean you're not staying?"

"I think it's best if I leave. I gave her a lot to think about."

Nora nodded, her gaze thoughtful. "Thank you for coming."

"All of you need to be careful. Evil is on Skye, and it isn't going anywhere."

"Is that why you reached out to Kirsi?"

Ferne glanced back through the doorway. "She can find it. And that scares her."

"She said you told her she had done it in past lives. Did it work then?"

"I can't answer that since I didn't see it. I just know what I've been shown."

Nora's cool fingers took one of Ferne's hands and squeezed.

"There is a presence on the isle that hasn't been here before. Be mindful if you see any mist."

Ferne nodded her thanks without sharing that she had already encountered the mist. Nora released her, and Ferne gave her a farewell smile before striding out of the co-op. She was nearly to her car when someone stepped into her path. She found herself looking into eyes the color of nutmeg again.

"Hello," the woman said.

Ferne was surprised to hear another British accent. "Hi. Can I help you?"

"We hope so."

Her gaze snapped to the side at the deep, Scottish brogue to find the auburn-haired man walking up. She was instantly on alert. "And what do you think I can help you with?"

"You're a Druid," the woman stated.

Ferne studied her, feeling the prickle of familiarity again. "So are you."

"I'm Esther. That's Nikolai," she said as she motioned to the man.

Ferne looked between them. "I'm Ferne."

"Something brought me here," Esther said. "I'm thinking something brought you, too."

A sudden gust of wind from the sea rocked Ferne and sliced through her. She trembled and wished she had put on her coat. "I could just be a tourist."

"I could say the same about us. But we're no'," Nikolai replied.

Esther held up her hands before her. "I know something is going on, but I can't pinpoint what it is. He doesn't sense anything wrong, which should alleviate my worries, but it doesn't."

Ferne raised a brow as she lifted her gaze to Nikolai's baby blue eyes. "You can sense magic?"

"Aye."

She waited for more, but he refused to say anything else. There was something different about Nikolai. Finally, Ferne blew out a breath. "I don't know much."

"But you know something," Esther said. "We'd love to hear it."

"Not before I know what he is." Ferne stood her ground, not looking away from Nikolai.

A slow smile spread over his face. "I'm a Dragon King."

Ferne blinked, unsure if she had heard him correctly.

"Let's talk somewhere more private," Esther said.

Ferne hesitated.

Before she could say more, Nikolai's gaze moved past her. "Henry?"

Esther looked behind Ferne. "Henry," she suddenly exclaimed and raced around Ferne.

Ferne turned and watched the couple greet a man with the same brown hair as Esther. As they talked, her mind tried to grasp what she had just learned. A Druid and a Dragon King. A *Dragon King*. She took a step back, wishing she wasn't alone. She didn't think Esther would harm her, but she wasn't sure she wanted to take the chance with a Dragon King. Ferne didn't wait for them to remember her. Instead, she got in her car and drove away.

CHAPTER THIRTEEN

Someone was watching her. Ferne felt the tingle on the back of her neck. She turned and looked into the back seat just to be sure no one was there, but it was empty. As she drove away, a glance outside showed Esther and Nikolai in deep conversation with the other man. No other cars followed her. So, who could possibly be watching?

Or maybe her imagination had gotten the better of her.

In the short time she had been on Skye, there had been an abundance of odd occurrences, beginning at the pools. With Theo. She would like to think he was the catalyst, but the truth was, only one person was to blame. Her. She was never meant to be on the isle, yet she had ignored generations of warnings. What did that say about her?

Ferne glanced at the time on the dash and grimaced. She only had a few hours before she expected Mason to contact her. She had mucked things up terribly with Kirsi. She couldn't do the same with Rhona and Mason. To be fair, her brother would listen to her ramblings and pick out the important things. Others didn't know her well enough to do that. But that didn't mean she shouldn't be prepared for her sibling.

Both she and Mason had been in protection mode with each other since their parents' deaths. His had ramped up over the last few months, and she now realized it was because he suspected that someone had killed their mum and dad. She was used to Mason's overbearing ways, but she could talk him out of things most times. But if he thought her life was in danger, he wouldn't listen to anything she said. He would get her somewhere safe and then let her talk. And *that* was what she wanted to avoid.

She needed to be on Skye. Had to help Kirsi. Needed to stand with the other Druids. To…well, she wasn't sure what exactly, but she knew in her gut that she needed to remain until they defeated the danger she sensed.

There was more traffic on the roads now as she drove to Rhona's. Once more, Rhona wasn't at home. Ferne decided to wait this time. She sat on the hood of her car, soaking up the warm sun on the cool day. After a while, she climbed back into the Mini and pulled out her phone to record some notes about Skye.

"I need to discover how my visions work. I know other seers also seek this, and I believe there has to be some kind of answer. I feel different here. It's difficult to explain. I…it's almost as if I've been freed. But from what, exactly? The magic on Skye is unlike anything I ever imagined."

She frowned then. "And it's also troubling. The way it responded to me at the Fairy Pools and last night was startling. It's easy to think that it's ignoring me now, but I believe it's more than that. I think it's what I felt in my vision. The great, malevolent threat. Could it be preventing magic?" She shuddered just thinking about it. "Rhona can help me connect the dots. If I could only find her."

Ferne swallowed and looked out the passenger window. "She's going to want to know who I am. Mason would likely tell me to hide it for as long as possible, but I think that way lies folly. I want…no, I need Rhona to believe me. The only way to achieve that is with honesty. To tell her the entire truth as I know it. Even if it gets me kicked off Skye."

She hit the STOP icon. Then, a moment later, she started recording again. "It would be very helpful with everything going on if I could stop thinking about Theo and those kisses. I have the worst timing in the history of the universe. And for all I know, he's just a normal guy who has no idea about magic. I can't imagine introducing him to such a world. He doesn't seem the type to run, but I'm just guessing. I know very little about him other than he's a police officer and helps people. If this trip were merely for a holiday, I'd drive straight to the station right now and ask for him. But it isn't. And I won't. That's too bad, Theo. I would've liked to know you better. And shared many, many more kisses, because… damn, can you kiss."

Ferne ended the recording and slid her mobile into her coat pocket. She used to write in a journal, but her mind moved too fast for that nowadays. Not to mention her hand always cramped. She had a journal app on her computer, and sometimes typing it out was what she needed. Then other times, saying the words, and hearing them aloud, helped her sort through things more clearly. Her father had taught her to always try new things and see if she could get anything to fit what she needed.

It seemed that everything in her life was a hodgepodge of images and details. It was vastly different from others, but it fit her.

Uniquely yours, her mother used to tell her. The pang in her chest began whenever she thought of her parents. They hadn't been perfect—no one was—but they had been hers.

Ferne waited an hour for Rhona before her stomach grumbled. She dug through her purse and found an old receipt. She turned it over and left Rhona a note with her name and number. Ferne stuck it between the door and the jamb of the house, then set out to grab some lunch.

She found a café and got a sandwich takeaway. The shop wasn't full, but she wanted to find somewhere scenic to enjoy her meal. Ferne got on the road and started driving. She passed signs alerting tourists to attractions, but she kept going. No doubt they were beautiful, but she wasn't interested in being around others.

The sun drenched the land from the cloudless sky. She drove, winding her way around Skye until she caught sight of the granite-covered peaks of the Red Cuillin mountain range, or the Red Hills as locals called them. She glimpsed water and pulled off the road to admire it. The sign read Loch Ainort. And surrounding the beautiful body of water were the Cuillins.

There was no mistaking the peace surrounding her. She drew it into her lungs with each breath and absorbed it into her skin as she walked around the isle. The longer she spent on Skye, the more she understood why the ancient Druids had called it home.

Her gaze kept returning to the Red Hills until she got back inside her car and found a parking area in front of the range to admire the view as she ate. The food was good, but nothing could touch the magnificent landscape. She almost snapped some photos and sent them to the London Druid elders just to raise their ire. But that would only cause Mason issues, so she refrained. Barely.

With a better view of the mountains, she let her gaze wander the peaks. The Black Cuillin range was near the Fairy Pools, and while roughly the same height as the Red Hills, that was where their similarities stopped. The Black Cuillins were more rugged and dramatic, with bolder hills, steeper scree slopes, and knife-edged ridges. It was the most challenging mountain range in all of the United Kingdom. The Red Hills were more rounded, but it didn't make them any less splendid. They had areas of steep, rocky terrain but were great for hillwalkers.

Ferne wrapped up the last of her sandwich and smiled as she realized why she had left some items in the boot of her car—specifically her waterproof hiking boots. She hurriedly got out and changed. She dug around, lifting the hidden compartment in the boot, and found the backpack she had stuffed there for emergencies. It had a hat and gloves inside. She added a water bottle, her leftover sandwich, as well as a bag of uneaten crisps. She hid her purse, locked the car, and settled the backpack in place. Then, she set out. She didn't intend to hike long, and she would keep the Mini in sight at all times. But she had to get on the mountain.

She looked at her phone as she set out, checking the compass, just in case. She had about thirty minutes before she expected Mason's call—just enough time for a quick hike.

Ferne hadn't gotten far before she encountered the wind. It pummeled her relentlessly in places. The higher she climbed, the more stunning the views. Every so often, she looked back to check her path and ensure she hadn't deviated too far. At the thirty-minute mark, she knew she should start down. She eyed the top. It was close, and there wasn't a certain time Mason would be there, much less contact her. She could take the time to climb to the summit.

Ferne kept going. The air grew cooler, forcing her to pull out the gloves and beanie and zip her coat. Along with the wind came a short rainfall. She laughed as she looked up at the one cloud in the sky that hung over her. But it didn't deter her from her quest.

She'd spent too many years hiding behind walls instead of really living. And that's what she was doing now. Living. It was stirring and petrifying, but that's what life was supposed to be. She had let her thoughts of becoming an editor for a publishing house go when she left university. She had toyed too long with the idea of her own bookshop until she wasted five years doing little more than helping Mason run the estate.

Skye had opened her eyes—and her heart—to life once more. She couldn't turn her back on it now. The isle called to her. The blood of her ancestors coursed through her, binding her to the magical island as nothing else could.

All the jumbled thoughts in Ferne's head quieted one by one with every step upward until she reached the apex. Then she gloried in the moment, basking in the cool air that slammed into her lungs, the way her wet jeans stuck to her thighs and chilled her, and the bright sun that showered her with its rays. She didn't snap any photos. She didn't take a video. She simply stood and took it all in, locking it away in her memories piece by piece so she could revisit it anytime she needed to remember the exhilarating feeling.

Ferne spread her arms wide and leaned her head back as she closed her eyes. One of her ancestors might have stood on this very spot. Even if they hadn't, it didn't matter. Because she was here. A place that had been forbidden.

But somewhere that welcomed her.

Ferne lowered her arms, but she couldn't stop smiling. Finally, she checked her phone and saw that it had taken her much longer to reach the top than expected. Mason still hadn't contacted her, but she wasn't worried. His meeting had probably run over. That gave her more time on the mountain.

She turned to look for the Mini. A moment of panic set in when she couldn't find it. She retreated a few steps, thinking it was just behind a section of rock, but it wasn't. That's when she checked her compass and realized she had let herself get carried away in the moment and moved far from the vehicle.

The alarm subsided, though. All she had to do was go straight down. She might have a little hike back to the Mini, but it wasn't a big deal. Ferne decided to replenish her energy. She removed the pack and dug out the rest of her sandwich and water as she rested. Once she had finished both, she started walking.

It wasn't a straight trip down as she'd imagined. She had to wind around sections that didn't look at all familiar. Once, she became flustered and lost her footing. She slid about fifteen feet. Ferne managed to slow and then stop herself on a small boulder. Her heart tripped in her throat when she saw a sheer drop past the rock.

Maybe the isle wasn't as welcoming as she'd believed.

In order to get down, she had to climb back up and find another route. She was tiring quickly. Once she found firm ground to stand on, she began searching for the simplest way down. Then she saw what looked like a cave. She looked at it for several minutes. Something was in there. She was sure of it.

Even though she was tired and knew she should get off the mountain, Ferne made her way toward the cave. She reached it easily and stepped inside to find a dark tunnel. She used the torch on her mobile to light the way. The passageway went on for some time, winding one way and then the other. The ground undulated beneath her feet and caused her some alarm when she misjudged and tripped. Then, finally, she reached a low-ceilinged cavern. Beyond it were six smaller hollows that formed a semi-circle.

Recognition slid through her. She knew this place. Not from a vision but from deep within her.

CHAPTER FOURTEEN

SKYE DRUIDS

Theo was mildly surprised to get a message from Sabertooth in his private email, but he probably shouldn't have been, with as skilled as the hacker was. Theo needed a lesson from Finn on how to decode the encrypted files, but once Theo had, he got his first look at just how talented Saber was.

Financials, social media information, email accounts, and phone records for all five of Rhona's deputies, as well as those who had been murdered, waited for him. The only one missing was Kerry, but Theo knew Saber was still sorting through her accounts.

The Knight highlighted anything in the records he felt might be worth a second look. It was the most comprehensive report Theo had ever received. He wanted to hire Saber for himself. With someone like him on hand, Theo could get twice as much work done in half the time.

Theo set about poring over the reports. A part of him wanted to find something. Only because they could finally have a suspect. But he was happy when he agreed with Saber's assessment that there was nothing to be found with any of the deputies. That didn't mean nothing was there, though. It meant there wasn't anything digital. Still, it was one step closer to clearing them.

He moved on to the reports for the victims. There was some crossover, but then again, everyone had lived on the isle. It was bound to happen. Yet Theo couldn't find anything to link them that pointed him in any one direction. Which frustrated him.

Theo pushed back the chair and stood. While on his way out of the room, he nearly collided with Elodie. "Sorry," he muttered.

"Oops," she said with a laugh. "Just the guy I was looking for."

"Something wrong?"

She shook her head. "I was going to call until I realized I didn't have my mobile." She pointed inside the room and let out a sigh as she walked to pick it up off the floor. "It must have slipped out of the back pocket of my jeans this morning when I sat down."

"Call me about what?"

"It's probably nothing."

"Everything is something, even if we doona know it right away. Something caught your attention. What was it?"

Elodie swallowed and tucked her mobile into her back pocket. "I was watching Lyra when she went into the co-op."

"Okay," Theo said. Lyra was the youngest of Rhona's deputies, but also one of Rhona's biggest supporters.

"The woman you were with last night at dinner was there."

Theo hoped there was no reaction on his face. "It's a co-op."

"True, but she looked troubled when she walked out. Not long after, Kirsi Brown ran out the back of the store, really upset. Nora followed and tried to talk to her, but Kirsi didn't seem to want to listen."

"Interesting." Theo knew from experience that it could be nothing. But it could be something.

Elodie drew in a deep breath. "There's more."

"Tell me." He just hoped it had nothing to do with Ferne.

"The woman…" Elodie began.

"Her name is Ferne."

"Ferne," Elodie corrected. "She was stopped by a man and a woman around our age."

Theo shifted his weight to his other foot, instantly on alert. "Stopped?"

"They walked in front of her. She seemed surprised by their appearance."

"Did you catch their conversation?"

"I didn't have a clear view of Ferne's face from my position in the car, but she looked tense. The man and woman were both at ease and smiling."

Theo wished for the hundredth time that he had Ferne's number. He told himself that what Elodie saw could mean anything or nothing, but that didn't stop his worry. "What happened then?"

"The man noticed another guy walking up. That got the woman's attention. Ferne turned to see who it was, but she quickly slipped off and drove away."

"Perhaps they thought she was a local and wanted directions or something."

Elodie shrugged. "Maybe. It didn't look that way to me, though. I thought you might be interested."

"I am. Thanks."

"She's pretty."

Theo nodded absently. "Aye."

"Are you going to see her again?"

"It's no' as if I have a lot of time."

Elodie shot him a grin. "Everyone has to eat."

"I doona know how to contact her."

"I bet Saber could find out."

Theo couldn't believe he hadn't thought of that. It would take seconds to ask Saber to find her, but should Theo be using his resources that way? "If you saw the couple again, would you be able to recognize them?"

"Definitely. A person doesn't forget a man like him. He was pretty distinctive."

"Distinctive how?"

"Tall and broad-shouldered with auburn hair. He held himself with confidence, but also...I don't know how to describe it exactly."

Theo filed that away. "You do realize we're Scottish, right? Lots of redheads walking around."

"You'd spot him. Trust me," she replied.

They walked out of the room together and headed down the long hallway. Theo couldn't stop thinking about what Elodie had told him. "I never asked if Ferne knew anyone here. It's her first time on Skye. At least, that's what she told me. Truth be told, we have no' known each other verra long."

"Long enough for you to be interested."

He glanced at Elodie to find her grinning. He couldn't quite make himself return it. "She could be a Druid."

"Lots of people have Druid blood in them but can't do magic. Just because they come to Skye doesn't mean anything."

"Does it no'?" he questioned as they descended the stairs.

Elodie trailed one hand along the railing as she walked. "The only way you'll know, I suppose, is by talking to her."

Which he wanted to do. Even though he shouldn't. Despite that he needed to focus everything he had on the current situation. Ferne hovered in his mind, waiting for the most inopportune moments to flutter into his awareness. Her smile, her voice. Her kisses.

"You're a detective, Theo. Use your skills to learn who she is."

"I doona have the time."

They reached the bottom floor, and Elodie stopped to face him. "You're obviously worried about her. And you can always say it's to figure out if she's a Druid so you can question her about the goings-on."

"You make it sound so rational."

"Because it is." She laughed and shook her head. "Don't make it more convoluted than it needs to be."

He snorted. Elodie had a valid point.

"What worries you more? That she came here with a mission about Druids? Or that she didn't?" Elodie asked.

"I wish I knew."

She gave him a sad smile. "I'm rooting for you."

Theo followed her out of the manor, locking the door as he did. She drove away while he walked to his car. He had hours before he was supposed to meet everyone back here to go over the day. Hopefully, those watching the deputies and Kerry would have something. Actually, he hoped everyone had something to report. The case needed to move forward. It had been stalled for too long.

As he drove, Theo couldn't help looking for Ferne's black Mini convertible. There were others on the isle, but hers was a distinctive John Cooper Works model with red mirrors and red-trimmed racing stripes on the hood. Unfortunately, he didn't spot it. He wasn't sure what he would've done if he had.

Theo called the chief and checked in with her as he went to his destination. He didn't give her details over the phone. They'd meet later for that, but he wanted her to know that he was working the case.

"I had no doubt," she said. "And your team? Are you happy with things? You've not asked for anything."

"I've no doubt I will. We're just getting sorted."

"And you don't know who you can trust."

He flattened his lips. "Right now, everyone is a suspect."

"Whether they're from your group or not?"

Theo noted the statement and treated it as such. "Aye, ma'am."

"Can't say I blame you. Keep me posted," she said before hanging up.

Theo found his target's address and looked for a place to park. It was because of Elodie's and Elias's words the night before that he had decided to make Edie his priority. Not because he didn't believe Elodie or Elias could be impartial when it came to their sister or her children, but because he was making sure they didn't have to make that choice. Theo also didn't want either of them worrying about whether their sister might be a suspect. He hadn't told anyone he planned to follow Edie. Theo didn't think he'd find anything, but he wouldn't stake his life on it either. Not with how things had been going on the isle over the last weeks.

Edie and Trevor's kids would likely get marked off the suspect list quickly. After all, they were children and spent the majority of their days in school. Not to mention, it would take someone with impressive magic to wield the mist. That wasn't to say a Druid child couldn't have magic that potent, but if they did use it, it was because an adult had instructed them how.

That was why he focused on Edie. Trevor wasn't a suspect because he didn't have magic. Theo would feel better if he could clear Edie sooner rather than later. And he was sure Elias and Elodie felt the same way.

CHAPTER FIFTEEN

Henry stood on the back porch and gazed at the mountain rising imposingly from the ground. He knew his place was with his sister. They were a team. Esther was the TruthSeeker, and he was the JusticeBringer. The Ancients—long-dead Druids—had chosen the Clacher family to regulate Druids. In each generation, one female was born a TruthSeeker, and one male the JusticeBringer.

Their ancestors had been so feared that a powerful *drough* named Deirdre had wiped out all the Clachers. Or so everyone thought. The Warriors and Druids of MacLeod Castle had fought and vanquished Deirdre, but the swath of destruction she wrought across Scotland had lasting effects.

Everything Henry and Esther thought they knew about themselves had been obliterated not long ago. It was more than them being adopted. It was more than learning they were part of an age-old game set up long before they even walked this Earth.

It was so much more than accepting a destiny they had no control over.

At one time, Henry had thought his days working as a spy for MI5 would be the most dangerous thing he ever did. But that was before he learned his friend, Banan, was much more than a rich Scot. He was, in fact, a Dragon King. It seemed a lifetime ago that Henry had tumbled into a world of shapeshifting Highlanders who made the world's most sought-after whiskey.

Henry had walked away from MI5 without a backward glance. The dangers he'd thought inhabited the globe were nothing compared to what he discovered after aligning with the Kings. He didn't have magic and couldn't shift, but he was the eyes and ears to the human world the Kings couldn't reach.

Henry had naively believed he could keep his sister unaware of things. While he had held his confidences close, she had secrets of her own. Namely, working for MI5, as well. That had led to Esther getting caught up with some bad people who used her against him and the Kings. Things could have gone terribly wrong then, but with the help of the Dragon Kings' magic, along with the Druids and a few special Fae, Esther had survived the ordeal.

And found love with a Dragon King.

The cool wind ruffled Henry's hair. He kept his hands in his coat pockets and tried not to think about coming back to Earth. That was a sentence he'd never imagined would go through his mind. Zora. It was where the dragons that had once roamed Earth now lived. All of the unmated Kings were on Zora now, fighting a new enemy.

Henry had gone to the new realm because he'd felt an undeniable pull to it. Esther had been devastated. They were a team. They were supposed to remain together. Yet he knew he had to be on Zora. Everyone, including Constantine, the King of Dragon Kings, had believed it was because of Mel—

"I'm not sorry you're back."

Henry drew in a breath and released it at the sound of Esther's voice. "I know."

"Are you ever going to tell us what happened on Zora? Why you returned so soon?"

"I'm sure Nikolai can find out from Con."

Esther walked around him, stopping before him. She raised a slender brown brow. "I'm not asking Nikolai. I'm asking you."

"Things are…unstable on Zora. The dragons aren't thrilled with the arrival of all the Kings."

"But the Kings are there to help keep them safe," she said with a frown of confusion.

Henry shrugged. "Try to tell them that."

"But what does that have to do with you?"

"I'm human. On Zora, the humans keep to their area, far from the dragons, so as not to repeat what happened here."

Esther's lips flattened. "I see."

"Yet, there I was, riling them up."

His sister tucked a strand of brown hair caught in the wind behind her ear. "Not on purpose. You belong on Earth, though. I know you don't want to hear that, but it's a fact. This is where the Druids are. There aren't any Druids on Zora."

"Maybe. Maybe not." He looked over her head to the mountain again. "There are plenty of other beings there. Banshees, Amazons, elves, and redheaded warriors that live for hundreds of years."

"And you think there are Druids among them."

He dropped his gaze to her. "Something pulled me there."

"We both know it wasn't something. It was some*one*."

Henry clenched his jaw. Just like Con, his sister didn't look any further. "This has nothing to do with her."

"It has everything to do with Melisse, and the sooner you accept that, the sooner you can figure out why."

"Drop it," Henry demanded and walked away.

Esther followed, dogging his feet as she had since the moment she learned to walk. "The hell I will. You love her."

He whirled around so fast that Esther collided with his chest and staggered back a step. Henry let his anger fill his face, his eyes, and his voice. "I don't want to talk about her. Ever. So, I'm only going to say this once. I wasn't on Zora for her. Whatever was between us, if there ever *was* anything, is gone."

"Henry…" Esther began.

He held up a hand. "I mean it. No more, or I return to Dreagan."

"You're on Skye because you know something is wrong," she stated indignantly, her nutmeg eyes narrowing. "Don't use me as an excuse to run away. I'll figure this out without you. I was doing that anyway."

She spun on her heel and stormed back inside the house, slamming the door behind her to reaffirm her fury. Henry dropped his head back with a sigh and closed his eyes against the bright sunlight.

He straightened and walked out onto the grass. It would be easy to run to the mountain and let it take him. He loved this world of magic and mayhem he found himself in. But, sadly, it didn't seem to love him. After the embarrassing and catastrophic events of believing he was in love with Rhi, Con's mate, Henry had somehow found his footing again. Then along came Melisse.

He'd sworn after his years of living lies as an agent with MI5 that he wouldn't go through that again. Yet he found himself falling for someone who turned out to be a liar wanting only to use him. It had been too much.

The sound of the door opening alerted Henry that he was no longer alone. He tensed, waiting to hear more of Esther's tirade, but a deep, Scottish brogue filled the air instead.

"I thought you could use this."

Henry looked to the side to find Nikolai holding out a glass of familiar amber liquid. Henry accepted the whiskey with a nod of thanks and downed it. "If you've come to tell me I need to apologize to my sister, you should go back inside."

"I'm no' taking sides."

"Right," Henry said with a snort.

Nikolai chuckled and turned to look at the mountains with Henry. "As far as your sister goes, she believes I'm here to talk some sense into you."

Henry turned his head to the Dragon King and quirked a brow.

"She's my mate. I go to bed with her every night," Nikolai said with a shrug. "I'm always going to do anything and everything I can to help her. She does the same for me. It's what couples do."

Henry rolled the empty glass in his hand. "You said she thinks you're out here to talk to me."

"You're a grown man. You can make your own decisions. You doona need anyone telling you what you should or shouldna do. No' even your sister."

"That's the problem. I don't know what to do."

"That's no' entirely true, is it?"

Henry blew out a breath and looked away. "I can't go back to

Zora. I might not like what I was told, but I understand the reasons."

"Did you tell Con something pulled you there?"

"I did. I appreciate that Con is walking a fine line. He doesn't rule there. His children do, and the dragons are rebelling at the appearance of all the Kings. My arrival made things worse."

Nikolai scrubbed a hand over his jaw. "If something drew you, it will continue to do so. In the meantime, your sister needs you. I can no' feel anything is off on Skye, but she insists it is. Have you felt anything?"

Henry inwardly winced before looking at Nikolai. "No, but I've not been paying attention either. As soon as I got to Dreagan, they told me you and Esther were here. So, I came."

"Esther hasn't said anything to you, but she's worried. Verra worried. We stopped a Druid today. I'm no' sure why Esther wanted to talk to Ferne, but then we saw you."

Henry's brow puckered as he recalled the woman standing with them on the sidewalk outside the co-op. "Why that particular Druid?"

"Something sparked Esther's interest. You know her need to seek out the truth."

"So, we need to find Ferne again."

"I think we should."

Henry gently tossed the glass into the air and caught it in his palm. "Let's get started, then. Esther and I might not have magic, but our positions don't leave us entirely adrift." He handed the glass to Nikolai. "Let me get a feel for the isle before I go inside."

Nikolai nodded and left without another word. Most all the Kings were that way. Then again, if he lived to be millions of years old, he probably wouldn't waste words either. Henry turned his back to the house and walked toward the mountain.

He and Esther had visited Skye with their adoptive parents when they were much younger, but it was nothing like being on the isle now that they both knew of the hidden world of magical beings that lived alongside humans.

Henry had discovered his ability to sense where a Druid had been killed. It had come unexpectedly while they were after one of the Kings' fiercest enemies, a Fae named Usaeil. She had slain Druids and took their magic. The world had collectively sighed when they finally defeated her.

One of the things Henry had the hardest time with was being part of an ancient line that policed Druids without having magic himself. It didn't make sense to him. How could he and Esther regulate Druids without it? Yet, somehow, they did. Esther would know that something was off and search for the truth. Once she found it, he was there to mete out justice.

There were several generations without a TruthSeeker and JusticeBringer, but the titles were known among the Druids. Maybe not all, but large congregations like those on Skye, for sure. He didn't want to make himself known yet, but he might not have a choice. Esther was seeking, and that usually meant justice would soon follow.

He halted and closed his eyes as the quiet of Skye drowned out the rest of the world. On the surface, everything felt normal. He went deeper, still without noticing anything. Then, just as he retreated, he felt something. It was gone in an instant, but it had been there.

Henry's eyes flew open. He spun around and lengthened his strides as he made his way inside the house. He found Esther and

Nikolai in the kitchen. Both paused in their conversation to look at him.

Henry's gaze locked on Esther's. "There's something here."

"I knew it. What did you feel?" she demanded.

Henry shrugged as he glanced at Nikolai. "Just something that didn't feel right."

"Well," Nikolai said, "perhaps *now* it's time we speak to Rhona."

Esther rolled her eyes. "He's been after me to do that since we arrived."

"You mean you haven't?" Henry asked in shock.

Esther gave him a flat look. "I wanted to take a look around myself."

"We've done it. Now, we visit Rhona and Balladyn," Henry stated.

CHAPTER SIXTEEN

Ferne moved around the caverns, investigating each of the six smaller grottos. She wished Mason was with her. He would have an idea of what this place was. Thinking about her brother made her remember she was waiting to hear from him. She checked her phone but saw she had no signal. That meant she couldn't stay inside long. She didn't want to worry Mason needlessly.

Her gaze followed the trail of light from her phone. The place seemed ordinary, but she knew it wasn't. She instinctively knew Druids had created it. But for what? She turned the light to the six caverns. If she didn't know better, she'd think they were holding cells, given how they were set up. The only thing missing was metal bars. Not that Druids would need actual doors to hold another Druid.

Ferne set her backpack aside and walked to a nearby wall. She studied a section, and before she knew it, she removed her glove and placed her bare hand on the cold granite. The edges of her eyesight became fuzzy, causing her to blink rapidly to clear it.

Not once in her life had she ever touched anything and gotten a vision, yet it felt like that was trying to happen. She pushed her magic into the rock. It didn't make the vision come, but it did light up the entire area in a golden glow.

How she wished she could communicate with stone. It had a story to tell, and she wanted to hear it. But that wasn't her gift. She left her hand on the wall and lowered her phone to see the sparkle along the walls. It was like thousands of tiny gold stars lighting up. Around her. Above her. Below her. They were everywhere. To think, if she hadn't come to Skye, she wouldn't have experienced this.

The lights began to blink out one by one. Ferne pushed more of her magic into the rock to ignite them once more, but they kept going out. Until she was swathed in darkness once more. Ferne had never been scared of the dark, but this felt different. Even the light from her phone barely extended a few feet past her when it had once shone easily.

Ferne suddenly felt nauseous. Her knees went weak as if her blood sugar had plummeted. The mobile slipped from her fingers. She put both hands on the wall to keep herself upright, but even that became impossible. She turned and put her back to the wall, sliding down it when her legs gave out.

It wasn't long before she found herself flat on her back, looking up at the darkness above. Then she saw it. One tiny, golden light.

Theo had prepared to watch Edie for the rest of the afternoon and into the next morning. He was happy to finally be parked near her house after all the nonstop running around. Between the rentals and the kids' after-school activities, the woman never stopped. He'd had no idea Edie was so busy.

He had a good view into the house, helped by all the windows. The kids were upstairs in their rooms while Edie was in the kitchen preparing dinner. Theo glanced at the two protein bar wrappers. He had more, but he craved something with more substance. Too bad he wouldn't get it anytime soon.

Theo returned his gaze to the house to find Edie staring out a window, seemingly lost in thought. She was so out of it that she didn't realize her daughter had walked up. It took the girl shaking her before Edie finally snapped out of it. There was an exchange between the two, and while he couldn't read lips, he did see Edie's exasperation and the daughter's frustration before she stormed off.

No family was perfect, no matter what they showed the world. Before this, he would've said Edie's family seemed to have a good life. That made him think back to when he was in his teens, and Edward MacLean was killed.

All anyone could talk about was how great the MacLean family was. Now that Theo knew the truth, he wondered how Elias, Edie, and Elodie had kept it all inside. Especially Elias, when his father began physically abusing him.

People showed the world what they wanted others to see. Theo was guilty of that, too. He didn't want anyone to know how overworked he was. Or lonely. Or tired. Damn, was he ever tired. There seemed to be no rest for the wicked. The minute he dealt with one foe, another popped up. He understood there was a balance, but sometimes people became exhausted. Weary.

Sapped.

He rubbed his eyes. He had a long night ahead of him. He

wasn't particularly happy about spying on his friends' sister, but it had to be done. His phone vibrated. He looked at the screen to see Rhona was calling.

"Hey," he answered.

"I hate to cut your night short, but you need to come to the manor."

"Something wrong?"

She paused for half a second. "There's more information coming in."

"From?"

"Nikolai. And Esther and Henry."

"A Dragon King?"

"Aye," Rhona said. "And the TruthSeeker and the JusticeBringer."

He frowned. Why did those words sound familiar? "Who?"

"Do you remember Corann teaching us about how the Druids used to be policed by the Clacher family?"

"I do."

"Well, Esther and Henry are from that family. She's the TruthSeeker, and he's the JusticeBringer. And Esther happens to be Nikolai's mate."

"I'll be there as soon as I can."

Theo got to the manor in record time. He wasn't the last one there, which meant he had to wait for the rest. They gathered in the front room. He greeted Nikolai, who stayed near Esther. Theo looked between her and her sibling, Henry, before welcoming them.

Once Carlyle and Filip finally arrived, introductions were made all around. They took longer than Theo was comfortable with since he wanted to get to the reason for the gathering. Henry had questions about the Knights, but he kept them minimal. Nikolai also displayed interest, but he didn't voice any questions. No doubt he would later.

"So," Rhona said as she looked at the siblings, "you said it was important."

Esther crossed one jean-clad leg over the other where she sat on the sofa. "I didn't expect such a large group."

"We're on a time constraint," Balladyn replied.

Theo nodded. "Too many Druids have been murdered recently, and we need to find the perpetrator."

"Why no' ask the Kings for help?" Nikolai demanded with a frown. "Or the Reapers?"

Rhona sat taller in her chair. "Do you ask for aid for every problem?" She paused for a moment. "We're trying to handle things ourselves. If we can't, then I have no problem calling on friends."

Theo saw the look that passed between Balladyn and Nikolai.

"Nikolai and I have been here for a few days," Esther said. "Something brought me here."

"She seeks," Nikolai explained. "It's what she does when there's a problem."

Elias grunted. "We've plenty of issues on Skye at the moment."

"I…" Esther began and then stopped. She pressed her hands together in her lap.

Henry looked at his sister and then continued. "I arrived today. I was too caught up in other things to notice, but once I was reminded why Esther came, I tried to sense if anything was amiss."

"We know the answer to that," Bronwyn replied.

Theo nodded. "We do, but I'm curious to know what you found out."

Henry's brown eyes met his. "It was quick. Barely a blip, really, but there's something here. I couldn't tell you what, but it feels…" He paused, searching for the right word.

"Wrong," Elodie supplied.

Esther nodded. "Yes. Something's off."

Rhona put her hand to her head. "The mist is killing Druids. Someone controls it, and we're trying to figure out who that is. On top of that, some Druids are seeing their magic wane. Not just a little. They're losing it."

"Bloody hell," Henry murmured.

Theo frowned at Rhona. Why hadn't he been told that?

As if sensing his gaze, she turned to him. "I made a judgment call in not telling anyone. I didn't want word to get out and scare our people more than they already are."

"How did you find out?" Theo asked.

"Druids either went to their deputies or came to me directly."

He gave her a nod of acceptance. She wouldn't have kept it from anyone if it had to do with the murders. Though it might very well be connected. He needed to think on that some more.

"And then there are the Ancients," Rhona finished.

Esther shook her head. "What about them?"

"No one's heard from them in weeks," Sabryn answered.

Nikolai crossed his arms over his chest, his frown deepening. "You know for sure that no one has heard from them?"

"They are selective about who they speak to," Henry said. "We know that from the Druids at Dreagan and MacLeod Castle."

Rhona released a long breath. "Those I've spoken to said the Ancients have gone silent. Isla from MacLeod Castle said they've not said anything to her since the Reaper and Fae battle on Skye."

"Fuck," Henry murmured.

Theo agreed with the sentiment.

"There is a Druid who might know something," Esther said. "I saw her earlier today. She's British and visiting Skye."

Theo stiffened, his mind immediately going to Ferne. But what were the odds Esther was speaking about her?

"She was visiting the Druid-owned co-op," Nikolai added.

Theo scooted to the edge of his seat, remembering what Elodie had said about Ferne going to the co-op. His heart started to race. He didn't believe in coincidences. "Why do you want to talk to this Druid?"

All eyes turned to him, but he was focused on Esther.

She held his gaze for a heartbeat before saying, "I seek. And she's not only a Druid. I believe she is here on a mission."

"What makes you think that?" It couldn't be Ferne. It just couldn't. Theo's mind raced with the probability.

"You know Ferne?" Esther said.

Theo's lungs seized. Out of the corner of his eye, he caught Rhona and Balladyn exchange a look. "What?" he asked them.

"Ferne left a message at our house," Balladyn explained.

Theo slowly sat back in the chair. Why did everything lead to Ferne?

"Theo, do you know her?" Rhona pressed.

He cleared his throat and nodded. "No' well. I met her the night before last at the Fairy Pools. We went to dinner, but I got called to work."

"Scott and I saw them," Elodie added.

Theo looked at the ground, scanning the few memories he had of Ferne. He'd thought she almost said the word *magic* at the pools, but could he be sure of that now? Or was what he learned clouding his recollections? He couldn't be sure. And that's what bothered him the most.

The facts were simple. Ferne was on Skye. She had visited the co-op, though it was mere speculation that she spoke to the Browns. Though Esther and Nikolai confirmed Ferne was a Druid. An English Druid on Skye. It could mean nothing.

But it could mean so much.

He barely knew Ferne. So what if he was attracted to her and had enjoyed the bit of time he'd spent with her? And their kisses. Hot, steamy, hungry kisses. That meant nothing if she was somehow involved in the tangle he was trying to unravel. It wouldn't be the first time he'd had to set aside his personal feelings for a case. Nor would it be the last.

Then why did it feel as if he'd been sucker punched?

Theo drew in a breath and looked up. Once more, everyone watched him. He met Rhona's gaze. "We need to talk to Ferne."

"I'll ring her to meet," Rhona said.

Theo almost snatched the paper from Rhona's hands so he could have Ferne's number. Balladyn's brow quirked in response. Theo clenched his fists and waited.

After a short while, Rhona lowered the phone. "She's not answering."

"Then we find her. There's a connection between several of us and this woman. Let's not waste time," Balladyn said.

Filip straightened from the wall he'd been leaning against. "Skye isna that big. If she's here, we'll find her."

"Her Mini is unique." Theo described it, even as the knot in his stomach tightened. "Let's split up and search."

His feet felt laden as he walked from the manor and slid behind the wheel of his vehicle. As he started the engine, the passenger door opened, and Finn folded himself into the seat. Their gazes met. Theo wanted to say something, but he couldn't find the words.

"We'll find her, mate," Finn said.

There was no teasing, no judgment. Just a simple statement. But it was exactly what Theo needed to hear.

CHAPTER SEVENTEEN

SKYE DRUIDS

Somehow, Edie managed to keep a smile on her face and her thoughts to herself. The dinner had gone better than expected, and after the kids had retreated to their rooms, she and Trevor remained to watch the tele. She hadn't paid attention to anything, though. Her thoughts were on the meeting that morning.

Edie could hardly believe the things Kerry had told her—and shown her. The implications were serious, dangerous. Grave.

"Why me?" she had asked. "Why are you showing me this? And what makes you think I won't tell Rhona?"

Kerry merely laughed. "I've been watching you, Edie. You have exactly what I've been looking for."

"And what's that?"

"Rage."

Edie drew back as if struck. "I'm not angry."

"Aren't you?" Kerry asked in a soft voice.

Instead of replying, Edie crossed her arms over her chest. "Rhona needs to know about this. Everyone should know what you've done. What you are."

"You won't tell anyone."

Kerry's self-assured attitude bothered Edie. "You're a murderer."

"I'm cleansing our people." Kerry shrugged. "How do you know others won't think you're an accomplice?"

"Because I'll tell them I'm not."

Kerry smiled again. "You really think I'd let that happen? If for one second I think that you'll do something stupid, I'll send the mist after your children."

Edie's stomach dropped to her feet.

Kerry took a step toward her, her hands at her sides. "You're a smart woman, Edie. Soon, you'll see how beneficial this arrangement can be. Just take the blinders you're wearing off."

"Blinders?" What in the world was Kerry talking about?

"You came because you wanted answers about your husband."

"I do. But you don't know anything, do you?"

Kerry's lips twisted. "Oh, I know a lot. So could you if you'd just look. It's all right there."

"You're daft. Utterly mad. And so am I to come here expecting to get actual answers."

Her smile remained as Kerry said, "The magic that runs through your family's bloodline is stronger than you know. When I'm finished, the Druids will be as powerful as we once were—as we always should've been. I'm going to put us back on track. You can join me and reap the benefits. Or…wait to discover your fate. It's up to you."

Kerry walked away, leaving Edie alone with the weight of the words.

And it had stayed with her since. Edie wished she disagreed with Kerry about the Druids needing a purge. Their magic was dwindling, and everyone knew the cause. She was part of it by finding love with someone who didn't have magic. Trevor knew what she was, and he agreed with the kids being taught how to use their magic.

But how Kerry was going about what she called *cleansing* concerned Edie. Though how else could Kerry do it. But to join Kerry? Edie couldn't do that. It was enough that she knew what was happening and wasn't going to Rhona or the police. Part of that was Kerry's threat to the kids, but Edie didn't want to get involved with such things. She had a much more important matter on her hands.

She glanced at Trevor, who laughed at something on the tele. Before this rift between them, she would've immediately told him every detail. She missed the closeness they'd once had.

Edie reached over and covered his hand with hers. He didn't even appear to notice as he kept his attention on the screen. She scooted closer to him and tucked her legs against her, leaning against him. Finally, he briefly slid his gaze to hers and smiled.

"How was your day?" she asked as she propped her elbow on the back of the couch.

He shrugged. "A normal day."

She tried not to feel the sting when he didn't ask about hers. Closing the rift would take longer than she had hoped, but it didn't deter her. "I was thinking we could go away for the weekend."

"The kids have a full schedule."

"I could ask Elodie and Elias to help. They're here now."

Trevor sighed and paused the show. His mouth was tight as he faced forward, not bothering to even look at her. "This isna a good weekend. I've got too much going on, and it's last-minute."

"We used to take impulsive, last-minute trips all the time. I think we should get back to doing that again. I'm trying, honey. It would be great if you could meet me halfway."

He turned his head to look at her then, his eyes meeting hers. His expression softened as he nodded. "You're right. I'm sorry. This weekend will be difficult."

"But it can be done?"

He considered it for a moment and then nodded. "I might be able to pull it off."

"Okay. Where do you want to go?" She could barely contain her excitement.

"Doesna matter. You pick."

She grinned and played with his hair. "Why don't we do what we used to do and just get in the car and drive until we find a place?"

"We can do that."

"Could you take half a day on Friday so we can leave early?"

Trevor considered that for a moment before shrugging. "I might. Depends on how the week goes, but I'll do my best."

Edie threw her arms around him and kissed his cheek. Whatever had pulled them apart was being mended. And that was all that mattered. "I love you."

He gave her a kiss and a smile and then restarted the show.

The one pinprick of light was growing bigger. Brighter. Ferne couldn't take her eyes off it. She felt heavy, like something pressed down on her to keep her pinned to the ground. She should be cold, but she was strangely comfortable.

She became the light. Or the light became her. All she knew was that, eventually, she was within the golden glow. The feeling of warmth and safety surrounded her before it slowly began to dissipate. Out of the corner of her eye, she saw shadowy silhouettes, but each time she tried to look at them, they disappeared.

Her eyes grew heavy. Ferne fought against it, but there was no escaping whatever was happening. Soon, she drifted between consciousness and sleep.

"Help."

The voice was barely a whisper. Neither male nor female. She was lucid enough to realize it wasn't a dream. Someone was attempting to communicate with her as she had with Kirsi. In her mind. *"Who are you?"* Ferne asked.

"Help."

"Who are you?" she asked again.

"Help."

Ferne tried another approach. *"What do you need?"*

"Help."

"How? I don't know what to do."

"Don't fight."

Before Ferne could ask what the voice meant, it retreated. She didn't see anything, but she felt it. Someone needed assistance, and they had gotten her into the cave to do it. It would be foolish to rush off and give aid to someone who could be part of the malevolence surrounding the isle.

But it had her. Ferne wasn't sure she had a choice.

Yet she wasn't afraid. Somehow, she had recognized the cavern and had known to use her magic. Ferne basked in the light's glow and trusted whatever was happening.

"Got it," Finn said and hung up the phone. He looked at Theo. "They found the Mini at the Red Hills."

Theo glanced behind him to ensure no one was there and then jerked the wheel around, swinging his vehicle in the opposite direction. He slammed his foot down on the accelerator and gunned the engine. The tires squealed as the car leapt to do as he wanted.

Finn put his hands on the dash. "Easy, Frasier."

There was no holding back. Theo had to get to Ferne before the others did. He had to interrogate her. No. No, he needed to talk to her. But what if she was a suspect? Then he should question her. He slammed his hand on the steering wheel. Why did everything have to be so fucking difficult?

"We're close," Finn told him. "We'll beat most of them."

Most. But not all. Sabryn and Carlyle had found Ferne's vehicle. No doubt Balladyn had teleported himself and Rhona already. Theo took a corner too fast. He saw Finn reach for the handle above him.

Theo demanded too much of the car. It gave what it could, but it couldn't get him there as quickly as he wanted. The drive took too long, mounting his frustration to an all-new high. He exchanged no more words with Finn. Theo's mind ran through various situations as he sped his way to the Mini and Ferne.

"Ah, you might want to slow down, mate," Finn cautioned.

"You're going to run over Carlyle. I mean, he does need a kick in the pants occasionally, but I'd rather him not be squished."

Theo slammed on the brakes, the car skidding to a stop on the gravel and dirt. He nearly forgot to put the vehicle in park before he was out and striding to Ferne's car. Sabryn, Carlyle, Balladyn, and Rhona stood aside as he looked inside the Mini.

"She's not here," Sabryn said.

Theo straightened and looked up at the dark mountain range standing against the night sky. Was Ferne a good climber? Had she come prepared? Few remained on the slopes after nightfall unless they camped. What if she had fallen and hurt herself? What if she was lost?

"Hey," Rhona said, touching his arm to get his attention.

Theo whirled on her so fast he knocked her arm away. Behind him, Balladyn growled. Someone turned on the flashlight app on their phone to give some light, allowing Theo to meet Rhona's gaze.

"We want to talk to her, Theo," Rhona continued. "That's it. Talk. No one is doing anything else."

Carlyle leaned against Sabryn's vehicle and said, "In other words, calm down."

He was calm. Or as calm as he could be. Theo took a deep breath and then released it. He didn't feel any better. He didn't understand the need to find her. Or the urgency that had suddenly overtaken him.

"You're in charge here. Tell us what you want to do," Finn said.

Theo rubbed his forehead, trying to clear his thoughts. "The only reason for Ferne to park here would be to hike."

"Unless she met someone," Sabryn said.

Carlyle looked around. "There are plenty of tracks. We'd never know if she got into another vehicle."

"Then we check the mountains," Balladyn stated.

Finn frowned. "Shouldn't we wait until light?"

"Nay." Theo turned to the mountain. "She's there."

"How do you know?" Rhona asked.

Theo shrugged. "I'm not sure."

He started walking, realizing too late that he wasn't wearing the right shoes or clothing for a climb. But he wasn't going to retreat now. Rhona fell in behind him, and then Balladyn joined. Sabryn, Finn, and Carlyle followed in that order. Theo had no idea where he was going. He used the light from his phone to look around, but it would be so easy to walk right past Ferne in the dark.

Rhona suddenly stopped. Theo halted and followed her line of sight to something in the distance. He couldn't see much in the dark, but something had gotten her attention.

"What is it?" he asked.

She sighed and swung her head to him.

The longer she remained silent, the more uneasy he became. "Rhona?"

"There's a secret place only I, Balladyn, and the deputies know about." She winced and glanced over her shoulder. "Well. A few others know about it."

"Aye," Scott murmured.

Finn chuckled softly. "Not so secret anymore, then."

Theo shifted his weight impatiently. The rest of the team had paused to listen to the conversation, but he paid them no heed. "How close is it?"

"Too close for my comfort," Rhona answered.

Theo lifted his gaze in the direction she looked. What were the odds that Ferne knew about a secret place in the Red Hills?

Carlyle paused with one foot on a boulder. "Is it a coincidence that Ferne parked here instead of any of the dozens of other sections around the mountain?"

Balladyn came up beside Rhona. "We should check it out, regardless."

"Jump us?" Rhona asked.

Theo shook his head. "Ferne could be hurt on the mountainside. We need to walk it."

"Phones out, lights on," Sabryn advised.

Theo tipped his chin at Rhona. "We'll follow you."

"I'll bring up the rear," Balladyn added.

Theo gave him a nod and followed Rhona upward. They had to climb and scramble down in a zigzag pattern to keep on good ground. Theo knew the range well, and he also knew the dangerous regions. Climbing at night was never advised, especially without being dressed for it.

Finally, they reached the hidden entrance. He paused outside the cave and looked back at their cars. It was so dark he could no longer see them. Theo turned to enter when Balladyn made a sound. That was when Theo saw the glow coming from within the tunnel, growing brighter as it came closer.

His mouth fell open when Ferne stood within the entrance. Her eyes were open, but she didn't seem to see any of them. A golden glow covered her silhouette like millions of tiny lights. She walked past them without a word.

"Ferne," he called, but Sabryn put a hand on his arm to quiet him.

Theo watched Ferne walk away before she turned and faced him. But it wasn't him she looked at. It was the sky. Theo looked behind him just in time to see the mist.

A shout sounded behind Theo. He spun toward Ferne and saw the others move into battle stances. But not Ferne. Her arms hung at her sides, and her eyes were locked on the mist. Theo rushed toward her, ready to get between her and the enemy.

"Theo!" someone shouted.

His shoe slid, causing him to lose his balance. He righted himself and rushed to Ferne, his heart beating frantically. Just as he was about to reach her, someone grabbed him. In the next moment, Balladyn yanked him to a stop and teleported him back to his spot.

"What the fuck?" Theo bellowed.

But Balladyn wasn't looking at him.

Theo slid his gaze to Ferne. His heart sank when he noticed the mist weaving around her tighter and faster. Still, she did nothing. There was no fear on her face. And if she wasn't scared of it, that could only mean one thing. He didn't want to believe she controlled it. He wouldn't have if he weren't seeing it with his own eyes. But there was no denying it.

"What's it doing?" Carlyle whispered.

No one answered.

Theo might be furious—and hurt—that Ferne was their suspect, but he had what he needed now. He would have to forget her laugh and the way her kiss had made him ache to his soul. He knew who to stop now, who he had been searching for. Why, though, did it have to be someone he found so charming?

He shook himself, but he still couldn't dislodge the sadness. At least no more Druids would be murdered. Theo motioned to Rhona and Balladyn to do their mixed magic thing. They needed to stop her. Rhona and Balladyn could do that. Easily. Quickly.

Theo wished he could talk to Ferne and ask her why. Why had she killed? Why had she resorted to such drastic measures? He took a step toward her. The mist suddenly halted. It hung suspended for a heartbeat before completely covering Ferne, canceling out the light around her. Something was wrong. Theo fumbled with his phone to shine a light on her. He had to know that she was unhurt, but there was only darkness. The mist wasn't moving.

"Ferne?" he called.

The six of them watched and waited. Theo glanced around, trying to think of a way to get the mist away. There was nothing but boulders and a slippery slope all around them. Theo spotted movement and watched Finn slide slowly around and behind Ferne. Theo held his breath. If she or the mist noticed, neither gave any indication.

Seconds became minutes, and the only sounds were their breathing and the wind. Just when Theo was about to call out to

Ferne again, the mist pulled away from her, retreating a fair distance into the sky in a large ball.

Ferne stood in the same position and appeared unscathed. The golden glow around her remained. Theo was confused at what he had witnessed. Nothing made sense, and he feared it wouldn't until he could talk to Ferne. If she spoke to him. He might have caught their suspect, but the mist could take them out in a heartbeat. But why hadn't it?

Ferne lifted her face to the sky. Theo followed her line of sight to see the mist swirling angrily. Then it darted toward them. Magic pooled in his hands. There was no time to shield himself before the mist was there.

Except it didn't touch him. The light that had clung to Ferne's silhouette expanded outward, blocking the mist. It wasn't deterred, however. It moved around her. Theo remembered Finn and shouted his name, but Ferne was faster. In an instant, she was at Finn's side. She shoved him down and stood before him, her hands out, the light impeding the mist once more. Theo heard the mist swarm furiously before speeding away.

His gaze lowered to Ferne to see the light around her fading. She blinked, her eyes coming into focus on him.

"Theo?" she asked, confusion furrowing her brow.

She swayed then. He rushed to her, dropping to one knee to catch her as she fell.

"What the bloody hell just happened?" Carlyle asked into the silence that followed.

Theo gathered Ferne in his arms and got to his feet. He faced the others. "We'll figure that out off the mountain."

"I can take her," Balladyn offered.

Theo turned away from the Reaper. "I have her."

"Do you really want to slip on the way down?" Rhona asked.

He didn't, but Theo also couldn't release Ferne. He didn't understand his feelings or his need to protect her. Later, he'd take a look at it all, but now wasn't the time.

"Stubborn human," Balladyn mumbled and grabbed Theo's shoulder.

In the next second, the Reaper teleported them to the vehicles. Seconds later, Balladyn had jumped the others down, as well. Finn said nothing as he opened the back door to Theo's car. Theo gently laid Ferne on the back seat and debated whether to climb in with her. But he withdrew and softly closed the door.

"To the manor?" Sabryn called.

Carlyle rested his arms on the hood of the SUV. "Of course."

"Maybe not," Rhona said. "I don't think Bronwyn would appreciate us bringing the one controlling the mist within the walls of her home."

Balladyn nodded once. "Agreed."

"It went after her," Theo felt the need to point out.

Finn walked around to the passenger side of Theo's car. "And then us. Which she stopped."

"You doubt she's controlling it after what we just saw?" Sabryn asked.

Theo scrubbed a hand down his face. "I doona know what to think."

"That doesn't solve where to take her." Carlyle shrugged when Theo looked at him.

Balladyn jerked his chin to the cavern. "The prison is there for a reason."

"That wouldn't stop the mist from getting to her," Finn replied.

Rhona shook her head. "There's nowhere to take her."

But Theo knew of a place. It might be the wrong thing to do, but at this point, he wasn't sure there was a *right* one. "Mine." When the others looked at him, he cleared his throat. "My house."

"Theo," Rhona said, her brows drawn together, "are you sure?"

"Nay," he answered honestly.

Balladyn glanced inside the dark car. "Let's start there. Between my magic and all of yours, we can ward Theo's place to keep her locked inside and the mist out."

"And if we need to move her somewhere, we can." Rhona nodded. "We'll follow you, Theo."

Sabryn patted the back of her vehicle. "We'll let the others know where to go."

Theo said nothing as he started toward his car.

"What about Ferne's Mini?" Finn asked. "Want to leave it here or drive it to your place?"

Theo looked around to discover that everyone was waiting on his decision. "She might have the keys on her."

A quick look came up with nothing. No keys, and no mobile. They must be up in the cave, but Theo didn't want to linger. The mist might come back. Or worse, it could be picking its next victim.

"I'm sending a text to the deputies, telling them to keep an eye out for the mist. We'll get Ferne's car later," Rhona said as if reading his mind.

Everyone climbed into their vehicles while Rhona and Balladyn teleported away. The drive to Theo's house seemed to take forever. Finn didn't attempt to fill the silence, which Theo was grateful for. So much had happened tonight, and he couldn't begin to process any of it. He knew what he saw, and he knew what he wanted, but they weren't meshing.

He pulled into his driveway. Sabryn parked behind him. Theo tossed Finn the keys to unlock the door as he picked up Ferne. As they walked to the front door, Theo heard Basher meowing.

"Wait," he said after Finn had unlocked the deadbolt.

Theo removed the wards on the house and nodded to Finn, who opened the door. Theo was the first one in. Basher glanced at the others behind him, but the cat was more interested in who Theo carried. He glanced toward the sofa but decided to put Ferne in the spare bedroom instead. Sabryn was there to pull back the covers on the bed and help remove Ferne's jacket and boots. Once Ferne was tucked in, Theo straightened and looked down at her.

"You can't make her wake up. Give it time," Sabryn said in a soft voice before walking past him and out of the room.

Theo turned on his heel and started out when he caught a blur of white jumping onto the bed. He sighed when he saw Basher. "Let her rest," he said as he gathered the cat in his arms. "You can get to know her once she's awake."

Basher looked at him with big blue eyes before glancing back at Ferne. The cat jumped out of his arms after Theo closed the door, darting toward the kitchen to await his evening meal, no doubt. Sure enough, by the time Theo walked into the kitchen with the others, Basher was weaving around their legs, headbutting calves in an effort to get fed.

"He's beautiful," Sabryn said as she squatted to run her hands through Basher's long, white fur. "I love the seal point coloring on his ears and tail."

Theo smiled and got out the food. "He's spoiled."

"As all animals should be," Finn replied.

Carlyle eyed the feline as it headed his way again. He leaned as far back on the counter as he could. "I'm more of a dog person."

"He knows. That's why he's going to you," Sabryn said with a chuckle.

A knock sounded then. Carlyle happily went to open the door while Theo filled Basher's bowl and moved it into a quieter room. It wasn't long before everyone had claimed a spot in Theo's small living area after warding his home. He chose to remain standing near the doorway, one ear tuned to the back of the house where Ferne slept.

He stayed quiet as the others filled Scott, Elodie, Filip, Bronwyn, and Elias in. Theo didn't ask about Saber. He assumed the Knights would share details with him later. Everyone had a theory on what had happened. Everyone except him. Unfortunately, the others soon noted that he hadn't spoken.

"What are you thinking?" Elias asked.

Theo shrugged. "I'm trying no' to until I can question Ferne."

"Is that a good idea?" Elodie asked.

He knew he shouldn't take offense to the question, but he did. "Why?"

"Well," she said, drawing out the word, "you two went to dinner."

"A dinner that never happened," he snapped. Theo pushed away from the door and squeezed the bridge of his nose. "I'm sorry, Elodie." He dropped his arm and looked at her. "You're concerned that I'll let my feelings get in the way. I can no' say I willna," he admitted. "That's why I doona intend to be the only one there when I talk to her."

Bronwyn tucked her hair behind her ears. "I don't think we should all be here. It'll be overwhelming and appear as if we're ganging up on her."

"We are," Elias said.

Sabryn wrinkled her nose. "But we shouldn't all be around. Why don't we take shifts? Some of us can stay now while the others get some sleep at the manor. We can swap come morning."

"Sounds reasonable." Rhona turned her head to him. "Theo? What do you think?"

She didn't have to ask him, but he appreciated the effort. He nodded. "It's a good plan."

"Now that that's settled, I'll stay," Finn announced.

Sabryn, Elias, Bronwyn, and Filip remained behind while the other five returned to the manor. It was decided that two of them would stay awake while the others tried to get some rest, changing every three hours. Elias and Bronwyn opted to take the first watch.

Theo made his way down the hall and stopped to check on Ferne. She was on her side facing the door. He quietly closed the door behind him and made his way to his room. But even as exhaustion weighed him down, he knew he wouldn't get any rest.

Not until he had answers from Ferne.

CHAPTER NINETEEN

Ferne shifted beneath the covers, loving the feel of the weighted blanket atop her. She saw sunlight behind her eyelids. She blinked open her eyes and stilled when she found herself looking into the large blue eyes of a cat that sat atop her chest. There was no weighted blanket. It was the animal.

The feline blinked and immediately began purring so loudly she could feel the vibration through the covers. She carefully pulled her hand from under the blankets and reached up, letting the feline sniff her. He butted his large head against her hand, which made her smile. Ferne slid her fingers through his white fur. And if it were possible, he purred even louder.

"You're a handsome one." Ferne frowned. "I assume you're male with the sheer size of your head, but I suppose that's rather sexist, isn't it?"

The cat closed his eyes and leaned his head against her palm as she petted him. He had the color of a Siamese but was much larger. She didn't want to move him because he looked so comfortable, but her bladder had made itself known. Which begged the question, where was she? She was almost positive the cottage she had rented didn't have a cat. But she could be wrong.

Though, more troubling was that she didn't remember getting back to the house. Or how comfy the pillows were. To be fair, she had only spent one night there, but still…

Ferne took the time to look around the room, and her stomach dropped. This wasn't her rental. There were no curtains on the window, only wooden shutters. And the cover was navy instead of the cream and yellow in her cottage. Where was she?

And how had she gotten here?

"I'm sorry," she whispered to the feline as she sat up.

The cat moved away, but he didn't go far. He plopped down and stared as she shoved aside the covers and looked down to find herself fully clothed except for her boots. She saw them beside a chair with her coat draped over the back of it. Then she took the time to inspect her body to make sure nobody had assaulted her. She discovered nothing other than a sore spot on the back of her left arm. It hurt enough that she imagined there would be a bruise eventually.

Ferne rose and walked silently to the windows. She slowly opened the shutters to look outside. The sun was low in the sky. It looked more like morning than evening, but she couldn't be sure. She then felt in her back pocket for her mobile. When she didn't locate it, she searched her coat and the room, to no avail. Her backpack was also missing.

She bit her lip, trying to think of what to do. She couldn't remember anything after trekking up the mountain. There was missing time, and that was troubling. The sound of muffled voices reached her right before a burst of laughter.

The only way Ferne would find out what was going on was to leave the room. If she dared. She felt something against her hip and looked down to find the cat rubbing against her. She absently petted him. Something about his presence calmed her. She slipped her feet into her boots, just in case she needed to make a run for it. She wasn't sure where that would be, but it was better to be prepared.

Then she slowly and quietly made her way to the door. Ferne pressed her ear against it, her eyes dropping to the cat at her feet. He stared up at her as if wondering what was taking so long. She didn't hear anyone outside. The next step would be to test the handle to see if she was locked in. Her hand rested on it as fear thundered through her.

She turned it with measured, painstaking slowness, expecting the lock to stop it at any moment. But the door clicked softly open. She glanced at the feline. He was no longer interested, washing his face with his paw instead. Ferne opened the door a crack to peer outside. The voices were louder now, and while she was interested to see who owned the house, she needed a toilet more. And she'd rather do that before making her presence known.

Ferne slipped out of the room and stood in the empty hallway. There were no pictures on the walls. She moved across a carpet runner when she spotted the bathroom. Then she was inside, closing the door just as carefully as she had opened the other. After she finished emptying her bladder, she stopped at the sink and looked at herself. She winced at her wild, frizzy curls. Her mouth was dry, so she rinsed it with water from the faucet. Then she splashed more on her face.

As she patted herself dry, the door opened. Her heart skipped a beat as she focused on the place where someone should be. Yet no one was there. Movement caught her attention, and she looked down to see the cat.

Ferne squatted next to him and whispered, "Did you just open that?"

He looked at her, purring. She straightened and decided it was time to let whoever was out there know she was awake. Hopefully, the situation would be easy, and she could get back to her cottage.

A soft meow pulled her attention back to the feline as he stood on his back legs and put his front paws against her thigh. She had always wanted a cat, but her father had been allergic. Her mother had been allergic to dogs, which meant she and Mason never had a pet. She didn't know why she hadn't gotten one when she went to university or after her parents' deaths. Ferne picked up the cat, grunting at his heft. He settled in her arms, proving that was exactly where he wanted to be.

She opened the door wider with her foot and peered down the hallway. It was as empty as before. She moved to the left, where the voices were coming from. She paused and listened to the conversation.

"Oh, I meant to ask how the date went," a female said with a soft Scottish accent.

A male with a deep brogue replied. "I doona want to talk about it."

"You took my advice, I hope." This from an Irishman.

There was a snort. "Of course, not. He took mine."

The British accent brought her up short. Something about it tugged at her memories, but she didn't get a chance to delve into them as the conversation continued.

"He wouldna listen to either of you. He'd take my advice," stated another Scotsman.

A woman laughed in reply. "He knew better than to listen to any of you. He took mine."

A round of chuckles came from the men before the Irishman said, "I'm sure you mean well, Elodie, but we men know what we're talking about."

"Really?" Elodie asked. "And how many of you have a significant other?"

The Scotsman had a smile in his voice as he said, "Me."

"You don't count," she replied playfully.

It was the Englishman who stated, "I choose not to date."

"Oh, that's the biggest pile of shite I've ever heard," the Irishman said.

Another round of laughter rose that had Ferne grinning. The group sounded near her age, and they obviously got along well.

"I'm done with dating," declared the Scotsman, who hadn't wanted to talk about it to begin with. "I doona understand why it has to be so difficult. Perfect picture, perfect profile, perfect answers. No one is perfect. So, I'm done."

There was a beat of silence before everyone began chiming in at once with suggestions for how to help. Then the hairs on the back of Ferne's neck rose. Someone was behind her. She turned to see who it was. Shock ran through her when she looked into familiar dark eyes.

"Theo?"

He stood as still as a statue, his face blank. She didn't know what to make of that. Or him.

"Where am I?" she asked.

He glanced at the floor. "My home."

"How did I get here?"

"We brought you."

She realized then that the conversation in the kitchen had ceased. Ferne looked over her shoulder to see a group of people standing at the entrance to the hallway, watching the exchange. She swallowed and turned back to Theo. "Why?"

"You don't remember?" asked a voice from behind her.

Ferne didn't look away from Theo. She wanted—no, she *needed* him to answer. "What happened?"

"I was hoping you could tell me."

There was no kindness in his deep voice, none of the openness that had been there before. It was like he had shut a door between them. Ferne didn't know any of these people, why she was here, or why she was missing time. But she knew one thing—she had to leave.

She dropped the cat to the floor before spinning on her heel and stalking toward the group. They parted immediately. She scanned the kitchen before her quick search located the door. Ferne reached it, her hand on the knob, before a man with wavy brown hair and deep brown eyes blocked her.

"Sorry. We need to talk to you."

So, he was the Irishman. Ferne glared at him before stepping to the side, keeping her hand on the doorknob as she located Theo. "I have to leave."

"We need a few moments of your time," said a Scotswoman with long, straight blond hair and light blue eyes.

Ferne began to shake. It was from nerves, but also from lack of food. "Give me my mobile. I have to call my brother."

"In a bit." This from a Scotsman with black hair and pale gray eyes, the one who had trouble dating.

Fear, cold and shocking, threaded through her. "So, I'm a prisoner?"

Another man held up his hands before him. He had short dark hair and deep blue eyes. His brogue was deep as he said, "We need to talk first."

"And I need to call my brother!" Mason was no doubt worried when she hadn't answered him yesterday. He was probably scouring Skye for her right now. She couldn't imagine the dread and horror he'd felt when she hadn't been there to meet him.

Ferne yanked on the door, but the Irishman banged it closed. She gathered magic in her other hand, ready to use it to get him out of the way. Because nothing would stop her from getting to Mason.

"Stop. Everyone stop!"

That voice again. Something on the edge of her memories told Ferne she should recognize whoever it was. The kitchen had gone silent at his bellow. Ferne glanced away from the Irishman to the man who had shouted. He stood on the opposite side of the round table, his hands upon it. His auburn waves were perfectly styled, but it was the startling turquoise eyes that made her frown and sparked another memory.

"Ferne," he said softly. "Do you remember me?"

She wasn't the only one to startle at his words. Several of the others in the room snapped their attention to him. Including Theo.

The looks didn't faze the man. He kept his attention on her. "It's been some years, sadly. Mason and I lost touch." The man's lips twisted. "Actually, that was my fault. I...well, things happened."

As he spoke, she saw a flash of him and Mason on horseback, racing across the estate.

He straightened. "Some of my favorite times during uni were at Brannelly."

Her hand fell from the doorknob. She took a step toward him as more memories filled her mind. She scoured them, trying to put a name to his face. And then she had it. "Carlyle?"

His face split into a grin. "Hey."

Ferne suddenly fought a wave of tears. She was overcome with nostalgia but also uncertainty, especially when the Irishman let more people into the house. "I have to talk to Mason."

"I know," Carlyle said as he came around the table.

The Irishman behind her made a sound. "Care to fill the rest of us in, Carlyle?"

Carlyle didn't say anything until he reached her. He gave her a reassuring smile that she couldn't quite return. With a small nod, he stood beside her and said, "Everyone, this is Lady Ferne Crawford. Her brother, Mason, is the Earl of Brannelly. We were inseparable at uni." Carlyle then glanced at her and pointed to the Irishman, "Ferne, that's Finn. The tall one is Scott. Next to him is his better half, Elodie. Next to her is Filip."

Carlyle cleared his throat and pointed to a beautiful woman with deep blue eyes. "That's Sabryn, my American friend. Next to her is Bronwyn, and beside her is Elias. The scowling one with the silver eyes ringed in red is Balladyn, and the flame-haired woman is Rhona. Of course, you know Theo. Well," he said, clearing his throat again, "that's everyone."

Ferne couldn't look away from Balladyn. "A Dark Fae?"

"I've been many things," he replied.

Rhona caught her attention. "He's a Reaper, and with me. You left a note for me. What did you need to say?"

Ferne squeezed her eyes closed as the room began to spin. "I'm not saying more until I talk to Mason."

"We need answers," Rhona said in a firm voice.

Ferne lifted her chin defiantly. They could bully her all they wanted, but she wasn't saying a word.

"It's fine," Carlyle said. "She needs to talk to her brother."

Finn's dark brows lowered as he came up on her other side. "Why?"

"It's not a big deal," Carlyle snapped.

As the two traded words, Ferne's gaze found Theo. He stood off by himself, his arms crossed over his chest as he watched her. She didn't understand why he was treating her so coldly—why *any* of them were acting how they were toward her. And then she did. She was from London. Mason had warned her that they wouldn't welcome her. Ferne thought she'd at least get to say what she needed before they turned on her.

"Their parents died!" Carlyle bellowed over Finn.

Ferne flinched at the outburst. After so many years, she should be used to hearing those words, but it never got any easier.

"Bloody hell," Carlyle mumbled as he put a hand on her arm. "I'm sorry, Ferne. I was trying not to blurt it out."

She shook her head. "It's fine." Even though it wasn't. She turned to Carlyle. "Mason was coming to Skye. He should've arrived yesterday afternoon." That drew her up short. "Wait. What day is it?"

"We found you last evening. You've only been unconscious for a night," Carlyle explained.

Ferne blinked. Unconscious? She'd ask about that later. Right now, she had to talk to Mason. "I need my phone."

"We couldn't find it," Scott said.

At least she thought that was his name. Too many people had been introduced at once. It was difficult to keep up.

"I'll go look," Balladyn said.

Ferne tried to make her lips curve into a smile at the Dark Fae's—no, the *Reaper's* offer. "I'd appreciate that."

Her stomach chose that moment to growl loudly.

Carlyle pulled out a chair at the table and motioned her to it. "Sit. You need to eat."

"I need my mobile," she argued.

Rhona waved away her words. "We'll go back to the mountain and look. You stay."

Then she and Balladyn vanished. Ferne barely had time to register that before Carlyle set a plate of food in front of her.

"My specialty," he stated proudly. "It's my British take on the American breakfast burrito."

There was a groan as Sabryn plopped into another chair. "Please, tell me you didn't put baked beans in it again."

"Even I didn't like that," Finn stated.

Carlyle flipped a towel over one shoulder and huffed. "Since you two complained so loudly, no. They're on the side for me."

As soon as Ferne smelled the food, she realized how famished she was.

CHAPTER TWENTY

If anyone noted that he hadn't spoken, Theo was glad they hadn't pointed it out. He had been waiting near the hallway in hopes of hearing Ferne when she woke. She must have come out of the room when he went in search of Basher.

Theo was glad she was awake, but that mixed with what they had all witnessed the night before. He liked Ferne. Liked her more than any other woman before. The fact that she could be involved with the mist and he'd missed it didn't sit well. He was a detective. He should've seen something, anything, that would've hinted at who she was.

A file on her was on his bed. Saber had sent it to him last night. Theo hadn't been able to look at it. He'd tried several times and finally gave up. If he'd read it, he might have known that Carlyle was friends with her brother. And about the death of her parents.

Theo couldn't take his eyes off her. Not since he had found her in the hallway listening to the others while holding Basher. The way she kept looking at him made him want to shove everyone aside and stand protectively beside her. But she didn't need anyone to guard her. She had proven that the night before.

She pushed away the plate and the second half-eaten burrito. Theo noticed that Carlyle and Finn kept the conversation going to put her at ease. Even Sabryn, Elias, and Bronwyn joined in.

Theo spotted Scott making his way over. He knew what was coming even before Scott asked, "Want to talk about it?"

Balladyn and Rhona returning with Ferne's backpack in hand saved Theo from answering. As soon as Ferne saw it, she jumped up and went to retrieve it. She began searching the pockets when Balladyn held out a mobile.

"Thank you," Ferne told them. "I had it in the…"

Theo dropped his arms to his sides when she trailed off, her brows furrowing.

"In the what?" Rhona pressed.

Ferne looked at Rhona. "I went for a hike while waiting to hear from Mason. I found a cave entrance."

"Then what?" Rhona asked.

Ferne shook her head slightly. "I had my mobile out for the light, and then…" She paused a second time, her head tilted slightly as if she were trying to remember. "I put my hand on the wall."

"You used magic," Carlyle stated.

Ferne glanced at him. "Yes."

"What happened?" This from Rhona.

Ferne's green gaze slid to him. Theo stood on a knife's edge, waiting with the others. He wanted to be done with the mist and whoever controlled it. Needed things to get back to normal. But he didn't want Ferne to be involved. Anyone but her.

"Tiny lights lit up the entire cavern," Ferne explained. "Others were there, though I couldn't see them clearly. It was like something was between us that made them all appear like dark silhouettes moving around."

"Did they say anything?" Balladyn asked.

Ferne licked her lips as a flash of unease passed over her face. "They did."

"Someone spoke to you?" Rhona glanced at Balladyn. "What did they say?"

Ferne looked down at her mobile. Whatever she saw—or didn't see—made her brow pucker. "I'll tell you everything, but I need to call Mason first."

Rhona let out a long sigh. "Please make it brief. This is important."

"So is letting my brother know I'm not dead," Ferne replied stiffly.

She turned to go outside when Finn moved to block her again.

"She's going outside for privacy," Carlyle argued.

Ferne's mouth was tight when she turned back around. "Carlyle can come with me."

"Sure," Carlyle said. "Theo, join us."

He almost declined but then realized he *wanted* to go with them. He was the last out of the house and closed the door behind him. Ferne paced back and forth in agitation as she searched her phone.

"What's wrong?" Carlyle asked.

Ferne pressed her lips together. "He didn't call. He didn't text."

"There's probably a good reason," Carlyle said.

She stopped and looked into the distance. "No. There isn't."

"Ferne, what's going on?"

Instead of answering Carlyle, she lifted her mobile and punched in some numbers, then went back to pacing. Theo watched her avidly. Carlyle was right. Something else was going on. The way she reacted to not getting in touch with her brother was a little odd. It made more sense when he learned about the death of her parents, but that didn't explain everything.

"Billings," Ferne said as the call connected. "Yes, yes. I'm fine. I…lost my mobile while hillwalking yesterday. I expected to have messages and calls from Mason, but there's nothing." The fingers on her free hand flexed as she paused to listen. "I don't understand."

Theo noted that Carlyle's frown grew with every word. The Brit stood with his arms crossed. A muscle moved in his jaw. A flare of jealousy rose in Theo. Had Carlyle and Ferne been lovers? He had no right to be envious. It wasn't as if he and Ferne were anything but acquaintances who had shared a couple of kisses. Nevertheless, the emotion was there.

And not going anywhere.

"That doesn't make sense," Ferne said. Her pacing slowed. "When does he get back?" There was a long pause where she halted and put a hand to her forehead. "And you're sure nothing is going on with—? I mean, in London."

Now, Theo wanted to know what was in London that would make her change her words so quickly.

"Something isn't right," Carlyle whispered.

Theo shrugged. "People change."

"True, but there's an undercurrent here that doesn't make sense." He looked at Theo. "Tell me you don't feel it."

Theo twisted his lips. "I can no'."

"That's what I thought."

A few moments later, Ferne ended the call. She remained where she was, her gaze distant. She drew in a breath and then faced them.

"When is Mason getting here? I'd like to catch up with him," Carlyle said.

The smile Ferne gave him was tight. "Mason is dealing with something back home. He's not coming."

"What's more important than his sister?" Theo asked.

She hastily looked away and brushed at her eye. "I don't know. He was adamant about coming before."

"This has to do with the London Druids, doesn't it?"

Theo's head snapped to Carlyle. London Druids? Theo didn't know there was such a group, but he shouldn't be surprised. What else didn't he know was out in the world? Probably a lot more than he was ready to learn.

"How did you…?" Ferne stopped and blew out a breath. "Mason told Billings it had to do with the estate, but that would never keep Mas from coming when he thought I might be in danger."

It felt as if Theo had been kicked. "Danger?"

"What happened with the London Druids?" Carlyle asked her.

Ferne slid her mobile into the pocket of her jeans. "They kicked me out."

"They wouldn't," Carlyle said, shock pitching his voice lower.

She shrugged one shoulder. "Things have been different with them since Mum and Dad died."

"Did they know you came here? Is that why?" Carlyle pressed.

Theo frowned at that. Why would any group of Druids care who came to Skye?

"They knew I used magic to contact a Druid on Skye."

Carlyle blew out a harsh breath. "If they know you're here, they might have stopped Mason."

"From coming to his sister? Why?" Theo pressed.

Carlyle swung his head toward him. "It's against the rules. Families disown those who come to Skye."

CHAPTER TWENTY-ONE

"Excuse me?" Theo's voice rose higher with disbelief.

Ferne couldn't quite meet his eyes. Yesterday, she'd had a plan, one that seemed simple enough. Today, that plan had been decimated. She was still bewildered—and, frankly, alarmed—at not remembering the previous evening. Having a group of people gang up on her hadn't helped matters.

Then there was Mason.

Her brother would move mountains to get to her. Just as she would for him. Tragedy did that to people. So, his lack of communication was worrisome. She had thought to remain on Skye and help the Druids. Now, she wanted to tell Rhona everything and get back to Mason as quickly as she could. In order to do that, she should get back inside and give them all the answers.

Ferne walked past Theo, whose frown had intensified, and Carlyle, who seemed lost in his thoughts. She said nothing to either of them as she opened the door and stepped inside the house. Theo's house. She had been in his home. Had he found her? Had he carried her inside? Was he the one who'd tucked her into bed?

It shouldn't matter. They hardly knew each other. A few kisses and an *almost* dinner didn't count. He had barely spoken to her since she woke. It was difficult to determine if he was angry or just didn't want her here. Though she couldn't imagine what he was upset about. Unless he felt as if she had trespassed in the cavern.

It wasn't as if she had known he was a Druid. She wasn't even sure of it now. She assumed since he was with Rhona and Carlyle. It was wrong to presume everyone in the house had magic, though. However, she was interested in knowing what a Reaper was.

The moment she passed the threshold, everyone halted their conversations and looked at her. She felt a presence behind her and knew without looking it was Theo. She could feel him close. Or maybe she just wished that she did.

Ferne had never felt as if she belonged with the London Druids. Her mother had been a high-ranking member, which meant that both she and Mason were heavily involved with the group. It didn't matter how powerful her magic was, it seemed as if she were on the outside looking in. Not so with Mason. Everyone welcomed him.

When Ferne walked the trail near the Fairy Pools, there had been a connection she had never experienced before. She realized it was the thing that had been missing with the London Druids. Perhaps that was what made her want to remain on the isle and lend aid to the Druids.

Those inside the house were in two groups. One in the kitchen, and another in the adjoining living space. Uncertainty returned to Ferne now that she was within sight of the others. She didn't know whether to stay in the kitchen or go into the other room. There was more seating in the living room, so she decided to go there.

Ferne chose a comfy-looking chair in a maroon plaid. As she sank into it, she noticed a tablet on the small table next to her and realized she had taken Theo's spot. She started to rise, but he shook his head and motioned for her to sit. The cat jumped into her lap and turned in a circle several times before curling into a tight ball.

She stroked his thick fur, and the sound of his purring helping to ease the building stress. With so many eyes locked on her, it made Ferne feel as if she stood before the elders again. The only way she would be able to do this was to find someone to focus on. Carlyle was the safe bet. Yet her gaze slid to Theo. He stood near the kitchen entryway, leaning against the wall with his thumbs hooked in the front pockets of his jeans.

Ferne took a deep breath and then began. "I came to Skye with a purpose. In order for you to understand that, I need to start from the beginning."

"Please," Rhona said with a nod.

"It started about a month ago. I'm not a normal seer. I don't get flashes from touching people or things. It's only when I meditate that I get anything. I've heard the Ancients three times in my life. The first was the summer I turned sixteen. The second was, I later learned, the same time my parents' plane impacted the ground."

"What did they say?" Carlyle asked.

Ferne kept her gaze on Theo. "They've never said anything. They sang."

Theo's brows snapped together as a murmur went through the room. Ferne looked down at the cat to find his blue eyes looking at her. She smoothed her hand over his big head and scratched behind his ears.

"Go on," Rhona urged.

It wasn't in Ferne's nature to open up like this. She was private to the extreme. It was the importance of what was happening on Skye that pushed her out of her comfort zone and brought her to a forbidden land. The danger lurking here grew every day. What she liked or didn't like wasn't of any concern at the moment.

She lifted her head and found her gaze snagged by Theo's. He had offered comfort when they first met, and she longed for that now. "The third time I heard the Ancients, their screams were so loud my eardrum burst."

"That's impossible," someone said.

She turned her head toward the sound of the voice and found herself looking at Scott. "I assure you, it isn't. I've never sought them out. Maybe that's why they've come to me as clear and loud as our conversation now." Ferne paused, thinking back. "That day, I felt off the moment I woke. Meditating helps to ground me when I'm feeling particularly out of sorts. I had just sat and closed my eyes when the screams bombarded me. Then, they stopped, all at once. Not gradually, mind you, but as if someone had muted the volume."

"We all heard that," Bronwyn said.

Ferne was surprised to learn that, but she decided to ask about it later. She wanted to finish her explanation. She focused on Theo once more. "The silence that followed was unnerving. There was a wrongness about it that is difficult to describe. For the first time, I sought out the Ancients, but I got no response."

"No one on Skye has heard them since either," Rhona said. "I suppose someone could lie about it, but we ask regularly."

Ferne touched the ear which still sometimes hurt when the altitude changed quickly. "It was just a few days after that when I sat for meditation that I started getting flashes of places and people. I saw a landscape on repeat. A quick search brought up Skye, but what was more concerning was the threat I felt looming over the isle. Each day, it and the danger grew."

"And you just came now?" Elias demanded from his position on the sofa beside Bronwyn.

Carlyle stood on the opposite side of the room, a muscle jumping in his jaw. "You speak of things you don't understand."

"Then explain them."

The command came from Balladyn. Though spoken softly, there was no denying it was an order. Ferne watched Carlyle struggle to find the words, and she took pity on him.

"The London Druids are the largest sect in England, though they don't come close to the size and clout of Skye." Ferne wondered if the elders' ears were burning. She hoped they were. "The group is ruled by elders, of which my mother used to be a member. From the moment of their inception, there has been a strict rule that no one can come to Skye. If any London Druid breaks that decree, they are kicked out of the group and banished from their family."

Filip scooted to the edge of the cushion on his chair. "What the hell? Why?"

"They fear us," Elodie said.

Rhona shook her head. "It isn't fear that created such decrees. It's hatred."

Ferne briefly closed her eyes as she lowered her head. Rhona knew. Of course, she did. It had been foolish for Ferne to think that maybe the past had been lost.

"Someone want to explain it for those of us not in the know?" Sabryn asked.

Carlyle blew out a harsh breath. "I... Fuck!"

"He's never at a loss for words," Finn stated, concern in his voice. "Never."

Elias stood and walked across the room to be near Carlyle. "Someone talk. Now."

Ferne was glad Carlyle had found such friends. The anguish on his face was something she understood all too well. "The London Druids originated in Skye. They were banished long ago for corruption. Their actions put the reputation of the Druids here at risk. So, they were forced out. The anger and loathing for Skye and the Druids who call it home have been passed from generation to generation. My family and..." She paused and looked at Carlyle. "Others."

"You want to know why I won't go home," Carlyle said to no one in particular. "That's why. I've had my fill of those bastards and their bloody rules."

Obviously, something had happened with Carlyle and the London group. Ferne wondered if Mason knew what it was. She'd have to ask when she finally spoke to him. Ferne took pity on Carlyle and brought the attention back to her. "It wasn't only places on Skye the visions showed me. There was a person, too. Repeated over different lifetimes, in different eras. But always the same face."

"It was you," Rhona said, her eyes wide. "You're the one who spoke to Kirsi."

Ferne nodded as she looked at Rhona. "It was me. When I saw her face, I knew her. I can't explain it, but I recognized her and knew she was from Skye. Once I accepted that knowledge, I saw that she's the answer."

"I hate to keep saying this, but what?" Sabryn asked, her frustration clear.

Filip threw up his hands. "I doona know either."

"None of you do," Rhona explained. "Kirsi came to me recently, and I've only told Balladyn."

As a collective, everyone turned to Ferne. She was prepared for it now. Not that it made finding the words easier. "Speaking to someone through their mind isn't something I do often—it takes so much out of me. But I thought it would be the quickest, safest way. I thought I could contact someone on Skye without breaking the rules ingrained in me since birth."

"Holy shit," Sabryn murmured.

Scott's eyes widened. "That's impressive."

"That's what you did?" Carlyle said.

Ferne swung her gaze to him. She didn't reply. There was no need.

"They knew and kicked you out," Carlyle stated, shaking his head.

It was Rhona's turn to frown. "Are you telling me the London Druids know you did magic?"

"They felt it," Ferne said. "That kind of magic takes a considerable amount."

Elias ran a hand over his jaw. "That doesna explain how they felt it. We can no' do that."

"We're brought before the elders as infants so they can use a spell that allows them to keep an eye on us. You know, to make sure we don't venture to Skye or contact a Skye Druid," Carlyle explained.

Theo caught Ferne's gaze. "Is that true?"

She nodded.

"And you reached out to Kirsi anyway?"

Ferne nodded again. "It was important that she go to Rhona."

"Wait. Just…wait," Finn said tightly as he held up a hand before him. "I'm still reeling from these arseholes spelling you two. Who the hell does that?"

"People who hold that much animosity and fear," Balladyn replied.

CHAPTER TWENTY-TWO

What Theo had learned about Ferne and the London Druids had rocked him. It still didn't clear her from having a connection to the mist, however.

"It took some time, but I had the spell on me removed," Carlyle told the silent room.

Theo watched Ferne sink her fingers into Basher's fur over and over again as if the cat kept her calm. And Theo supposed he did. Basher loved something about her. He had been with her from the moment Theo brought her into the house—even through shut doors.

"What about yours?" Bronwyn asked.

Ferne shook her head. "Mine is still in place. It didn't matter what they knew. I was no longer a part of the group, and Mason understood why I had to come."

"Is Mason still involved with them?" Carlyle asked her.

Theo had been about to ask the same thing. He hoped for her sake that Mason had gotten out.

"Mason remains," she replied.

Carlyle's face went slack. "Why the bloody hell would he do that?"

Theo's gaze narrowed on Ferne when she parted her lips to speak but hesitated. There was something she wasn't comfortable telling others. None of them had earned her trust, so he didn't blame her for keeping whatever it was to herself. That didn't make him want to know any less, though.

"We're getting off topic," Rhona said to the room. She turned her gaze to Ferne. "Why didn't you contact me instead of Kirsi?"

"I couldn't take the chance of you ignoring my warning. Besides, this falls to Kirsi, but you needed to be aware," Ferne explained.

Balladyn placed his hands on the back of the sofa. "Aware of what, exactly? You never told Kirsi, nor have you told us."

"Didn't I?" Ferne retorted. She licked her lips. "There's evil here. And it's growing. The threat to Skye is multiplying exponentially every day. If the Skye Druids fall, the rest of us will soon after. I had to do something. I couldn't take the chance that Kirsi wouldn't see the path she's been destined to take."

Theo had the urge to move closer to Ferne. "Which led you to the isle."

"Yes," she replied, their gazes locking.

"You went to see Kirsi."

"I did. I thought I could explain things better in person, but it was too much for her. She needs time."

"Time we doona have," Theo guessed.

Ferne bowed her head in acknowledgement. "Exactly."

"And last night?" He should wait to bring it up, but he had to know if, after all his years learning his trade, his skills as a detective were waning. "Better yet, start with your movements from the moment you arrived on the isle."

Her green eyes were clear as she stared into his. "You want details?"

"Aye." He needed them more than she knew.

Ferne remained still except for the hand that continued stroking Basher. "I arrived on Skye two days ago. I wanted to see the isle for myself, and the first place I went was the Fairy Pools. Where I met you."

How could he ever forget? He had thought to be alone and found a beautiful woman instead.

"I found the rental cottage, and then met you for dinner. You barely arrived when you were called away for work."

So far everything lined up, but Theo kept that from showing on his face.

"I stayed for my meal. A woman at a nearby table stared at me. She smiled as if she knew me. Later, when I left, I saw her sitting in her car watching me," Ferne said.

Theo jerked. "What woman?"

"Did she say anything to you?" Rhona asked.

Theo almost snapped at Rhona to stay out of his investigation, but he caught himself in time. He held himself stiffly as he waited for Ferne to answer.

Finally, Ferne said, "Nothing. She just looked at me. Her smile was a tad unnerving, though."

"What did she look like?" Theo asked.

Ferne wrinkled her nose. "Older. Graying brown hair that was straight and on the shorter side. She sat alone."

"That could be anyone," Elodie said.

Rhona twisted her lips, nodding.

"Did you see what she drove?" Theo questioned.

Ferne winced. "Sorry, I didn't. She just stared at me in that same disturbing way."

"Anything else happen?" Theo knew the moment she glanced down that something had.

Ferne's breathing quickened. "I was driving to Rhona's while on a call with Mason. That's when a wall of…it sounds insane, but it was mist. It just appeared in front of me, so dense I couldn't see through it. I slammed on the brakes. I swear I'm not making this up, but an arm and hand formed out of it."

Theo's mind was racing. "What happened then?"

"It seemed to wave," Ferne said. "Then it moved all around the car before flying off."

Elias grunted. "Well, that's no' what it normally does."

"You mean…you believe me?" Ferne asked dubiously.

There were many reasons the mist could act that way. He couldn't get the night before out of his mind. Or the fact that she could be making it all up to look innocent.

"The mist has been killing Druids for a few weeks," Bronwyn said.

Ferne's eyes widened. "The mist…? Damn."

"Which is why we need to know about last night," Scott said.

Ferne looked around the room and settled on Theo once more. "What about it?"

"Finish your movements, please," he requested.

She swallowed and gave him a firm nod. "After the mist, Mason demanded that I come home. He was terrified that something would happen to me. He expected Rhona to kick me off the isle, but he thought she might listen first. The mist was something new. He stayed on the phone with me as I drove to

Rhona's, but she wasn't home. I convinced him to join me here, and said I'd return with him after we went to Rhona's together. Then I went back to the rental. The next morning, I went to see Kirsi."

Elodie raised a hand. "I can confirm that."

"Then what?" Theo pressed.

She gave a half-hearted shrug. "A man and a woman stopped me. She knew I was a Druid. Said she was one, as well. Her name was Esther, and the man with her was N—"

"Nikolai," Rhona said over her.

Ferne turned her head to Rhona. "That's right. He also said he was a Dragon King."

"Because he is," Balladyn replied.

Theo ran a hand down his face. There were a lot of factors right now, and he didn't know how it would all play out—or what part Ferne played. She could be innocent in all of this. Or…she could be the mastermind. She did come from a group of Druids who loathed those on Skye.

"Another man arrived and took their attention," Ferne said. "I used that opportunity to return to Rhona's. When she still wasn't home, I left a message."

Rhona nodded to confirm.

Ferne drew in a deep breath and slowly released it. "I had some time before I expected to hear from Mason. As I already explained, I went for a hike and found the cave."

"With the lights," Carlyle said. "We remember. You were going to tell us what they said to you."

Ferne glanced at Theo. "Yes. Of course. They asked for help." Ferne shrugged. "Then they urged me not to fight."

That caught Theo's attention. "Not to fight what?"

"I've no idea. I don't remember anything after that."

Carlyle scratched his neck. "That's weird, because we saw you."

"You did?" she asked, sitting up straighter. "What did I do?"

Balladyn crossed his arms over his chest as he straightened. "You came out of the cave glowing."

"Glowing?" Ferne asked, startled.

Theo nodded when she looked at him. "It looked like the light edged around your entire body."

"Then the mist came for you," Finn said.

Carlyle rocked back on his heels. "It swirled around you and then just covered you without moving. It didn't harm you, though."

"But it was pretty pissed," Sabryn added.

Rhona nodded. "It came for us. You used the light to block it. It wasn't until it left that the glow around you dimmed."

Ferne's brow furrowed deeply. "I don't remember any of that."

"You passed out after. We brought you here," Finn stated.

Ferne leaned her head back on the chair. "I can see why you wanted to know who I was, but I can assure you, I don't have anything to do with the mist. I didn't even know about it. I came here for something else."

"But what if the mist is just one part of things?" Balladyn asked. "It could be why the Ancients aren't speaking anymore."

Theo briefly squeezed his burning eyes shut to relieve them. Sleep. One full night of undisturbed sleep was all he needed to shake off the fog in his brain. Caffeine could only do so much.

"Ferne, you came to help," Rhona said. "Esther thinks you can. I'm hoping you can."

"But you're not sure because of how the mist treated me," Ferne stated.

Scott shrugged and asked what everyone was thinking. "Do we have a choice here? We have to stop the murders. I say we use anything and everyone we can."

"Agreed," Filip replied.

Elias twisted his lips as he nodded. "Scott's right. We have to trust Ferne. She did save you all from the mist."

"But I don't know how," Ferne interjected.

Elodie said, "We go back to the cavern and see if we can replicate what happened."

Theo's mobile vibrated in his pocket. He withdrew it and saw it was the chief. He stepped into the kitchen to answer it. "Morning, Chief."

"It's not a good one, Frasier. I take it you haven't heard?"

His heart sank. "Doona tell me there was another murder."

"I'm texting the address now. Come alone. Once we clear the scene, you'll be able to bring in your team."

"Yes, ma'am."

"Oh, and Frasier?"

"Ma'am?"

"Hurry. The residents are getting unruly."

He stared out the kitchen window at the beautiful day beyond, one soured by more death. "I'm doing my best."

The call disconnected. Theo stood for a moment before walking back into the living area. His gaze immediately went to Rhona. As soon as she saw him, she held up a hand to quiet the conversation.

"There's been another murder," Theo announced.

Rhona's face went ashen. "Who?"

"The address just came in. I'm headed there now. Once the

body has been removed and the scene released, all of you will be able to come. Until then, it's just me."

Rhona got to her feet. "Nay. I need to be there."

"I'll make sure neither of us is seen," Balladyn said from beside her.

Theo nodded. Before he turned, his gaze caught Ferne's. He hadn't wanted her to be involved with the mist, and maybe she wasn't. But there wasn't proof either way. The simple fact that they needed help didn't bode well, but if Ferne was working against them, she could impede the investigation.

But if she really had come to help, she could be exactly what they needed to find their suspect.

CHAPTER TWENTY-THREE

Today had been one of the longest days of Ferne's life. After Carlyle and Sabryn brought her to the Mini, she drove back to the rental. No one cautioned her to remain on Skye, or whatever authorities told persons of interest. If she even was still a suspected perpetrator. She really didn't know.

Though with a Fae—ugh, a Reaper….she needed to remember that—at the ready, Ferne couldn't go anywhere Balladyn couldn't find her. She told herself that was why she remained on the isle. The truth was, she didn't know what to do. There was still work to be done on Skye. She wanted to help. Would anyone let her? Should she allow them to dictate that?

Ferne shook her head at herself. Tough talk from someone who had shuttered out the world then came to a place that didn't want any part of her. Sure, the others might want what little information she had, but they clearly didn't want her around. She was a complication, a difficulty they didn't have time to deal with.

She could reach out to Kirsi again. Ferne had mucked that up, and she needed to fix it. Kirsi was an integral part of defeating the malevolence on the isle. Maybe even the mist. Ferne scrunched her nose. Did she believe what Theo and the group had told her about her glowing and the mist from the night before?

Ferne looked at her mobile. She wanted to talk to her brother. He'd see the right path for her as he always did. But no matter how many times she tried to get ahold of Mason, he hadn't done more than send a text promising he'd call when he could.

As she sat beneath the dark sky, gazing at the rising moon perfectly situated over the water, she found herself searching for the mist. Perhaps she should be concerned about it coming for her, but at this point, there wasn't anywhere she could get away from it either. She'd meditated several times throughout the day in an effort to remember the missing time from the night before, but she couldn't bring up a single memory. It was like someone had wiped it from her.

Or firmly blocked it.

She kept her phone with her, waiting for Mason to call. And Theo. She really wanted to talk to him. Neither had reached out. Actually, after being questioned that morning, no one had contacted her. It was almost like they had washed their hands of her. It was an illusion, but a good one. Their interest in her and the mist was too great for her to miss. Ferne didn't believe they had all the information they wanted. They were busy dealing with another murder. Attention would swing back to her soon enough. She hoped she would have something worthwhile to tell them by then.

Her hands were curled in the pockets of her coat. She missed the cat. Petting him had soothed her as much as it had him, and she could use more of that. It wasn't until today that she realized just how heavily she leaned on Mason. She was on her own this time. He could still swoop in and rescue her, and for a short time this morning, she had wanted exactly that. But now? She'd had time to think about things, and it all came back to the very thing that had brought her in the first place—danger.

There was an argument to run and save herself from whatever lurked on the isle, the mist, and even Theo and his friends. Ferne could even hear Mason giving that exact argument. Grief and heartache had caused her to retreat into herself. Mason had tried everything to get her to resume her life, but she hadn't been able to.

Then came the visions. Nothing else mattered but stopping whatever was happening on the isle. She hadn't hesitated, hadn't thought too much about the dangers that might await her. She'd just acted.

And now…she wondered where she fit in the world. London had been nice, but she wouldn't go back there for many reasons, none of which were the London Druids. Derbyshire was her home, a place she could always return. However, it wasn't where she wanted to be at the moment. That was Skye.

The isle was nothing like she'd thought it would be. The beauty was breathtaking, but what she'd experienced at the pools had made the most impression. No matter how she looked at it, Skye felt like a homecoming. Such an odd thing to think about a place she had never visited or cared much about, but there was no getting around the simple fact.

The crunch of tires over gravel pulled her from her contemplation. Ferne didn't rise from her chair. Whoever it was could look for her around back. The fire that helped warm her could be seen from the drive. Sure enough, she heard the sound of approaching footsteps. She craned her head around and spotted Carlyle.

"Can I join you?" he asked with a quick smile.

She motioned to one of the other chairs. "What brings you here? Checking to make sure I didn't leave?"

"That's not really an issue with Balladyn."

Ferne chuckled. "I expected as much."

Carlyle sank low in the chair, his legs out before him as he gazed at the dancing flames. Their gazes met. He rubbed his lips together, and his face creased with unease. Ferne watched him. Something had brought Carlyle to her. He would speak when the time was right.

"There was a time I considered your family mine," he said after several long minutes.

She nodded before he looked away.

"Things…happened." Carlyle swallowed loudly as if uncomfortable admitting even that much. "Mason tried to be there for me, but I wouldn't let him. I wouldn't let anyone. I lashed out at anyone close to me. I ruined a lot of friendships and burned a lot of bridges. It was about nine months later that I learned about the plane crash. I wanted to be there for you and Mason. I just…I wasn't sure I'd be welcomed," he said and lifted his gaze to her.

"We never would have turned you away. Never. Mason knew you were hurting, but he never told me why. I don't think he knew, and that bothered him tremendously."

Carlyle blew out a breath. "I'm sorry about your parents. They were good to me."

"Thank you. They adored you." Ferne hesitated, wondering if she should say more. With Carlyle no longer involved with the

London Druids, she wasn't concerned about it getting back to them. It would also be helpful to have someone else looking out for her brother. Because Carlyle would. "I'm going to tell you something no one else knows."

His turquoise eyes grew intense. "I was hoping you would. It's obvious something is going on. I'm here for you and Mason. In whatever capacity either of you needs me. I wasn't before, but I'm a different person now."

"I hope we won't have to ask anything of you, but...I'm worried, Carlyle."

He straightened in his chair. "Go on."

"After the plane crash, Mason and I became very close. A tragedy like ours can do that. He stood with me before the elders when they expelled me from the group. He was furious, of course."

Carlyle grinned. "I can well imagine."

"But he kept it inside."

"Just like we Brits are told to do."

She tightened her coat around her. "He didn't try to talk me out of coming here. That alerted me that something was going on that he didn't want me to know about. I was so wrapped up in what I'd find on Skye that I didn't piece it together until the drive up here."

"What, exactly?"

"Mason thinks it's possible our parents were murdered."

Carlyle's face went slack with shock. "Bloody hell," he murmured.

"Precisely."

He ran a hand down his face before he got to his feet and walked to the edge of the deck to look out at the water. Carlyle was silent for several moments before he faced her and shook his head.

"Fucking Mason. He shouldn't be doing that kind of investigating alone. *Especially* if they did kill your parents."

"It's why I convinced him to come to Skye. He was worried, and I wanted to be there to help him. But I need to take care of things here first."

Carlyle sat on the edge of the chair. "He agreed to that?"

"After my run-in with the mist and a little persuasion. He wanted to fly here two nights ago, but he had a meeting he assured me was about the estate and not the elders. He told Billings to contact the pilot for the chopper so he could leave as soon as the meeting wrapped."

"And he isn't here."

Ferne twisted her lips and shook her head.

"Have you spoken with him?"

"I got one text an hour ago that said he'd call when he could."

Carlyle rose and began to pace. "I don't like this, Ferne. Mason has always been a man of his word. He wouldn't leave anyone, much less his sister, hanging on something as mundane as an estate meeting."

"I believed him about that, but I don't now."

Carlyle sighed heavily before turning to her. "I'm going to help, and I know the rest of the Knights will, too."

"Knights?"

"It's what we call ourselves. You met Sabryn, Finn, and Elias, today. Technically, Bronwyn is part of our group now, too. Then there's Sabertooth. He's our hacker extraordinaire. If there's something on the net, he'll find it. We've each had someone close to us killed. Friends, lovers, family. All Druids. And all murdered."

She wondered if that was what had driven Carlyle to push everyone away. "Like those on Skye?"

"Similar, yes. We hunt down Druids who have killed, and we offer help to others who have nowhere to turn."

Ferne sat forward and rested her forearms on her knees. "You and I both know what it means to go up against the London Druids. Do you really want to do that? What about your father and the rest of your family?"

"Everything I've done, I've done for them and all the other Druid families out there. I let Mason down before. This is my chance for redemption."

She studied him, recognizing the resolve in his turquoise eyes. "You should probably clear it with the others."

"The Knights are my family. They'll back me." He pushed to his feet. "I'll go fill them in on everything. Saber will pull up information on your family. He…ah…he already did on you."

Ferne shrugged and sat back. There wasn't anything she could do about that now. She just hoped there wasn't anything too cringe-worthy in what had been uncovered.

"Meanwhile," Carlyle continued, "you should go see Theo."

She let out a little snort and looked away. "He's busy. Besides, he made it clear he doesn't want anything to do with me."

"You didn't see him when we were searching for you. He was a man on a mission."

Ferne slid her gaze to Carlyle, a burst of hope blossoming in her chest. Yet, she cautioned herself. "Because he thought I was a suspect?"

"Because he thought you were in danger. He tried to jump between you and the mist. I haven't known him long, but from everything I've seen, Frasier's a good guy. There's obviously a connection between the two of you. Life's too short not to explore it."

She looked at the stars and laughed. "Low blow, throwing my mother's words back at me."

"Seemed fitting," Carlyle said with a wide smile. He grew serious then. "You're right. Something is going on here. Keep following those instincts. Theo brought us all together to help him. You're an asset, Ferne. Make him see that."

"I don't know," she said hesitantly. That would be putting herself out there in a way she hadn't done in so very long. She touched her lips, remembering the soul-stealing kiss they had shared.

"Live," Carlyle urged. "That's what your parents would want you to do. You disregarded a lifetime of decrees and threats about Skye to contact Kirsi, and then came yourself. You were never meant to sit on the sidelines. Take your place where you belong."

She watched him walk away, his words ringing in her head. Ferne looked at her mobile. Nothing from Mason or Theo. Carlyle was right about one thing. She hadn't heeded the London Druids' laws or considered the risks involved. She had done what was right. She would do it again.

And she wasn't controlling the mist.

It was time to prove that to Theo. She didn't know how she'd do it, but she would. Ferne rose and turned off the gas feeding the firepit. Then she gathered her purse and locked and warded the rental.

The drive to Theo's was quick. Her heart thumped eagerly, excitedly as she pulled into his drive behind his car. She rubbed her clammy hands on her thighs.

Fortune favors the bold, Ferne.

She smiled at her father's voice in her mind. It had been his favorite quote. She used to be bold in all aspects of her life.

Nothing had ever stopped her. It was time she found that stride again. She liked Theo. A lot. She liked the way his warm brown eyes looked at her, the crinkles around them when he smiled, and the steadfast approach he exuded.

Ferne hoped they could get back to how they were at the Fairy Pools and the start of the dinner they'd never gotten to have, but she wouldn't know unless she tried. Impending danger had sent her to the isle, but she stayed because she wanted to. But that wasn't the only reason. She could help. She *wanted* to help Theo and the others find and end whatever was disrupting Skye.

She glanced at her mobile one more time. Disappointment filled her when there still wasn't anything from Mason. She would tackle him next. First, however, was Theo.

Ferne exited the car and nearly closed the door on her hand. She mumbled to herself and reached back inside for her purse. Then she walked to the house. She didn't know what made her glance upward. There was no sign of the mist. Nor did a glow surround her. Ferne inwardly shook herself and knocked.

A smile touched her lips when she heard a familiar meow. Could the cat sense her? Her thoughts scattered when the door opened, and she found herself ensnared by deep brown eyes.

"Hi." Ferne put a smile on her face and hoped her voice didn't sound as squeaky to him as it did to her ears.

CHAPTER TWENTY-FOUR

Theo's shite day turned around the moment he opened the door to Ferne. And he wasn't the only one happy to see her. Basher rushed out to wind around her legs, purring loudly. Theo watched the easy way Basher showed his affection. His hand tightened on the door because he knew just how good Ferne felt against him.

She smiled and bent down to give Basher a scratch under his chin before glancing up at him through her lashes. Did she know he had been thinking about her? That he couldn't get their kisses out of his mind?

That he wanted to toss aside any doubt just to hold her once more?

"Hi," Theo finally managed when she straightened.

She looked behind him expectantly. "Is it too late for a visit?"

For her? Never. Thankfully, he kept those words inside. He stepped aside. "Come in."

As she walked past, he inhaled the same clean, warm scent that had clung to him from their first meeting. Her hair was gathered at the back of her head in a loose bun with curls dangling around her face. He closed the door behind her, barely missing Basher's tail. The feline shot him a dark look and hurried after Ferne.

"Traitor," Theo whispered, though he had to stop himself from also running after her.

She turned and raised a brow. "I'm sorry?"

"Nothing."

He rubbed the back of his neck and turned into the living area. She unzipped her coat to follow him before shrugging out of it. Did that mean she planned to stay? God, he hoped so. Theo paused beside the fireplace. He couldn't get too close to her, not when all he could think about was kissing her again. He let his eyes roam over her. The beige sweater she wore showed off her dark skin and highlighted her extraordinary eyes. The denim clung to her legs and was tucked into brown boots.

"Do you want to talk about it?"

He started at her words. "Talk about what?"

"Your day. The…um…murder."

"Murder*s*."

She visibly cringed. "I'm so sorry."

"Me, too." He realized he was being a horrible host and motioned to the sofa. "Please, sit."

Ferne lowered herself onto the cushion before setting her purse on the floor and her coat beside her. Basher jumped onto the arm of the couch and sat, eyeing them both.

"I will do whatever it takes to prove that I'm not controlling the mist," she said.

Theo waved away her words. "It would've been difficult for you to do that when you were unconscious here."

She held his gaze, her head tilting slightly to the side. "Though

I suspect you're not entirely sure I'm not working with whoever is doing this."

"The thought has crossed my mind." There was no reason *not* to be honest. He was a cop. He always thought the worst.

"It isn't me. I came here to help, to *warn*."

Theo sank onto his chair, bringing him perilously close to her. Apparently, he wanted to test his resolve to the fullest. He looked into her green eyes and saw her earnestness. "I want to believe you. I know several of the others do, too. Carlyle specifically."

"What's stopping you?"

He glanced at the floor. "I have to be certain."

"We had a connection. At the pools. I didn't misinterpret that."

"Nay, you didna." Connection? They'd had *way* more than that.

She looked around the room as if trying to find something to say. He was at a loss, too. Too many thoughts swirled in his brain, and when he was like this, he didn't want to talk.

"Maybe this was a bad idea," she began.

At the same time, he said, "Want some whiskey?"

He didn't know what had possessed him to offer. No one liked to be around him in his present state, but he really didn't want her to go. He sat and waited with bated breath for her response. The way she held his gaze, it was almost as if she searched for something.

"That would be nice. Thank you."

Theo hesitated, unsure if he had heard her right. It finally hit him that she had said yes. He made his way to the kitchen. As he got the glasses, he noticed that his hands trembled. All the desire, the longing—the hunger—from the pools returned with a vengeance. He placed his hands on the counter and closed his eyes in an effort to get himself under control. But there was no banking the raging need coursing through him.

He didn't care who she was or why she was on Skye. He just wanted her in his arms once more. And Theo was very aware of how dangerous that was.

He shook himself and poured them each a dram of whiskey before carrying the tumblers into the other room. He handed her one, their fingers brushing softly. His gaze jerked to her face just as her eyes lifted to his. Breathing became difficult. Images of them at the pools flashed in his mind.

How *right* it had all seemed.

Theo slowly pulled his hand away and took a couple of steps back. His last relationship had exploded epically, and he had accepted that he couldn't be a cop *and* be in a relationship. He was dedicated to his career, and that left no room for anything else. Women said they understood when he warned them, but they never did. It was *always* the reason for the relationship ending.

Ferne would be even worse. She might have fibbed about being on holiday, but there was no getting around the fact that she wasn't staying on Skye. And he would never leave. Which left them exactly nowhere.

So why start something that would lead to a dead end?

Another affair that would inevitably go up in flames. He'd had enough of being hurt, of putting all of himself into a relationship and coming out with nothing. Though a few of his past lovers would argue that he hadn't given all of himself. They weren't wrong. He gave as much as he could, which was never enough for anyone.

Then there was his family. His parents were divorced. His grandfather divorced. His great-grandfather and great-great-grandfather had both lived separately from their wives and families when divorce wasn't something people did. Why do that to himself and potentially any children that would come from a relationship? He didn't care if his family's line ended. The Frasiers had all served Skye and the Druid community with their blood, sweat, and tears, giving up any sort of family and life except for keeping Skye safe.

Even as Theo told himself all of that, he had a dozen reasons at the ready for Ferne to stay.

She sipped the whiskey and looked around the room. He studied her profile and considered how she had handled herself earlier that day. He wasn't sure he would've reacted as calmly as she had. In fact, he knew he wouldn't have.

"I'm sorry we ganged up on you."

Her head swung to him. "It was a bit daunting, but I understand why. I wish I could remember what happened in the cavern."

"Did you go back today?"

"I thought it might be better if someone was with me. Just in case it happened again."

Theo nodded and took a drink. "That's probably a good idea."

"Carlyle visited me earlier."

"Did he?" Theo had thought he might since all Carlyle could do was talk about Ferne and Mason.

She held her glass in her lap. "He suggested I join your group to help out where I can. I would like to do that. If you can trust me enough."

He was trapped by her beautiful eyes, swayed by her compelling voice. What was it about her that pulled at him? She had gotten into his blood, and she would remain there forever. "I doona find it easy to trust. It's partly because of my job. You learn early on that people will do and say anything to save themselves. And yet…" He paused, trying to put his thoughts into the right words, to try and articulate what it was he sensed when he looked at her. "I knew when I saw you at the pools that you were unlike any other. I still see that."

"But?" she pressed when he didn't continue.

"Is that to get close and ruin our chance of stopping the killer?"

She set aside her drink and stood. "Did you ever think it was because I'm here to help you catch them?"

"Aye." Every fucking time she came to mind. Which was about every other second.

"If you want me to go, I will. I'll leave Skye tonight and never return."

His fingers clenched around the glass in his hand. She couldn't leave. "Nay."

"I don't want to impede your investigation. I warned Kirsi about her role, but I came to alert all of you to the growing threat."

His gaze briefly lowered to her lips. She had the most captivating mouth. He hadn't slept at all the night before as their kiss replayed over and over. His thoughts had tangled from what he had seen her do, and wanting to hold her against him once more. Now that they were alone, nothing was stopping him from going to her, from giving in to his need to know the taste of her lips again.

To feed the flames of desire that licked against him even now.

Yearning. Need. Passion. They had relentlessly thrummed through him from the instant he had laid eyes on her. Even when he worried she might be a suspect, he couldn't stop his longing for her.

Theo drank the last of the whiskey, squeezing his eyes shut as it burned a trail down his throat before settling warmly in his stomach. What had they been talking about? Ah, yes. The danger. "What's the threat?"

"Something very powerful."

"Some*thing*?" he asked.

Ferne shrugged and walked closer to him. "It could be a person."

"You said something else that got me thinking. The Ancients said not to fight. Do you think they meant not to stand with us?"

She slowly shook her head. "I don't know."

"You didna battle the mist at first. I suppose they could've meant that. But then you did fight it."

"Because it went after you."

He frowned. "You remember that?"

"That's what I was told."

She rose to her feet. Close enough to touch. Theo swallowed as he glanced at her lips again. He bit back a moan as the fire within him roared. She was a temptation he didn't have the strength to resist.

"You feel this," she said in a soft voice. "I know you do."

"It would be wrong."

"Because you don't trust me?"

"There are many reasons."

Her lips curved into a seductive smile. "Give me one."

"I doona have time for anything."

She placed her hands on his waist and closed the space between them. "Seems you have time now."

Heat slid through his veins as his cock hardened painfully. He didn't try to come up with a response because there wasn't one. His free hand rested on the swell of her hip. Was it to push her away or keep her close? Theo wasn't sure. All he knew was that he had to touch her.

Her nose brushed against his as she rose on tiptoe. With her soft breath fanning his cheek, she said, "Stop fighting this."

All Theo's defenses crumbled the moment her mouth touched his. Her lips were soft and pliant. A shiver of longing shot through him when her tongue swept over his bottom lip. His hand splayed on her back, holding her as he plundered her mouth, giving in to the need. He found his other hand free, and he tangled it in her hair.

The kiss was explosive. It was fever and flame. Hunger and heat. It was a deep ache that was finally filled. A longing Theo had never believed would diminish.

She was all he had ever wanted.

The ringing of a mobile broke the spell. He blinked as he looked down at Ferne. Her lips were swollen, her eyes heavy-lidded. He wanted to rip her clothes off and spend hours making love to her.

The shrill ring of his mobile once more pulled him back to the present. He dropped his arms from her and stepped back, his heel knocking into the tumbler that had fallen to the floor. He frowned at it even as he went to the table for his cell. He saw the number for the lab and answered the call.

Theo listened with half an ear as he watched Ferne. He ended the call and tossed the phone aside.

"Don't you dare tell me you regret that kiss," she said.

He shook his head. "I regret nothing involving you."

"But?" she pressed.

"It's no' the right time."

She quirked a perfectly arched brow. "When is it ever? Life will always get in the way. You're a police officer, and there will also be another crime that needs solving."

"If we're going to work together, this would be wrong."

Instead of becoming angry, she nodded and twisted her lips ruefully. "I can see where that could be an issue."

"Then there's my job. I wasna jesting when I said there was never time for anything. My duties will always come before anything else. Before *anyone*."

"Even your own pleasure."

He tried not to flinch at that. "People are being murdered."

"And life can end for either of us at any time. I didn't figure you for someone who ran scared."

"I'm realistic," he retorted.

She started past him. She was leaving. He knew it and understood that it was for the best. Before realizing it, Theo had taken hold of her wrist. She spun around, and they were again in each other's arms. He backed her to a wall and claimed her lips.

CHAPTER TWENTY-FIVE

Explosive. Scorching. Passionate. With every sweep of his tongue against hers, Ferne was lost, swept away on a surge of desire too vast and deep to withstand. Time stood still, and the outside world fell away, leaving only the two of them deep in the rapture of lust.

His mouth was firm and insistent. His hands gentle and searching. His body, oh so hard. She moaned as he rocked his arousal against her. She had never felt such a burning need before where nothing mattered but having him inside her, their bodies joined in a lover's dance.

She slipped her hand beneath the hem of his shirt and met warm skin and solid muscle. Her sex clenched eagerly as he ground against her once more. She wanted to run her hands over him and taste every inch of his amazing body, but right now, all she could think about was him sliding inside her.

Ferne skimmed her fingers along the waistband of his jeans. It took both hands for her to unhook the button and slide the zipper down. She didn't get any further as he tugged her sweater over her head. Instantly, he claimed her lips again.

He turned them and began slowly backing her up. All the while, they were a tangle of limbs and lips as they yanked off clothing. She managed to remove one boot and get her jeans open. Theo had one leg out of his pants when they toppled onto the rug. Their laughter rang through the room. It died when they looked into each other's eyes, and the passion returned.

His hand caressed her hip up to her waist. Her eyes slid shut on a sigh as his head lowered. Their lips touched just as he cupped her breast through her bra. Her nipples hardened into tight peaks. His mouth moved down her jaw to her neck while he slid his hand to her back and unhooked her bra. The instant it loosened, he was at her breast again, his fingers moving the garment aside to reach her nipples.

Ferne moaned as he rolled the tips between his fingers, desire shooting straight to her core. She wrapped a leg around him, bringing him closer, even as she rocked against the hard length of his cock.

His low, rumbling groan sent a thrill through her. She smoothed her hands down his chest over his shirt until she found the waist of his jeans. She tugged them down his remaining leg as far as she could, then hooked her toe in the denim and lowered them even more. Leaving only the thin, clingy material of his boxer briefs.

They both realized her pants were still on at the same time. He rolled them to their sides as they each wriggled out of their jeans. One leg got free, but the other was stuck. She inwardly cursed as she sat up long enough to remove her remaining boot and toss it across the room. With one yank, the jeans were gone. She started to pull down her panties when his hand stopped her. He slowly ran his finger around the lace edging from her hip to her stomach, then traced a line down to her sex.

It became impossible to breathe. Ferne couldn't take her attention from his face as he looked at his finger gradually skimming over the fabric, coming closer and closer to her core. She sucked in a breath when he caressed a fingertip over one side of her labia and then up the other. Her legs shook with wanting as wetness flooded her panties.

Theo cupped her sex, grinding the heel of his hand against her. Pleasure rocketed through her. It was too much. And it wasn't nearly enough. She had to have all of him. The sooner, the better.

She lifted her hips when he pulled at her panties. He glided them down her legs while she slipped the bra straps from her arms. She then reached for his shirt. Theo was faster. In seconds, the shirt and underwear were gone. Then he was on top of her.

Their lips joined once more as his hard length rested at the junction of her thighs. Her arms wrapped around him as he held himself up on either side of her head. He began to slowly rock back and forth, sliding his arousal over her sensitive flesh. She sank her nails into him while attempting to shift her hips to draw him inside her.

Theo managed to evade her. She barely had time to register that before his lips wrapped around a turgid peak. The soft pull on her nipple made her moan as her sex clenched. He was merciless in teasing her to the point of abandon. Then he moved to her other breast and did it all over again.

Ferne just needed the right amount of friction to orgasm. She was that close. And he had barely touched her. Her entire body hummed with hunger like never before. She didn't try to understand or decipher it. All she could do was hold on during the incredible ride, with the best yet to come.

Theo barely held it together. He fought against the need to thrust deep into Ferne, to meld their bodies completely. He ached for her to the deepest recesses of his soul. He could get drunk on her kisses, and her touch made him shiver with wanting. The very air crackled with desire. Deep and incalculable.

As if it were of their making.

Perhaps it was. He couldn't bring himself to think too much on that when his cock throbbed. He suckled on her nipple. She moaned and arched her back. Her sex was slick with need, with wanting for *him*. He reeled from the knowledge.

He raised his head and looked down at her. Her pulse beat wildly in her throat, and her chest rose and fell rapidly. Her eyes were closed, her lips parted as her moans grew louder. He had imagined this moment since their first meeting. It almost seemed impossible that she was in his arms.

Theo lowered his gaze to the rounded globes of her breasts. They overfilled his hands just a little, and he couldn't wait to spend more time teasing them. The way she responded to his slightest touch was extraordinary.

His cock jumped when she lifted her hips to rub against him. His control was breaking fast. She was ready for him, her entire body trembling with expectation. He had wanted to drag out this exploration more, but he couldn't wait. He had to be inside her.

He slowly rubbed his arousal against her swollen flesh one last time. As he drew back, he let his rod slip down and press against her entrance.

Ferne held her breath, her body rigid as she waited. She opened her eyes to see him hovering there, his gaze locked on the apex of her thighs. The feel of him at her opening, knowing what was about to occur, made her even wetter.

He reached for something on the table. It wasn't until she heard the crinkle of a wrapper that she realized it was a condom. He tore open the seal and unrolled it down his length. Then he looked at her. She became lost in the warmth of his brown eyes while he gradually pushed inside her. Ferne gasped when her body stretched to accommodate him. She tried to nudge him faster with her foot, but he ignored her.

Finally, he was fully inside. She held him tighter, sinking into the amazing feel of him. Then he began to move. Desire, sharp and true, spiraled through her, gathering at her center and plunging her deeper into its depths with each thrust of his hips.

Her body held him like a glove, her wet heat tempting him with the ultimate pleasure. He sank into her again and again, each time needing more, hungering for more. He was starving, and she was the feast.

Theo plunged into her hard and fast. She met his movements,

her moans turning into soft cries that urged him on. He felt her body tense and slowed his thrusts. She sobbed, her head moving side to side as she begged him to let her finish. But he had more in store for them. So much more.

His tempo increased as he pushed them both to the point of no return. It was right there, all he had to do was give in, but it wasn't time. He slowed again, barely moving his hips. Ferne wrapped her legs around his waist and rose. He stilled her with one hand. Sweat dotted her brow and slickened their bodies when he once more built his rhythm.

He had never pushed himself or a partner this far before, but he knew the pleasure would be mindblowing. His hips pumped faster and faster, his body slamming into hers as their breaths and moans filled the room. He focused on Ferne so as not to give in to his orgasm. It was the only reason he saw a change in her expression. He immediately stilled. She tried to move, but he held her down.

She was going to pass out from the unquenchable desire. Ferne was past coherent thought. Her body tingled with a craving that only one man could ease. Her sex pulsed around his rigid arousal. She saw how he fought his need. She could send them both plummeting into orgasm, but it all felt too good to end it so soon.

He released his grip on her hips, and excitement flooded her. He was going to bring her to the edge again. Would he allow them to succumb to the climax this time? Or would he push them even further? She wasn't sure which she wanted. Yes, she wanted to orgasm, but she knew he would give her that. It was the ride there that counted.

A lock of dark hair had fallen over his forehead. She clenched his cock with her body, sending a surge of pleasure through her. His rod jumped inside her. That was all it took to get him moving once more.

There was no gradual build-up this time. It was deep and hard, the tip of him touching her womb each time. And nothing had ever felt so good. Her orgasm built rapidly. It was too intense to try to hold back. Theo's gaze was locked on her. When she stiffened, he didn't stop. He continued thrusting.

The climax was incredible. It swept over her, blinding her with its potency. It rolled through her, gaining strength as he continued plunging into her. Just as the first orgasm ended, another began. It stole her breath and engulfed her in pleasure.

A faint shout pulled her back to the present. She forced her eyes open to see Theo thrusting rapidly from his own climax. He was breathing heavily when he stilled. She touched his face, and his eyes opened to meet hers. No words could describe what they had just experienced.

She pulled him down atop her, and he readily lowered himself. Ferne held him tightly and closed her eyes. Her body was satiated. In fact, she wasn't sure she would be able to stand. Her fingers played with his hair as their breathing began to even out.

"Stay tonight," he whispered.

Ferne smiled. "All right."

CHAPTER TWENTY-SIX

A persistent sound woke Theo. He was on the floor with Ferne nestled against his side. He blinked wearily, noting the light from the lamp shining into his eyes. He craned his neck and glanced outside to see that it was still dark. The sound soon became one he recognized—specifically, the ringtone he used for the chief. Theo gently rolled Ferne over and jumped to his feet. He glanced her way when he reached the phone, but she remained fast asleep.

"Ma'am?" he answered and walked to the brightly lit kitchen so as not to wake Ferne.

"I've been calling."

He rubbed his tired eyes, noting the irritation in her voice. "I'm sorry. I didn't hear it."

"I need you dressed and on the road, Frasier. It happened again."

It was like being run over. Theo stood at the doorway to the living room and saw Basher curled up next to Ferne. His gaze lingered on her naked body, his blood heating when he remembered how she had shattered in his arms.

"Where?" he whispered.

"Two different places."

"What?" He turned away and headed toward his room.

She sighed. "I'm beginning to wonder if you can solve this."

"I can. I *will*," he stated and yanked open his closet.

The chief was silent for a moment. "Maybe I've asked too much of you."

"You didna. You gave me your trust, and I willna let you down."

"Then move quickly. Because I've been on the phone with the higher-ups wanting a piece of my arse over this."

Theo tossed jeans and a sweater onto the bed before grabbing underwear and socks from his dresser. "Consider it done."

"Be careful out there."

She ended the call before he could reply. He dropped the phone onto the mattress and hastily dressed. He was about to walk from the house when he thought about Ferne. He paused and decided to leave her a note. He glanced at his phone as he set it aside and noticed that it was a few hours before dawn.

Something wasn't right. His instincts were shouting a warning he needed to pay attention to. Theo slowly lifted his head to the front door to look out the panes of glass. The porch light normally illuminated the area. It was programmed to come on at dusk and go off at dawn. And it was a brand-new LED bulb, which meant it should be on. Yet only darkness met his gaze. The electricity wasn't out, because the lights were on inside.

He took measured steps to the door and peered outside. He couldn't find a single light from the houses near him. He moved to another window, and then another. He walked across the house and tried that window, all with the same outcome.

It was the mist. It was here. He backed up, his heart thumping in his chest. And it waited for him. Had he walked outside without noticing anything, it would have had him. The only reason it couldn't get into the house was because of all the wards.

Theo pulled his mobile from his pocket and dialed Rhona. She answered on the third ring.

"Theo?" she asked sleepily. "What is it?"

"I could use your help," he said, staring out the window. "Or rather, Balladyn's."

Her voice was clear and strong when she asked, "What is it, and where do you need us to go?"

"The chief just called about two more murders. I was about to walk out of the house when I realized I couldna see any lights outside. I'm positive the mist is here."

"Do you need us to come get you?"

He swallowed and turned toward the living room. "First, I need to know if I was set up."

"By your chief?" Rhona asked in confusion.

"Aye."

Rhona was silent for a heartbeat. "Text me the addresses. Once we find out, we'll come to you. If it is her…" she began.

"I know," he replied.

"Talk soon," Rhona said and disconnected.

Theo turned on his heel and walked to Ferne. He knelt and touched her arm. When she didn't wake, he gave her a little shake. That only managed to stir Basher, who rose and yawned widely before stretching.

"Ferne," Theo said, shaking her harder.

She made a sound, her brows drawing together as she tried to roll over. He stopped her and called her name again. This time, she opened her eyes. A smile curved her lips when she saw him, but it vanished when she noticed he was dressed.

"There's a situation." He then explained everything.

Her head swung to look out the window as she sat up. She wrapped her arms around herself, shivering from her nakedness and the long-dead fire. He straightened and held out his hand. She took it, and he pulled her to her feet. She began to dress without a word.

He used the time to pick up his discarded clothes, tossing hers to her when he found them. Theo had just put the garments into the hamper when his mobile rang, Rhona's name popped up on the screen.

"I take this to mean there has been a murder," he said.

She hesitated. "Actually, no."

He closed his eyes, a mixture of relief and regret twisting his insides.

"We looked at both the places, and there's nothing," Rhona continued.

"I can no' say I'm sad to hear no one's life was taken, but that leaves the chief for me to handle." He shook his head and opened his eyes to find Ferne before him.

"I think we should be there to back you. There's more," Rhona said before Theo could argue the point. "We can't get to you."

Theo's brows rose at that. "Excuse me?"

"Every time Balladyn tries to jump inside your home, something stops him. We're looking at your house now. You're right. The mist has it surrounded."

"Well, fuck."

"I've notified the others. We'll figure this out. Just stay there. You…and Ferne."

"This isna her." At least he hoped it wasn't. She was here. The mist was here. It was easy to connect them.

"First things first. The mist."

Theo slid his gaze to the door. "The sun will burn it off as soon as it rises. We wait it out. Doona do anything that could get one of you hurt."

"You're starting to sound like Balladyn," she teased. "Besides, when do I ever do anything rash?"

Theo said, "Always," and heard Balladyn say the same thing in the background.

Rhona snorted. "Hold tight. And don't go outside."

"I'm more worried about the rest of you."

The call ended. Theo lowered the phone. This wasn't how he wanted the morning with Ferne to go.

"It isn't me," she said.

He nodded and pocketed his mobile. "I know."

"Do you? I'm not sure I would if I were you."

The worry in her green eyes didn't sit well with him. "We just have to wait. The mist can no' get into the house. We've made sure of that."

"If it isn't letting a Reaper in, then perhaps we should be concerned about it finding a way inside."

"We have no idea how long it's been out there."

"And it could've been working at getting past the wards all that time."

Theo shrugged one shoulder. "It hasna gotten in yet."

They both looked at the door.

"I've got a bad feeling about this," Ferne murmured.

"We wait," he said again. Theo wasn't sure if he repeated it for himself or Ferne.

The mist was there for one of them. Or maybe both. It'd had the chance to kill Ferne on the mountain, but it hadn't. Why? That lingering, unanswered question bothered him. Was it because she was part of it—unknowingly or not? Could it be because it wanted to use her for something? Which wouldn't be good. There was a chance it might fear her. Nothing else seemed to faze it in the weeks since it had begun its murdering spree.

No matter how he looked at it, Theo couldn't figure out who the mist targeted and why. Obviously, the one controlling it had a reason, but he damn well hadn't worked it out yet. And he wasn't ready to think about his chief and her role. He would have to sooner than he liked, but first, he needed to survive until dawn. And make sure the mist couldn't come back for him this evening.

"Don't fight."

He looked at Ferne and frowned. "What?"

Her gaze was locked on the door. "That's what I was told. *Don't fight*. I wasn't sure if the Ancients were urging me not to fight them, whatever was happening to me in the cave, or…"

"The mist," he finished.

Ferne swung her head to him. "Yes."

"When we saw you at the Red Hills, and the mist surrounded you, you didna fight it. At least no' until it came after us." Theo rubbed the back of his neck. "You stopped it from getting to us. You didna fight it."

"Some might consider that the same thing."

"You didna go after it, and you certainly didna try to hurt it. I think you could've."

She blew out a breath and returned her gaze to the door. "You said it surrounded me. Has it done that with anyone else?"

"No' that I know of."

"Why me?" she whispered. "Why didn't it take my life?"

Theo was glad it hadn't, but he had the same questions. "I was hoping you knew."

Ferne pulled out a chair and sank onto it. Almost immediately, Basher jumped into her lap. She stroked his fur absently while lifting her gaze to him. "If the Ancients did speak to me, and the mist is killing Druids, why tell me not to fight it?"

"Are you sure it was the Ancients?"

Her head lowered as she shook it. "It felt like them, but how can I say that when I have no idea what they feel like."

"You said they sang to you before."

Green eyes glanced up at him. "They weren't singing this time."

"They spoke to you in your mind like you talked to Kirsi."

"Yes, and if they can do that, why not keep doing it?"

Theo sat in the chair on the opposite side of the table. "Maybe they needed you in the cavern."

"What was that place?"

"A prison, of sorts." He wrinkled his nose. "No' of sorts. It's a prison. A place where my—*our*—ancestors kept Druids who broke the law."

"The six smaller caverns. Those are the cells."

"Aye. We hadna used them in…" Theo blew out a breath. "*Years*. But we did recently."

Ferne lifted a brow, her interest clear. "Why?"

"Have you heard of the Druid Others?"

She rolled her eyes. "Unfortunately. There was a small sect

within the London Druids who pushed for them to join, but the elders dismissed the notion. Those Druids left to join the Others."

"What do you know about the organization?"

Ferne continued to pet Basher as her brows knitted. "I know they're different from the London Druids in that they actively sought out *droughs* to join. If I remember right, they then connected their magic to become more powerful."

"That's exactly it."

"I thought that would alarm the London branch, but they didn't bat an eye."

Theo snorted. "My guess is that's because they were either already a part of it or formed it themselves."

"I can see them doing both." Her lips twisted with disgust. "But why is it suddenly so important for Druids to be more powerful?"

"That's a verra long story, and it began with a Druid from another realm, searching for a new home. She found Earth with its abundant magic, but there was one problem. The Dragon Kings were already here. She decided to defeat them, but she couldna do it on her own. It took a *drough* from her planet, a *mie* and *drough* from ours, and a Dark and Light Fae. The might and magic of the Dragon Kings was unstoppable. No group had more power than they did. Until the Others."

CHAPTER TWENTY-SEVEN

Ferne opened her mouth to talk, then shook her head as she tried to process what she'd just heard. "I just met a Dragon King. I'm not even sure who that is, but they're still around, right?"

"The dragons once ruled this realm. Then humans arrived. We now know it was the Druids who put them here. The Dragon Kings welcomed the mortals and gave them a home, but it didna last long. Many of those humans were born without magic, but a few had it."

"Our ancestors," she murmured.

Theo nodded. "They settled on Skye. The humans multiplied quickly and needed more and more land. Some hunted the smaller dragons."

She winced at that.

"And the dragons retaliated by having humans as a snack."

"I think I see where this is going."

"Aye. War."

Ferne glanced down when Basher's rough tongue scraped along

her finger as he decided to bathe her. "The dragons have magic. They could've wiped us out. Or did the Druids step in?"

"As far as I know, the Druids were no' involved in the war, but who knows for sure? You're right, though. The dragons—the Kings specifically—could've ended us at any time."

"Why didn't they?"

Theo rose and heated some water. He held up a bag of coffee beans and raised a brow in question. After she nodded, he continued. "From what I've been told, the magic of this world chooses a King for each clan—the clans being the color of the dragons. When a stronger, more powerful dragon is found, the magic tells it to take over."

"And the previous King just steps aside?" she asked in disbelief.

Theo shook his head and leaned back against the counter, his arms folded over his chest as the water boiled. "It's a fight to the death. The Kings had two choices. They could kill the mortals, thereby forcing the magic to remove every one of them as a King, or they could hold to the vow they'd given when the mortals arrived. They chose to protect the humans."

"What became of the dragons? Are they still around? They can't possibly be." Suddenly, she had to know.

"The Kings sent the dragons away to another realm. They've only recently located them."

Ferne was mesmerized by the heartbreaking story. "So, Earth was home to dragons, and now, there are no more here?"

"The Kings remain. They're the realm's guardians."

As she looked around the kitchen, she spotted a bottle of Dreagan whiskey. Suddenly, the double-headed dragons on the label made sense. "Dreagan. That's where the Kings are."

"Verra good," Theo said with a smile. "They remain hidden for obvious reasons."

"Hidden? Nikolai looked like a human."

"The Kings can shift from dragon to mortal form."

She couldn't wait to share all of this with Mason. "That's incredible."

Theo ground the beans and then added a heaping spoonful of ground coffee to the French press pot and poured the hot water over it. Then he stirred before adding the plunger to the pot and setting a timer for four minutes.

He reassumed his stance against the counters. "The point to me telling you all of that is that the Kings defeated the Others, but it gave the Fae and Druids ideas. The Fae nearly gained control. If it were no' for Death and the Reapers, they would have. The Druid Others targeted Rhona. One of her deputies, Kerry, worked with the Druid Others to lure Rhona away from Skye and attempt to kill her. Balladyn found her just in time. It took our healers a while to mend the numerous wounds on her body."

"Bloody hell," Ferne said. "I didn't know."

"Why would you? It happened here."

She shrugged. "That kind of event makes people talk."

"Rhona lived, and there was a huge battle on Skye." Theo's gaze went distant before lowering to the floor. "It took all the Druids on Skye, plus Death and the Reapers, *and* the Dragon Kings, and we still couldna defeat them. No' until Rhona and Balladyn combined their magic. It was something to witness, that's for sure."

Theo dropped his arms as the timer went off. He slowly pushed the plunger down. He poured coffee into two mugs and brought them to the table with cream and sugar. Neither of them added anything to their cups.

"Balladyn is Warden of Skye," Theo said. "He's still a Reaper and has duties with Death, but he aids Rhona in watching over the isle."

"Can you explain the Reapers to me?"

Theo took a drink of coffee. "They're Dark and Light Fae, chosen by Death to keep the balance between the Fae."

"Ah. I thought he might reap souls," she said with a smile.

He looked at her over the coffee mug. "They do."

"I see. Why haven't they gone after the mist?"

"Rhona and Balladyn would like nothing more than to fight it, but it's never around them."

Ferne took another drink of the delicious coffee. "It's scared of them."

"Or biding its time."

She could see the argument for that. "Who did you have to put in the caves?"

"We call them the Red Hills. And it was Kerry. Rhona removed her as a deputy and allowed her to remain on Skye so long as she promised to behave."

"Has she?"

"As far as I know."

Ferne found her attention drawn to the door. "Are you sure the mist isn't acting on its own?"

"What do you mean?"

Her head swung back to Theo. "If it was the Ancients I heard, then they can't speak as they normally have. Perhaps that's what allowed the mist to be controlled."

"Perhaps."

"But…there's also a chance it wasn't the Ancients I heard. That it was something else. The Ancients' silence is what made me reach out to Kirsi, but once I got here, I sensed something was off."

Theo leaned one arm on the table, his fingers curled around the handle of the mug as he turned sideways. "You're no' the only one who's said that. Esther felt the same. She wants to talk to you."

"Just as soon as we can get out of here," she said, looking at the door again.

Something kept drawing her gaze. Nothing had moved. At least as far as Ferne could tell. That didn't mean it hadn't, though. She felt Basher move and looked down to see him awake and staring at the door. He then lowered his head back down.

Theo's phone rang. Ferne heard Rhona's voice coming through the speaker, but she couldn't make out what the Druid leader said. She thought about Mason. After gently setting Basher on the floor, she rose to find her purse and mobile. But one look showed Mason still hadn't gotten in touch. That troubled Ferne. She needed to talk to him and know everything was all right. Things had been odd since she arrived on the isle. Or perhaps *she* was the one who was…off. It was difficult to tell.

She sent Mason another text. Not that she expected him to respond this early. Once the ordeal with the mist was over, she'd phone the estate again. Maybe she would get lucky and catch him. At the very least, she'd get to speak to Billings.

Ferne hadn't flown in the helicopter or a plane since her parents' accident. But she needed to get back to England in a hurry. She'd only stay long enough to talk to Mason, and then she'd return to Skye to finish things here. It was too bad she didn't know Balladyn well enough to ask him to just pop her over to the estate. She wouldn't have to deal with the trauma of flying—or the fear of crashing.

Even if she were friendly with the Reaper, she wouldn't ask. There was too much turmoil on Skye for him to leave just because she wanted to talk to her brother.

Ferne kept her mobile with her and headed into the kitchen when she heard a tapping at the door. She glanced at Theo, but he was deep in conversation, his brow furrowed, and his lips compressed. She had just decided it was her imagination when it happened again. There was no mistaking the sound of a fingernail tapping on glass.

Her heart skipped a beat because she knew the mist was trying to get her attention. But for what? Did she dare find out? What if the Ancients had told her not to fight the mist because it was trying to help them? What if the mist was killing the Druids responsible for the Ancients being unable to talk?

Another tap. She took a step toward the door. All she had to do was open it and find out what the mist wanted. She assumed it would talk to her. If it had at the Red Hills, she didn't remember. She couldn't recall anything after passing out. All she had was Theo's word. But she trusted him.

She looked at him over her shoulder. He had his back to her, pouring another cup of coffee. More patter drew Ferne's attention to the door once more. There was a fifty-percent chance the mist was evil, and another fifty percent that it was helping the Ancients. She took another step. This was one situation that fell definitively into either the good or evil column. There were no shades of gray here. If she made the wrong decision, it could end her life.

Another step. Then another.

Ferne was near the door now. She peered through the glass into the blackness beyond and decided to look at the facts.

The mist had killed.

But it hadn't harmed her.

Of course, that didn't mean it hadn't changed its mind.

The doorknob wiggling caused her gaze to lower. Ferne felt something at her legs at the same time she heard a hiss. Basher faced the door, his back arched and his long fur sticking out everywhere.

The cat's reaction gave her pause. She wasn't sure of her own judgment anymore. Was she so off-kilter that she had been debating opening the door and walking out into the mist in the hopes that it talked to her? Basher hissed louder.

"Ferne?" Theo called. "What are you doing?"

She heard the concern in his voice. "I don't know."

The tapping repeated. Theo was at her side in a heartbeat. Basher backed up against their legs as if pushing against them. Theo drew them back a few steps. The feline followed, though he never took his eyes off the door. The cat kept himself between them and the door until they were away from it. Then he turned and fastened his blue eyes on her.

"What just happened?" Theo asked.

Her legs were shaking so badly she could barely stand. Ferne resumed her seat. "I–I heard tapping, and I wondered why the mist hadn't harmed me. I thought maybe it was being directed by the Ancients to stop whatever was being done to them."

"You thought the mist was, what? Good?"

She grimaced at his icy words. "I was trying to make sense of the situation."

"Shall I show you how brutally the mist is killing?"

"It's killing, yes, but what if it's attacking those responsible for silencing the Ancients?"

Theo opened his mouth, then his face hardened with anger as he paused. Slowly, the scowl transformed into lines of concern.

Ferne nodded. "Exactly."

"Nay," he said with a shake of his head. "It tried to kill Elias. Twice. It went after Elodie, Scott, and Filip. It also recently went after Bronwyn and the rest of the Knights. We're working with Rhona and Balladyn. The Ancients would know we're on their side and wouldna have the mist going after any of them."

She deflated. "Oh. That makes sense."

"Your theory gave me pause, mainly because there could be some truth in it."

"Are you sure the mist is being controlled?"

He looked around for his coffee before finding it on the counter and retrieving it. "When it went after Bronwyn at the manor where Elias and the Knights were, she saw someone. She didn't see who it was and could only make out a form in the shadows, but they were off to the side, watching."

"Hmm. That would cause me to think they were controlling it, too. Is there a chance they just happened to pass, saw the commotion, and stopped to watch?"

"The manor is set far from the road."

Ferne felt the pull to look at the door again, but she kept her gaze on Theo. "Why do I get the feeling it wants me?"

CHAPTER TWENTY-EIGHT

Edie woke suddenly from a deep sleep. She looked across the room into the doorway to the bathroom. She lay there listening to see what might have disturbed her, but the house was silent. She rarely woke in the middle of the night.

She slipped from the covers and padded to the bathroom to empty her bladder. It wasn't until she was on her way back to bed that she noticed Trevor's side of the bed was empty. She figured he must have gone downstairs for a drink. She could use some water herself. Edie walked out of her room, along the hall, and then down the stairs.

The cool tile as she stepped off the wooden stairs chilled her bare feet. She walked noiselessly to the kitchen but didn't see Trevor. She did a quick walkthrough of the downstairs without finding him. She returned to the kitchen for her water and happened to look out the wall of windows to the outside. There, she spotted him on his phone.

No matter how hard she tried, Edie couldn't think of a reason for him to leave the house to take a call. Well, she could think of one reason, but Trevor would never cheat on her. They had a great marriage. Okay. *Great* was pushing things right now, but they had a solid relationship. As with any couple, they had their ups and downs, but they got through each one. Whatever was going on now was no exception.

Was it?

She fought the need to burst out of the house and demand to know who he was talking to. But after the past few days and how everyone kept telling her she was overreacting to everything, Edie thought better of it. That still didn't dampen her need for answers.

Her husband had left their bed to make a call. The fact that he had snuck downstairs—what else *could* she call it?— then went outside into the cold night to talk to whoever was on the other end of the line made her stomach knot painfully.

This wasn't something she was making up. She saw this with her own eyes. But what could she do about it? The logical thing would be to confront him. Calmly, of course. If she could even do that. With how rocky things were, if she lost her temper, Trevor would refuse to talk. She was doing everything she could to put their relationship back on track. Not to mention her bond with the kids.

Trevor turned towards the house, and she saw him smiling. A huge smile that lit up his entire face. Her heart sank. *Was* he having an affair? Could he do that to her? To their family? Had her behavior pushed him to do something so drastic?

Edie rushed upstairs when he ended the call and started toward the door. Her heart was racing when she jumped into bed and turned on her side with her back to the door. She lay as still as she could when he came into the bedroom and quietly climbed into bed. He didn't reach for her, didn't touch her.

She didn't know how long she lay there staring into the darkness before she heard him snoring. Edie debated whether to creep downstairs to check his phone. But what if it was a number she didn't know? She didn't want to call it. Or did she? She could write it down and look up the number later.

Those were the actions of a woman who didn't trust her husband, and Edie had spent too many years loving Trevor to do something like that. No, she only had one course of action. She needed to talk to him and ask him outright if they were going to be okay. Depending on how he answered, she would then ask if he was having an affair.

Trevor had pursued her when they were younger. She hadn't wanted to be involved with anyone—not after what had happened to her father. But he hadn't given up. Now, it was her turn to show him that she wasn't giving up. She would be the wife she used to be. She would set aside the anger and resentment she felt toward her siblings and move forward.

In order to do that, she *had* to tell Trevor everything. She'd had the opportunity earlier but chickened out. They were getting along so well, and learning the truth would cause him to get upset that she'd withheld it from him for so long. But she didn't have a choice. The trip would be the perfect time. It would just be the two of them without any interruptions or distractions. Once she explained everything, Trevor would understand. It might cause some friction at first, but they would work it out. They always did. Just like this…whatever it was going on.

As Edie mulled things over, her thoughts drifted to Kerry. The Druid claimed to know things about Trevor. Edie could ask her, but that would make Kerry aware that something was amiss in their marriage. There was, of course, but Edie didn't want her to know that. Though Kerry's smirk suggested she already did.

Edie rolled onto her back and sighed as she stared at the ceiling. She'd had a good life. Hectic, but good. Right up until Elodie returned to Skye. Edie had been happy about it. At first. It didn't take long for everyone on the isle to take note of Elodie's arrival, and just like when they were children, everyone tripped over themselves to do things for her sister.

Even Elias had come home. Elias, who barely made time to phone Edie, much less take her calls. It was like they were teenagers again, leaving Edie out. Being the middle child was never easy. As the eldest, Elias got the most freedom.

Then there was Elodie. The youngest, and their father's favorite. Their mum's, too, it seemed. Emily McLean always tried to treat the three of them equally, but Elodie's powerful magic had singled her out early on.

That left Edie. The eldest daughter, but that didn't seem to mean much to either of her parents. Neither did having perfect grades, doing all of her chores, and never making a fuss. It seemed that by being a good child, she had gotten overlooked. And left out.

Of everything.

Childhood issues shouldn't return to an adult, but it happened. Elias and Elodie could keep their secrets. Edie wouldn't tell them that she knew. If her brother and sister didn't have time for her, then she didn't have time for them. She shouldn't have allowed herself to let her resentment and anger fester. Look what that had done to her marriage.

It was time she focused on Trevor and the kids. They were

what mattered. They would always be here. Elias and Elodie might be blood, but they weren't family. Not really. They'd proven that time and again, but she hadn't wanted to see it. She certainly did now.

Even Kerry with her crazy thoughts and outlandish claims didn't matter. Even if all she'd said was true, Edie wouldn't let herself be pulled into it. She'd allowed her concentration to be diluted with insignificant matters. Not any longer.

No matter how hard Edie tried, she couldn't go back to sleep. To stop herself from checking Trevor's phone, she planned their upcoming weekend. That meant she needed to contact Elodie or Elias to watch the kids. She might not care about being a part of their lives, but she had no compunction about using them. Besides, the children barely knew their aunt and uncle. It was time her siblings stepped up.

Edie rose just before five and went downstairs to work out. She eyed Trevor's mobile as she passed, but she was proud of herself for not looking at it. She showered and took a little extra care when she dressed for the day. She woke the kids and then returned to her bedroom as Trevor got up. She offered him a kiss and a tight hug, both of which he accepted enthusiastically.

"Shall I close the door?" she whispered when she felt his arousal.

He kissed her forehead and twisted his lips in regret. "I can no' be late this morning. I'm trying to get everything done so we can have the weekend."

"Right." She tried to hide her disappointment. "We won't have to close the door on our getaway."

He winked and walked around her to the bathroom where he

started the shower. Edie pressed her lips together before turning on her heel when she heard the children arguing.

"Come on, kids," she called as she walked downstairs. "If you hurry and dress, I'll make hotcakes."

Their shouts of joy brought a smile to her face. She would get things back to normal. It would take one slow step at a time, but she owed it to her family to do exactly that. They needed her, and she had let them down in a big way.

Edie busied herself getting breakfast together, but again and again, her gaze went to Trevor's mobile. When the kids came down, she had them make their lunches while she finished the first batch of hotcakes.

"Something smells good," Trevor said as he entered the kitchen dressed in a navy suit, a pink dress shirt, and a navy tie with pink stripes. She had picked out the outfit on their shopping trip a few months ago. The fact that he chose to wear it today said he was also trying.

Their gazes met. He gave her a smile, but instead of coming over to her and grabbing her arse, he went straight to the table. Edie was hurt, but she reminded herself that she had done a lot of damage to the family. This morning was a vast improvement from the past few, and that was a win in her book.

"It's been a good morning," Trevor said as he looked at the kids.

Both of them nodded, smiling. Then, all three looked at her. Edie's eyes burned with tears. She had missed this so much. She hadn't realized how badly she had sunk into old habits about her family until her husband and children called her on it.

"Who wants more hotcakes?" she asked as she brought a second plate to the table.

All three reached for another. Edie added one to her plate and ate as casual conversation began. She didn't interject or join in. She was too grateful to do more than bask in the fact that her eyes had been opened to what she had nearly ruined.

Trevor glanced at his watch and wiped his mouth before rising. "I have to go. I'll see all of you tonight."

He paused to kiss the top of the kids' heads before stopping beside her chair and giving her a soft, lingering kiss. "Have a good day," he said.

Nothing would wipe the smile from Edie's face. The kids were quick to get moving that morning, too. They didn't even argue on the way to school. She was in such a good mood that she decided to bake a cake as a surprise for everyone. She dashed to the co-op and parked.

She reached for the handle to open the door of the SUV when she looked up through her windscreen and saw Kerry watching her.

CHAPTER TWENTY-NINE

It took eons before dawn arrived. The entire team gathered with Rhona and Balladyn, which didn't seem to faze the mist one iota. Theo and Ferne promised they were unharmed, which was the only thing that kept the group safely away.

Theo knew they had to figure out what the mist wanted. And quickly. The way Ferne kept looking at the door troubled him. The list of other things they needed answers to lengthened continually.

He was running out of time. He felt it deep in his bones, a sixth sense that went beyond being a Druid or a cop. The lives of everyone on Skye rested on his shoulders. Each minute he didn't gain answers was another tick on the clock that counted down to the next death.

He was drowning under the lives already lost. He couldn't lose anyone else. His gaze moved to Ferne, who used a string to play with Basher. Theo had been sure she wasn't a part of anything. Then he had been sure she was. Then, he couldn't decide. He was back to being sure she wasn't involved.

The more he learned about Ferne muddied the waters of truth even more. He never should've crossed the line and slept with her, but he hadn't been able to stay away. Even now, he wanted to reach across the table and hold her hand, touch her hair. Draw her into his arms for another long, languid kiss that would incinerate them both.

She was firmly in his blood. A drug he was utterly, completely addicted to.

Ferne laughed when Basher jumped high to catch the string, flipping dramatically and landing softly on feline paws. The cat had actively kept both of them away from the door. Some would say Basher had a good sense of people. He was utterly taken with Ferne, when he hadn't willingly gone to anyone else but Theo before.

"Look," Ferne said.

He followed the line of her finger to the door to see portions of the mist burning off with the sunlight, revealing the outside world. Theo got to his feet and walked around his home. Finally, he was able to see outside in multiple places.

His mobile rang, Rhona's name on the display. Theo put it on speaker as he made his way back to the kitchen. "It's working."

"It is. Thankfully, the front door faces the sunrise. Stay there. We're coming to you."

He met Ferne's gaze as he ended the call. "Do you still want to work with us?"

"I do, but I understand if you have doubts."

Theo ran a hand through his hair. He wanted her with him, but was that purely because of his desire? Or did his instincts realize she could be helpful? No matter how many times he tried to figure it out he couldn't. "We both need answers, and I think it'll go better if we work together."

"I agree."

"Can you let them in? I'm going to grab a quick shower."

Her lips twisted. "Wish I could."

His balls tightened when he thought about taking her in the shower—the water running over her slick body, her long legs around him as he thrust inside her. His cock got instantly, achingly hard. "You can. Here," he added, hearing the roughness of his voice.

A slow smile came to her lips. "Don't tempt me."

Fucking hell, she made him burn with a hunger that scalded him. An image of their bodies coming together flashed in his mind. She was the only one to sate his hunger. The only one to match his desire. The only one…

"Go," she said in a voice husky with need.

Her eyes had darkened. She was thinking about their lovemaking, too. He wanted to know what she saw in her mind's eye. He would ask, but later, when they were alone. Now, he required a cold shower. It would do little to dampen his yearning, but if he didn't at least try, he would take her right here on the table regardless of who walked inside.

Theo pivoted and strode to his room. He turned on the shower and stripped. His need for Ferne was growing out of control. The passion between them was unlike anything he'd ever experienced. She was easy to talk to, effortless to be with. She would, in fact, be perfect if she weren't potentially tied to a killer mist.

He turned off the water and toweled himself dry. Voices from the other side of the house reached him, alerting him that the team had arrived. He dressed in a charcoal gray sweater, jeans, and his boots. He raked his fingers through his wet hair after brushing his teeth. His lips twisted when he saw the dark shadow of a beard. He shaved every morning, and by evening, he needed another pass of the razor. But he didn't want to take the time this morning. There were too many other things to do.

Theo entered the kitchen to find Carlyle frowning at a box of donuts on the table. On the other hand, Finn grinned from ear to ear as he bit into a pastry.

"Want a donut?" Finn offered Carlyle.

The Englishman turned up his nose. "My body is a temple."

"Mine isna," Filip said as he snagged one with powdered sugar.

Theo noted that nearly everyone was eating one of the sugary confections. Only Ferne, Carlyle, Bronwyn, and he were not.

"I can cook something quick," Carlyle offered as if he also noticed others had chosen to refrain.

Theo's gaze slid to Ferne, who stood at the doorway into the living area with Basher in her arms. The feline looked content, his eyes half-open as he lazily surveyed the room.

"What happened last night?" Elodie asked into the silence.

Carlyle slapped his hands together. "Breakfast it is. Something simple. Eggs, sausage, and toast."

"There isna much left from yesterday," Theo told him.

Carlyle flashed a grin. "I anticipated that and bought some items."

"And I brought these," Finn said as he held up an iced donut.

Carlyle began preparing breakfast. Theo set about making more coffee and heating water for those who wanted tea. He got out as many mugs as he had, which wasn't nearly enough.

"I came by to see Theo," Ferne said in answer to Elodie's question.

Theo dumped out the cold coffee in his mug and nodded. "I got the call from my chief, and, well, you know the rest. No' much to tell." Which was a lie. There was a lot to say about him and Ferne, but no one else needed to know that.

"What happened after you knew it was the mist?" Balladyn asked, his eyes on Ferne.

Theo glanced at Ferne. She didn't look away. Instead, she raised her chin. She didn't lie. Instead, she told everyone what had gone through her mind about the mist and their subsequent discussion.

"You think it wants you?" Bronwyn asked with a concerned frown.

Ferne's shrug was small. "I might be wrong. It's just…"

"She wanted to go to it," Theo said when her voice trailed off. Her eyes met his. "She might be right about it coming for her. I never wanted to get near it. In fact, I always want to go the other way."

Scott snorted. "Och. Me, too."

"What do you think it wants with you?" Rhona asked.

Ferne shook her head. "I've no idea."

"And you still doona remember anything from the Red Hills?" Elias questioned.

Ferne shifted Basher to her other arm. "I don't. I want to go back, but as I told Theo, I want someone with me in case something happens. At the very least, I'm hoping it'll jog my memory."

"It couldn't hurt," Elodie said.

Theo rubbed his eyes. "There's a lot we need to do. I think the best thing is for us to split up. I need to confront my chief." Which he wasn't at all thrilled about. He liked Alisha. It would be a blow if she were on the opposing side.

"You really think she's mixed up in this?" Finn asked around a mouthful of donut.

Theo shifted his weight to one foot as he leaned against the counter. "I hope no', but I can no' think of another explanation for her call and the lie to get me out of the house."

"Unless it wasn't her," Sabryn stated.

Carlyle held a bowl as he whisked the eggs. "You mean someone used her?"

"Maybe," Sabryn said. "She could've been forced to call Theo. Or, it might not have been her on the phone at all."

Theo's head throbbed, thinking through all the scenarios. He was beginning to wonder if he would ever solve this mystery. If he failed…he didn't even want to think about it, but it was becoming harder not to.

"Did she—or whoever called—know Ferne was here?" Finn asked.

Theo threw up his hands. "Your guess is as good as mine."

"Regardless, you shouldn't go to see your superior alone," Rhona told him.

Balladyn crossed his arms over his chest. "I'll be shadowing him."

Theo bowed his head to the Reaper. To think that he had wanted nothing to do with the Fae once. Now, Theo couldn't imagine Skye without Balladyn.

"Then I'll take Ferne to the cavern," Rhona stated.

Theo saw Balladyn's lips pinch as if he were getting ready to protest, but he held it in. Theo knew how he felt. He didn't want Ferne going without him either. Not because he didn't trust her, but because he wanted to be there to witness anything for himself. Also, so he could be there if she needed him.

As if reading his mind, Ferne said, "Actually, I'd like for all of us to go. Just in case."

Sabryn leaned her head to the side and popped her neck, making Finn wince. "We don't know how long it'll take Theo with his chief. There are things the rest of us can do in the meantime."

"Finish the surveillance for one," Theo pointed out.

Elias nodded from his seat at the table. "Agreed. And doona worry," he said to Theo. "Elodie and I willna watch our sister."

Carlyle lifted a hand as he scrambled eggs on the stove. "I can do that."

"I'll join him," Filip said.

Theo cleared his throat, and the others divvied up posts with the deputies and Kerry. "Something is out there. It could be the same thing that's been killing Druids around the world. Or, it could be something different. I know two things for certain today: Druids are being targeted, and time is running out."

"You forgot something," Sabryn said.

Theo raised a brow in question.

Sabryn's deep blue gaze slid to Ferne. "She's an integral part. Ferne sensed the danger here."

"When I didn't." Rhona's lips twisted. "Trust me, I've been able to think of little else."

A knock sounded, interrupting them. Theo wound his way through the bodies in the small area and spotted the trio standing outside through the window. He opened the door to Nikolai, the TruthSeeker, and the JusticeBringer.

"We're here to talk to Ferne," Esther said as she looked around Theo.

He didn't need to turn to know that she stared at Ferne. These three could help them get to the bottom of their current mystery.

And right now, Theo could use all the help he could get. He stepped aside. Esther entered first, followed by Nikolai. Henry brought up the rear.

Everyone shifted to grant the newcomers room, but Theo's attention was on Ferne and Esther, who stared at each other.

"You feel it," Esther said.

Ferne nodded.

"What do you feel?" Henry pressed.

Ferne licked her lips. "The growing darkness."

CHAPTER THIRTY

Ferne longed for a shower. She was grateful for the breakfast Carlyle had cooked, and the two cups of tea afterward, but she wanted a change of clothes. Food was quickly eaten, and the kitchen was cleaned just as rapidly. Now, everyone was readying themselves to head out to their respective assignments—everyone except her.

"Have you heard from Mason?" Carlyle asked as he walked up.

She shook her head. "I'm getting worried."

"Saber can find him. It'll only take a quick text."

"You sure he won't mind?"

"Positive."

Ferne nodded. "Please. I need to know my brother is safe."

"Consider it done."

Something tugged on Ferne's arm. She turned to find Theo on her other side. Ferne set Basher down when Theo tugged her after him. He took her into his room and closed the door behind them. Basher quickly opened it and sauntered in.

Theo pushed it closed again before turning to her. "Are you okay?"

"I'm not the one about to confront my boss, who might be aligned with the opposing side."

"Esther, Henry, and Nikolai want to stay behind and talk to you."

"I assumed as much."

"I can ask Rhona to remain."

Ferne smiled, heartened by his worry. "I might learn something from them. I'm not afraid if that's your worry. They want the truth, and they can help."

"I…" He blew out a frustrated breath and ran a hand down his face. "I doona like leaving you on your own."

"I've been alone most of the time. I can take care of myself. Unless you're afraid I might hurt one of them."

One side of Theo's lips curved into a grin. "I doona think you'd get one over on a Dragon King."

She closed the space between them. "I'll be fine. I'm more nervous about you."

"I'll have a Reaper with me. That gives me a definite leg up should something go wrong."

"You're right. Time is running out for us. The darkness I saw in my visions has multiplied."

"What do you mean when you say *saw*?"

She flattened her hand on his chest, feeling the softness of his sweater and the heat of him beneath. "Imagine a storm cloud growing larger and darker as it approaches. That's what I see. It hung over Skye before, but now, it's everywhere."

"You had another vision?"

"No. I've tried. I *feel* this. I have ever since I woke up yesterday."

He reached for her and slowly wound his arms around her. "Do you think it has anything to do with the mist covering you?"

"I don't know. Maybe."

"You'll wait for me to go to the Red Hills?"

"Promise," she replied with a nod.

"What if Mason wants you home?"

There was no mistaking the worry in Theo's deep brown eyes. She wondered if it was because of the feelings developing between them, or if he didn't quite trust her yet. "I'm not going anywhere until we solve what's going on."

"*We?*" he asked with a wry grin.

She shrugged. "You said we work better together."

"I did."

"We've not discussed last night."

His gaze lowered to her mouth. "Nay. I enjoyed myself. I'm pretty certain you did."

"I did, yes," she said with a smile that quickly slipped. "I hope it wasn't a one-time thing."

"I couldna stay away from you if I tried."

Prickles of pleasure ran over her skin. "Are you going to keep talking or kiss m—"

His mouth slanted over hers, his tongue sweeping in and laying claim to her in a way that made her sex clench hungrily.

As quickly as it began, the kiss ended. He steadied her, his eyes brimming with desire. "I'll finish that tonight."

Theo walked to the door and opened it, waiting for her. Her legs were jelly after such a wickedly hot kiss. It surprised her that her knees didn't buckle as she put one foot in front of the other and made her way back to a nearly empty kitchen. Balladyn spoke to Nikolai as he and Rhona waited for Theo. And then the three of them were gone.

"So," Esther said when it was just the four of them remaining. She pulled out a chair and patted the table. "Can we chat?"

Henry sat across from Esther while Nikolai remained standing and off to the side.

Ferne took one of the other seats and met Esther's gaze. "Do you know what's here?"

"I don't. I was drawn here."

"To seek the truth," Ferne said.

Esther nodded once. "Exactly."

"I came to warn Rhona and stayed to help."

Henry lightly drummed his fingers on the table. "Rhona told us what you said about the Ancients. How do you know you spoke to them in the cave?"

"I just do." Ferne shrugged. "If you're looking for evidence, I don't have any."

Nikolai leaned a shoulder against the wall. "You took a big chance coming to a land you were forbidden to visit to help Druids, who might have turned you away."

"I did what I had to do. What I know is the right thing to do." Ferne felt Basher rub against her leg before jumping into her lap. "If the Skye Druids fall, the rest of us are doomed."

Henry's drumming ceased. "That's a bold statement."

"It's the truth," Esther said. "I can sense it in her."

Ferne nodded as she met Esther's brown gaze. "It's no mistake that whatever is going after them did it for a reason. They're the biggest, strongest group."

"You claim to be a seer," Henry said.

Ferne swung her head to meet his brown eyes. "I don't claim anything. I have visions. That is the definition of a seer."

He shrugged as if her word choice didn't make any difference. "How many of your premonitions have saved others?"

Ferne frowned at that. She lowered her gaze to Basher as the cat lifted his blue eyes to hers. "None."

"Because you didna interpret them in time?" Nikolai asked.

Ferne rarely talked about this. The only person she had ever shared such information with was Mason. She took a deep breath and then slowly released it, lifting her gaze to the Dragon King. "I've never known anyone in my visions."

"No family? Friends?" Henry asked in surprise.

Ferne shook her head. "Never."

"How did you know about Kirsi, then?" Esther's voice was soft, even.

Ferne shook her head helplessly. "I didn't know her. I saw her face over and over in different time periods. One of the visions she was in showed a landscape, and I suspected it was Skye. Once I confirmed that, I reached out to her."

"And you're sure you're a seer?"

"Again, I have visions. What else would you call that?"

Nikolai's lips twisted. "Aye, but visions of what?"

"Of people. Places." Ferne rubbed her temple. "Sometimes… sometimes, they don't feel as if they're from this time period."

"How interesting," Esther said.

Henry slowly sat back in his chair. "What are you thinking, sis? She sees the past?"

"I think Ferne's right. I think the mist wants her."

Ferne's stomach dropped to her feet. "What?"

Esther shot her a reassuring smile. "Don't worry. We're going to find out why."

"You don't need to worry about Ferne. She's safe with Nikolai, Esther, and Henry," Rhona said.

If Theo didn't know that Balladyn and Rhona were veiled in his back seat, he could think they were conversing through his mobile. But they were in his car. All because there was a good possibility that Chief Superintendent Alisha Cunningham, a cop he liked and admired, could be involved in the very crimes she had him investigating.

He adjusted his grip on the steering wheel and glanced in the rearview mirror to where he thought Rhona sat. "*Safe* is a relative term at this point. I've yet to narrow down the pool of suspects. How can I know where to look to locate the bastard responsible if I think *everyone* is guilty?"

"You split us up as you have," Balladyn stated.

Theo pressed the brake as he came upon a slow-moving vehicle where the occupants gazed out the window at the attractions instead of paying attention to the road. "It's no' going to be enough."

"You have all of us. We'll do this," Rhona assured him.

Theo wished that were his only problem. He wasn't sure what he would say to the chief. If things had gone to plan, he would most likely be dead. It wasn't as if he could storm into her office, slam the door, and tell her he knew about her involvement. Because he didn't.

It might not have been her who called. It would almost be easier if it were her. Then he could spend the next few hours interrogating her in the Red Hills. Time would tell when he stood before her.

"I've been going over this thing with your chief," Rhona's disembodied voice said, dragging him from his thoughts. "If she is on the opposing side, then other police could be, as well."

Theo had already thought of that. It left a sour taste in his mouth. Being a cop was like a special kind of family. One others who weren't on the job never understood. "Aye."

"I wouldn't even know where to begin interrogating the force. Perhaps you should ju—" There was a short pause before Rhona said, "Sorry, Theo. I was thinking aloud. I know what being a police officer means to you."

"You're no' thinking anything I've no' already," he told her.

Balladyn grunted. "That doesn't mean we shouldn't be aware of the tricky situation you're in."

Theo finally got around the tourists and sped up. He wanted this thing with the chief over with so he could get back to Ferne and the assignment. "Can we do this? Can we stop whatever is happening on our isle?"

"We're going to bloody well try," Rhona replied.

Balladyn let out a long breath. "We halted the Fae Others. We might need to bring in all the Skye Druids again, but the answer is aye."

Theo grimaced at the thought of another large battle. "It may come to that, but we can only hide such battles so many times before regular people take notice."

"Magic will conceal things," Balladyn reminded him.

Theo put his turn signal on and slowed before taking a right.

"Magic is life here for many of us. But no' even magic can hide all the ugliness. Eventually, it'll leak out. It always does."

"I've long believed the Dragon Kings never should've remained hidden," Rhona said. "I understand why they did, but they've had to live in secret. And there's no coming back from that now. It has only happened to us for a few generations, but once we hid who we were, it was hard to reveal it."

Balladyn chuckled. "The Fae have never had an issue letting anyone know what they are."

"Which of us is right? I'm no' sure anyone can claim victory. There are pros and cons to hiding and revealing yourself," Theo said, shrugging. He found a spot to park and cut off the engine. Then he released a long breath. "I suppose it's time for answers."

He didn't wait for Rhona or Balladyn to reply. Theo exited the car and made his way into the building. He knew the couple would stay with him, hiding until they either had to reveal themselves or contain a situation. There was a chance things could go tits-up quickly.

His stomach knotted, the breakfast he'd had not sitting well thanks to his heightened stress level. He needed a holiday. A very long one. Somewhere warm and sunny. With Ferne. And without any interruptions or evil to fight. He just had a long list of things to take care of beforehand.

Theo nodded at the cop at the front desk and keyed in his code to get to the back of the station. He scanned the offices as he made his way down the hall. At a glance, everything appeared normal. He saw the chief's door was closed when he reached her office at the back of the building.

"Tom," he called to the nearest detective. "Is the chief in?"

Tom shook his bald head without looking up from his computer screen. "She's been out for a couple of days."

There was no use staying if she wasn't here. Theo retraced his steps and got back into his car. He didn't bother saying anything to Balladyn and Rhona as he pulled onto the road and headed toward the chief's house. Theo tried to look at the upside. If there ended up being an altercation with the chief, it wouldn't be done in sight of the entire police force now.

Theo put the car in park. As he reached to turn off the engine, he felt a hand on his shoulder. He looked in the rearview mirror. Balladyn had lowered his veil, his silver and red eyes troubled.

"Don't go in."

Theo squeezed the steering wheel so tightly he heard it crack. There was only one reason the Reaper would say that. "How long has she been dead?"

"A day. Two tops. I'm sorry, Theo."

He nodded. "Me, too."

"At least we know she wasn't working with the enemy."

That was little consolation. A good cop, a good *woman* was dead. And her life was taken because she knew about Druids and had given him the authority to run his own team.

CHAPTER THIRTY-ONE

Kirsi didn't want to be at work. She didn't want to be anywhere. She hadn't been able to sleep or think clearly since Ferne approached her. At least her parents were giving her space. Though for how long, was anyone's guess.

She made sure she had a smile on her face to greet customers, but that was all Kirsi could manage. There was no small talk, no cheery hellos. She wouldn't be at the front for long. As soon as her parents returned from her mom's doctor's appointment, she had the rest of the day off. Kirsi didn't know what she would do. She didn't want to talk to her friends about things any more than she wanted to discuss them with her parents. Sitting in her room only made her aware of her parents' anxiousness.

No. She needed to get away. The isle was big enough that she could find a spot to just sit and be. Maybe the muddle in her mind would clear, and she could figure out what to do. That made her snort. According to Ferne, she already had the answers. What a load of shite. Kirsi didn't know anything. Ferne had to be wrong.

Or she got the wrong Druid.

The clank of items on the counter made her turn around to find Edie. Kirsi smiled at the woman, but Edie kept looking out the door. Kirsi followed her line of sight to see Kerry standing outside. She continued scanning Edie's items and putting them in the woman's reusable bag. Edie barely spared her a glance as she paid and left.

Kirsi walked to the door as she watched Edie. It was blatant spying, but something was going on. The women's exchange was brief. Edie mostly spoke. Kerry just smiled and waited to talk. Whatever Kerry said seemed to stun Edie into silence. Kerry walked away, but it took Edie a few moments before she put the bag of groceries in the boot of her SUV and drove off.

The sound of Kirsi's parents coming in the back got her attention. She went to greet them, only to have her mother place a key in her hand.

"We should've done this years ago," her father said sheepishly.

Kirsi stared at the key. "I don't understand."

"It's for the upstairs flat," her mum explained. "We selfishly wanted you at home, but you're young and need your own space."

She shook her head. "But…you rent that out for extra income. I don't mind living at home. I'm here to help."

Her parents shared a look. It was her mum who leaned forward in her wheelchair and took her hand. "You already do too much, and we've taken advantage of that. We have help coming twice a week now. Live your life, pet. We'll be fine."

"It isna as if you'll be far off. We're just a few blocks away," her dad said with a watery smile.

Kirsi had wanted to ask for the flat since she was eighteen, but then her mother got sick, and it was never the right time.

"We've been talking about it for a few months." Her father shrugged. "That's why we didna rent it out again."

Kirsi looked from her dad to her mum. "You don't need to do this."

"We want to. Now, go take a look at your new place. I've already contacted Scott and Filip to do some repairs. It's up to you if you want to wait until they finish to move in," her mum said with a wink.

Kirsi looked at the key, then at her parents, happiness spreading through her. "Really?"

"Really," they replied in unison.

She gave them each a hug and a kiss before running out the back and up the stairs to the flat above the shop. The studio wasn't large, it wasn't much of anything really, but it was hers now. Kirsi sighed, her smile wide. She walked around the space and tried to figure out how she would decorate, but her confused head prevented it and diminished her joy.

Kirsi quietly left the flat and started walking to clear her mind. She had no destination in mind. She just needed to be on her own. She walked for miles until she found it. Beacon Cove was one of the prettiest spots on Skye, and not overtaken by tourists. It was partially hidden and difficult to get to, which helped the locals keep it a secret. She picked her way through the jagged boulders and headed down the slope to the beach.

The lapping water was soothing as it rolled onto the sand and pebbles. She spotted a boulder she knew would hide her from anyone walking past and hurried to it. Kirsi rounded the rock and came to a halt when she found someone else already there. It wasn't just anyone, though. It was Skye's bad boy himself—Callum Kilmuir.

He sat against another boulder with his arms resting on his bent knees, his feet spread. His shoulder-length, wavy hair couldn't decide if it was blond or light brown and was shoved to one side as if he had raked his hands through it. Those hands sported a silver ring on his right ring finger, as well as a mix of leather, metal, and beaded bracelets on his left wrist. A short-sleeve, blue tee, faded from washing and frayed around the neck, covered his wide shoulders. His jeans had holes in the knees from wear.

"Sit or leave. Doona just stand there."

Her gaze snapped to his face and the amber eyes locked on the sea. He had the kind of magnetic face you saw in magazines or the on the tele. Intense eyes, an amazing jawline, full lips, and a don't-fuck-with-me defiance.

Not to mention a hard, muscled body to match.

His voice wasn't harsh, but it was a command, nonetheless. Kirsi had thought to be alone here. If she left now, it would be rude. Callum would think she'd left because of him. Everyone kept their distance from him and his father.

Except the girls who had a thing for guys like Callum.

Which she certainly didn't.

He sighed irritably. "Sit or leave."

Kirsi quickly looked around and spied the rundown house up on the hill to the right. The one where Callum's father lived. She sank down and heard someone shout, the wind snagging the word.

"It's my dad. Ignore him," Callum told her.

She settled more comfortably about two feet from him and stared ahead at the water. The air off the water was cold, but her coat protected her. Callum didn't have a jacket on, but if the temperature bothered him, he didn't show it.

"I didn't mean to invade your spot," she said after a long while.

He shrugged. "It's a public beach."

"Callum! You sorry excuse for a son! Where are you, ye bastard?"

She tried not to flinch at Joseph Kilmuir's incensed voice growing nearer. "You obviously wanted privacy."

"I wanted to disappear. This was as far as I got."

His candid admission surprised her. "I was trying to find a place to clear my head."

"This will do it. No one will find you here."

"A place to disappear."

His head turned, and his amber eyes met hers. He stared at her for a full minute. "Aye."

"If only we could."

He raised a brow at that but didn't pry any further. She was grateful. She didn't want to think about her problem, much less discuss it with anyone.

"Be careful when you come," Callum said as he leaned his head back against the rock and closed his eyes. "Joe Kilmuir's a mean bastard. He likes to say this cove is his. If he sees you, he'll run you off, and he willna care if he hurts you in the process. It's why the cove is usually empty. He always spots them on their way down. There's a route by the water that's easier and quicker to get to and from the path you took."

"You don't mind sharing?"

"As long as you don't mind not talking."

"It's what I'd prefer."

"Good."

A ding had Ferne reaching for her mobile. The text was from a blocked number, but the message itself made her decide not to dismiss it.

Your brother's at the family estate. Saber.

She was relieved, but also furious. Why wasn't Mason phoning? Why hadn't he answered any of her texts? Ferne sent a quick reply of thanks to Saber before calling the estate. As usual, Billings answered.

"Hello, Billings," she said, trying to keep her voice unemotional when she was anything but. "Have you heard from Mason?"

"I'm afraid not."

Ferne ignored the trio at the table and surged to her feet, Basher jumping to the ground as she did. Billings was lying. She had to figure out why. She walked to the living area and circled the room as Basher watched her from atop the back of the sofa. "I'm worried about him. He still hasn't contacted me. It's not like him."

"I can add another message to give him when he returns," Billings offered.

Ferne stopped beside the place she and Theo had fallen into each other's arms the night before. She had to handle this delicately. Which she wasn't sure she could do. She wanted to shout and demand that he hand the phone to her brother. That's when she knew that she had to go home. Immediately.

"I'm on my way home. I'll find a helicopter to get me there shortly. I must find Mason. Be ready for me, Billings."

She hung up and turned to the doorway where Henry, Nikolai, and Esther watched her. Ferne made her way to them. "I'm coming back as quickly as I can, but something is wrong with my brother. I think..." She was really about to say it out loud. "I think Mason is in danger. Nothing would stop him from talking to me."

"We can help with the ride," Esther said. She looked at Nikolai. "Can you get Lily here with the chopper?"

Nikolai grinned. "I've got another idea that'll be even quicker."

"With as many of you that borrow the bracelet from Ulrik, you'd think he would have a sign-out card like a library so he knows who has it," Henry said with a chuckle.

Ferne listened to everything with interest. "Theo needs to know I'm coming back."

"He'll know. We'll be the ones getting you there and bringing you back," Nikolai replied.

Of course. She should've realized that. Ferne turned in a circle, trying to think of what she needed to do. She'd only rented the cottage for one more night. She could extend it or find a hotel.

"I heard you mention a shower earlier. I can take you back to your place so you can wash and change clothes since you don't seem in a fit state to drive," Esther said as she pushed the chair back to stand.

Ferne was far from good to drive. "Thank you."

In short order, Esther led her outside and to the white Range Rover. Then they were off.

Ferne's worry for Mason doubled with every minute. "I should've known something was wrong. I should've returned home immediately. I actually believed Billings when he said Mason was dealing with estate business."

"And you know Mason isn't because?"

"Saber found him at the estate."

Esther maneuvered the roads easily. "Playing Devil's advocate here, but can't that mean he's doing exactly what Billings said?"

"For two days after being distressed with my first encounter with the mist?" Ferne shook her head before looking at Esther's profile. "He's not answering because he can't. It has nothing to do with the estate, and everything to do with the London Druids."

Ferne had spent the last hour filling the three of them in on the group in London and Mason's suspicions about their parents' deaths.

"Would those in London keep Mason from talking to you?"

Ferne sighed and looked out the passenger window. "I'd like to say they wouldn't, but it's possible. And I hate to admit that. If he's not getting in touch, it's because they're preventing it somehow. I need to help him. He's all I have."

"I know how that feels." Esther shot her a sad smile. "Henry means the world to me. When siblings are that close, the bond is strong. We've gone through a lot over the last few years. I had Nikolai as another shoulder. Henry didn't have that."

"Then you understand why I need to get to Mason?"

Esther briefly met her gaze. "I do. We wouldn't be helping if we didn't get it."

CHAPTER THIRTY-TWO

SKYE DRUIDS

Theo watched his chief's covered corpse being rolled out of her home on a gurney. She hadn't been a Druid, but it was obvious by the way she'd so savagely been killed that the mist had done it. She had been deceased before he received the call, which meant someone had mimicked her voice—and tried to lead him to his death.

The crime scene techs were doing their jobs, but they wouldn't find anything. Theo, Balladyn, and Rhona had scoured the scene before they arrived. There was nothing. Just like all the others.

Theo heard reporters' shouts behind him. The story was growing, the panic on the isle escalating. Someone would step into the chief's place, and they likely wouldn't be so open about him working outside the lines of protocol. Theo already felt the pressure of time, but now he could hear the ticking clock louder in the background.

This entire time, he'd been trying to go at this like a regular crime, when it was as far from it as you could get. He needed to rethink things. He was good at his job. Now, he had to prove it to himself and the others. It was time to take back the peace for Skye.

There was nothing more for Theo to do at the Cunningham scene, so he made his way to his car. Balladyn and Rhona were veiled, walking among the others. He didn't have long to wait before they noticed and jumped inside the vehicle.

Before he drove off, Balladyn asked, "Did you find something?"

"A new plan. Or at least a new thought. Rhona, can you contact the team and have them head to the Red Hills?"

"You want to take Ferne now?"

He shrugged. "I'm trying a different approach. Instead of hunting for the suspect, we bring them to us."

"Are you sure about this?" Balladyn asked as he dropped the veil.

Theo looked in the rearview mirror to meet the Reaper's silver and red gaze. "It'll be up to Ferne."

"She thinks the mist wants her. Maybe this is what we should do," Rhona said with a shrug.

Edie drove to the next rental to check everything over before the new arrivals came the following day. She was shaken by Kerry waylaying her. She didn't like that it felt as if Kerry were spying on her. The only good thing that had come out of the interaction was that Edie had convinced Kerry she couldn't be a part of anything now.

Kerry's mention of the two Druids on Skye about to move

things along quicker managed to sway Edie. She'd almost asked who they were out of curiosity, but something had told her not to. A part of Edie enjoyed the way Kerry pursued her. It reminded her of how Trevor had been so certain of his love, even in the beginning.

Could there really be something that important about Edie? It had given her pause when she was about to refuse Kerry again. Instead, she'd relented. A little. If Kerry was giving the Druids a much-needed overhaul, Edie wanted to come out with her family on the other side. The only way to do that was to stand beside the one in charge. Which was why Edie had agreed to join Kerry, but not right away. Edie wanted to get things back to normal with Trevor first.

Kerry's smile had been triumphant, but Edie hadn't minded. If Kerry wanted her that badly, then she was worth the wait. However, Kerry's parting remark about Trevor had shaken Edie.

"You care about your family. I admire that. But don't let them stand in the way of your greatness. I doubt your husband would hesitate if he were in your shoes."

Edie shoved that from her mind and took the bumpy drive to the rental. As she emerged from the trees, she was shocked to see Trevor's car. They were partners in their rental properties, but she usually did the day-to-day things. He only ever came out during work when she told him it was important. So what was he doing here now? Was he putting cameras inside?

God, she hoped not. She hadn't confronted him about the ones Elias had found in his rental. Had it been anyone else who'd found them, they could be in a lot of trouble. Edie needed to know if there were others. But she had to know why they were there first.

And she wanted to know what Trevor was doing at this rental when he was supposed to be at work.

She parked and climbed out of her vehicle. Glancing inside his car, she saw a red Chanel purse on the passenger seat. Suspicion shot through her. Edie swung her gaze to the house. It felt as if her feet were weighted down as she walked to the door. The knob turned without resistance beneath her hand. As soon as she entered, she heard a woman's laughter coming from the deck area, Trevor's joining in a heartbeat later before they both quieted.

Did she burst into the room? She might find them together. Would they be kissing? Hugging? Tearing off each other's clothes?

She fought the sudden nausea the images brought and kept moving toward the sound. She came to a doorway and paused. Was this the truth she wanted? Or did she turn and leave, never to know?

The woman's renewed soft laugh made the decision.

Edie walked around the doorway and saw Trevor standing beside a beautiful woman with long, black hair, a red coat, a black leather skirt, and long, shapely legs. Trevor was a leg man. It would've been the first thing he noticed. Edie hated the woman immediately.

At least she and Trevor weren't kissing. They weren't in an embrace either. But the way her husband smiled at the woman took Edie's breath away. Not so long ago, he had looked at her like that. The jealousy that swarmed her was quick and choking.

Suddenly, Trevor saw her. Surprise flickered across his face, followed by a flash of what she could only describe as annoyance. "Here's my lovely wife," Trevor said, motioning her forward with a warm smile.

Had it been irritation on his face? Maybe she wanted to see

that. He wouldn't greet her so cheerfully if he were displeased. Edie put a smile on her face and nodded at the woman. "Hello."

"I'm Sheila," the woman said, extending her manicured hand.

Her makeup was impeccable. Her skin perfection. The coat fit her as if it had been sewn specifically for her. Edie's smile felt frozen as she shook Sheila's hand. "Nice to meet you. I'm Edie."

"Trevor has told me so much about the rental properties the two of you manage," Sheila said. "I thought I'd see if one was available."

Trevor wound an arm around Edie. "I thought of this one because of the view. This is Sheila's first trip to Skye."

"Work keeps me in Edinburgh. I'm glad it finally brought me here. I've fallen in love," Sheila said with a wide smile.

The tightness in Edie's chest loosened with Trevor beside her. She took a breath to relax. "This is one of our best rentals. As Trevor said, it's the view that does it for everyone. Getting up here isn't easy, but once you are, you don't want to leave."

"I'm surprised you don't live here yourselves."

She and Trevor exchanged a look before he said, "We did for a time, but we built a house with views just as good."

"Well, I'm envious," Sheila said, laughing.

Trevor gave Edie a quick kiss. "We got out of a meeting early. I need to get us back for the next one to wrap things up for the week."

"Oh, right. Trevor gave me your card, Edie. I'll be in touch soon about renting this place."

"Sounds good."

"Sheila gets the friends discount," Trevor said with a wink.

Edie felt herself prickle as she walked with them to the door, but she kept it hidden. Trevor gave her another kiss. She watched them walk out to his car and drive away, wondering why her thoughts kept going to him having an affair when he obviously wasn't.

Ferne gathered her wet hair at the back of her head and bound it. The shower had been quick but refreshing. The change of clothes helped tremendously. She took one last look at herself in the mirror on the back of the door before going to find Esther.

Their phones dinged at the same time. They looked at each other and then their mobiles.

"Looks like we're headed to the Red Hills," Esther said.

Ferne nodded. "I'd rather go during the day, anyway. Less chance of running into the mist."

"Good point. Ready?"

Ferne locked and warded the door behind her and was climbing into the Range Rover when her mobile rang. Relief filled her when she saw Mason's name. "Where have you been? Are you okay?" she asked by way of answering.

He didn't laugh at her harried questions, nor did he try to calm her. Mason's voice was clipped with aggravation instead. "I've busy running a large estate, Ferne. You were told that the multiple times you called. *I* told you I'd call you when I could."

She stilled, her heart tripping over itself. She and Mason argued like all siblings, but he hadn't spoken to her like this since they were teenagers. This wasn't the brother she'd talked to on their last call. "You were supposed to come."

"Things changed."

"They don't for us."

"They did."

She swallowed and glanced at Esther. The phone wasn't on speaker, but Mason's voice was loud enough that the Druid could hear. Ferne's stomach clenched painfully. "Estate business has never pulled you away like this. Is it...did your investigation find anything? I wanted you to wait, but I understand if you couldn't."

"For the last time, I'm working," he snapped.

She flinched as if he'd slapped her. His words were so unfeeling. "Mason, what is going on? You don't treat me like this."

"How else am I supposed to treat you?"

Her blood turned to ice. Something about his tone was unusually cruel. "What?"

"You broke a cardinal family rule."

Ferne couldn't breathe. She opened her mouth, but air wouldn't pass into her lungs. This couldn't be happening. She wanted to toss the phone aside and scream at him to shut up, but she was frozen as his next words filled her ears.

"You went to Skye. You know what that means."

If Ferne hadn't been sitting, her knees would've buckled. Her hand shook as she placed it on the still-open SUV door. "Mason, don't."

"Don't put this on me. It's all on you."

"Y-you accepted what I had to do."

"That doesn't mean I liked it. You're an adult, Ferne. You knew what would happen if you went. Even after you were kicked out of the London Druids. And you *still* went to Skye. You showed where your true loyalties lay."

This couldn't be happening. Tears blurred her vision as her throat clogged with emotion. "Mason, we're all each other has."

"You chose your side. Don't call again. And don't come back. You won't be welcomed."

The line went dead. Even then, she left the mobile at her ear, thinking he would come back on the line and tell her it was all a joke. But he didn't.

Esther gently took the phone from her. Ferne squeezed her eyes shut. She fought against the tears because if she gave in to them, she knew she wouldn't be able to stop.

"We can still take you to him." Esther's voice was filled with sympathy.

Mason's aloof, icy tone told Ferne everything she needed to know. She opened her eyes once the tears were at bay. She would cry, but not now. "No."

"Could the London Druids be responsible?"

"I'd like to lay the blame on them. And in a way, it *is* on them. Between them and the families, it's a rule we all know never to break. Mason hates the London Druids. This has nothing to do with them. This is him."

There was a slight pause. "Like you said, you two only have each other. He'll change his mind."

Ferne tried to close the door and pinched her foot in it instead. She brought it inside the vehicle and then shut the door. Mason had just banished her from her home—and his life. She could leave Skye right now, but the damage had already been done. There was no going back.

She was so lost in thought that she didn't realize they had driven anywhere until Esther got out of the vehicle. Ferne blinked and found herself looking at the hulking mounds of the Red Cuillin mountains. Something had happened to her here last time. Regardless of what was going on with her brother, she was here to save not just those on Skye, but also Druids around the globe. If that cost her Mason, then she would somehow learn to accept that.

Ferne squared her shoulders and exited the Range Rover. Theo was beside her before she could close the door.

He studied her face. "What happened?"

"I heard from Mason."

"Is he all right?"

"He's fine."

Theo's brow furrowed deeper. "You're ashen. Something happened."

"He exiled me."

Theo's hand found hers, his long fingers firm as they held hers. "I'm sorry. We can postpone this. Go to him. Talk. Do whatever you need to do."

"I have to be here."

"We can take some time," he insisted. "We'll go wherever you want to go and talk. Or just sit. Whatever you need."

"No," she said and squeezed his hand. "We'll talk later. This is about saving people. I have to do this."

"I should warn you about the risks," he said hesitantly.

She shook her head. "I'm aware of the risks. It's daylight. That helps."

"The mist could still be in there. It has been before."

Despite that nugget of information setting a stone of worry in her stomach, it didn't change anything. She had to do this. Just as she'd had to contact Kirsi, travel to Skye, and go into the cave the other night. There was no backing out of this.

"Will you stay with me?" she asked.

"I willna leave your side."

CHAPTER THIRTY-THREE

Something was off. Theo tried to pinpoint what it was as they scaled the mountain. He looked to Ferne, who was ahead of him. It was more than her being upset. He turned his gaze to the mountains. The answers they sought were there—if they dared to go. It was what he wanted. It should be what he wanted. Why then did he want to turn back and get away as fast as he could?

Sometimes, the answers didn't give the solace or relief a person needed—or required. In some instances, the answers only made things worse. There was pain, sorrow. Loss. And knowledge that, while not literally killing a person, could destroy in other ways.

That's what they toyed with.

That's what they sought.

"What is it?" Finn asked once they had gotten halfway up the mountain.

Theo shrugged and shook his head. "I doona know."

"The Red Hills have been sacred to us for generations," Rhona said as she reached them. "It's why the prison was created here."

Sabryn shoved hair from her eyes as the wind whipped the black locks. "Just because it's sacred doesn't mean it isn't dangerous."

"The mist brought Scott here," Elodie pointed out.

Scott nodded solemnly. "And took you."

"As I said," Sabryn added.

Elias sighed as he looked toward the cave entrance. "Are we doing this or no'?"

"It isna up to us," Theo stated with more force than intended.

Ferne met his gaze as she gave his hand another squeeze. "We are. I just need a moment alone. I want to meditate to center myself before I go inside. I won't be long."

"Take whatever time you need," Theo said. After what happened with Mason, he wasn't sure Ferne should be here at all. The ticking clock reminded him they didn't have time to waste.

Balladyn nodded. "We're not in a hurry. Do what you must."

Theo reluctantly released Ferne's hand and watched her walk up another incline to the right, where the ground leveled out in a small section. She kept her back to them and faced the mountain as she sat cross-legged. Only then did Theo turn toward Esther. His voice was low when he asked, "What happened? I need details."

Everyone looked at the TruthSeeker. Misery crept over her face as Esther glanced at Ferne. "Mason finally called."

"Saber came through, then," Carlyle said.

Theo briefly looked his way as Esther nodded.

"The call didn't go well." Esther paused, her face twisting with anger and disbelief. "He…after she told me how close they were, I was surprised to hear his tone. It was beyond cold and callous. It was heartbreaking to see her devastation. He cut her out of his life as if she didn't matter."

Theo wanted to find Mason and punch him. Repeatedly.

"He wouldn't do that," Carlyle said in disbelief.

Esther shrugged. "He did. I heard him."

"Damn. Poor Ferne," Finn murmured.

Theo turned to look at her. After such heart-wrenching news, she was there, helping them. Helping all Druids.

"I'm going to talk to him. He…Mason…*fuck*," Carlyle muttered in frustration.

The team was silent for a long time before Bronwyn asked, "What can we do for Ferne?"

"We'll figure that out when we're done here," Theo said. "We owe her that."

"I agree," Rhona replied.

Theo looked at the group and squeezed his eyes closed for a moment. "I know we want answers, but are we prepared for what they are? What we might learn?"

"Is anyone ever?" Balladyn asked.

Elodie shrugged and looked around. "We don't have a choice. We have to end the killings. Even Ferne believes she has some kind of connection."

"It didna hurt her last time," Filip pointed out.

Nikolai made a sound in the back of his throat. "That doesna mean it willna now."

"We need to be prepared for anything. Ferne is going to do this. She asked us to come as witnesses, but I think she would've come alone if she had to," Henry said.

Theo grunted. "She wants the same answers we do."

"Truth is here," Esther said. She was looking at the mountains, a frown beginning to crease her forehead. "And I think we're about to get it."

Unease slid down Theo's back like a bony finger. He whirled around to find Ferne levitating above the ground. Her body slowly rose. As it did, her legs straightened, and her arms stretched out at her sides.

"What the actual fuck?" Sabryn asked.

Theo took a step toward her. "Ferne?"

A hand grabbed his arm, holding him in place. "Don't," Esther warned.

Ferne continued drifting higher before moving forward toward the top of the mountain. They scrambled after her, Theo in the lead. He had proper shoes this time, which allowed him to get the traction and grip he needed to scale the rocks. He kept his eyes on her, glancing down to ensure where his hands and feet needed to go.

"She didn't mention this happening when she came before," Elodie said through tight breaths.

There was a grunt and the sound of small rocks falling. Then Scott said, "Maybe it didna."

Theo climbed as fast as he could. He had to get to Ferne and catch her. He would get Ferne off the mountain and back to his house so the team could regroup. He had known something was off. If only he had listened to his gut. He couldn't let himself dwell on that now, though. She was his focus, the only thing that mattered.

And then she stopped moving.

Theo hurried up to her. Just as he reached for her foot, she levitated higher out of his range. "Ferne!"

"I'm not sure that is her, mate," Finn whispered, out of breath.

Ferne gradually rotated to face them. Her eyes opened, and she looked down at Theo, pausing for a moment before looking at the others' faces. Her arms lowered to her sides as she hung several feet above the mountain—still out of reach. At least for him.

Theo could use magic to reach Ferne, but he wasn't sure what had her. He might do more damage. Instead, he searched for Balladyn and found him and Nikolai standing together, both apprehensively watching Ferne. He caught Nikolai's eye and mouthed, "Can either of you get to her?"

Nikolai looked at Balladyn. The two slid their gazes to Ferne and then to him, giving a single nod. Theo let out a breath he hadn't known he was holding. Nikolai and Balladyn would get to Ferne, and then they could all go back to his house. They wouldn't have answers, but Ferne also wouldn't be levitating.

"Finally."

Theo's head snapped to Ferne. The voice had come from her, but it didn't sound like Ferne. Far from it. In fact, it sounded like more than one voice. As if… It couldn't be.

"Oh, shit," Henry murmured.

"We've been kept silent for so long," Ferne said.

There was no mistaking it now. It was definitely more than one voice. Theo didn't know what the Ancients wanted with Ferne, but it couldn't be good if they were using her to speak. "Ferne? Can you hear me?"

Her green gaze lowered to him as her head tilted to the side. The Ancients ignored him as they scanned the group again. "Too much to do. We have been silenced. Find the cause."

"Oh, my God. She's a conduit," Esther said.

Ferne swung her gaze to the Druid. "A strong one. She heard us beckoning."

"Who silenced you?" Rhona asked. "Who do we look for?"

"The Ageless One."

Theo fisted his hands. "We need more than that."

"No time," the Ancients said. "This life force is waning."

"Then get out of her!" Theo lunged for Ferne, but arms held him back. He fought against them, his fist connecting with a jaw.

"Bloody hell, Frasier," Elias muttered. "Stop."

"Get the fuck off me!" Theo fought like hell to get to Ferne. He had to reach her before it was too late.

Theo slipped free, only to have more hands and arms grab him. He shoved at Filip, kicked Scott, elbowed Finn, and headbutted Elias before tripping Carlyle. He was free again and raced up the last few feet to Ferne. He spotted a boulder. He could use it to launch himself and get to her. His foot found purchase, and he pushed off, only to find himself tackled to the ground by Balladyn.

Theo looked to Ferne and saw her eyes roll back in her head. He watched helplessly as she sank to the ground unconscious. "Ferne!"

He shoved Balladyn away and sprinted to Ferne, dropping to his knees beside her. Theo reached for her and paused. Then he gently put his fingers to her neck for a pulse. It was faint.

"Is she alive?"

He glared up at Rhona. "Barely. If you had let me get to her, things might be different."

"You'd be dead," Henry said.

Nikolai's lips twisted. "Balladyn and I deflected the Ancients' magic from striking you."

He didn't know what they were talking about. He hadn't seen anything. Theo had been too engrossed in the fact that they were killing Ferne. He owed them gratitude, and he would tell them.

Just not now. He gathered Ferne in his arms as he had a few days ago and got to his feet.

"She's breathing. We need to call the Healers," he told Rhona.

She nodded, swallowing. "I'll do it now."

"Where do you want to go?" Balladyn asked.

Theo looked down at Ferne. He could almost tell himself she was only sleeping, but he knew it was so much more than that. "Home. Take us home."

Half a second later, he stood in his kitchen. Balladyn was gone, but he didn't care. Theo took Ferne to his room. He lay her on the bed and removed her boots and coat, just like before. Basher jumped onto the bed and sniffed her before letting out a soft, forlorn meow.

"I know, lad," Theo murmured.

He sat beside Ferne on the mattress and took her hand in his. Basher curled up next to her on the pillow. Together, they waited. Each second felt like an eternity. Theo watched her chest move up and down. She breathed, and right now, that's what he clung to. It was all he had.

If she hadn't come over the night before, he wouldn't know how incredible they were together. She'd gone after what she wanted while he stood back, ready to watch the world pass him by. All because he'd thought it was the right thing to do. That was a load of horseshit, and she called him on it.

He'd tell her that once she woke. The alternative wasn't an option. He had lost too much. He couldn't lose her, too. Even if nothing ever came of it but a night of amazing sex, she was too special to leave this world so early. Even the Ancients had known that. It took someone strong in mind and spirit to hear the Ancients. Ferne might not have known that's who brought her to

Skye, but she had come regardless. Even knowing she might not be welcomed. Even knowing that she put herself in danger. She had done it because it was the right thing to do.

How could he have possibly thought she was aligned with the malevolent force killing Druids?

"Theo?"

The whispered voice drew his attention to the door where he found Rhona. He stood and motioned to her while still holding onto Ferne. The five Healers filed into the room and took up positions around the bed. The last was a middle-aged Druid with her black hair shorn to her head, wearing brightly colored clothes that contrasted nicely with her dark skin.

The last Healer took up a position at the foot of the bed, then put her hand out, palm down. She closed her eyes, and almost immediately, her brow furrowed, creasing into deep lines. She opened her eyes, her gaze locking with Theo's as she lowered her arm. "Nothing can be done. I'm sorry."

"You have no' even tried," Theo stated.

"It would be a waste of our magic."

His eyes narrowed as fury ripped through him. He had never known a Healer to refuse aid to anyone. He opened his mouth to speak, but Rhona talked over him.

"Why not? This isn't like you, Lucy," Rhona said.

Lucy closed her dark eyes as sadness filled her face. "Her soul, the essence that gives this body its persona, is gone. Doctors would call it brain death. The body itself is functioning, but it won't for much longer."

"Nay," Theo said. He wouldn't believe it. Couldn't.

Lucy clasped her hands in front of her. "I wish I had better news. I'm sorry."

CHAPTER THIRTY-FOUR

Carlyle finally understood what *silent as death* meant as he stood with the others in Theo's house. Most everyone arrived after the Healers had departed. It was Rhona who shared the outcome of the visit with the team. Carlyle couldn't believe that Ferne was gone. How could the Ancients do that to her? How could they so easily take a life?

But he knew the answer. One life was worth the cost of saving others.

That didn't mean he had to like it. He wished he could say that Ferne had known what she was getting into, but he didn't think she did. He wasn't sure he could forfeit his life so easily if he were in her position.

Carlyle looked at Finn, Sabryn, Elias, and Bronwyn, who stood around him, everyone lost in thought. Saber might not be with them physically, but he was there in spirit. The Knights were his family. And he would do anything for them. Even sacrifice himself.

Thinking of family brought Mason to Carlyle's thoughts. What he had done to Ferne was inexcusable. Unforgivable. It didn't matter what they had been taught or believed. No one should give up on their family. He stalked from the house to the backyard and dialed Mason. He never expected his old friend to actually answer.

"Hello?" Mason asked.

"It's Carlyle."

"Carlyle?" he repeated in surprise. "It's been quite a while. How are you?"

"I didn't call to exchange small talk."

There was a beat of silence. Mason's voice hardened when he asked, "Then what do you want?"

"I want to know what it feels like to be horse's arse. I want to know what happened to the man who was once my best friend, whose word meant everything."

Mason released a long, exasperated sigh. "What is this about?"

Carlyle looked at the puffy clouds moving above him. "Tell me the London Druids are controlling you. Give me a reason not to hate you."

"What are you going on about?"

"You know exactly what I'm calling about. Or have you so easily forgotten you have a sister?"

Mason grunted. "I take it you're on Skye, too, then."

Carlyle knew in that instant that Mason would tell Carlyle's father and the London Druids. After years of secrecy, Carlyle would find out how his father responded to what he had been doing. "You have no idea what's happening here."

"You shouldn't either. It doesn't concern us. Those Druids made their beds."

It had been a long time since Carlyle had felt such seething hatred for another. "Spouting the same rhetoric that was given to us... You'd think with as smart as you pretend to be, that you'd come up with something different."

"I don't have time for this. Or you."

"Your sister was braver than you'll ever be."

Silence stretched. Carlyle knew his words had struck, just as he had meant them to. If he couldn't be there to deliver the hit in person, this would have to do.

"Was?" Mason asked in a barely audible voice.

Ferne never would've retaliated against her brother. Carlyle, however, didn't have any such compunction. He hung up the phone.

He turned to walk toward the house. He paused outside the door and let his actions wash over him. He hoped Mason had many sleepless nights, wondering if his sister were dead or alive. He deserved that and so much more for following the stupid rules they had all once rebelled against. When Carlyle heard voices, he pushed away from the door and walked around the corner of the house. He spotted Nikolai and Balladyn and made his way to them.

"He won't do it," Balladyn said.

Nikolai shrugged. "We doona give him a choice."

"Did you see him? He threw off five men to get to Ferne."

Carlyle looked at each of them as he came to a halt. "Tell me the two of you wouldn't do the same if it came to your women."

Balladyn and Nikolai nodded in unison.

"That's what I thought. Now, what do you want Theo to do?" Carlyle asked.

Nikolai crossed his arms over his chest. "We need to be at Carwood Manor where it's safer."

"I agree," Balladyn said. "I'm merely pointing out that Theo won't want to leave."

Carlyle felt his mobile vibrate with a call. He looked down to see Mason's name and declined it. "You think the mist is coming back."

"You saw it this morning. Do you think it will give up so easily?" Balladyn asked.

Carlyle ran a hand over his jaw. "I don't. We also don't know if it was after Ferne or Mason."

"Another reason to get them both to the manor," Nikolai stated.

Balladyn's silver and red gaze briefly moved to the house. "I'll have Rhona talk to Theo."

"Let me." Carlyle shrugged when the two raised their brows in question. "He's suffered a loss that few understand. It hasn't sunk in yet because her body is still alive. But it will soon enough."

Nikolai inclined his head. "Good luck."

Carlyle slapped the Dragon King on the shoulder as he passed and entered the house. His gaze immediately went to Sabryn, who was on her phone, no doubt updating Saber on what was happening. Carlyle wove through the others to get to the hallway. Everyone was too lost in thought to pay attention to him, which suited him just fine.

He stopped outside Theo's bedroom and knocked softly. Carlyle waited for a response. When he didn't get one, he cracked open the door. "Theo?"

"I doona want company."

Carlyle put aside his hurt and anger and slipped into the room. Theo sat on the bed beside Ferne, holding her hand. He hadn't even taken off his coat.

"This won't take long."

Theo didn't look at him. "Say whatever you need to say, then go."

"We need to get everyone to the manor. The mist will return tonight. You know that."

"No' if it was after her," Theo mumbled.

Carlyle remembered sitting in a room by himself all those years ago, letting conversations replay in his head in different ways to change the outcome. But you couldn't reverse death. He should know. He had looked for a way. "We don't know that it was. We were split up last night. It was your idea to gather at Carwood. It was a good plan, and we need to keep to that."

"I'm no' leaving her behind."

"I wouldn't let you."

Theo's head swiveled to him. "Basher comes, too."

"I'll carry him myself," Carlyle said with a grin.

Theo released a long breath and returned his gaze to Ferne. "How did this happen?"

"I wish I knew."

"She told me last night that life was too short. I tried to turn her away. Can you believe that?"

The pain in Theo's voice was almost too much to bear. Carlyle's voice broke when he said, "Aye. We're stupid like that sometimes."

"She wasna. She knew what she wanted, and she wasna going to let it go without trying."

Carlyle leaned back against the door. "She could be relentless like that. I had forgotten that about her. She never complained or griped. She just found another way to get whatever it was she was after. This time, it was you."

"I want more time. We barely had any."

Carlyle didn't have a reply for that. There was none. Nothing he could say would make the situation better.

"Esther called her a conduit. What did she mean?"

Carlyle could answer that. "We can discuss it at the manor. We all want to know."

Theo dropped his head into his free hand. "I should call her brother."

"I took care of that." No one needed to know what Carlyle did or didn't say to Mason. The fucker. Mason was the last person Carlyle would expect to embrace the code of the London Druids. But there was no getting past the truth. He'd heard Mason himself.

"Thanks."

"Now, tell me what I need to get for Basher."

Kerry walked out onto her back porch with a cup of tea and a small plate of biscuits. She sank into her favorite chair and tapped her finger on the porcelain mug. Things with Edie were going exactly to plan. She would fall in line first, and the others would follow. Kerry knew Edie's potential, especially with the magic running through her veins.

Everyone had a tipping point. Edie was about to find hers. Kerry could facilitate things, but it would have a greater impact if Edie experienced it herself. It would be like a switch being flipped. And Kerry could hardly wait.

"The time is nearly at hand. Are you ready?"

She smiled at the sound of the Ancient's voice. One single voice that proved they had chosen her to begin the restructuring of the Druids to become the powerful group they were meant to be. "I am."

"*Tonight.*"

"Really?" Kerry was shocked it was so soon. She had been waiting for this for some time. Now, it had finally arrived. Tonight would be Rhona's last night.

"*Retrieve the target you didn't get last night. That's the only way you'll get the two we need. Rhona will come later.*"

"Consider it done," Kerry said as she popped a biscuit into her mouth.

It would be a terrific night.

CHAPTER THIRTY-FIVE

Theo walked into the command room after settling Ferne and Basher down the hall. He wanted to stay with her, to be there when her body gave up, but Theo owed it to Ferne to make her life count. He would do that by locating—and destroying—his suspect.

He fought not to fidget beneath the sorrow and regret he saw in his friends' eyes. But he was a Frasier. And a cop. Too many were counting on him. He would deal with the tempest of his emotions later. When he was alone. In his home. Until then, they were shut tightly away.

"Does anyone know who the Ageless One is?" he asked.

Rhona rubbed her eyes. "This is one of those times I wish Corann were still around. He would've known."

"Someone has to know something," Finn said.

Bronwyn looked at Elias. "The book Sydney stole would be useful. It had a bunch of stuff in it. It might have something about this."

"We talked about looking for it," Elias said.

Sabryn leaned her hips against a table. "It was last seen in Edinburgh."

"It's probably still there. Sydney hid it," Bronwyn said.

Rhona shook her head as she straightened from her spot against a wall. "We don't have time to search for it at present. I'd love to have it, but you heard the Ancients. Time is running out."

"Then we do a search. Good thing we have someone working on that," Carlyle said with a sly grin.

Esther sat in a chair with her husband on one side and her brother on the other. "I've asked the Druids at Dreagan about the Ageless One. No one has heard of such a person."

"Have the Dragon Kings?" Theo asked.

Nikolai stretched his legs out before him, crossing them at the ankles. "No' that I'm aware of. Word is spreading through Dreagan. If any of the Kings knows anything, they'll contact me."

"I'll reach out to the Reapers and Death," Balladyn said. "The Ancients didn't give us a clue if this entity is human, Fae, or something else."

Finn suddenly frowned, his gaze jerking to Bronwyn.

"What is it?" Theo asked him.

Finn swallowed loudly. "We saw a monster when Bronwyn opened the space between dimensions."

"I closed the portal. It can't get to us," she said.

Theo slid his gaze to her. "Are you sure?"

"Positive." Then she wrinkled her nose. "Well, mostly positive."

"Check on that, will you?" Theo ran a hand over his jaw and felt the thick growth of whiskers. "What about the MacLeod Druids?"

Rhona nodded. "I'll contact them."

Theo looked at the still-blank whiteboard and walked to it. "We like to take care of our own issues on Skye, but something has come here right under our noses." He stood before the others and crossed his arms over his chest. "Thanks to Ferne and whatever connection she has with the Ancients, we know they've been silenced. Ferne also believed the mist wanted her. Is it because she's a conduit?"

"The answer is: possibly. The mist could want to remove her so the Ancients couldn't communicate through her," Esther explained.

Theo had already come to that conclusion. "Just for clarification, why do you call her a conduit?"

Esther rubbed her palms on her thighs and looked around the room. "We all know the Ancients choose who they talk to and when. They're not only extremely powerful, holding the magic they had in life, but it's been debated that they can intervene in situations if they wish to."

"Debated. Not proven," Henry added.

She nodded at her brother. "The only thing we know for sure is that we don't know much of anything regarding the Ancients. Druids trust their guidance, but does anyone know when that began? Who started it?"

"Corann probably would have known," Elodie said.

Rhona chuckled. "He seemed to know everything. Too bad he didn't have time to impart such knowledge to me. Or even leave it for me to find."

"So," Esther continued, "we go by what other Druids have been taught to do and trust the Ancients. Yet we know they speak to some more than others. They highly favor Isla at MacLeod Castle while ignoring the vast majority of other Druids." Esther took a deep breath. "The Ancients said Ferne heard them. She claimed she felt the need to get to Skye and help. She had an experience in the cave that she couldn't remember."

Theo rocked back on his heels. "That was the Ancients glowing? Do they do that?"

"I'm going by what all of you told me, but it seems probable."

"They had a chance to talk to us, then. Why did they no' do it?"

Esther shrugged one shoulder. "Maybe they couldn't."

"That is something to think about," Filip said. "They should've spoken to us that night. They had time."

Sabryn nodded slowly. "I'd also like to point out that no lasting damage was done to Ferne at that point."

"I doona think they had the control over Ferne then that they did today," Scott said. "Would they have wasted an opportunity to speak if they had?"

Bronwyn sucked in a breath. "It was the mist. That's why the Ancients couldn't speak. The mist surrounded Ferne. It might have prevented them from communicating."

"Or maybe it didn't want the mist to know it was them," Balladyn added.

Just when they were making headway, they took two steps back again. It was enough to drive a person crazy. Theo dropped his arms to his sides. "Let's get back to the conduit bit."

"Right." Esther cleared her throat. "I read something about it on one of the Druid forums. Oh. We should check there for information on the Ageless One."

Sabryn lifted her phone. "Already contacting Saber."

"Anyway, there are instances where Druids can act like a conduit. I've also seen others call it channeling or being a medium."

Concern lined Rhona's face. "Aren't all Druids channeling magic already? The Windtalkers, Healers, and such?"

"The simple answer is yes." Esther shifted in the chair. "This is different, though. These Druids have magic, and they are powerful, doing things others can't even dream of doing."

Theo smiled wryly. "Like speaking to Kirsi in her mind."

Esther nodded. "Exactly like that. While these Druids can pull off those special feats, their truest gift lies in channeling one thing."

"Like what?" Carlyle asked.

Esther's gaze slid to Theo. "The Ancients."

"Did Ferne know and not tell us?" Rhona asked.

Theo glanced at the floor and shook his head. "If she had known, she would've told us." She would've told him.

"Are you sure about that?" Filip asked.

Theo looked into Filip's pale gray eyes. "I'm positive."

"Is your cop's brain telling you that?" Sabryn asked in an even tone. "Or your emotions?"

It was a fair question. Theo ran a hand down his face, briefly wondering if there would ever be a time when things were normal again. Ferne's face popped into his mind, her smile wide as she leaned in to kiss him. He pushed the image aside before it consumed him. "A little of both."

"I agree with Theo," Esther said.

Sabryn inclined her head to Esther and then Theo. "I do, too. I just thought it was something that needed to be asked and answered."

"All this is great, but what does it give us?" Carlyle rose from his chair and walked to a wall to lean a shoulder against it. "It's good knowledge for the future, but the Ancients have already used Ferne. We can't help her now."

Balladyn grunted. "But we can find the Ageless One. I'm going to the Reapers to see if they know anything or have heard about this being." He leaned down and kissed Rhona before teleporting away.

"We have information from tailing, ah…" Filip trailed off and glanced at Elias and Elodie.

Theo fought against rubbing his tired eyes, which would only make them hurt worse. "If you know something that can remove someone from our suspect list or make them more of a focus, you need to tell me."

"It's okay," Elodie told Filip. "We know you and Carlyle were watching Edie."

Elias sat forward in his chair and nodded. "Tell us what you found, though we're no' expecting anything. Edie is completely absorbed with her family."

Theo saw the grin Elias and Elodie shared. Then he looked at Filip and Carlyle, who exchanged a cryptic look. Theo was about to tell everyone to leave so he could hear what the two had discovered about Edie, but it would all come out in the end. It was better if everyone heard it together.

"Go on," he urged Filip.

It was Carlyle who said, "We saw her with Kerry."

"That could be nothing," Bronwyn said. "Kerry was a prominent figure for a long time."

Scott put a hand on Elodie's leg. "But it could be something."

"We didna hear what was said," Filip quickly told the room.

Carlyle twisted his lips with a look of doubt. "Whatever it was, Edie didn't like it. Kerry was calm. Very calm. But Edie seemed pretty rattled at the end."

"The thing we noticed was that Kerry appeared to be waiting for Edie outside the co-op," Filip added.

Carlyle looked at him and nodded before swinging his gaze to Theo. "It did seem that way. Kerry didn't speak to anyone or go into the store."

"Where did Edie go after that?" Theo asked.

Filip pulled out his mobile and read the notes he'd taken. "It was one of their rental properties. I have the address here."

"She wasn't alone. Her husband was there with another woman," Carlyle told them.

Elias frowned at that. "What woman?"

"We didna recognize her," Filip said. "We had to hide the car and make our way to the rental on foot. The three of them had a conversation. We missed Edie arriving, so we can no' say what happened at the beginning, but things appeared fine."

Carlyle nodded. "Edie remained behind and walked the property before leaving. We don't know anything after that because we got called to the mountains."

"I want to know what Kerry said to her," Rhona stated.

Theo rubbed his chin thoughtfully. "As do I. Like Bronwyn pointed out, it might be nothing."

"I believed Kerry when she promised to abide by the rules. I allowed her to remain on Skye." Rhona's jaw clenched. "If she's—"

"We doona know anything," Theo quickly told her. "There's no need to go down that path." *Yet*, he added to himself. "Let's take some time to call around and see what we can learn about the Ageless One. Anyone else who was trailing the deputies, give me that information."

Nikolai and Henry left the room, followed by Rhona. Theo wrote down anything to do with the deputies for the next twenty minutes. So far, the only ones who had drawn his attention were Edie and Kerry.

He stared at the whiteboard, wishing he had something on there, some direction to take so he could find the culprit. But it was still blank. Time was running out, and there weren't any suspects. What kind of cop was he that he couldn't find a single clue? Was he really that incompetent? Or was he too blind to see something right in front of his face? He wanted to go to Ferne, but sitting beside her would do nothing for all the other Druids in danger. Solving this mystery, finding the murderer, and bringing them to justice was what he could do. It was what he was born to do.

"Hey," Rhona said softly as she walked up.

He briefly looked her way. "Hey."

"I spoke to Isla. No one at MacLeod Castle knows about an Ageless One."

Theo tried not to feel defeated. A lot of his hope had rested with those at the castle since they had been alive for hundreds of years. Maybe the Dragon Kings would know something, but he doubted it. If they did, the Kings would've killed it already. They protected this realm from such things. And Nikolai hadn't seemed to recognize the name. So, that left the Reapers and Death, who focused on the Fae. Which meant, again, there was a slim chance they knew anything.

"Maybe the Ageless One has other names," Theo said.

Rhona put a hand on his shoulder. "You need to rest. Carlyle is making dinner. Go sit with Ferne until it's time to eat."

"I'm fine."

"You look about ready to fall down, and we need you."

He relented grudgingly. "Just for a wee bit."

"I had Balladyn check in on your father."

Theo grimaced at the reminder. He was a bad son to have forgotten his ailing father.

"Don't do that," Rhona chided. "You've had a lot on your plate. Besides, he's well taken care of. Balladyn reported that all was good."

What she didn't say was that he wouldn't know anyway. His father's dementia had grown steadily worse over the last year, causing Theo to put him in a home so he could be watched around the clock.

"Go rest," she repeated and gave him a little shove.

CHAPTER THIRTY-SIX

Ferne came awake suddenly. The instant she saw the mist, she bolted upright. But it didn't attack. It hung still and lifeless. That didn't mean it was. She couldn't see well in the washed-out light of dusk. That, along with the mist, made it nearly impossible to see anything past a few feet in any direction. Dread tightened her chest as she climbed to her feet and turned in a slow circle. She was outside. At least, she thought she might be. There were no trees, mountains, houses, or anything else in sight. Nothing gave her any clues to her location. She had no idea where she was.

Ferne took a second to do a quick scan of her body. Thankfully, she didn't detect any injuries. It was neither warm nor cold, which was good since she wasn't wearing her coat. She bent and put her hand on what she thought was the ground. It was hard and smooth, like a floor, but it wasn't that either. It was possible she was in the cavern again, but she remembered how cold it had been there. She couldn't be in the cave.

She straightened. Her stomach clenched with trepidation. Her breathing was rapid and ragged, bordering on hyperventilation. Ferne had to keep calm, which was asking a lot. She didn't know where she was or how she had gotten here. She didn't know anything. Had no idea where even to begin.

Theo. Ferne closed her eyes and pictured his face in her mind. She could imagine him standing before her, his brown eyes locked on hers as he grasped her arms.

"You can do this. Find your way back to me."

Her eyes flew open. *That's right.* All she had to do was get back to Theo. And she couldn't do that by standing still. Ferne strained her ears to pick up any sounds. Eery silence met her. She couldn't see well, couldn't hear anything, and had no idea where she was. This was a bad situation.

Then she realized she could ring Theo. She reached for her coat pocket, belatedly realizing she wasn't wearing it. She checked the back pockets of her jeans, but they were also empty. Maybe it was on the ground. Ferne dropped to her knees and blindly felt around but came up empty-handed.

She blew out a breath, the panic trying to take hold of her once more. She thought about Theo and shoved the thoughts away. So much for calling for help. She was well and truly on her own. Ferne lifted her gaze. In a place where every aspect felt foul. Wrong.

Ferne stood. It would be so easy to give in to the dread and alarm that clung to her like wet clothing. She had turned in circles so many times she didn't know which direction she'd faced when she first woke. Her only choice was to pick a direction and start walking. She didn't get far before she collided with some kind of barrier that gave beneath her touch.

Ferne bit back a startled cry as she lurched away from whatever it was. Magic surged in her palms as she waited for an attack. But nothing happened. Gradually, she lowered her arms and took a tentative step forward. The mist parted to show a thin membrane before her. She hesitantly pressed her palm against it. It was warm and elastic-feeling. She then tried to puncture it with a nail, but the material was stronger than she'd first thought.

It didn't appear as if she could get through it without something much stronger and sharper—if she wanted to cut it at all. The barricade was there for a reason. It could be keeping her out.

Or keeping something in.

Ferne turned her back to the membrane. Did she yell? Shout for Theo or Carlyle? The quiet made it feel as if things *should* stay that way. Kind of a don't-wake-the-fiend kinda vibe. Mason would say her overactive imagination had kicked in.

The thought warmed her until she recalled their last conversation. Her stomach tightened, and her heart lurched at the memory. Mason had said ghastly things. She couldn't understand why. And that troubled her the most. It wasn't him. It *had* to be an outside influence.

It would be easy to stay in that troubling mindset and sink into the despair that had claimed her. But she had another purpose. She had been with Esther, going…where? Ferne frowned as her memories became as wispy as the mist. She shook her head in frustration when Theo's face filled her mind again. She had reached for him, needing his solid presence and the comfort it provided. His eyes had been filled with concern because she…told him about Mason.

And just like that, her recollection cleared. She had been at the Red Hills with the team because she was going back into the cave.

They had started up the mountain. Ferne recalled the trek up. She even remembered wanting a few moments alone to meditate and ground herself after the call with her brother. The place she'd chosen had been away from the others and out of the wind. The ground had been cold and damp, but the sun had warmed her. She had been at peace after closing her eyes and clearing her mind. And then…she couldn't remember anything until she woke in this horrid place.

Ferne might not have seen much, but she knew she didn't belong here. The problem was, how did she get out? If there was a way in, then she would find the exit. More lost time troubled her profoundly, but she would delve into that dilemma later. First, she had to find Theo and the team. It didn't matter if she'd gotten herself into this, or worse, if someone had put her here. She was in the same predicament either way.

Ferne licked her lips and began walking again. Standing would get her nowhere. She had no concept of time, and her mind wandering interrupted her attempts to count. Finally, she gave up. The mist around her didn't seem alive, but Ferne remained alert. She was deep in the middle of it, and she had no idea if her magic would be enough to keep it at bay.

Her foot struck another barrier. She reached out to prevent herself from slamming her face into this one. It had the same texture and composition as the other. Maybe if she retraced her steps, she could count them and try to get an idea of how far apart these were. That was if she hadn't somehow gotten off course and found the same barrier.

Ferne was just turning around when she froze, her blood turning to ice as she heard a low, rumbling growl. A shadow moved on the other side of the membrane. She stumbled back, tripping over her feet and nearly falling before spinning around and running.

Ferne didn't stop until she was out of breath and the stitch in her side wouldn't let her go any farther. She dropped to her knees, her chin to her chest as she dragged in huge mouthfuls of air. She wasn't alone, and whatever was with her seemed terrifying, even just from the sound. But how to get out? She didn't have any way to contact anyone, so how… A smile curled her lips. She had one trick to play.

It would mean putting herself in danger, but she didn't know any other way. Ferne had never tried this without her usual setup.

"Desperate times and all that," she whispered.

She sat cross-legged on the ground. She was out in the open, at least she thought she was, and with no blindfold, she would have to drown out everything on her own. She closed her eyes and took a few deep breaths.

Fear of what might come upon her prevented her from achieving the grounding she so urgently needed. Ferne didn't give up, though. She couldn't. Everything hinged on her being able to reach out. Each time she cleared her mind, she held on a little longer. Until she finally found the focus she sought.

Then she reached across time and space to the one person she knew would hear her.

Theo deepened the kiss, holding Ferne too tightly, but he couldn't make himself loosen his hold. He rolled them until he lay atop her soft body. Her legs parted as he settled between them. His cock jumped, impatient to be inside her, to have them connected, body and soul. He kissed along her jaw and down the column of her throat. He would never let her go again.

Never.

"Theo?"

Her voice, seductive and enthralling, drew his attention. He lifted his head and looked into fern-green eyes. She was so beautiful. He gently ran the pads of his fingers across her cheek. To his horror, she started to fade. No matter how hard he tried to hold her, she withered like smoke. Leaving nothing but the memory of her against his skin.

He fisted his hands and squeezed his eyes shut as a wail of despair rose. It couldn't get past the lump in his throat.

"Theo."

For a brief moment, he had believed it to be real. But there was no denying this was a dream. He rested on his forearms and looked at his hands. Empty. Hands that had known the warmth of her body, the silkiness of her skin. The passion, the pleasure. The ecstasy. Now, all he had was her voice. Something he would never hear again in the waking world. He wanted to rail at the unfairness of it all. Strike at the ones responsible. Ferne hadn't deserved such an end.

"Theo. I'm here. I'm right here."

Her body was protected, but the part that made her Ferne was gone.

"I don't know what happened, but you have to pay attention to what I'm saying. I need your help. Theo. Hear me. Please. I need you."

It was such an odd dream, but of course, he would want her to need him to save her. He wanted to be her protector, and what a shite job he had done of that. He hadn't been able to do anything. He felt as helpless as a human without magic.

"This isn't a dream. I'm...I don't bloody know where I am. I'm stuck somewhere I can't get out of, with a...kind of wall. A barrier. Something. I'm not sure what it is, but I don't want to run into it again."

What a strange thing for her to say in a dream.

"It's not a dream. It's me, Theo. I lost time again. Find me. Please. This place is unsettling."

If this were real, he'd need details to locate her.

"Okay. Um...there's mist everywhere. Not the killing mist—or maybe it is. Hard to tell. It hasn't done anything to me. It's deathly quiet, except for when that thing growls. It's also dark, like it's dusk, but it hasn't gotten lighter or darker since I woke. I'm not sure how long that's been. Sorry. And then there are these membrane-like walls that move beneath my hand but don't puncture easily—or at all from what I've tried with my fingernail. I'm stuck, and if I don't get out soon, I get the feeling I may never."

That was good information, but he needed more.

"I'm not on the ground, at least not the kind of ground we're use—"

Someone shook him and called his name. He fought against it to stay with Ferne.

"No. Don't leave!" Ferne cried. *"Theo!"*

His name faded as his eyes snapped open. He sat upright in the chair and found Rhona beside him. Theo swung his gaze to Ferne, who hadn't moved. Basher sat beside her, his eyes locked on her. The cat meowed softly and butted his head against hers.

"What is it? What's wrong?" Rhona asked.

Theo jumped from the chair so fast it toppled backward. He

pressed a kiss to Ferne's brow and raced out of the room to the team downstairs, Rhona at his heels. He followed the sound of voices to the kitchen and skidded to a stop inside. Everyone stilled and looked up at his rushed entry.

He scanned the room until he found the person he wanted. The minute he located Bronwyn, he urged, "Tell me what it's like."

"What are you talking about?" she asked with a shake of her head.

"The place between dimensions. What does it look like?"

Finn made a choking sound. "Trust me, mate. You don't want to know."

"Bronwyn," Theo pressed as he stepped toward her. "What does it look like?"

She set her empty plate on the table. "It's gloomy. Empty. Silent."

"And the walls? Are they still like ours, or do they move when you touch them?"

Her face paled. "They're thin, and yes, they sway and bend when you press against them, but they don't tear."

"Yet," Finn added.

Elias caught Theo's gaze. "How do you know about the walls?"

Theo bent at the waist and braced his hands on his knees to catch his breath. It hadn't been a dream. It hadn't been a fucking dream! Ferne had used her magic to reach him. Now, he was going to find her. Somehow. However long it took.

He straightened. "Ferne told me."

"What?" Bronwyn murmured as her eyes widened.

Finn dropped his head back against the wall and blew out a breath as he said, "Feck me."

"She reached you," Rhona said as she walked around Theo to look at him.

He nodded. "Just as you woke me. She's terrified. She mentioned something was in there with her."

"Because there fecking is!" Finn shouted. He scowled at Bronwyn. "You can't open the doorway. Not again. It'll get out."

Carlyle gaped at him. "Did you not hear Theo? Ferne's in there."

"Her soul. Not her body."

Theo realized the truth of Finn's words, and it dampened some of his hope.

Finn resolutely shook his head again. "You're all assuming Bronwyn can just open another portal and we'll find Ferne right there. But none of you," he said, pointing to those who hadn't seen it, "were there last time. You didn't see that…thing…inside. It was trying to get to us."

"And it could be after Ferne. I'm no' leaving her," Theo stated. He met Bronwyn's hazel eyes. "Open the portal. I'll go in myself."

Elias snorted. "The hell, you will. Finn is right about one thing. We doona have a clue where Ferne is or how we can get to her, but we'll try."

Theo ran a hand down his face. If he did this, he would be taking time away from finding the murderer and discovering the Ageless One. But he couldn't leave Ferne. He *wouldn't*. He'd have to trust that the rest of the team could pick up the slack.

"I don't know if that monster can be held back," Bronwyn said. "Finn's right to caution us about it. I opened a small room between dimensions. I don't know if I can do more."

Rhona met Theo's gaze and nodded once. "Do what you can, Bronwyn. Theo will do the rest."

CHAPTER THIRTY-SEVEN

Ferne tried—and failed—to catch herself as she pitched sideways. Her cheek slammed against the ground or floor, whatever it was. She wished she had some orange juice to replenish herself. She wished Mason would storm to her and demand, in that high-handed voice of his, that she stop exerting herself with such magic.

She didn't have the juice, Mason, or Theo. And she might never have them again. She had reached Theo, but it had taken much more time, power, and energy than it ever had. His thoughts had been almost too soft for her to hear. What if he hadn't heard her? What if she didn't have the magic needed to give him the details he required?

Her throat clogged with unshed tears. She had held them off, clinging staunchly to hope, but it was waning rapidly. Exhaustion tugged at her. She tried to stay awake. That thing was still around, and she didn't want to be caught unawares. Ferne endeavored to get her hands beneath herself to push up, but her arms shook too much to manage it. She gave up with a sigh, even as her eyes drifted shut.

The tumbler slipped through Kirsi's fingers to hit the wooden floor. She watched it bounce and roll away, thankful it was plastic and not glass. She took a step back, reaching for the chair, but bumped into the kitchen counter instead. Her hands gripped it, even as her legs buckled, and she slid to the ground. She drew her knees up to her chest and wrapped her arms around her calves as she struggled to figure out how she had heard the exchange between Theo and Ferne.

While fully awake.

The magic had been so potent it had felt as if she were drowning in it. Then it was gone. Like the snap of fingers. She couldn't begin to theorize what had just happened, but the one thing she knew was that Ferne was in trouble.

Kirsi hadn't processed her feelings about the Druid yet. In truth, she hadn't done much of anything but ignore the very thing Ferne implied she couldn't run from. Kirsi was beginning to think Ferne was right. Especially now. But what could she do? She didn't know where Ferne was, and she couldn't begin to come up with ideas. How could she with the descriptions of mist, a dusk-like setting, and walls that flexed?

She had picked up on one important clue that Theo hadn't seemed to catch, though. Ferne had mentioned something was in there with her. Something that *growled*.

Kirsi lowered her forehead to her knees and closed her eyes.

Had all of that really happened? Or was it her mind playing tricks after all the stress of the past few days? A person could only handle so much, and Kirsi had always known her threshold was lower than most people's. It was difficult to know how to deal with anxiety when the worst thing she had ever endured was schooling and dealing with tourists. It wasn't as if she knew much of anything beyond Skye. Or the business world.

She loved the low-key lifestyle she had been raised in. It was idyllic at times, but it had its drawbacks. Like now. If she were in the corporate world of cutthroat competition, she probably could've figured out her current quandary in her sleep. Instead, she was losing said sleep because of it.

But this wasn't about her. It was about Ferne.

Kirsi surged to her feet. She walked on unsteady legs to the door of her flat and down the stairs to the co-op. She entered the back to see her father standing with his palms face up as he stared at them.

"Dad?"

He lifted his eyes to her. "Something's wrong. I can no' feel my magic."

"What?" she said as she rushed to him, her problems forgotten.

"My magic is...gone," he said in a weak voice.

She shook her head. "You've just had a long day. Go home and rest. Everything will be fine in the morning."

He didn't appear to hear her. Kirsi hurried through the doorway to the store. She thought her mother was there, but all she found was a line of people waiting to check out. Kirsi glanced over her shoulder, but she couldn't see her father. She did the only thing she could, she helped the customers.

The last one to approach was Ariah. Outsiders would call the tea maker a hippie with her flowy skirts, billowy shirts, scarves tied in her long, brunette hair, and various moon jewelry. But the Druids knew her for what Ariah truly was—a child of the forest.

Kirsi waited until the previous customer left the store before leaning toward Ariah and whispering, "Did you feel anything?"

"I did."

"Can you still feel your magic?"

Ariah's dark brows drew together. "Aye. Can you not?"

"I can." She cast a quick look behind her. "Dad can't."

Ariah sighed. "He's not the only one. Some others have been afflicted thus."

"What? Th-that can't be." How had Kirsi not known about this?

"It is."

"Does Rhona know?"

Ariah nodded. "She does."

"What is she doing about it?"

"All that she can."

But that wasn't enough. Kirsi flattened her hands on the counter. "Ariah...I..." She trailed off and tried again. "Someone reached me through my mind. It was to warn me about, well... something." Kirsi didn't want to get into specifics at the moment. "Is it possible that I could then hear a conversation between her and another?"

Ariah studied her for a long moment. "You're made of magic. You know anything is possible. This Druid, whoever she is, appears to be very powerful."

"And in trouble."

"If you heard her, then you should help."

"I don't know how."

Ariah gave her a small smile. "One day, you'll stop doubting yourself. It'll be a glorious sight when it comes." She handed money to Kirsi. "Keep the change."

Kirsi was so taken aback by the woman's words that she could only watch Ariah depart. When the door closed behind her, Kirsi put the money in the register and then hurried to her father. He was just as dazed as before. She couldn't leave him, and her mother had overtaxed herself the day before. No one else could watch the store. Kirsi had no choice but to stay. Her mind raced with what Ariah had said as she made her father a cup of tea. He barely acknowledged her when he accepted it.

Kirsi returned to the front of the store and pulled out her mobile. She was about to call Evan. The deputy might know what to do. But it would take forever to explain everything to him. Kirsi's finger moved, hovering over Rhona's contact information for several moments before she finally tapped to call.

The line connected, ringing once before going to voicemail. Kirsi decided against leaving a message. She hung up and wondered what to do next. Then she remembered that she had Ferne's number. She tried it on the off chance someone would answer the phone, and she could tell them what she knew. Once again, no one picked up. She tried Rhona again before tossing her mobile on the counter in frustration as the bell over the door chimed, announcing a customer.

She looked up and spotted Callum. His amber eyes met hers. She got lost in the copper-tinted light brown depths. He wore an army green-colored coat that had a tear at the hem and a couple of stains on one arm. Beneath it was a black sweatshirt and faded jeans. Silver flashed on his finger before he put his hands into his pockets.

"Hi," she said.

He nodded before turning toward the aisles. Kirsi rubbed her hands together and stared at her mobile. Who else could she phone to help? It was on the tip of her tongue to call for Balladyn. It was said the Reaper could hear his name from anywhere and would come, but she was certain he could choose if he wanted to answer a summons or not. He didn't know her. Why would he respond to her call? But things weren't that dire. Yet. They were close.

Very close.

She checked on Callum. He was still looking around, so she took the time to dial Ferne again. The line was still ringing when Callum headed her way. She set the mobile aside when he placed a bottle of water and a bag of crisps on the counter.

"He'll call."

"Excuse me?" she asked with a frown.

"Ben. I'm sure he'll call."

Kirsi waved away his words and rang up his things. "Ben and I are done. Have been for weeks."

Callum pulled out some coins from the front pocket of his jeans and began counting out the amount.

"It's okay. It's on the house," she said when she realized he might not have enough. It was embarrassing for her and the customer when that happened. She wanted to save him that.

He stilled before lifting those unusual eyes to her. Then he carefully placed the money on the counter. "I can pay."

"I didn't mean that," she began, "I was just..."

He grabbed the items and walked from the store.

Kirsi leaned her elbows on the counter and dropped her head

into her hands. "That couldn't have gone any more awkwardly." She sighed and looked at her mobile. "Ferne, how did I hear you?"

Ferne's eyes opened as she came instantly awake again. She knew that voice. It had been Kirsi. Ferne felt marginally better but not nearly back to normal. She pushed herself into a sitting position, all the while wondering what Kirsi had meant. What had the Druid heard?

Ferne glanced around but didn't see anything near, nor did she hear any growls. She knew she was taking a huge chance, but she was impatient and scared. And people did crazy things when backed into a corner.

She licked her lips and prayed her idea worked. It was reckless and risky, but did she really have another choice? She closed her eyes and let herself sink into the quiet of her mind. Then she reached out to Kirsi.

"Can you hear me?"

"Ferne?" Kirsi's voice was clear, as if she stood right beside her.

Tears burned Ferne's eyes behind her lids. Emotion clogged her throat so badly it took her a moment to answer. "Yes."

"Where are you? Has Theo found you yet?"

"How do you know about that?"

Kirsi blew out a breath. "I, ah, I heard your exchange. And I'm a wee bit freaked about it."

It was on the tip of Ferne's tongue to question her, but there were more pressing matters at hand. "Find Theo. Help him."

"I can't leave my father. He's…he can't feel his magic anymore."

Ferne was stunned. "How is that possible?"

"It's been happening around Skye."

"Kirsi," Ferne said softly. "Things are getting worse. I need your help. I know you're scared, but you can do this."

"Do what?" Kirsi asked in a strangled voice. "I don't know what I'm supposed to do or even how."

"You'll figure it out. Until then, contact Theo or Rhona."

"Rhona isn't answering her mobile."

"Try Theo. Go to them." The hairs on the back of Ferne's neck rose. She wasn't alone anymore. "Hurry, Kirsi. Please."

CHAPTER THIRTY-EIGHT

SKYE DRUIDS

"Open the goddamn portal!" Theo bellowed as he stood in the hallway. He was tired of waiting, tired of talking about it. The plan had been decided, but Finn wouldn't let it go.

Finn took a step toward him, his brown eyes narrowed angrily. "You're risking all of our lives for one person."

"I'm risking my life," Theo stated, stabbing his finger into his chest. "*Mine*. No' yours."

"Hey, hey!" Carlyle said as he stepped between Theo and Finn, pushing them apart. He faced Finn and said, "Take it easy."

Finn shook his head, scrunched up his face, and looked at everyone as if they had lost their minds. "What is wrong with all of you? Don't you understand what could happen?"

"I understand what Theo is willing to risk for Ferne," Bronwyn replied in a calm voice.

Finn slid his gaze to her, sighing. "And you're fine with Elias going with him?"

"Of course. I'll be with them."

Theo crossed his arms and begged for patience as Elias, Finn, and Carlyle all began talking at once, each having a reason for why Bronwyn shouldn't go with him. Every second was one less he could use to rescue Ferne. Someone touched his shoulder. Theo turned to see Sabryn and Esther.

He stepped away from the others, the voices rising, and followed the two. "What is it?" he asked when they finally stopped.

"Are you sure it was Ferne who reached out?" Sabryn asked.

This was the third time someone had asked that. It exasperated him, but he also understood. "I do. She's the only one I know who could connect to me like that. She did it with Kirsi, remember?"

"We remember," Esther said. "We don't know what you're going to find in there."

"I know." He was more than aware.

Esther pursed her lips. "Putting a soul back into a body is… It's beyond any of us here."

"My main goal is to get her out of that place. We'll deal with the rest when the time comes."

Sabryn nodded gravely. "We know you care about her, and it says a lot that you're willing to risk your life to find her."

"But?" he pressed when she paused.

Sabryn exchanged a look with Esther. "Something isn't right about any of this."

"You're just now figuring that out?" Theo snorted and fisted his hands at his sides, the last of his tolerance evaporating. "The Ancients took her. They *used* her. And they didn't think twice about it. Her soul was taken and put in a place we may never find. Nothing's right about anything having to do with Ferne, the mist, or Druids losing their magic."

"One person versus billions," Finn said from behind him.

"Ferne's life compared to the mass loss of life if that creature gets loose."

Theo realized the arguing had stopped behind him. They had obviously been listening to his conversation. He stepped to the side to see everyone but locked his gaze on Finn. "I'm no' going to continue this row. You have your opinion, and I respect that. Respect mine."

"You're too good of a cop—and a man—to throw your life away like this. We need you. Skye needs you," Finn said.

Theo briefly lowered his gaze to the floor and released a deep breath. "I appreciate that, but I have to do this. For Ferne. For me."

"Then go find her," Sabryn said. "The rest of us have our assignments. We'll carry on until you return."

Theo nodded. "Thank you."

"Is everyone ready, then?" Bronwyn asked.

"I'd be happier if you stayed behind," Elias murmured.

She shot him a look. "And just who do you think is going to open the portal so you can come back through? I need to be there."

"Doesna mean I have to like it."

Finn leaned a shoulder against the opposite wall, his face grim. "Good luck."

Bronwyn turned to an open bedroom door on the second floor. She then lifted her right hand and placed her open palm against the invisible enchantment that stood at the threshold. "*Nochd*, reveal," she whispered.

Magic charged the air. It crawled over Theo's skin, causing the hairs on his arms to stand up. Bronwyn's power was vibrant and strong, her control absolute. A *mie* who had turned *drough* to avenge her family but then learned to wield the powerful magic instead of letting it overtake her. She was a formidable ally.

Once she used the Gaelic command, Theo felt a vibration around him. His gaze was drawn back to the doorway as he saw the air begin to spark and spin around Bronwyn's hand. The vortex expanded, and the whirling increased, getting faster and faster until the sections merged into one spiraling maelstrom.

Bronwyn dropped her hand as an opening appeared. Theo craned his head to the side to peer within. The split grew larger and larger, and as it did, the whirlpool slowed until it finally halted altogether. The bedroom was gone, replaced by a platform draped in dark fabric. The air was ashen, the murky atmosphere thick as it twisted and arched as if alive. This had been where Bronwyn had hidden her cousin.

Elias was the first to enter. Theo sensed all eyes on him as he followed. He felt little as he stepped through. He halted and looked around. So, this was what it was like to stand between dimensions.

"It was there," Elias whispered as he pointed to a section of wall.

Wall was a loose term, Theo realized. Ferne had called it a membrane, and that better described it. Theo made his way to it and put his palm against it. It was thin enough to know something was on the other side. He pushed against it, feeling the wall stretch like elastic, but it held firm.

"I don't know how far sound carries," Bronwyn said in a low voice as she joined him. "I'd keep the talking to a minimum and at a whisper. Just in case."

Elias's lips twisted. "Aye. I doona want to run into that thing again. It was huge. With talons that tried to cut the barrier."

Theo snatched his hand back. If that thing was out there and after Ferne, he needed to get to her quickly. He faced the couple and asked, "Where do we go?"

"That's the thing," Bronwyn said with a sad smile, spreading her hands out. "This is all I've ever done."

Theo turned in a circle to see that the area was no larger than the bedroom. There were no doors to exit or openings leading anywhere other than back to their world.

"I did warn you," Bronwyn murmured.

She had, but Theo had been so sure he would find a way to Ferne. "She's here," he said and faced the back wall. "She's out there, waiting for me to find her and bring her home."

"We can always try this," Elias said and held up a knife.

Bronwyn looked sick at the thought. "What are you doing?"

Elias touched her face with his free hand. "I know what I'd do to get to you. I know what I did to keep you safe. How can I refuse someone else seeking to do that verra thing?"

"Elias," she began.

He pressed a kiss to her lips. "Stay here and guard the door. If that thing comes, close it."

"And seal you two in? No," Bronwyn stated firmly.

Theo walked to Elias and took the blade from him. "Stay. I've got this."

"No," Finn said as he walked through the opening with a dramatic sigh. "I'm coming with you. Nope," he said stubbornly when Elias opened his mouth to argue. "You two have been through enough. Besides, I'd rather have you here in case we're chased."

Bronwyn took hold of Finn's and Theo's hands as she looked at each one. "Be careful."

"Do what you need to do to keep everyone safe," Theo told her. Then he walked to the wall across the room and lifted the dagger above his head, ready to stab it into the membrane. He glanced at Finn. "Last chance to turn back."

"Just do it already," Finn grumbled.

Theo took a breath and plunged the blade into the barrier.

Kirsi's hands shook as she dialed the police station. She asked for Theo, tapping her finger nervously on the counter as she waited to be connected. It was all in vain as she found out he wasn't there. She rushed to the back to find her father had a little more color in his cheeks.

"Dad, I need to get ahold of DI Theo Frasier. Do you have his number?"

He shook his head. "I doona have it? What do you need Frasier for?"

"It's important. Ferne's in trouble. Who else would have his contact information?" she asked, trying to remain calm but failing miserably.

Her father shook his head helplessly. "Rhona, maybe?"

"She's not answering."

"Try the police station."

"Already did that. Theo isn't in."

Her father threw up his hands in defeat. "I doona know who else."

She covered her face with her hands and let loose a cry of

frustration. Ferne was counting on her, and Kirsi was going to fail. She couldn't even do one simple thing.

"Go."

Her head jerked up. "What?"

"Go," he urged her. "You're needed."

"I can't leave you. Not after…" She trailed off, not wanting to bring it up. But even not saying it brought it to his attention.

Her father straightened from the stool. "I can handle the store. Ferne needs your help. Go, give it to her."

"Dad," she began.

He grasped her shoulders, his brown eyes unwavering. "I'm fine, Kirsi. Go."

She nodded and spun around, ready to dash out, when he called out. Kirsi paused to look back just as he tossed her the keys to his car. He nodded and smiled. Then she was out the door.

Her hands shook so badly it took her several tries to unlock the door. She slid behind the wheel and wasted more time adjusting the seat so she could reach the pedals. When she tried to stick the keys into the ignition, she dropped them twice. The last time, she slammed her hands against the steering wheel.

"Fuck!" she yelled. Couldn't anything go right?

"Need some help?"

The sound of a deep voice had her head swinging around to find Callum standing next to the open door.

His brow furrowed when she met his gaze. "What's wrong?"

"I have to get somewhere, and I can't stop shaking."

"You shouldna be driving."

She dropped her head back. "Ugh. Who else is going to do it? You?"

"Move over."

Kirsi studied his face. She had been joking, but evidently, he wasn't. She hesitated only a half-second before pushing him aside and walking around to the passenger side. By the time she got in, he was already buckled in with the engine running.

"Where are we going?" Callum asked as he looked at her with his amber eyes.

She tried to calm her racing heart. "I have to find Theo Frasier."

"The cop?"

"You know him?" she asked hopefully.

Callum shrugged, his face impassive. "You could say that."

"Do you know where I can find him?"

"He isna exactly a mate. Nor do I go looking for cops."

She fisted her hands in her lap. "I *have* to find him! Someone's life is in danger."

"All right," Callum replied evenly. "Let's see what we can find."

Tears of gratitude burned her eyes as he put the car in drive.

CHAPTER THIRTY-NINE

Ferne caught herself with her hands this time, but it didn't stop her arms from giving out, and her from once more face-planting on the ground. She tried to open her eyes, but they were too heavy after using her magic to talk to Theo and Kirsi. She couldn't believe she had managed it both times. Kirsi had been so much clearer than Theo. All of Ferne's hopes rested with her.

A nearby rumbling growl nearly stopped her heart. It was so close. For all she knew, it could be right on top of her. She tried to force herself to get up and run, hide. But she couldn't even open her eyes. Her magic was at the ready, but it wouldn't do her much good if she couldn't see where to aim it. Besides, she was horrible at using it to defend herself. No matter how many times her parents and Mason had tried to teach her, she hadn't been able to do much of anything. At the very least, she could shield herself.

Yet every instinct told her to remain perfectly still. Her heart hammered like a drum against her ribs, and she was sure it was loud enough for someone to hear. She swallowed nervously. There was nothing but silence, but she *knew* something was out there. Waiting. And watching.

Her.

When Ferne journeyed to Skye, she'd imagined she would come up against Druids who didn't want her around. It had never entered her mind that she would face some mysterious being in an otherworldly setting. She had been prepared to stand against her kind. She wasn't equipped for whatever waited for her in the shadows.

But if she was to make it out alive, she only had herself to turn to. Theo wasn't here. Mason had disowned her. She was more alone than she had ever been. It would be easy to cave under the terror of that. So easy. And a part of her wanted to do just that. She wouldn't have to dig deep to find the strength that had vanished in an instant after her parents' deaths. She wouldn't have to fight. She could just…accept whatever happened.

Her fear grew and consumed her. Cautiously, slowly she curled onto her side, tucking her knees against her. All she needed to do was sink into the waiting exhaustion. She would never feel a thing.

"I've waited a long time for you."

Ferne stilled as the eerie voice slid over her like a wet rag. It was neither male nor female.

The being laughed. "Such a long time. Finally, you're here."

Ferne squeezed her eyes closed even tighter when she felt breath on her cheek. She thought of all the strong, powerful Druids she had been around the past few days. None of them would be curled into a ball if they were in her place. They would fight.

"It's better if you don't fight. You've tried a few times. It's never worked in your favor."

Ferne held her legs tighter. All she had to do was hold on. Kirsi would find Theo, and Theo would find her.

"I scare you. Good. You should be terrified. Now that you're here, things can begin. I should warn you not to cling to hope. It's so…pedestrian. Besides, there is no hope. Not for you."

Something touched her face. Ferne tried not to flinch but failed. The being laughed as if it knew how much she hated it. An image of her parents flashed in her mind. Then one of Mason, shouldering all the responsibilities of the title. She was a Crawford. She owed it to them to act like one.

Ferne forced open her eyes. She didn't see anything in the haziness around her, but it was there. It took her two tries to find her voice, and when she spoke, it shook. "Wh-who are you?"

"Give it time. You'll remember."

"Why did you bring me here?"

The voice cackled as it moved away. "Oh. This is brilliant."

Ferne's frown deepened. Just what was that supposed to mean? The thing was toying with her. It irked her. She pushed up on an elbow. She might regret it, but she wanted to see what planned to do her harm. And if it hadn't dragged her to this awful place, who did? "Are you saying you didn't do this to me?"

"I might have wanted you here, but I didn't bring you. I would've done it long ago if I'd gotten the chance."

"You expect me to believe you?"

A large shape lunged from the shadows toward her. Ferne instinctively raised her arm to shield her face. It didn't touch her, though. Just remained close so that the growl issued was loud enough to shake the air around her. She flinched but somehow managed to remain where she was.

"You'll see the truth. It won't do you any good, though. Not in my world."

Ferne opened her eyes to see large cloven hooves and bony and scaly skin, like an alligator's. She lowered her arm enough to look over it and found the being's face inches from hers. She stared into eyes so dark they seemed to swallow all light. Before she could look at the face, it turned to smoke and twisted in on itself before taking the appearance of a human woman. In the next instant, it appeared as a man, a very gorgeous man.

"What are you?" she asked in a soft voice.

It smiled, showing even, white teeth as its black eyes watched her. "There is no name for me."

Ferne dropped her arm as the creature idly walked back and forth before her, a grin on its face. "Where are we?"

"You don't recognize it?" It stopped and tilted its head of blond hair to the side, its look curious. "We're in The Grey. The place separating dimensions."

The hits just kept coming. "The what?"

Its smile grew as if it delighted in her apprehension. "I've waited centuries for this encounter. I admit, I'm a bit let down. I expected more from you."

Ferne watched it take a step toward her. She realized her disadvantage of being on the ground, but what could she really do about a shapeshifting entity? She was still drained from using her magic. "I think you have me confused with someone else."

It laughed, slowly shaking its head. "I could never forget you and the part you played."

"What part?"

"This innocent act is grating on my nerves," it snarled.

Ferne slowly regained her feet, which was an achievement. Her legs threatened to buckle beneath her again. She had to hold out her arms to steady herself, and as soon as she stood, she wished she hadn't. It took everything she had to remain upright. "If you're going to kill me, then do it."

"Oh, I'm definitely going to take your life. But I'm going to do it slowly," it said, drawing out the word. "You're going to feel the same pain, fear, and dread I did."

The simple way the being stated her impending death sent chills of foreboding down Ferne's spine. It meant every word. She almost curled in on herself again to await the inevitable. But that wasn't who she was. She'd lost a part of herself with the death of her parents, but since coming to Skye, she was finding herself again.

After meeting Theo.

Theo. He carried so much responsibility on his wide shoulders. She had hoped he'd find her, but that was before she realized just how screwed she was. Now, she prayed Theo never came to this place. It was a place of ruin.

Of death.

The being's lip curled in a sneer. "Fading hope is such a beautiful sight. I wonder how loud your screams will be. The louder, the better, I say."

Ferne braced herself as it lunged for her.

"We'll be lucky to find our way out," Finn whispered.

Theo flicked off the sticky goo-like substance that clung to his hand after cutting the wall. "It isna as if I knew we'd need anything."

"Good thing I'm here."

Theo watched the Irishman create a bright green light that resembled a glow stick. "Nice."

"I'm smart like that," Finn said with a smirk. It faded as he came up beside Theo. "Shall we?"

"Aye."

"Keep the dagger handy in case we need to cut our way back through."

Theo tapped the handle of the blade he had tucked into the waistband of his jeans. "It's right here."

"This is a bad idea."

"Then why did you come?"

"Fek if I know."

"Maybe because you're a good man."

Finn grunted. "Doubtful."

Theo wanted to shout Ferne's name. He couldn't see more than a few feet around him. He could pass right by her and never know. "There are two of us versus one of those things."

"That we know of," Finn muttered.

Theo jerked out a hand to stop him. "Shh."

"What?" Finn asked in a soft voice.

Theo squinted into the distance. "I thought I heard something."

They stood still for several minutes. Finally, Finn shrugged. "I don't hear anything."

"This place is eerie."

"We don't belong here."

Theo shook his head. "Neither does Ferne."

"Turn! Now. Turn now!" Kirsi shouted.

Callum made sure no one was behind him before slamming on the brakes and jerking the wheel. He had driven Kirsi for the last thirty minutes as she wrung her hands and bounced her knee up and down nonstop. She had barely said two words. Each stop he made netted no results for Frasier. Callum still wasn't sure what had prompted him to offer Kirsi assistance. He never let himself get mixed up with others.

"Go faster," she urged him.

He glanced over and saw her face set in hard lines as he maneuvered the twisting drive through the trees. They emerged a short time later in front of a manor house with a vibrant sunset on display. Several vehicles were parked at the front. Callum took his foot off the accelerator, hovering it over the brake as they coasted. All the while, he wondered if it wouldn't be better to turn around.

"Are you sure about this?" he asked.

Her pale green gaze met his. "Nay."

He parked the car and turned off the engine. "I'll wait here."

Her brow creased.

"Or I can go with you."

Relief smoothed out the worry lines. "Thanks."

What the fuck was wrong with him? He didn't help people. It wasn't his thing. Yet he had offered twice now. He shouldn't have gone into the co-op earlier. He hadn't needed anything. He certainly didn't need to waste money.

Kirsi was already out of the car. Callum exited and followed her to the manor's imposing double doors. He didn't belong here.

In fact, he didn't belong many places. But he really shouldn't be here. As soon as they saw him, they'd run him off. That's what usually happened. He prepared himself for what he knew was coming. Kirsi raised her hand to the knocker, but the door swung open before she could grab hold.

"Kirsi?"

Callum hid his grimace when he spotted Rhona. Of course, she would answer the door. He searched the area for the silver-and-red-eyed Reaper. Callum had only seen him once, but that had been enough for a lifetime.

"I'm looking for Theo Frasier," Kirsi said in a rushed voice. "It's about Ferne."

Rhona's eyes cut briefly to Callum. "I think you'd better come in."

Callum turned on his heel and started walking away before he was told to leave. He could save himself at least that embarrassment. He had done what he'd said he would do. He'd brought Kirsi to Frasier. He didn't owe her anything more—not that he owed her anything to begin with.

"Callum."

He halted at Kirsi's voice. Why didn't he keep going?

"Come inside," Rhona urged.

He didn't want to know what was going on. It wasn't as if anyone in the grand structure would welcome him, and rightly so. He had his little corner of Skye, and that was where he belonged. Where he should've remained, instead of trying to…what? He was so out of his depth he didn't have words. He certainly had no business with the leader of the Druids, a cop, and whoever this Ferne lady Kirsi spoke about was.

Callum lifted his foot to walk away. Instead, he pivoted and retraced his steps to the manor. Rhona held open the door until he was inside, her eyes darting to the sky before she followed. The minute she shut the door, Callum wanted to throw it open again and leave. His work boots were clumped with mud and dirt. His clothes were stained with grease from boat engines. And everything inside the manor was clean, nice, and expensive. If he moved wrong, he might stain the rug or break something.

"Where is he? Where is DI Frasier?" Kirsi pressed.

Rhona gave her a placating smile. "Tell me what happened."

"There isn't time. Ferne's in trouble. She tried to reach him, but she didn't think he was able to hear her. So, she contacted me."

"Theo heard her."

Kirsi sighed, her eyes closing for several heartbeats. "Ferne is safe, then?"

"Ah…no."

Callum looked between the two women. Rhona was on one side, her long, red hair and commanding presence on display. Kirsi was on the other, her light brown strands shining red in the sunlight. Kirsi was gentle and kind, always ready with a warm smile for everyone—even him.

She wrapped her arms around herself. "Why isn't Theo going after her?"

"He is," Rhona clarified. "It's complicated."

"Then I'll find her. I found Theo."

Callum's gaze slid to Rhona as the Druid leader studied Kirsi.

"How did you find us?" Rhona asked.

Kirsi crossed her arms over her chest and refused to answer.

Callum shrugged when Rhona's attention swung to him. "Doona look at me. She told me to turn in here."

"Kirsi, you did your job. You found Theo, and he's trying to locate Ferne. There's nothing more you can do," Rhona said.

Kirsi blinked, her arms dropping to her sides. In that instant, the urgency smoothed from her face. Then she turned toward the stairs and slowly lifted her eyes to the ceiling. "It's going to get out. But first, it's going to kill Ferne."

"How…?" Rhona began as her brows snapped together in concern. She shook her head and pointed to Kirsi as she looked at Callum. "Watch her. Don't let her go upstairs. And neither of you leave. You're here until sunrise, so get comfortable."

Callum opened his mouth to reply, but Rhona was already racing up the stairs. He followed Kirsi's gaze upward as he heard raised voices above them. Just what fuckery had he gotten himself into?

CHAPTER FORTY

SKYE DRUIDS

Ferne slammed into the ground, losing her breath at the impact. Her vision blurred as the being remained on top of her. It was no longer in the form of a human. Its long, misshapen head loomed over her, its mouth open on a terrifying snarl. Saliva dripped from the razor-sharp teeth, hitting Ferne's cheek. She turned her head away and saw the hands on either side of her, digits with incredibly long, unbelievably sharp talons.

She squeezed her eyes shut as it leaned closer, its foul breath making her stomach churn. Ferne gathered magic in her hands. Oh, how she wished she had done better with combat magic. She had never thought to be in a situation where she'd need it. And it had just felt wrong to use her power that way.

Her magic rushed to her and then waned with the onslaught of dread that gripped her. At this rate, she would never be able to defend herself. But she had to try. She focused on her power, shoving aside the fear. Her magic rushed through her. She readied to release it when agony shattered her concentration.

The scream lodged in her throat as her left arm blazed with unimaginable pain. Tears poured out of her eyes as she looked to the side. Her gaze traced up her arm to see a talon pierced through her arm and embedded into the ground below. The being laughed at her agony. But it had warned her what it planned.

Shock dulled the pain enough that Ferne could look up at it, a retort on her lips when she heard…voices. And one cadence she recognized. Theo. Her heart leapt with joy. And alarm. She had to warn him. Almost instantly, the mist wrapped around the entity, and it was gone. Vanished.

She bit back a cry as she grasped her injured arm, cradling it against her and rolling onto her side. There was no time to think about the damage or the fact that no blood ran between her fingers or down her arm. She had to warn Theo. Ferne got to her knees and lifted her hand covering the wound to see a gaping hole. Her stomach lurched. Ferne gagged and turned her head away. She stumbled to her feet, holding her injured arm while her hand covered the wound.

The voices seemed to come from everywhere. She turned in a circle, frantic to locate the direction. A whispered curse reached her, and then silence. The creature had found them. Ferne fought to stay on her feet. She kept turning, trying her best to determine which direction Theo was in. She finally gave up and took another approach.

"Run, Theo! Go back before it finds you!"

She shouted the words three more times. Each time, it seemed as if the mist blanketed her voice, preventing her from reaching him.

But she had another way.

Ferne dropped to her knees and then onto her right hip. She

had no idea if this would work, but she had to try. She closed her eyes and thought about Theo. His deep brown eyes filled with such warmth and desire that it always made her stomach give a little flip. His sexy smile that made her breath catch. His hold that was both gentle and like iron, as if he had waited centuries to have her against him. Everything about him made her heart melt.

"Hear me, Theo," she whispered as she fought to connect her mind to his.

"Did you hear that?" Finn asked in a low voice.

Their eyes briefly met. Theo nodded. He'd heard something. It had sounded like a voice, but the words had been distorted. He couldn't be sure if it was Ferne or someone else. Some*thing* else. Because they'd heard a growl, too. It had been much closer.

The two of them turned, moving back to back as they looked around. The mist shifted and swirled. Theo didn't like the silence. He couldn't see anything, but something watched them.

"Hear me, Theo."

Ferne's voice shouting in his head made him gasp. He squeezed his eyes shut against the pain.

"Leave. Now, before the beast finds you."

"What is it?" Finn asked. He no longer whispered.

Theo grabbed one side of his head and shook it. He had tried to answer Ferne, but the pounding in his head was too much. "We've got company."

"Tell me something I don't know," Finn stated in a flat voice.

Theo picked up a sound from his left. He tapped Finn's right leg to warn him. Half a second later, something large rushed at them. Theo and Finn turned together. Theo's magic was a shield around them, while Finn targeted their opponent. Their attacker vanished before the magic struck. The chuckle that came from all around them only irritated Theo.

"It's playing with us," Finn murmured.

"Um…Kirsi, you shouldna be going up there," Callum said as he followed behind as she walked up the stairs. "Kirsi? Seriously. We should stay by the door."

She didn't seem to hear him. He flattened his lips. It was better to stay with her than leave her on her own. Kirsi had been acting differently since they entered the house. Actually, it wasn't until she looked up and made that strange comment.

Callum tried to step carefully, but he was leaving a mud trail in his wake. There wasn't time to clean it now, but he would just as soon as he could. They reached the second floor. Kirsi didn't pause as she turned down the hallway. He glanced up to see the stairs going up at least one more floor. It boggled his mind that a single family would live in such a huge house. No one needed this many rooms.

He had never been in a place like this before. Callum looked around discreetly, noting the wood, colorful rugs, pictures, and artwork. And that was just along the stairs and hallway. He couldn't imagine what the other rooms held.

"Whoa. What are you doing up here?" demanded a male with a British accent.

Callum moved up beside Kirsi when he spotted the small group of people standing in the middle of the corridor in front of an open bedroom door. The man had auburn hair and a deep frown. Had Callum walked in on some kind of sexual group? He never would've pegged Kirsi for that type of woman.

Rhona leaned around to peer at them. "What are you two doing?"

"She's no' answering," Callum informed them. "You can keep asking her things all you want, but I doona believe we'll get a response."

A woman with straight black hair cut at her jawline eyed Callum with her deep blue eyes. "What the actual fuck, Rhona?"

An American. Callum was growing more intrigued by the moment.

"I told them to stay downstairs," Rhona retorted and started toward Kirsi.

When Rhona stopped in front of her, Kirsi just moved around Rhona. The Brit then strode toward them.

Callum immediately blocked him from reaching Kirsi. He stood eye-to-eye with the Brit. "Doona lay your hands on her."

The man's turquoise eyes crinkled at the corners as he smiled, but there was no kindness in it. "And just who are you?"

"No one."

Something brushed his hand. Callum turned his head to see Kirsi walking around him. He expertly stopped the Brit before he could grab hold of Kirsi. Callum then faced her, holding his arms out so she would stop. Kirsi looked up at him with her green eyes.

"We need to go downstairs," he told her.

She shook her head. "It's going to kill her."

"Fucking hell. I knew I should've gone with them."

This came from a burly Scot inside the room. The man raked a hand through his dark blond hair and started pacing. Beside him was a woman with brunette hair.

Rhona moved to see Kirsi's face. "Kirsi, what are you talking about?"

"It already hurt Ferne," Kirsi said as she looked inside the room.

The American woman crossed her arms over her chest. "I think it's time we go after them."

"I'm ready," the Brit replied.

Rhona slashed her hand through the air. "We wait, Sabryn. That goes for you, too, Carlyle." Her head swiveled to look at the couple inside the room. "Bronwyn, can you close the portal quickly?"

"Aye, but I don't know if that will do any good. They cut the barrier."

That's when Callum looked past the couple in the room that wasn't a bedroom at all but something altogether different. Where a wall should be was a large gash big enough for a person to fit through.

"The house has been distressed since they went through," Bronwyn finished.

Callum wanted to ask how Bronwyn knew what the house felt when his attention snagged on Kirsi. She turned to face the room, her gaze directed at the gash.

"It's going after Theo and the other man now," she said.

Callum took a step back when he heard a growl that didn't sound like any animal he knew.

"Duck!" Finn yelled.

Theo saw the huge hand and even bigger claws coming at their heads. He bent forward, the momentum sending him rolling. He came up on his feet and could no longer see Finn.

"Finn?" Theo called.

There was no answer. Theo gathered his magic between his hands and dropped his gaze to the ground before him. He couldn't rely on his eyes. He had to tune into his other senses. His ears strained to listen for Finn, Ferne, or the creature. The longer it went without a response from Finn, the more worried Theo became.

Ferne was there, but she wasn't near enough that he could hear her. He'd find her, though. One way or another. First, he had to take care of the thing after them.

"Here," came a strangled voice.

Theo rushed toward it. "Finn?"

"Aye. I'm hurt."

He kept walking toward Finn until he spotted a shape bent over in the mist. Finn had his back to him, and the way he weaved told Theo that he wouldn't be on his feet for long. He had no idea how he would get Finn back to the others and find Ferne.

The mist moved, and then another Finn was there. Whole and unharmed. He put a finger to his lips. Theo halted and looked from one Finn to the other.

The figure turned and lifted its pained face to Theo. "Help me."

Theo looked from one Finn to the other. One of them was the

true Finn, and the other was…he didn't know who or what it was, but it didn't matter. The problem was figuring out which one was the real Finn.

"Theo?" the hurt Finn called.

The other Finn said nothing. Merely watched him. The wrong choice could doom them all. Theo turned to the one thing he trusted above all else—his instinct. Without warning, he hurled magic.

Ferne heard a bellow, and then the unnatural silence returned. That had to be the direction Theo was in. She tried to get to her feet, but her legs wouldn't hold her. With no other choice, she dragged herself with her right arm, using her legs and feet when she could.

She bit her lip and used whatever energy she had left to gain more ground each time. Worry festered and grew in the back of her mind. She had never used her ability so many times in quick succession, and she felt the effects. And that was before the injury. The wound made everything so much worse. She could practically feel her life force draining away.

The faster she got out of this place, the better. And there was a way out. There had to be. Otherwise, how had Theo gotten to her? It was Theo. She was certain of that. She had connected with his mind. He hadn't said anything, but it *was* him. Now, all she had to do was reach him, though at her current speed, it would take her months.

If the creature didn't find them first. The bellow could've been Theo or the thing. Either way, she was headed toward it.

She reached out her arm and dragged herself across the smooth ground. Her elbow hurt, but she couldn't let that distract her or stop her from continuing. Reach. Drag. Reach. Drag. Reach. Drag. She was so absorbed in staying moving that she didn't realize she was no longer alone until it was too late. Her arm connected with something that wasn't the ground. The mist moved, and she saw a hoof. Her head twisted to look up, just as long fingers wrapped around her neck and lifted her until her feet dangled above the ground. She weakly pulled at the grip tightening around her neck as she stared into inky eyes.

"They're out of time," Kirsi whispered and rushed through the doorway.

Callum watched in shock as she easily slipped past Bronwyn and the other man in the room to dash toward the cut opening.

"Elias, stop her!" Bronwyn shouted.

Callum didn't know what prompted him to run after Kirsi. He pushed Elias out of the way, hearing shouts behind him. Kirsi jumped through the gash without looking back. Callum heard someone yell his name as he stuck one leg through. He glanced back to see the others coming at him.

He climbed through and found Kirsi nearly swallowed by mist. Her pale green eyes were locked on him. She didn't move until he came even with her. Callum didn't like this place. Something about it felt tainted. It made his skin crawl while his brain screamed for him to leave.

They didn't get far before he heard the others come through behind him. Callum looked over his shoulder, but he couldn't see them. The mist was too thick, and the lighting too dim.

Kirsi took his arm and pulled him after her as she walked quickly. He lengthened his strides to stay in step with her. Callum's head swiveled from side to side, but he couldn't see anything but mist and more mist. The deeper into it they walked, the harder it became for him to stay. His feet were heavy, his knees locking and refusing to bend. The mist clung to him. He swatted it away, but it came back, wrapping around him. He realized Kirsi no longer held him. He looked for her, but she was gone. Swallowed by the mist.

Or maybe taken by it.

Theo flew backwards. The recoil of his magic on the injured Finn blew back on him, sending him tumbling hard to the ground. It knocked the breath from him. His shoulder was on fire, a pain he knew from the last time he had dislocated it. He held his arm against him and waited until his lungs stopped seizing so he could draw in a breath.

"Theo," Finn said as he knelt beside him. "Fek me. Are you hurt? Aye, of course, you're hurt. Where? What can I do? How did you know that wasn't me? Can you sit up?"

Finn fired the questions at him one after the other in quick succession. The air had never tasted so sweet as it did when Theo could finally breathe again. He opened his eyes to find Finn's hand outstretched. He took it and let the Irishmen pull him to his feet.

"I can fix the shoulder," Finn offered.

Theo shook his head and looked around. "Where is the bastard?"

"He wasn't thrilled with you. He'll be back."

"I don't plan on waiting."

"I'm open to suggestions," Finn replied.

Theo glared around him. "We need this damned mist gone."

He pooled his magic between his hands once more. Then he tugged back his good arm and shot his hand out, palm forward. The gust of magic cleared away the mist for a few seconds. Theo repeated the action, widening the area more each time.

"There," Finn whispered.

Theo had already spotted the dark shape in the distance. He started running toward it when he saw another figure he recognized. Ferne.

Finn was faster and moved ahead of him. The creature looked up and spotted them. Then its head jerked to the side. The snarl was loud and ominous. Angry. Theo glanced over to see what had caught its attention when he saw two other figures headed toward the beast.

Theo readied his magic as he neared. The creature lowered its head to Ferne before tossing her toward Theo. He tried to catch her, but he was too far away. Theo dove, slamming his injured shoulder onto the ground but missing her. He had been sure he'd had his good hand on her, but he had sorely misjudged.

Finn got to Ferne's unmoving body first and tried to turn her over, only to have his hand go through her. Theo's heart skipped a beat as he pushed to his knees.

"Uh…Theo? We might have a problem," Finn said.

Theo crawled on his knees and one hand to her. He would be able to touch her, he was sure. But his hand went through her, too. "Ferne," he called. "Can you hear me?"

"Is it her?" Finn asked.

"It's her," said a female voice.

Theo looked up, surprised to see Kirsi standing at Ferne's feet. There was also a second person. Theo peered behind Kirsi to see a slower-moving male. It wasn't until they were closer that Theo recognized Callum.

"Kirsi," Theo began.

She didn't look his way as she squatted down and placed her hand on Ferne's leg. It didn't pass through Ferne. Theo exchanged a look with Finn, who appeared as bewildered as he felt.

"We must get her out, and quickly," Kirsi said.

Theo tried to gather Ferne in his arms, but he still couldn't grab her. "I can no' help."

Kirsi stood, and Ferne's body floated. The girl turned and pulled Ferne along beside her. Theo climbed to his feet as Finn helped a struggling Callum, who didn't look well at all.

"Doona touch me," Callum snapped and yanked his arm away from Finn.

Finn held up his hands. "You're not going to make it out if you don't accept some help."

Theo walked to the duo. He quickly shook his head at Finn before meeting Callum's gaze. "We'll stay with you, but we need to keep Kirsi in sight. I'm no' sure how long the mist will stay away. You can take hold of one of us if you need."

Callum nodded and managed to keep moving. Theo gave him credit for staying within sight of Kirsi when he was so obviously hindered. Thankfully, the creature was nowhere to be seen. It had run when Kirsi and Callum neared. He wondered which of them the being feared. Theo eyed them both but couldn't decide.

He and Finn kept their magic at the ready and an eye out for an attack. But none came. The closer to the cut in the wall they got, the better Callum looked and the easier he walked.

"Thank fuck," Callum muttered when Kirsi entered the opening.

Finn snorted a laugh. "Ditto."

Theo waited for them to go through before looking behind him. The mist was rolling in steadily now. He slipped through the opening just as a growl reached them. Callum turned and lost his balance, tipping backward. His hand reached out to grab hold of something to steady himself, landing on the gash Theo had cut. Beneath his palm, the barrier stitched itself back together.

"Do it again," Theo urged.

Callum jerked his hand back. "Do what?"

"That!" Finn shouted. "Mend the tear before that thing gets through."

Callum started to say something, then thought better of it, putting his hand on the next section. Each time, the membrane sutured itself. Just as Callum finished, the creature arrived, its talons pushing against the wall in an attempt to tear it.

"Out!" Bronwyn shouted.

The three of them ran out of the room. Theo didn't budge until the vortex was closed, and the only thing he saw was the bedroom.

"That was close," Elias said.

Bronwyn leaned heavily against him. "Too close."

Others tried to talk to him, but Theo leaned one way and then the other to search for Kirsi and Ferne. He spotted Rhona standing at the doorway where he had brought Ferne's body. She motioned him over. Theo squeezed through the others and ran to Rhona. He reached her and looked inside the bedroom to see Kirsi standing next to the bed where Ferne lay. Yet above the body was the Ferne Kirsi still held.

His lips parted in shock as he slowly walked into the room. Kirsi said nothing as she slowly lowered her hand, bringing Ferne down until the two were one. There was a quick flash of golden light that caused Theo to shield his eyes with his arm. When he lowered his arm, Kirsi looked around in confusion.

"DI Frasier? I've been looking for you."

He glanced at Ferne. "You found me."

"Ferne needs you," Kirsi told him.

Theo moved to stand beside Kirsi. He saw Ferne's chest moving as she breathed and then motioned to the bed. "We got her."

"We?" Kirsi eyed him suspiciously. Then she looked around in shock. "How did I get up here?"

Theo swallowed, trying to coat his dry mouth. "There are many questions we'd also like answered."

"There certainly are," Rhona said.

Theo and Kirsi turned to see everyone standing just inside the room, watching them. Kirsi wrapped her arms around herself.

"Food," Carlyle said into the silence. "That's what we need."

Finn rubbed his eyes. "And the biggest glass of whiskey ever to be had."

"Dreagan, right?" Elias teased.

Finn elbowed him. "Irish whiskey for an Irishman. Have I taught you nothing?"

The conversation continued down the hall as they walked away one by one. All but Rhona, Kirsi, and Callum, who remained in the hall. Callum looked ready to bolt at any second, but his gaze kept going to Kirsi. They owed Callum for keeping that thing out, but Theo was intimately acquainted with the Kilmuirs. They were shunned by others on Skye for a reason.

As if sensing Theo's thoughts, Callum's gaze met his. The younger man lifted his chin before walking away. Rhona shrugged when Theo looked her way. Then Rhona jerked her chin to Kirsi, letting him know Callum had come with her.

"Come," Rhona urged Kirsi. "You look like you could use a drink, too."

Theo closed the door once he was alone then returned to the bed. He linked his hand with Ferne's. "I've quite a story to tell you. I think you have one, as well. Open your eyes. Come on, Ferne. You found me through all of that. Come back to me now."

CHAPTER FORTY-TWO

Ferne's eyes snapped open. She lay frozen, waiting for the mist to swallow her. Or the being to return. Her heartbeat didn't slow until she became aware of the light. She turned her head and saw the lamp on the bedside table. Her fingers curled into something soft. She blinked and finally realized she was in a room, on a bed. Another strange bed. Another strange room. This needed to stop. At least the mist and murkiness were gone.

She slowly sat up and took stock of her body. Her attention shifted to her left arm. She couldn't see a wound, but she felt it as if it were still there. She rubbed her right hand over it, just to make sure. The limb was intact—at least from what she could see and feel. On a good note, the lethargy that had plagued her was gone.

Ferne rose from the bed. The sound of water drew her to a door, and she put her ear to it. Someone was taking a shower. Slowly, she peeked inside. Through the shower glass, her eyes landed on Theo, rinsing his hair.

Without hesitation, she walked inside the bathroom before

quickly undressing. Steam filled the room as she opened the stall door and stepped inside. Theo wiped the water from his face and opened his eyes. He stilled at the sight of her. She had feared she'd never see him again. She still didn't know what had happened, but right now, that didn't matter. He mattered.

A muscle in his jaw jumped. She didn't know which of them moved first. One minute, they were staring at each other. The next, they were in each other's arms. She buried her head in the crook of his neck, holding him tighter than was probably comfortable. She had been so scared and had felt so alone.

He leaned back and searched her face as his hands cupped her head. "You came back."

"Always." She smiled as tears welled in her eyes. "You found me."

"Always."

Then his mouth was on hers. The kiss was deep and hungry. It sparked their passion, and it ignited in an instant. Ferne groaned when his cock hardened. He turned them, pressing her against the tiled wall. The surface was cool, the water hot, and his body slick. She lifted one leg to wrap around his waist.

His back and shoulder muscles flexed and bunched beneath her hands as he lifted her. Ferne locked her ankles together behind him as he groaned. She tore her mouth from his to suck in air. His dark eyes blazed with a need she recognized, a desire that burned within her. He dipped his head and circled her nipple with his tongue.

"Now. Please. I need you inside me now," she begged.

Theo answered by sliding deep within her with one thrust of his hips. She dropped her head back against the tile, a soft moan falling from her lips. He began to slide his cock in and out, spiraling her toward an epic orgasm. She found his mouth again, needing to taste him. Her fingers tangled in his wet hair as their tempo increased, and their bodies rocked together.

This was what she needed. Theo. And their explosive passion. It had a way of wiping away the horrors, erasing the bad, and leaving nothing but pleasure and love. Unfettered bliss. And a future bright with potential.

Desire tightened and spread as he filled her again and again, tugging her ever closer to the pinnacle. She dug her fingers into him when the climax hit. It shot through her, making her gasp and then sigh in ecstasy.

Ferne watched the euphoria cross Theo's face when he buried himself deep and orgasmed. The bond they had forged strengthened, tightened. She splayed her hand on his cheek to look into his eyes. Without a doubt, she loved him. Maybe from the first time they'd met at the Fairy Pools. And they had been swept away by desire even then.

He slowly released one of her legs and then the other. He closed his eyes and pressed his forehead against hers. "Ferne."

She heard the joy in his voice at her return, his fear of what had happened, and his worry about what might yet come. She wound her arms about him. She wished she had words to comfort him, but they would be hollow. Things weren't finished. Not by a long shot.

He straightened and turned her toward the water. Without a word, he washed her, taking a long time around her breasts. She leaned against his chest as he teased her nipples, sending pleasure straight to her core. His lips lingered on her neck as his hands lowered to the junction of her thighs. He thoroughly cleaned her before squatting to wash her legs.

Ferne smiled as she held on to the wall with one hand and the shower glass with the other. Theo then worked his way up her back. He took as much time rinsing her body as he had washing it. Only then did he turn to her hair.

No one had ever washed her hair before. Her eyes closed as he massaged her scalp until she was boneless. It was all she could do to stay upright. Even as he rinsed the strands, she didn't want the pampering to end. It gave her ideas for him, however.

She leaned her head back into the water and sighed. That turned into a cry of pleasure when his tongue licked her sex. He nudged her legs apart, and she quickly obeyed. Then his mouth was on her. He took his time licking her slowly, seductively. Until he found her clit. She cried out his name when he circled it with his tongue and added just the right amount of pressure.

Her hand slipped on the glass as she fought to stay standing amid the onslaught of pleasure. He slid a finger inside her, slowly twisting one way and then the other. He added a second digit to the first and began thrusting in time with his tongue flicking over her clit.

Desire tightened low in her belly, her body humming. Ready, eager. She reached for it, sought it. The orgasm took her breath. She clamped down on his fingers even as he continued to move within her, sending her higher and higher. The pleasure was exquisite, blissful. It filled every portion of her soul and shot outward.

Ferne slowly came to and found herself held by Theo's strong, tender arms. The water beat against her back, and his heartbeat was beneath her ear. She looked up to find him grinning.

"That was...incredible to watch. And feel," he said.

She gave him a dubious look. "What do you mean?"

"You used magic when you climaxed."

"What?" she asked in shock. "Are you sure?"

He nodded and turned off the water before handing her a towel. "There's no mistaking it."

"That's a first for me."

"Me, too," he said with a wink.

She pressed the towel against her cooling body for warmth. "Where are we?"

Theo's head swiveled to her as he stilled. He searched her face. "Carwood Manor. Bronwyn's home."

"How did I get here?"

"There's a lot I need to tell you."

"I remember that being having a hold over me. And then nothing. Until I woke here."

Theo went back to drying himself. "You doona remember anything else?"

"I remember the mist. The silence. I remember trying to reach out to you and Kirsi. I know you were in that place with me. Where was that? How did we get out? I'm missing time again, and I can't tell you how scary that is."

He hung up his damp towel. As he dressed, he shot her a quick glance. "There are many moving parts and players in this. I didna know how soon you'd wake. Or even if you would."

Ferne tried not to let that last statement affect her, but it did. Like a kick to the stomach.

Theo put his arms around her. "I'm no' trying to keep anything from you. I know it may sound like it, but the truth is, I doona know everything. Everyone is downstairs waiting."

"For me?"

"We decided the manor was the safest place for all of us tonight."

"The mist." How could she have forgotten about that?

He nodded slowly. "As I said, there are many moving bits and people, and we willna know the entire story until we're all together."

She started to turn away to dress when he tightened his hold.

"I thought I'd lost you."

The flare of panic in his eyes made her heart trip. She placed her hand on his chest over his heart, and he covered it with his. "I was lost. But I'm back now."

"Ferne, I'm no' good with words. I'm no' good at much of anything but being a cop." He paused and briefly looked away. "My work takes up most of my time. Ask any of my past relationships, and they'll give you the same reason why they ended things."

"I don't care about your past."

His fingers tightened over hers. "You're th—"

A knock interrupted him. Ferne wanted to yell at whoever it was to go away. She knew whatever Theo had been about to say was important, and now she might never know.

Theo sighed and stepped back. She let her hand fall from his chest, missing his touch and warmth. He shut the door behind him, locking in what little heat was left. She dried herself and put her clothes back on, then pulled her hair atop her head in a messy bun. When she opened the door to walk into the room, she saw Rhona standing in the doorway with Theo.

Rhona's vivid green eyes locked on her. "It's good to see you up. Are you hungry? Carlyle made enough to feed an army."

"We practically are one," Theo said with a grin.

Rhona chuckled. "The rest of us ate, but there's plenty left over. If you're up for it, Ferne, we'd love to know what happened."

"I have questions of my own," she said and walked toward them. Ferne spotted her boots beside the bed and paused to put them on. As she stood, she saw white cat hair on the bed. "Is Basher here?"

Theo grinned. "I wasna going to leave him at the house. He spent hours with you. Carlyle lured him away with some chicken earlier. He willna admit that Basher is growing on him, though."

The three of them walked out of the room and down the hall. A door drew Ferne's gaze. She stared at it as they passed. Something about it made her skin crawl. When Theo's hand reached for hers, she eagerly took it.

And was happy when they were well away from the door and whatever might be in that room.

CHAPTER FORTY-THREE

Edie hummed as she selected clothes from the closet and laid them out on the bed for herself and Trevor. She would have everything packed and ready so they could leave as soon as he was free the next day. They used to have date nights religiously, but that had stopped somewhere along the way. It was time they began that again, to reconnect and remember why they had fallen in love and married.

Downstairs, the kids were watching the tele together, actually agreeing on a movie. It was a rarity, and she wasn't about to interrupt that. There were leftovers in the fridge, which meant she didn't need to cook. She had sent texts to both Elias and Elodie about watching the kids over the weekend, and both had agreed. Elodie and Scott would pick the children up from school and take them for one night, and Elias and Bronwyn would have them Saturday night through Sunday when Edie and Trevor returned.

The alarm system alerted her that someone had pulled into the drive. Edie paused in digging through the dresser for her sexy underwear to look up at the TV on the wall and press a button on the remote. The video came online, showing multiple cameras around the house. It was the camera facing the drive that she focused on, seeing a familiar car.

"What are you doing back here, Kerry?" she mumbled.

Edie hurried from the room and down the stairs. The kids didn't pay her any attention. She checked the clock. Trevor would be home at any moment, and she didn't want Kerry still around when he arrived. Yet Edie couldn't give her the tongue-lashing she wanted. Kerry's threat to her family had enough weight to keep Edie wary.

She opened the door as Kerry walked her bulk up the path. Edie stepped outside, glancing behind her to make sure the kids were still watching the movie. She pulled the door closed behind her and looked at the woman who was quickly becoming a thorn in her side. "What can I do for you?"

"It's time."

Edie drew in a deep breath and crossed her arms over her chest. "What?"

"It's time. You need to be ready."

Edie was unsure what to say. It wasn't as if she could tell Kerry that she was about to go away on holiday with her husband, and to wait to do whatever it was Kerry intended with the Druids. Probably more deaths. She should be more concerned about that.

"Be prepared for what's next."

"You're doing this now? Will my family be safe?"

Kerry studied her a moment. "A family could mean many different things."

"I want to know if my children will be okay," she pushed.

"You're not worried about your siblings? What about Trevor?"

Kerry hesitated, struck by the anger she felt toward Elodie and Elias that she couldn't shake.

"Stop by tomorrow," Kerry said. "We'll chat."

"I won't be here. I'm leaving on holiday."

Kerry's smile grew. She said nothing as she walked away. Edie didn't move until the car had driven off. She had never thought much about Kerry, besides her being a deputy for Corann and then Rhona. Edie had very little interaction with her, truth be told, even with Kerry as the deputy over her area. Not once, in all those years, had she ever given Edie the kind of dangerous, treacherous vibe she was getting now.

Edie went back into the house to stand in the kitchen and look into the next room at the children. She was a mother. It was her duty to protect her kids above all else. Edie was sorry that so many had died, but she had to think of her family and their future. That was her priority.

The security buzzed, and the tablet mounted on the wall flashed awake to show Trevor's car pulling into the garage. Edie shook off what had happened with Kerry and began taking out the containers of leftovers from the fridge.

"Hey," she called when Trevor walked inside. She greeted him with a kiss.

He set down his briefcase and tugged his tie loose. "What a day."

"I picked up a bottle of your favorite red. It's been chilling in the wine fridge." She got down two glasses as he retrieved the bottle. "I figured we could eat these before they go bad. I'd rather spend the night packing than cooking."

Trevor stopped mid-pour and met her eyes.

Her heart sank. "No. Please don't cancel."

"I'm sorry, babe. It's out of my hands. It all happened this afternoon, and if I doona sort out the legalities of everything, the deal willna go through on Monday."

A well of fury so strong and righteous surged through Edie that she became dizzy with it. She tried to keep the anger out of her voice as she asked, "No one else can step in?"

"I've been working on this for months. It would take days for anyone else to get caught up."

"Well, we won't be able to leave as early as I would like, but at least we'll still have the time away."

Trevor finished filling her glass and handed it to her. "I'm afraid that willna be possible. I have to go to Glasgow."

"What?"

"Doona do that, Edie," he retorted angrily and grabbed his glass with such force that some of the wine sloshed out. "It isna as if I'm trying to get out of our trip. Shite comes up, as well you know. It's one goddamn weekend. We can have another one."

She stared at him, shocked at his outburst. He was right, of course. This wasn't his fault. And it wasn't as if this were the first time something like this had happened. The entire point of this trip was for them to reconnect, and she had been looking forward to it. It was unreasonable for her to take her disappointment out on him.

"I'm sorry," she said. "I was just looking forward to the holiday."

He sighed and braced his hands on the island. "Me, too."

"What would you like for dinner? I'll cook us something."

He drained the rest of his wine and set the glass aside. "Doona worry about me. I'm headed up to pack."

"You need to eat."

"I'll grab something on the road."

Her stomach clenched. "On the road? You're leaving tonight?"

"I told you I had to go to Glasgow," he said as he started up the stairs.

Edie followed him, glancing at the kids to find them watching the entire argument. She raced up to their room and closed the door to drown out their words. "Do you have to go tonight?"

"I've no interest in waking up before dawn to get on the road."

He wasn't even looking at her while he shoved aside the clothes she'd set out for them and began packing business attire. His tone was disinterested, his mood unreadable. Or was she reading into things again? Edie was tired of questioning her every thought, every feeling. But what else could she do?

"I'll come with you."

"Doona be silly," he said, gathering his toiletries.

Edie moved to the bathroom doorway to block him. "Why not? It isn't the getaway we had planned, but we would still be together. When you're finished, we can enjoy ourselves in Glasgow."

His jaw tightened as he stood in front of her. "It'll most likely run into the weekend. You'll be stuck at the hotel."

"Relaxing. Reading. Maybe getting a massage. We can have dinner whenever you get done and do whatever. We can walk around naked, like you love."

"Edie. I'm tired. I've a long drive ahead of me and work I thought was complete. I'm no' in the mood for this." He shoved past her.

She spun, her anger breaking loose. "I'm trying here, Trevor! Ion't that what you wanted of me? Or is it only on your terms when you're ready for it?"

"Maybe time apart is what we need," he snapped as he zipped the suitcase. "Instead of time together. You've never had a problem with my work before." He straightened and met her gaze. "Why now? Why are you suddenly clingy and demanding?"

"Because I feel as if the solid foundation we've always had for our relationship is crumbling."

"And whose fault is that? Yours." He grabbed the suitcase and stalked out of the room.

Edie fisted her hands, hating herself for losing her temper. "Trevor, wait," she said and ran after him. She caught him on the stairs, grabbing his arm to make him stop. Finally, he turned his head to her. "I'm sorry. I'm trying. I really am."

"You're right. You need to relax. Let the kids go to your brother's and sister's. Have the entire weekend to yourself. You willna have to pick up after us or cook dinner for anyone."

"I'd rather be with you."

"We'll schedule it once this deal is complete."

Edie's eyes burned with tears when she heard the lie in the words. She didn't even need to use magic to discern it. It was in his voice, his eyes, and how stiffly he held his body. She dropped her hand from him. "Sure."

"I'll call when I get to the hotel," he said, giving her a quick peck on the cheek.

Edie slowly descended the stairs, barely seeing Trevor laughing and joking with the kids as he showered them with love. They walked him to the door, shouting that they loved him.

"Mum, we're hungry," her son called.

Edie was on autopilot when she walked to the kitchen and took out plates to heat up the leftovers for them. She didn't even lay into them when they began arguing. She couldn't stop hearing Trevor's words.

Kerry's smile grew as she drove to Carwood Manor. Edie was just where she wanted her to be. The start of her army, and the beginning of the new order of Druids. There was just one more thing she needed to take care of tonight.

The mist was already there, waiting for her. She didn't need to be around to witness things, but she wanted to be. Mostly, she wished to see Rhona's face. The Ancients wanted to be rid of her and so many other Druids who had lost their way. After what Rhona had done to her, it was fitting that Kerry would be the one to take her life. But that wasn't tonight. The Ancients had made that clear. They wanted Kerry to have the start of her army before she faced off against Rhona and Balladyn, the Warden of Skye.

So many powerful Druids gathered at Carwood, thinking they were safe within its walls. They couldn't be more wrong. She had been waiting for this night for so long. She had almost gone against the Ancient's wishes at times, but she had listened and obeyed. And they had delivered everything—and everyone—they'd promised.

Tonight was the beginning of it all.

Tonight was when Skye learned just who held everyone's life in their hands.

CHAPTER FORTY-FOUR

It was irrational for Theo to want to take Ferne back to their room and shut everyone out. They were his friends. They had risked their lives right alongside him and Ferne. There was no reason to retreat.

Other than wanting her to himself.

He hadn't finished what he'd wanted to say in the bathroom. Maybe that was for the best. He wanted to promise Ferne the world, but was that the right thing to do after someone nearly died? Honestly, Theo didn't know what was right and wrong in such a situation. He'd never been in something like this before. And he never wanted to be here again.

She clung to his hand as if he were the only thing keeping her rooted. All the while, she was the one who maintained his calm. He had been beside himself after Kirsi came back with what many of the team believed was Ferne's soul. Theo had watched every breath fill Ferne's lungs and then leave them. He had searched for any sign that she was waking. That she would return to him. Hours stretched into eons, each more horrendous than the last.

Then she was there. Awake and alive. Smiling and in his arms. He'd wanted to cry, to shout with joy. To hold her.

Rhona reached the bottom floor a couple of steps ahead of them. She made her way toward the front room. As he and Ferne followed, Theo heard voices.

"Leave him alone," Sabryn said with a laugh.

Finn made a sound. "It's just a cat."

"I doona like cats."

Theo reached the door as Callum spoke. His gaze swept the room and found Callum sitting off to the side as far from the others as he could get, with Basher sitting at his feet, staring up at him.

"Why no'?" Elias asked.

Callum's gaze never lifted from Basher. "They're…unpredictable."

"Well, he likes you," Kirsi said.

Callum sat so rigidly that Theo expected him to break apart at any moment. Was that because of Basher, the group staring at him, or his past with Theo? He knew Callum's family better than he'd like. Every police officer on Skye was acquainted with the elder Kilmuir, Callum's father, Joseph. Joe had a nasty temper and a foul mouth, and he didn't hesitate to use both on anyone who got near him. Joe's father had been the same. Callum had yet to fall into the same footsteps as his father and grandfather, but he would. If Theo knew anything about the Kilmuirs, he knew that. Every Kilmuir got the gene that turned them into arseholes sooner or later. At least Nancy Kilmuir had gotten out when she could and took Callum's younger sister with her.

Basher butted his head against Callum's leg. Then the feline spotted Theo and Ferne. Basher's tail snapped up as he trotted to them, meowing in greeting. Basher sat at Theo's feet and looked up at him. Theo snapped his fingers, and the cat jumped into his arms, purring loudly as he and Ferne greeted him.

"Ferne," Kirsi called excitedly.

Everyone turned their way. Theo stood silently as the team rushed to Ferne, their questions running together. It wasn't until Carlyle let out an ear-piercing whistle that everyone quieted and parted for him.

Carlyle walked to Ferne and held out a plate of his chicken and pasta dish. "Sit. Eat. We'll talk first."

Theo gave Carlyle a nod of thanks. He waited until Ferne found a seat before moving to stand near her. She looked calm as she ate, but he couldn't forget the fear in her eyes when she had asked how she'd gotten to the manor. He wanted to shield her, to protect her from everything and everyone that could hurt her. Especially after all she had been through.

His gaze slid to her. If he had learned anything from Ferne, it was that there wasn't much she couldn't handle. She had a quiet strength about her that others missed at first. He knew he had. But he saw it now. He saw *her*.

Rhona spoke first, describing everyone getting to the Red Hills the day before. Theo widened his stance to get more comfortable while Basher rested his head on Theo's shoulder. As he listened, Theo watched Ferne discreetly, noting the times she paused in eating. She listened raptly. Right up until Rhona described how Ferne had levitated at the mountain.

Ferne slowly lowered her fork, her face pale. A moment later, she set the plate aside and folded her hands in her lap. Theo clenched his jaw when Rhona repeated what the Ancients had said. He felt eyes on him when she described how he had tried to get to

Ferne. Even now, he knew he could've gotten the Ancients out of Ferne if he had been able to reach her. Or maybe he was just lying to himself. It didn't matter. What was done, was done. Ferne was back.

No thanks to the Ancients.

Theo returned his focus to the story in time to hear Rhona tell Ferne how she was brought to the man. As if sensing that Ferne needed him, Basher jumped from his arms to her lap and curled up.

Ferne's head turned, their gazes clashing. She reached for him. He sidled closer and linked their fingers. He saw the uncertainty in her eyes, and he wished he could tell her that everything was fine. But it wasn't. And they both knew it.

Rhona paused and looked at him, indicating it was his turn to talk. Theo quickly explained how he had heard her voice in his head and guessed that she was in the space between dimensions. He finished detailing how he cut the wall so he and Finn could get through and then looked at Kirsi.

Theo listened raptly as Kirsi spoke. He'd been curious about her involvement and how she'd found him. Yet the things he really wanted to know, she didn't share. Her tale ended upon her entering the manor.

"You doona remember going up the stairs?" he asked. He was used to people holding things back. There was no reason for her not to share. Unless she knew something the rest of them didn't.

Kirsi shook her head. "I recall feeling something. It drew my attention to the ceiling. The next thing I knew, I was at the table with a plate of food before me."

"Then you don't know how you did…the thing?" Finn asked.

Kirsi shrugged her shoulders. "I've no idea what you're talking about."

"What did she do?" Ferne asked.

Theo swallowed and looked down to find her green eyes on him.

"If I was unconscious on the bed, how could I have been in both places?" Ferne asked. "It's not possible. I was there. Not here."

He looked down at their joined hands. "I tried to touch you in there, but I couldna. My hand went right through you as if you were…" He couldn't even say it.

"A spirit," she said for him.

Theo nodded.

"I couldn't touch you either," Finn said. "But Kirsi could. She pulled you from that place back to the manor."

Ferne's throat bobbed as she swallowed. "To my body."

"It appears that way," Rhona said. "What happened while you were in there?"

Ferne adjusted her fingers on his hand. "It called the place The Grey."

"*It?*" Bronwyn asked.

Ferne sank the fingers of her other hand into Basher's fur. "The entity, the creature. Whatever it was. It could shift into anything it wanted. It told me that it had been waiting for me. That it would make me suffer."

"Why?"

Theo jerked at the sound of Balladyn's voice. He hadn't noticed the Reaper's return.

"I don't know," Ferne replied. "It expected me to know where I was, who it was, and why I was there. When I didn't, it didn't stay upset for long. It planned a long death for me, full of suffering."

Theo frowned when she absently rubbed her left arm.

Rhona turned to Kirsi. "Do you know the answers the being sought?"

"I don't have a clue," Kirsi replied.

Theo waited until Ferne looked at him before asking, "I saw it hold you up by your throat. Did it say something to you then?"

"Noth—" Ferne began, when her face suddenly went ashen.

Theo went down on one knee and held her gaze. "It can no' hurt you now."

"I'm not worried about it."

"Then what?" Rhona asked.

The stark terror in Ferne's eyes twisted Theo's gut. "What is it?"

"I know who put me in The Grey," Ferne whispered. Her voice shook as she said, "The Ancients."

A deafening silence followed her statement.

Filip said, "The Ancients are who we turn to for advice. They direct us in times of trouble."

"Do they?" Esther asked. "How many times have you called on them when they answered?"

Rhona shook her head. "The Ancients are good. They would never—"

"Never take control of someone's body without their consent," Theo stated indignantly as he squeezed Ferne's hand and stood. "That's exactly what they did to Ferne. Twice. They used her body without hesitation before putting her soul in a place we couldn't reach. And into the hands of something wanting to do her harm."

Elias lifted a shoulder half-heartedly. "Unless they put Ferne there knowing we'd go get her."

"And put all of us in danger? I'm not buying it," Sabryn said flatly.

Theo noticed Callum's gaze was locked on Kirsi, fiddling with the cuff of her sweater as if her life depended upon it. Rhona had kept the pair at the manor because of the mist, but they didn't need to be a party to all of this. Or at least Callum didn't. Kirsi was embroiled in it, whether she wanted to be or not.

And yet, if not for Callum, that creature in The Grey would've gotten through to their world.

"It isna as if we can ask the Ancients what their intention was for Ferne," Scott said.

Ferne jumped up so quickly that Basher let out a startled cry as he dropped to the floor. She was breathing quickly, her eyes wide. Then she turned those beautiful eyes to him. "It's back."

Theo didn't need to ask what. They had been expecting the mist.

CHAPTER FORTY-FIVE

Ferne could feel the swarm of the mist buzzing like a thousand bees as it approached. She wanted to squish herself into a corner and cover her ears with her hands. She might feel like the same person she had always been, but she wasn't. Lying to herself would only prolong the inevitable acceptance.

The truth, as difficult as it was to acknowledge, was simple. Her soul had been pulled from her body and put in a place she shouldn't have escaped. The Ancients had done that to her. Whether they had a good reason or not remained to be seen. That creature wanted her death, and it would've gotten it, too, had her friends not come for her.

All that was enough to send Ferne's mind spinning, but that wasn't what alerted her that she had changed. Fundamentally. Irrevocably. The mist did that. She could *feel* it, hear it. She knew it hung above the manor, waiting for its master to give the command. It had come for someone here.

But who? She looked at those around her. It could be any of

them. The mist had tried to kill many of them already. Perhaps it came back for another attempt. Or it could be after someone else entirely.

"We're safe inside," Bronwyn said.

Ferne sensed the mist testing areas of the structure for weaknesses. The people in the room had risked their lives for her. They didn't care about the past or what her ancestors had done. Dragon Kings, Reapers, and Druids found a way to not just become allies but also friends. They had a strong bond.

Her gaze slid to Theo. Strong, unwavering, remarkable Theo. The passion they shared had opened her heart again. It had forged a connection between them that still boggled her mind. He hadn't given up on her. And she wouldn't give up on any of them. The mist had come to her twice. Once at her car, and the second time at the cave. It wanted something from her.

And maybe, just maybe, she could figure out what they wanted.

She started out of the room. "Not this time. They will tear it down to get to us."

"Then we fight again," Elias replied.

Theo caught up with Ferne, a hand on her arm to halt her. "What are you doing?"

"It has wanted me from the beginning. I'm going outside to figure out why."

"You can no' be serious."

Ferne placed her palm over his heart. His hand immediately covered hers. The mist was moving faster outside. "I must."

"I didna get you back only to lose you again."

"I was drawn to this isle for a reason. I thought I knew what that was, but I didn't know anything."

Theo's brows knitted in confusion. "And you do now?"

"Yes."

"Tell me."

"There isn't time."

"Then I'm coming with you."

Ferne shook her head, wishing with all her heart that she didn't have to go out there alone. But there was no other way. "You can't." She stepped closer and lowered her voice so only he could hear. "Do you trust me?"

"Aye."

"Then trust that I know what to do."

His dark eyes were troubled. "Doona ask that of me. You've no idea what I've gone through today."

"I knew a little of it when I didn't think I'd see you again."

"Ferne," he began.

Her time was running out. She rose on tiptoe and pressed her lips against his. "Trust me."

"No," Carlyle said as he strode up. "I'm with Theo. There are enough of us here to fight the mist and whatever fucker controls it. There's no reason for you to go out there alone."

Ferne never looked away from Theo. "What were you going to say before we were interrupted in the shower?"

He blinked, taken aback by the change of subject. "I...I was going to tell you that I wanted to...that I wanted us to...have a... you know," he finished with a shrug.

"I do." She smiled. "We can discuss our relationship when I return. Promise you won't follow."

He clutched her hand tighter. "I can no' do that."

"You have to."

"Ferne," he said, his voice deep with warning.

"I love you." She slipped from his grip and rushed toward the front of the manor.

Ferne was out the door, slamming it behind her a second later. She put her palm on the wood and sent a wave of magic around the manor to keep those within from getting out. It wouldn't hold them for long, especially Nikolai and Balladyn, but she didn't *need* that long.

"Keep them safe," she whispered to the manor.

Then she turned and walked out onto the graveled area in front of the house. Her gaze scanned the night, looking for the one responsible for the chaos and death. All her life, Ferne had shied away from physical fights. She never saw the purpose in them. Why use a fist—or magic—when someone could use kindness, compassion, or understanding instead?

She had flat-out refused to learn battle magic. And look where she was now. On a field, getting ready to face a Druid hell-bent on domination by fear and death. Ferne was the last person she would choose to face this Druid, but she didn't have a choice. *This* was why she had been brought to Skye.

This night, this battle, this villain.

Her brother had disowned her, the London Druids had kicked her out. She'd found a man who stole her heart, and a group of powerful Druids who stood beside her. The mist had sought her out, the Ancients had talked to her, she'd had her soul ripped from her body, and faced an entity after her death, all to stand in this spot at this time.

Her skin prickled with awareness as her magic swelled and rushed through her entire body, ready and waiting. The vibration of the mist intensified. She didn't need to look up to find it. She had zeroed in on it before she left the house. And it had locked on to her.

Theo shouted her name from inside the house and banged on the door. She wished she'd had time to explain everything to him. He probably wouldn't have believed her. He was a protector. It wasn't in him to sit on the sidelines and let someone else do the dirty work. But that's exactly what she was doing. For him.

He was the one the mist hunted. Its master wanted Theo gone, removed, because he was too big of a threat. She knew because the mist had warned her the first time she went to the Red Hills. It hadn't been the Ancients as she'd thought. The mist had asked her not to fight, because it hadn't meant her harm.

Because it needed her.

She was the only thing that stood between her friends and certain death.

So, here she was. Standing in starlight to face evil. Oddly, she wasn't afraid. Her mind was clear of restrictions and the blocks erected to protect her until the time was right. Movement to her left caught Ferne's attention. Her gaze shifted in that direction. She saw a human-shaped shadow near a tree. She couldn't make out the person. Yet. But she would.

"What are you afraid of?" Ferne asked. "It's just you and me."

"Oh, I'm not alone," a woman replied.

Ferne grinned, settling into her stance as power sizzled through her veins. Potent magic that had always been there. Lifetime after lifetime. "Neither am I."

"Your friends let you come out by yourself to face the mist. I'm not sure I'd count on them if I were you."

Ferne shifted to face the woman. Her arrogance was tedious. "Who are you?"

"Just a Druid finally getting everything she deserves."

"Oh, you'll most certainly get everything you deserve."

The woman laughed and stepped out of the shadows. Ferne recognized her immediately. She was the older woman who had stared at the restaurant and sat in her car watching Ferne.

"Shocked someone my age could do all of this?" she asked.

Ferne shrugged. "Evil doesn't care about age."

"I'd watch my tongue if I were you. I can end your life with a mere thought."

The banging from inside the manor grew louder. They would get out soon, which meant Ferne needed to hurry this along. The woman's worried frown made her smile.

"What?" Ferne asked innocently. "Have you never seen someone trap others inside for their safety?"

The woman jerked her gaze to Ferne. Her eyes narrowed. "This conversation is wearisome. It's time for you to die."

Ferne stood her ground as the woman snapped her fingers. The vibration of the mist grew louder as it neared. Ferne locked eyes with her opponent as it dove from the sky, headed straight for her. It covered her instantly. Swarmed her, moving around her fast.

And through it all, she heard millions of souls screaming, begging for her help. For release. The mist was made up of souls forced to do another's bidding. But no longer. Ferne held out her arms and released her magic.

"Ferne!" Theo bellowed as he yanked on the manor door again.

He wasn't the only one trying to get out. No one was having

success. Not Nikolai, not Balladyn. Bronwyn had her hand on a wall, talking to the house as Nikolai debated with Esther whether to shift and destroy the manor in the process. Theo ran to a window to see Ferne. He caught a glimpse of her just as the mist swarmed her.

"Nay!" He grabbed a chair and tried to hurl it through a window, but it bounced away like a child had tossed it.

He bellowed his fury. Ferne was out there, alone, fighting the mist and the person controlling it. That monster might be human, but after such brutal murders, he considered them the vilest kind of fiend.

Theo slammed his fist against the glass before pressing his forehead to the cool pane. He could do nothing but watch Ferne being torn to pieces. She shouldn't have faced the mist on her own. He should look away, but he couldn't. She was too…he paused and blinked. Was that light? He blinked it again. He could hardly believe it when he recognized the golden glow.

The mist moved and swirled around her in the same hypnotic manner it had at the cave. And the longer she stood there with her arms outstretched and the light growing brighter, the less mist he saw. As if…nay. It couldn't be possible. Could it? But he couldn't doubt his own eyes. Her light was killing the mist.

"Un-fucking-believable," Carlyle murmured from another window, a smile in his voice.

Theo stopped looking at the mist and focused on Ferne. Her gaze was directed across the expanse. He followed the direction, shifting to see beyond what the window allowed. He spotted the silhouette of a woman.

He shoved away from the window and whirled around. "Balladyn!"

The Reaper was next to him in an instant. "I've already tried to get out. The same thing that kept me from getting inside your house is keeping me here."

"Try again," Theo urged.

Balladyn hesitated for only a fraction of a second before he vanished, reappearing almost instantly. Without a word, Balladyn grabbed Theo and Rhona. He jumped them outside behind Ferne and then went back for the rest of the team.

Theo drew up short when saw their adversary. Kerry.

"I should've known," Rhona said through clenched teeth.

Kerry glared at Ferne. "What did you do with my mist?"

Theo's gaze searched the area for anyone else who might have joined Kerry. He didn't see anyone, but that didn't mean they weren't out there. Kerry had yet to notice them. She was too intent on Ferne. And too furious to see herself being surrounded.

"I've set them free," Ferne answered.

Kerry's lips drew back in a sneer as she pulled her elbows up, her fingers curled angrily. An unnatural, spine-chilling scream-like howl left Kerry's lips as she hurled magic at Ferne. Theo rushed toward Ferne, magic pooling in his hand. Before he could warn Ferne to duck, she lashed out with her power. Kerry managed to turn so only a portion of Ferne's magic found its mark.

"Ferne!" he called in warning.

But it was already too late. Kerry had released a blast that slammed into Ferne and tossed her aside as easily as a leaf in the wind. Theo pivoted to go to her and saw his friends encircle Kerry while bombarding her with magic. He wanted to take part in her demise for all the pain she had caused, but he was more concerned about Ferne.

Her glow had vanished by the time he reached her. He dropped to his knees as she pushed up on an elbow. "I've got you."

"You shouldn't be here."

The pain in her voice was like a knife to his gut. "It's all of us. We're a team."

Theo helped her to her feet. She favored her left arm, and he was careful not to touch it. He turned her toward the manor. She had done enough.

"No," she stated firmly. "We belong with the others. It will take all of us."

"Kerry's magic isna strong enough to withstand them."

"She's taken the magic of the Druids she's killed."

Theo wanted to ask how Ferne knew such a thing, but that was for later. Now, was about bringing down a murderer. He tightened his arm around her and adjusted their route. The closer they got to their friends, the clearer it became that Kerry was indeed holding her own. She moved quickly, turning and pivoting to block magic and pitch hers.

Sabryn went down hard on one knee, gasping in pain as she held her stomach. Scott lay unmoving on the ground. Carlyle and Finn propped each other up to continue fighting. But they all delivered as good as they got. Kerry had been hit with an iridescent bubble of Fae magic and stood with the help of a tree at her back. One arm dangled uselessly at her side.

"Enough of this shite," Nikolai grumbled as he heaved a round of dragon magic.

Kerry ducked, the tree taking the hit. It gave a loud groan before toppling backward. Kerry popped up and lobbed a blast at Nikolai, who easily batted it away.

"Don't stop," Ferne shouted, just as they reached the others.

The team showered Kerry with magic. She was able to produce a shield that stopped all but Nikolai's and Balladyn's. Kerry's cry of pain filled the night. Rhona and the Reaper linked hands. The air crackled with the mix of Reaper and Druid magic. It had defeated the Fae Others. It would take down Kerry. The ground trembled as Nikolai shifted and slammed a huge foot down. The rest of the team tossed magic as quickly as they could.

"Theo."

He met Ferne's gaze.

"It's going to take both of us."

Theo nodded. "You have an idea?"

"We need to come up behind her while she's focused on everyone else. There's an opening there."

Theo scanned behind Kerry and saw where Ferne pointed. Elodie stood over Scott, leaving a section vacant. Ferne pulled from his hold and walked in a wide circle to come up behind Kerry. If this plan worked, he and Ferne would have a lot of magic coming their way, and he didn't want any of it to hit them. Hopefully, someone would see what they were about.

They didn't have to be stealthy. Kerry all but ignored the Druids and turned her full attention on Nikolai, Balladyn, and Rhona. Ferne moved faster. Nikolai spread his enormous ivory wings. He opened his mouth to show rows of incredibly sharp teeth. All the while, Balladyn's and Rhona's combined magic grew stronger. Kerry leaned a hip against the stump as she moved her good arm slowly around her.

Theo snatched Ferne back when Balladyn and Rhona released a surge of magic. It hit the invisible shield Kerry had erected, making it crackle and hiss.

"We can't wait," Ferne said as she faced him.

"And we can no' do this now," he argued.

She looked in his eyes, ignoring another sizzle of Kerry's shield as Nikolai's magic hit it. "Now is exactly when this has to be done. It's the only time we *can* do this. We need her stopped, not dead."

"I'd be all right with her death after everything she's done."

Ferne's mouth tightened. "We need her."

"Why?"

"She isn't the one who forced the mist, Theo. It's someone else. Kerry's just a pawn."

"Fuck," he muttered. Why couldn't anything ever be easy?

Ferne held out her hand, palm out. He drew in a breath and put his hand behind hers, curling his fingers over hers as he called for his magic.

"Together," Ferne said.

He inclined his head. "Together."

They turned as one to Kerry and made their way to her. Kerry's shield was losing strength, but just as quickly, it was in full force again. Theo was shocked to see it happen under the onslaught of such powerful beings facing her.

Ferne glanced at him as they neared Kerry. "Ready?"

"As I'll ever be."

A hint of a smile touched her lips. "Now."

They shoved their hands at the shield. To Theo's surprise, there was only a brief moment of delay before they got through. The moment they did, the shield went down. Ferne pulled their joined hands back and then thrust them forward. Theo released his magic at the same time she did. It slammed into Kerry's back, sending her face-first to the ground. In seconds, the team surrounded her.

Kerry's groan of pain reached him as she struggled to roll over.

Even when the Reaper yanked Kerry to her feet, the elder Druid didn't take her eyes off Ferne.

"Your reign of terror is over," Rhona informed Kerry.

Kerry directed her words at Ferne when she said, "You've no idea what you've done."

"I know exactly what I did," Ferne replied.

Kerry wiped the dribble of blood from her nose on her shoulder. "You will soon enough."

"That's enough from you," Balladyn said as he raised his hand, which took her voice.

"I know the perfect place for her," Rhona said.

The three of them teleported away to bring Kerry to her new home in the Red Hills. Theo probably should've said something about that, but it was the only place for Kerry. Regular jails would never hold her.

Theo saw Filip and Elodie helping Scott to his feet. Finn and Carlyle were on either side of Sabryn. Elias and Bronwyn held each other in a tight embrace. Nikolai, now back in human form, turned toward the manor. Theo followed his gaze to find Henry and Esther walking from the manor, along with Callum and Kirsi. He didn't know who had talked Kirsi and Callum into staying inside but he was glad of it.

"Is it over?" Bronwyn asked.

Like everyone else, Theo found himself looking at Ferne.

She smiled and nodded. "The mist won't be killing any more."

"But is it over?" Elias pressed.

Theo saw the look that passed between Ferne and Esther. "Nay," he answered.

"We scored a victory. We'll take it," Nikolai advised.

CHAPTER FORTY-SIX

Kerry had been stopped. A woman Ferne hadn't known, but who had taken an interest in her from the beginning. Had Kerry known who she was? Ferne might never know the answer. She didn't want to know badly enough to visit Kerry at her new home in the Red Hills. The Druid prison. She might not want to talk to Kerry, but she might have to.

It had been over an hour since Rhona and Balladyn left with Kerry. Wounds had been dressed, whiskey had been passed around, and eventually food, as well. They all sat sprawled in the front room to await Balladyn's and Rhona's return. Everyone except Henry, who had departed to who knew where.

The group awaited an explanation from her.

Theo hadn't left her side. Carlyle, Finn, and Filip kept the conversation loud and jovial. It even allowed her to think of things other than the horrors of the past few days. But not Theo. He smiled when others laughed, but Ferne saw his mind sorting through everything and piecing the puzzle together.

Basher contentedly wedged himself between them. His eyes were closed, but the twitching of his ears told Ferne the feline was awake. A calm had descended, not just over them but also over the manor. It wouldn't last nearly as long as everyone hoped.

The darkness Ferne had seen that'd first made her reach out to Kirsi was still very much a threat. Kerry had been a part of that. Were there others? Ferne looked at Kirsi, who was so lost in thought she didn't realize others were casting looks her way. Callum was once again off by himself. He looked as though he wanted to sink into the wall. They had both witnessed—and been party to—more than either had bargained for. Well, Callum, for sure. Kirsi was something different.

Had things become clear for Kirsi as they had for her? Ferne was desperate to know, but now wasn't the time to ask. That would come soon enough. Ferne would give her time to absorb everything.

Theo's hand moved from Basher to her leg. Ferne met his gaze. When she saw the worry in his dark eyes, she covered his hand with hers. There was much they needed to talk about, but only when they were alone. Her life had been altered dramatically in only a handful of days. It seemed a lifetime ago that she had moved her belongings from London. She tried not to think about Mason, but that was asking the impossible. He was her brother, and one way or another, she would find a way to reach him.

"Ferne," Theo whispered.

Before he could say more, Balladyn and Rhona appeared in the room.

"Fuck me," Callum muttered.

Filip chuckled. "Aye. The popping in and out takes some getting used to."

"Speak for yourself," Elias stated.

Esther sat on the arm of the chair Nikolai occupied. "Is Kerry secure?"

"She is." Rhona accepted a glass of whiskey from Bronwyn and passed one to Balladyn. "She isn't talking. She may never, but she's in a place where she can't take any more lives."

Ferne felt the attention turn to her. Theo's touch reminded her that she wasn't alone. She lifted her gaze and looked around the room. "If I'd had time to tell all of you everything, I would have. When I felt the mist, everything became clear. They wanted me, but not to kill me. They wanted my help. The mist was actually made up of Druid souls who were trapped and forced to do another's bidding."

"The Ageless One, I presume?" Sabryn asked.

Balladyn's lips flattened. "None of the other Reapers or Death knew of any entity by that name."

"Same with those at Dreagan and MacLeod Castle," Esther added.

Ferne scratched her forehead. "Someone controlled the mist, but not every second of every day. They had time to themselves. One of those was when they lured me into the caverns in the Red Hills. I assumed it was the Ancients who spoke to me, but it was the souls."

"Then why could you no' remember what they said?" Theo asked.

Ferne shrugged. "I wish I had an answer for that. But that's why they didn't hurt me that night. They knew I could free them."

"The light," Theo said.

She nodded in agreement. "I've felt different since I woke from,"—she paused, trying to find the words—"The Grey. I could sense the mist. Feel it, even. It was a vibration that was different than anything else. I knew if I freed them, most of the power of whoever controlled them would be gone."

"You took a huge chance," Elodie stated.

Balladyn eyed her. "One you shouldn't have taken alone."

"I was the only one who could free the souls. They couldn't hurt me. They could've hurt any of you. It was their directive." She looked at Theo. "They were sent to kill you first. Kerry thought to lure me to her side and then kill the rest of you."

Elodie twisted her lips. "She underestimated you."

Rhona wrinkled her nose. "How did you know how to bring Kerry's shield down?"

"I just did."

"Like Kirsi knew she could bring you back to this dimension," Finn said.

Ferne glanced over to see Kirsi ducking her head. Ferne licked her lips. "I do know a few things now. The mist is gone. I'm not saying the Ageless One couldn't trap more souls in the future, but we don't have to worry about that now. But the threat I originally felt is still over the isle."

"Kerry wasna working alone. We find out who's been helping her," Elias said.

Rhona nodded. "That's the plan. We've won a skirmish, not the battle."

"Something I'm intimately familiar with," Balladyn said as he crossed his arms.

Nikolai grunted. "Aye."

"Some of us are no'," Theo said and nodded toward Callum and Kirsi.

Callum stood still as a statue. "I willna be sharing any of this with anyone."

"We're not thinking about that," Sabryn said.

Rhona shook her head. "I'm more concerned about how you're both handling it."

"I'm fine," Callum said, a finality to his words.

Theo grunted. "We'll see."

"What now?" Filip asked.

Ferne tucked her hair behind her ear. "We keep looking for the Ageless One. It needs to be defeated."

"Was that the creature in The Grey?" Elias asked.

Ferne looked away and swallowed. "That thing wanted my death. Badly. I asked for a name, but it said it didn't have one. It could've been lying, but I also got the impression that if it were the Ageless One, it would've told me in order to scare me."

"We know how to find it," Scott said.

Finn gave a loud snort. "That's not a place I want to return to. Ever."

"We might not have a choice," Rhona said. "There is too much we don't know, and that bothers me. Unless Kerry starts talking, we're only guessing."

Bronwyn nodded toward Ferne. "Not true. We actually have a lot more now thanks to Ferne."

"We're going to need even more," Esther said.

Rhona quirked a brow. "I take that to mean you plan on staying."

"For the time being," Nikolai answered.

That seemed to be the end of the discussion. Bronwyn and Elias offered for everyone to remain at the manor. Callum and Kirsi left almost immediately. As did Nikolai and Esther. Balladyn offered to jump Ferne, Theo, and Basher to Theo's, and they accepted since they didn't have a car. Ferne wanted a change of clothes, but mostly she didn't want to pass by that door in the manor again.

And then, finally, she and Theo were alone.

Basher jumped from Theo's arms and went to find food, leaving her and Theo to stare at each other in the kitchen.

"Did you mean it?" he asked.

She knew what he spoke of. It had hung between them since the words had left her lips. "I only tell people I love them when I mean it."

"We barely know each other."

"We've had a crash course, I'll admit."

He ran a hand over his jaw with dark stubble. "I wasna sugarcoating things earlier. My past—"

"Is your past. Hopefully, you've learned from any mistakes. That's what we're supposed to do. I've had failed relationships, too. I'd like to think they showed me what I didn't like or want so that when I found someone, I would know they were exactly what I was looking for."

"And my job?"

She shrugged. "What about it? That there will be long hours? That you'll deal with the most horrid of humans? Isn't that what we've both been doing?"

His lips split into a grin as he laughed. "Aye. It certainly is."

"I want to give us a try because there's something special between us. I know you feel it, too."

"I do."

She walked to him and put her hands on his chest as he settled his on her hips. "I hid from the world after my parents' deaths. I thought it was safer that way. Just me and Mason. I kept my heart caged and my feelings locked away. Then I came to Skye and walked the Fairy Pools. Suddenly, that lock and cage were gone. There was just you. As if my life didn't start until that moment."

He gently caressed a finger along her jaw. "I'd locked myself away, too. Then there was you. Beautiful and smiling. Strong and kind. Determined and generous. You forced me to face the passion between us. Fool that I am, I was going to ignore it. To save myself heartache."

"Where love is concerned, there's always a chance of that. And for happiness."

He flashed a quick grin. "I doona want to just try. I want us to be together. To live. And love." He pulled her closer, his head lowering to hers. "No holding back."

"No holding back," she whispered.

He pressed his lips to hers, the kiss slow and filled with so much love and passion that her eyes filled with tears.

Theo cupped her face and looked into her eyes. "I love you."

"Say it again," she begged.

He quirked a brow and looked down at her. "First, we need to talk about no' locking me away when you next want to battle an enemy alone."

"I can't make that promise if it means saving you."

Ferne squealed when he bent and lifted her over his shoulder. He strode down the hall with one hand on her arse. Ferne looked into the kitchen to see Basher watching them from the table.

"We'll see what promises you make when I'm done with you," Theo said in a husky voice right before dropping her onto the bed.

She reached for him, and they came together in a tangle of limbs and scorching kisses.

EPILOGUE

SKYE DRUIDS

Five days later...

Theo looked out the kitchen window as he drank his morning coffee. It was time to meet the new chief superintendent assigned to Skye. He wasn't looking forward to it. After finally working as a Druid and a police officer, Theo was loath to go back to where he hid the other side of himself.

"It might be okay," Ferne said as she entered the room.

He turned to face her. "Maybe."

"I'm sure you've had bosses you've not liked before, but you don't even know who this chief will be. You might like them."

"That's no' my issue."

She offered him a sad smile. "I know. You've told me countless times that you're a cop through and through."

"I'm also a Druid."

"You hid that from the others in the department."

He dumped out the rest of his coffee and rinsed the cup. "I

know. I doona want to do that anymore. I doona want to hide from anyone. No' other cops, no' tourists, no' residents. Bloody hell. Is this what the Dragon Kings feel like?"

"Pretty sure it is. What are your options?"

She'd asked him that last night, and he hadn't answered. Mostly because he wanted to think through what those options might be. There were only two that he could see. "Remain in my position and go back to the way things were. Or I quit. Work privately for the Druids on Skye."

"Or work with the Knights."

He walked to her, dragging her against him. "That did cross my mind."

"There's a third option."

"Is there?" he asked as he nibbled on her earlobe.

"You could work with me at the bookstore."

His head lifted. "You found a place?"

"Well, not yet. But there are a couple of locations I'm considering. I'm looking at two more today, and then I want to take you and get your opinion."

"Anything you want."

She grinned. "We could build something and have our place above it."

"You doona like my house?" he teased.

"I love it. I just think it would be neat to have ramps on the walls everywhere so Basher could move around the store and go up to the house if he wanted."

"That would be neat. We could build those walkways here."

She smoothed his shirt and straightened his tie. "No doubt we will. Until then, go meet your new chief and figure out how you feel. No one said you had to decide anything today."

"Good point. Any other plans for the day?"

"I'd love to say there's nothing but the bookstore, but I can't. Until this thing with the Ageless One is taken care of, I'll be focusing on that. And dabbling with the Knights," she finished with a grin.

They shared a kiss. It wasn't until she passed the table where her mobile lay that a frown crossed her face.

"Call Mason," Theo urged.

She turned her phone over. "I do want my books. I can't open a bookstore without them."

"Then call him."

"He's made his position clear."

"Then we'll go see him."

Ferne poured herself coffee. "And have the door slammed in my face? No, thanks."

"That might no' happen."

She faced him. "I want to know what happened to my brother for him to have such a change in thinking, but I don't think I can."

Because she was scared. Theo kissed the top of her head as he wound his arm around her. Carlyle had admitted a few days ago that he'd allowed Mason to believe that Ferne was dead. Would seeing his sister alive change his thinking? Theo thought it might.

"What if the London Druids are controlling him?" Theo asked.

And just as he expected, Ferne's face tightened with anger. "They'll have to face me."

"They'll face us."

She met his gaze and nodded. "Us."

Kirsi sat in the chair in her flat with a blanket atop her. She couldn't stop thinking about the battle and Kerry. She had offered to drive Callum home, but he had gotten behind the wheel and driven her back to the co-op before walking home.

The ride had been quiet until he parked in front of the store. He'd turned off the engine and sat back in the seat. "Why did you lie to them?"

"What are you talking about?"

"Why did you say you didn't remember going into The Grey."

She gaped at him. "How did you know?"

"Why lie?"

"I don't know." She looked out the passenger window. "I was there, but it wasn't me."

Callum shoved his hand through his hair. "You saved her."

"I did."

"You're going back to The Grey."

She pressed her lips together and glanced at him. "I don't want to."

"Doona go alone when you do."

Kirsi looked at him. His hair had moved, showing a scar on his neck that disappeared behind his shirt. "Thank you for the help today. I'm sorry you got pulled into all of this."

"Keep yourself safe," he said and handed her the keys.

She watched as he climbed out of the car and softly closed the door before walking away.

Edie was doing the laundry, going through Trevor's clothes to make sure he didn't leave anything in his pockets. He was the worst about stuffing receipts and other papers into them and forgetting. Her phone chimed with a text. She finished filling the load and turned on the washer.

Things with her and Trevor had been rocky since he'd left for Glasgow. He returned from the trip and acted as if nothing had passed between them. That rubbed her wrong, and she reacted, which started a fight. They had reconciled. Sort of. Now, whenever she tried to talk about it, he changed the subject. He was present, but it didn't feel like he was in the relationship. And she was careful, oh, so careful, to keep her thoughts and questions to herself. She plastered a smile on her face and went about life as if nothing were wrong.

Trevor slept in the same bed, but he didn't reach for her as often as he used to. There were no playful slaps on her ass, no grabbing her for a quick kiss. No smile to his eyes anymore. At least with her. Around the children, he was the man she used to know, the one who used to share her bed.

Another ding came from her mobile, reminding her that she hadn't checked the text. It was probably Kerry. She had been trying to contact her about things, but the woman had been ignoring her. It wasn't Kerry but a blocked number. The text was images only. Her finger hovered over them, wondering if she should look.

Her curiosity got the better of her. Edie opened the text. The first picture loaded, and all the air left her lungs as she stared at a picture of Trevor kissing another woman.

Edinburgh

Willa rolled her tense shoulders. She was ready for the charade to be over. She didn't know how much longer she could go to meetings and smile at George as if she didn't know the truth.

"It willna be much longer," her father said from the seat beside her.

She turned her head to him noting the grey strands mixed with the dark at his temples. His blue eyes were solemn, earnest when they met hers. The same look he'd given her after her mother died. He was a man who never gave up, a man who moved mountains for his family.

And for what was right.

"We'll grab the book and make our way to Scott," Luke Ryan said with a nod. "We have a good plan."

"It has to go flawlessly."

He swung his eyes back to the flat they were watching. "It will. It has to."

* * *

Thank you for reading **HEART OF GLASS**.
I hope you loved Theo and Ferne's story as much as I loved writing it. Next in the Skye Druids series is ENDLESS SKYE.

BUY ENDLESS SKYE NOW
at www.DonnaGrant.com

* * *

To find out when new books release
SIGN UP FOR MY NEWSLETTER today at
https://www.tinyurl.com/DonnaGrantNews

Join my Facebook group, Donna Grant Groupies, for exclusive
giveaways and sneak peeks of future books.
https://www.facebook.com/groups/DGGroupies

* * *

Keep reading for an peek of ENDLESS SKYE…

EXCERPT OF THE NEXT SKYE DRUID BOOK

ENDLESS SKYE, SKYE DRUIDS SERIES, BOOK 4

New York Times and *USA Today* bestselling author Donna Grant returns with another seductive novel in the magical and dangerous world of the Skye Druids.

Passion comes with a price…

For Willa Ryan, family is everything. So, when her brother asks her to locate a book of unparalleled power, she doesn't hesitate. Except she does more than find it. She attempts to steal it, and in the process, ends up running for her life—straight into the arms of a man waiting to rescue her. Jasper is unlike anyone she's ever met, and she's helpless to resist the undeniable passion between them. But desire always comes at a cost.

Jasper McCabe is a master of disguise and deception, and he uses both ruthlessly. Yet nothing can prepare him when he comes face-to-face with the breathtaking women he's supposed to use for his ruse. Every instinct screams for him to run as far from Willa as he can. But there's no escape from the captivating Druid and the feelings she awakens. With his darkest enemies closing in, Jasper is forced to choose with his heart, or lose the woman who is his one chance at salvation.

Keep reading for an excerpt of ENDLESS SKYE...

ENDLESS SKYE EXCERPT

Edinburgh

Her ragged breathing was so loud she could barely hear her shoes slapping against the wet cobblestones. Willa Ryan slipped as she turned a corner and pressed her back against a building to listen and catch her breath. Sweat clung to her, driving away the cool March air and the dampness of the recent rain.

Her hands shook as she lifted her mobile to text her brother a warning, but her fingers wouldn't work properly, and it was one of the rare times when autocorrect didn't do its job. She wanted to scream in frustration as she deleted the message and tried again, only to mess up once more. It would be easier to call Scott. She'd have to keep her voice down, but at least she could warn him. Willa was about to dial when she heard her pursuers. She clutched her mobile as she raced through the city, the streetlamps seeming to reach out with their light to find her.

She needed to hide, rest, and think. And notify Scott.

Willa turned onto another street. She continued to weave around the clusters of people out for dinner or looking for some fun. She kept her attention in front of her, watching where she planted her feet, allowing her to move quickly when someone stepped before her.

"Sorry," she hurriedly muttered when she hit a woman's shoulder.

Willa didn't look back. She knew those chasing her were still there. They were relentless. And they wouldn't stop until they found her. Willa's eyes darted about, scanning faces as she came to another intersection. She glanced at the crosswalk lights and noticed the cars traveling across her path.

When she spotted a group of people crossing the large intersection, she hurried to join them. She hated slowing to a casual walk, but at least she blended for the moment. It allowed her to rest and look back the way she had come. She saw the man and woman who had been trailing her anxiously searching. She wouldn't stay hidden for long. Willa had to make the most of it.

She shoved a long strand of hair that had escaped her ponytail away from her face. Her chest burned, and her lungs ached. Her legs were so fatigued they could barely hold her up. She brought her mobile up again to call Scott. She navigated to her favorites and was about to press his name when someone bumped into her from behind. Magic pooled in her palms as Willa whirled, ready to launch it, only to find two very drunk women.

"Ooh. You're pretty," the blonde said as she wound an arm around Willa's shoulder. "You should come hang with us."

Willa saw they were pulling her toward a nightclub. It would be a good place to hide, but she had no money or ID to get inside. She forced herself to smile, but she wasn't sure it appeared as relaxed as she wanted since both women gave her a funny look. "I don't have my wallet."

"You're not gonna need it," the bleached blonde said with a wink.

Willa continued with the group as the women talked loudly in between whistling at people. She couldn't see behind her, which meant her hunters likely couldn't find her. Then she was at the doors of the club. Someone at the front held up a black credit card and slurred, stating he was paying for the entire group. A bouncer counted them, and then, before she knew it, Willa was through the door.

She quickly maneuvered off by herself. The music was so loud her ears rang. Clusters of people were everywhere, leaving her barely any room to move. She had to shove people aside just to get to the bar and order a water. She gulped it quickly.

Willa wiped her mouth and looked around the dark club. When she spotted some stairs, she made her way to them. She weaved between people as she headed up, hoping she could find a quieter place to call her brother.

The flashing lights bothered her, but she tried to ignore them. There was a second bar upstairs, and she snagged another water. She debated her location. Scott would never be able to hear her over the music. She needed to text him instead. At least now, she could do that without worrying about being found, and maybe her hands wouldn't shake so badly. Once she warned him, she would make her way out of Edinburgh. Her father was probably already on his way to Skye.

Willa found a column near the balcony so she could watch the entrance. She didn't see her pursuers. Still, she kept one eye on the door as she typed out her message. She was on the last sentence when something slammed into her ribs, shoving her painfully into the balcony railing. The impact snapped her head to the side.

She immediately ducked when she spotted a fist coming at her face. Willa recognized the woman as one of her pursuers. How had they found her again? Her only thought was getting away. Willa slid to the right to bolt when a thick forearm connected with her throat. The lights spun above her before vanishing out of sight as she gasped for breath. Then, she was falling. She panicked and reached out for something to grab. Anything. Her fingers latched on to the cool metal of the railing as screams filled the building.

Willa tried to lift her right arm, but pain shot through her. She bit back a cry and looked at her hand on the railing. Her palms were sweating. She wouldn't be able to hold on for long. She then lowered her gaze to see the dance floor cleared, people rushing out and glancing back at someone. No. Not someone. They were looking at *her*.

"What the fuck are you doing?" someone shouted from above her.

She tried to imagine how far she was about to fall. If she landed wrong, she could twist an ankle. Or worse, break something. She glanced at her left hand and then looked back at the floor below. Her only choice was to drop and land as best she could.

BUY ENDLESS SKYE NOW

at www.DonnaGrant.com

ABOUT THE AUTHOR

New York Times and *USA Today* bestselling author Donna Grant® has been praised for her "totally addictive" and "unique and sensual" stories.

She's written more than one hundred novels spanning multiple genres of romance including the bestselling Dragon Kings® series that features a thrilling combination of Druids, Fae, and immortal Highlanders who are dark, dangerous, and irresistible. She lives in Texas with her dog and a cat.

www.DonnaGrant.com
www.MotherofDragonsBooks.com

facebook.com/AuthorDonnaGrant

instagram.com/dgauthor

bookbub.com/authors/donna-grant

goodreads.com/donna_grant

pinterest.com/donnagrant1